8 TINY REINDEER

AN ADVENT CALENDAR ADVENTURE

Written by Robert Tinkler

Illustrated by Danesh Mohiuddin

THIS BOOK IS LIKE AN ADVENT CALENDAR!
READ ONE CHAPTER A DAY, EVERY DAY
THROUGH DECEMBER. (BUT WE WON'T BLAME
YOU IF YOU BINGE-READ IT ALL IN ONE
SITTING. IT'S A PRETTY ELF-TASTIC STORY ...)

Kids Can Press

For Jessica and my boys. "Love you a million times."
Thanks to Annette for sticking with me,
and to Katie for your creative support. — R.T.

For my two tiny reindeer, Lara and Daniel — D.M.

Published in Canada and the U.S. by Kids Can Press Ltd.
25 Dockside Drive, Toronto, ON M5A 0B5

Kids Can Press is a Corus Entertainment Inc. company.

www.kidscanpress.com

The artwork in this book was rendered digitally.

The text is set in Alter Ego BB, Comical Lite and Silver Age LC BB.

Edited by Yasemin Uçar, Jennifer Stokes and Katie Scott
Designed by Michael Reis

Printed and bound in Shenzhen, China, in 3/2023 by C & C Offset

MIX
Paper | Supporting
responsible forestry
FSC
www.fsc.org
FSC® C008047

CM 23 0 9 8 7 6 5 4 3 2 1

Library and Archives Canada Cataloguing in Publication
Title: 8 tiny reindeer: an Advent calendar adventure / written by Robert Tinkler;
illustrated by Danesh Mohiuddin.
Other titles: Eight tiny reindeer
Names: Tinkler, Robert, 1973– author. | Mohiuddin, Danesh, artist.
Identifiers: Canadiana (print) 2022047477X | Canadiana (ebook) 20220474796 |
ISBN 9781525304644 (hardcover) | ISBN 9781525308208 (EPUB)
Subjects: LCGFT: Graphic novels. | LCGFT: Christmas fiction.
Classification: LCC PN6733.T56 A618 2023 | DDC j741.5/971 — dc23

Kids Can Press gratefully acknowledges that the land on which our office is located
is the traditional territory of many nations, including the Mississaugas of the Credit,
the Anishnabeg, the Chippewa, the Haudenosaunee and the Wendat peoples, and is
now home to many diverse First Nations, Inuit and Métis peoples.

We thank the Government of Ontario, through Ontario Creates; the Ontario Arts
Council; the Canada Council for the Arts; and the Government of Canada
for supporting our publishing activity.

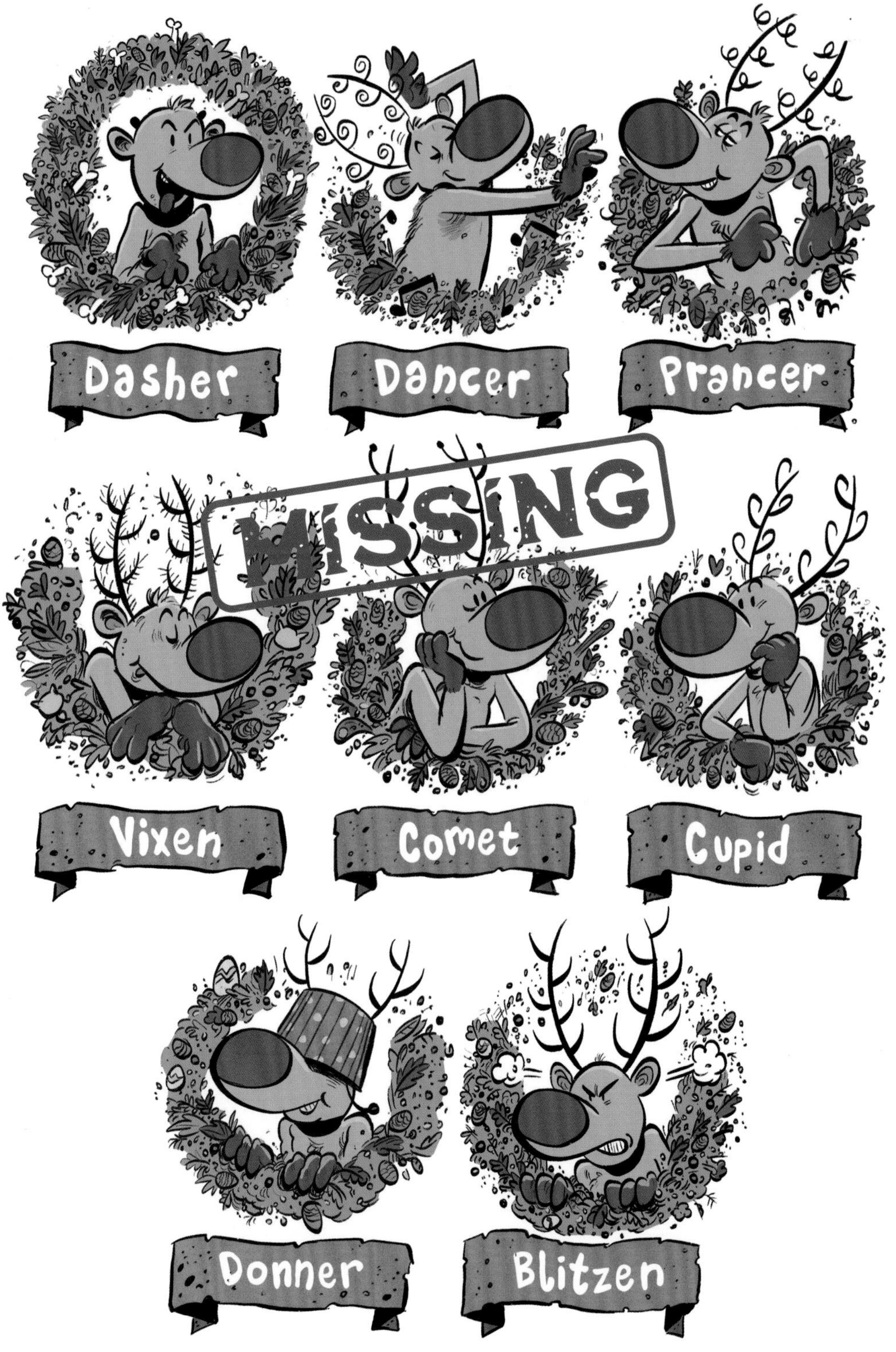
Dasher
Dancer
Prancer
MISSING
Vixen
Comet
Cupid
Donner
Blitzen

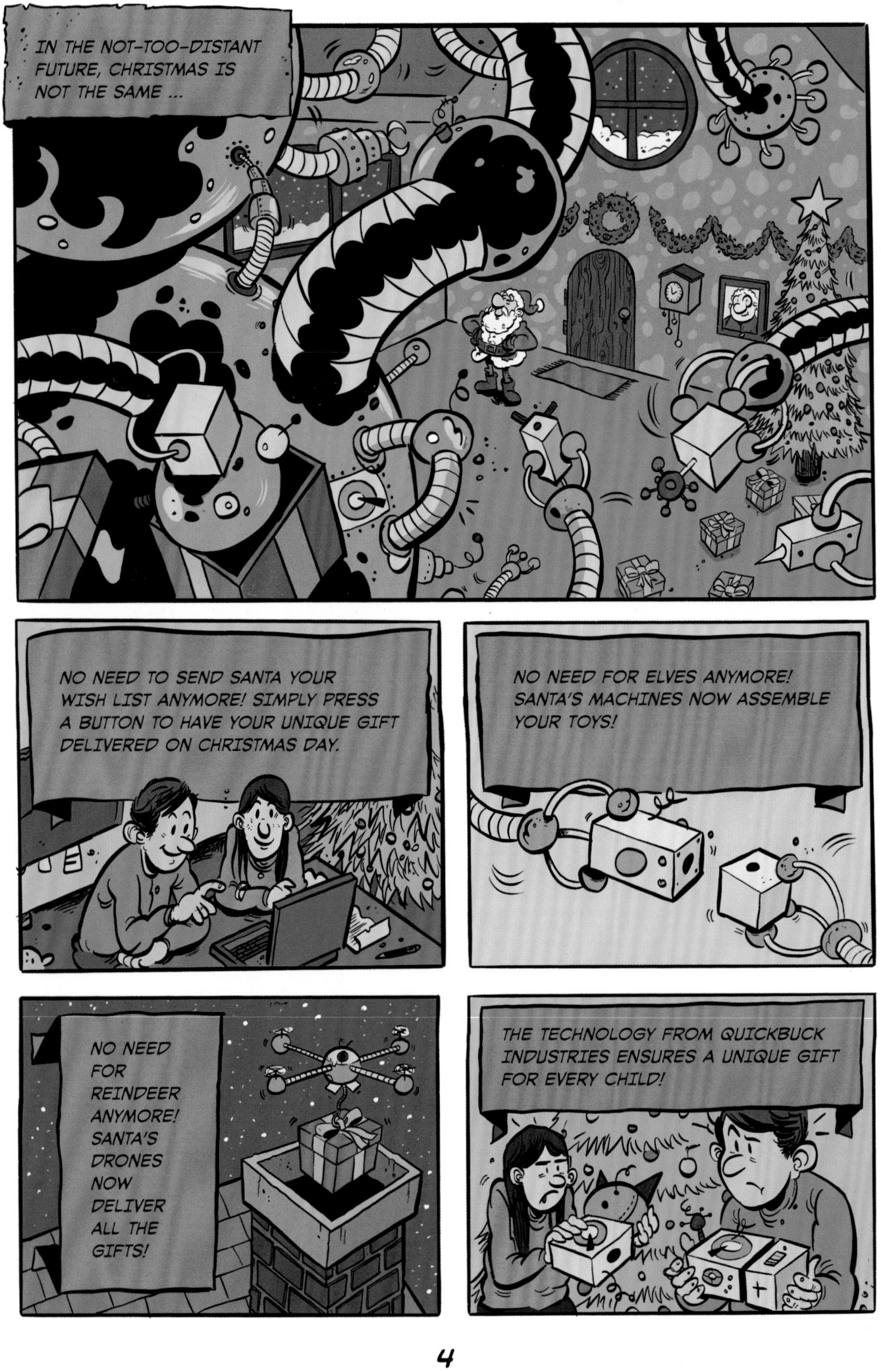
IN THE NOT-TOO-DISTANT FUTURE, CHRISTMAS IS NOT THE SAME ...
NO NEED TO SEND SANTA YOUR WISH LIST ANYMORE! SIMPLY PRESS A BUTTON TO HAVE YOUR UNIQUE GIFT DELIVERED ON CHRISTMAS DAY.
NO NEED FOR ELVES ANYMORE! SANTA'S MACHINES NOW ASSEMBLE YOUR TOYS!
NO NEED FOR REINDEER ANYMORE! SANTA'S DRONES NOW DELIVER ALL THE GIFTS!
THE TECHNOLOGY FROM QUICKBUCK INDUSTRIES ENSURES A UNIQUE GIFT FOR EVERY CHILD!

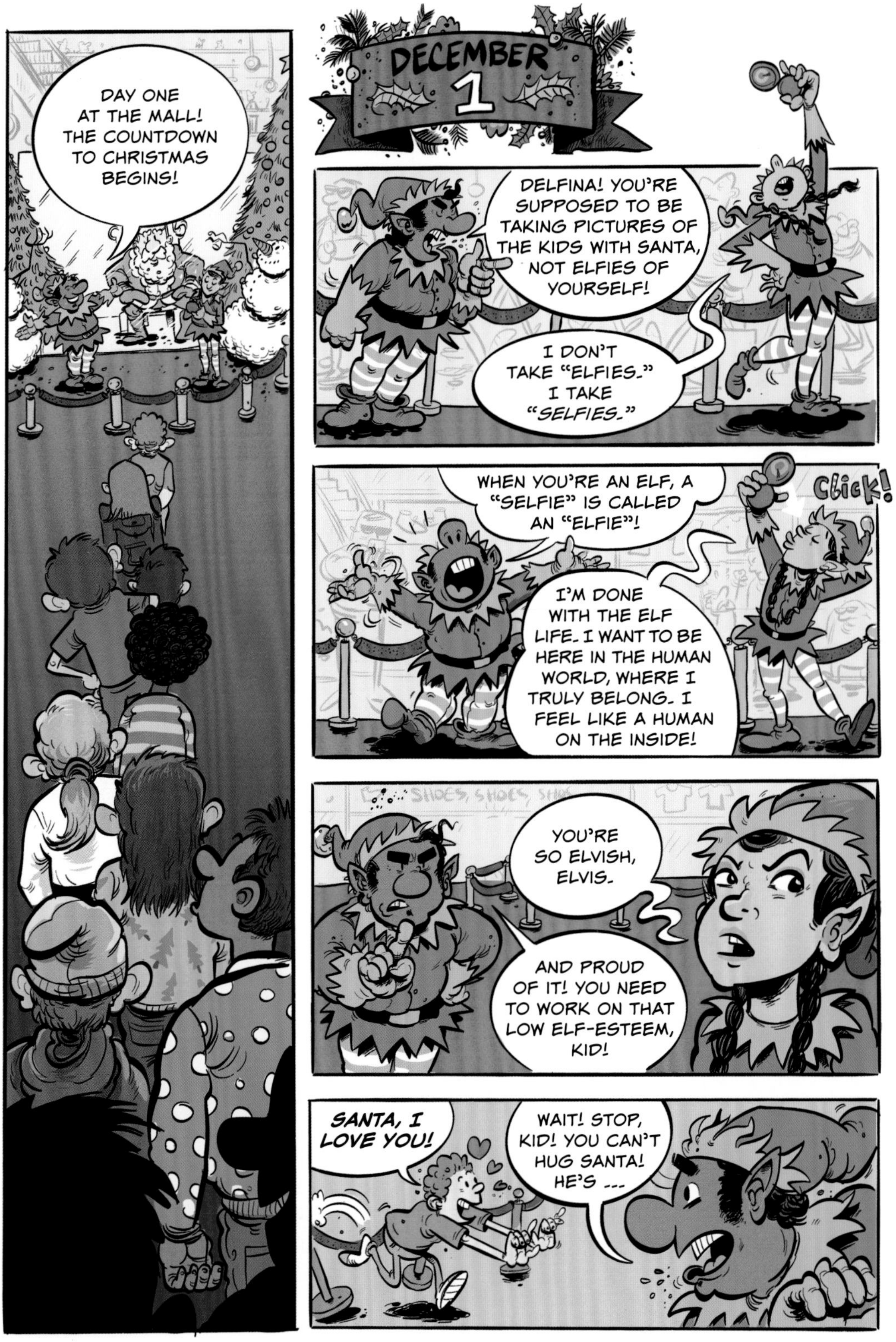
DAY ONE AT THE MALL! THE COUNTDOWN TO CHRISTMAS BEGINS!
DECEMBER 1
DELFINA! YOU'RE SUPPOSED TO BE TAKING PICTURES OF THE KIDS WITH SANTA, NOT ELFIES OF YOURSELF!
I DON'T TAKE "ELFIES." I TAKE "SELFIES."
WHEN YOU'RE AN ELF, A "SELFIE" IS CALLED AN "ELFIE"!
CLICK!
I'M DONE WITH THE ELF LIFE. I WANT TO BE HERE IN THE HUMAN WORLD, WHERE I TRULY BELONG. I FEEL LIKE A HUMAN ON THE INSIDE!
SHOES, SHOES
YOU'RE SO ELVISH, ELVIS.
AND PROUD OF IT! YOU NEED TO WORK ON THAT LOW ELF-ESTEEM, KID!
SANTA, I LOVE YOU!
WAIT! STOP, KID! YOU CAN'T HUG SANTA! HE'S ...

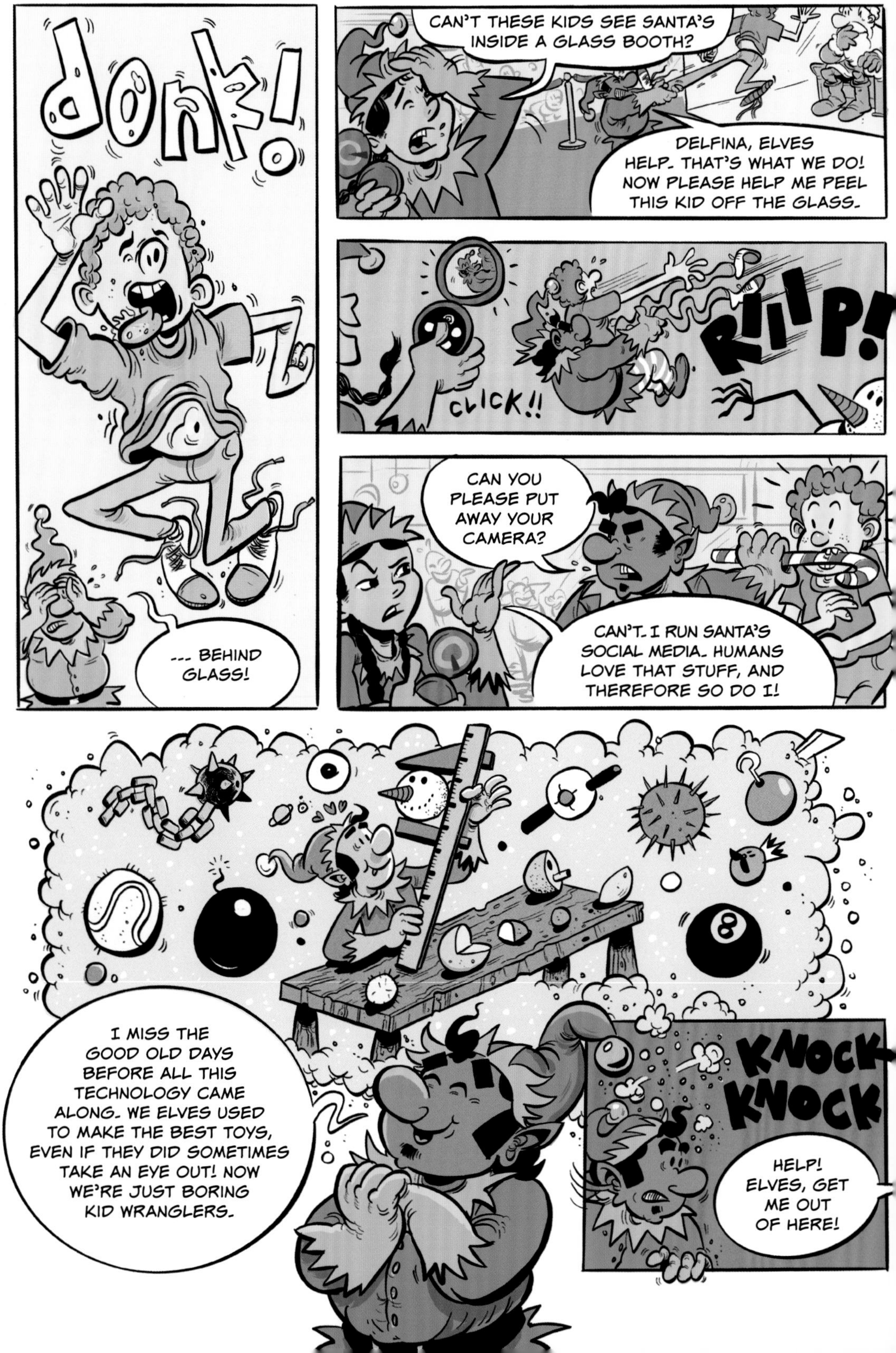
donk!
... BEHIND GLASS!
CAN'T THESE KIDS SEE SANTA'S INSIDE A GLASS BOOTH?
DELFINA, ELVES HELP. THAT'S WHAT WE DO! NOW PLEASE HELP ME PEEL THIS KID OFF THE GLASS.
CLICK!!
RIIIP!
CAN YOU PLEASE PUT AWAY YOUR CAMERA?
CAN'T. I RUN SANTA'S SOCIAL MEDIA. HUMANS LOVE THAT STUFF, AND THEREFORE SO DO I!
I MISS THE GOOD OLD DAYS BEFORE ALL THIS TECHNOLOGY CAME ALONG. WE ELVES USED TO MAKE THE BEST TOYS, EVEN IF THEY DID SOMETIMES TAKE AN EYE OUT! NOW WE'RE JUST BORING KID WRANGLERS.
KNOCK KNOCK
HELP! ELVES, GET ME OUT OF HERE!

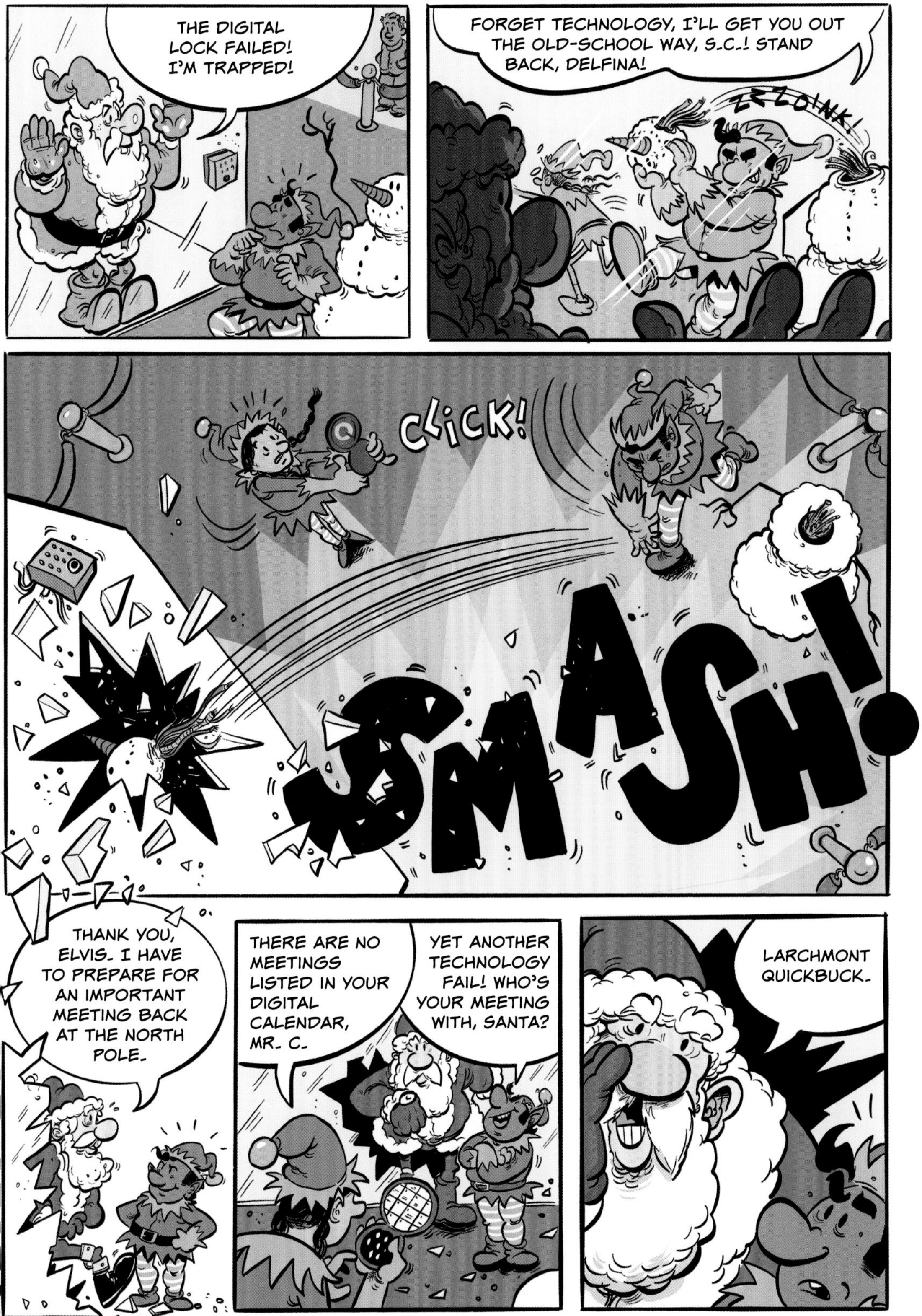
THE DIGITAL LOCK FAILED! I'M TRAPPED!
FORGET TECHNOLOGY, I'LL GET YOU OUT THE OLD-SCHOOL WAY, S.C.! STAND BACK, DELFINA!
ZZZOINK!
CLICK!
SMASH!
THANK YOU, ELVIS. I HAVE TO PREPARE FOR AN IMPORTANT MEETING BACK AT THE NORTH POLE.
THERE ARE NO MEETINGS LISTED IN YOUR DIGITAL CALENDAR, MR. C.
YET ANOTHER TECHNOLOGY FAIL! WHO'S YOUR MEETING WITH, SANTA?
LARCHMONT QUICKBUCK.

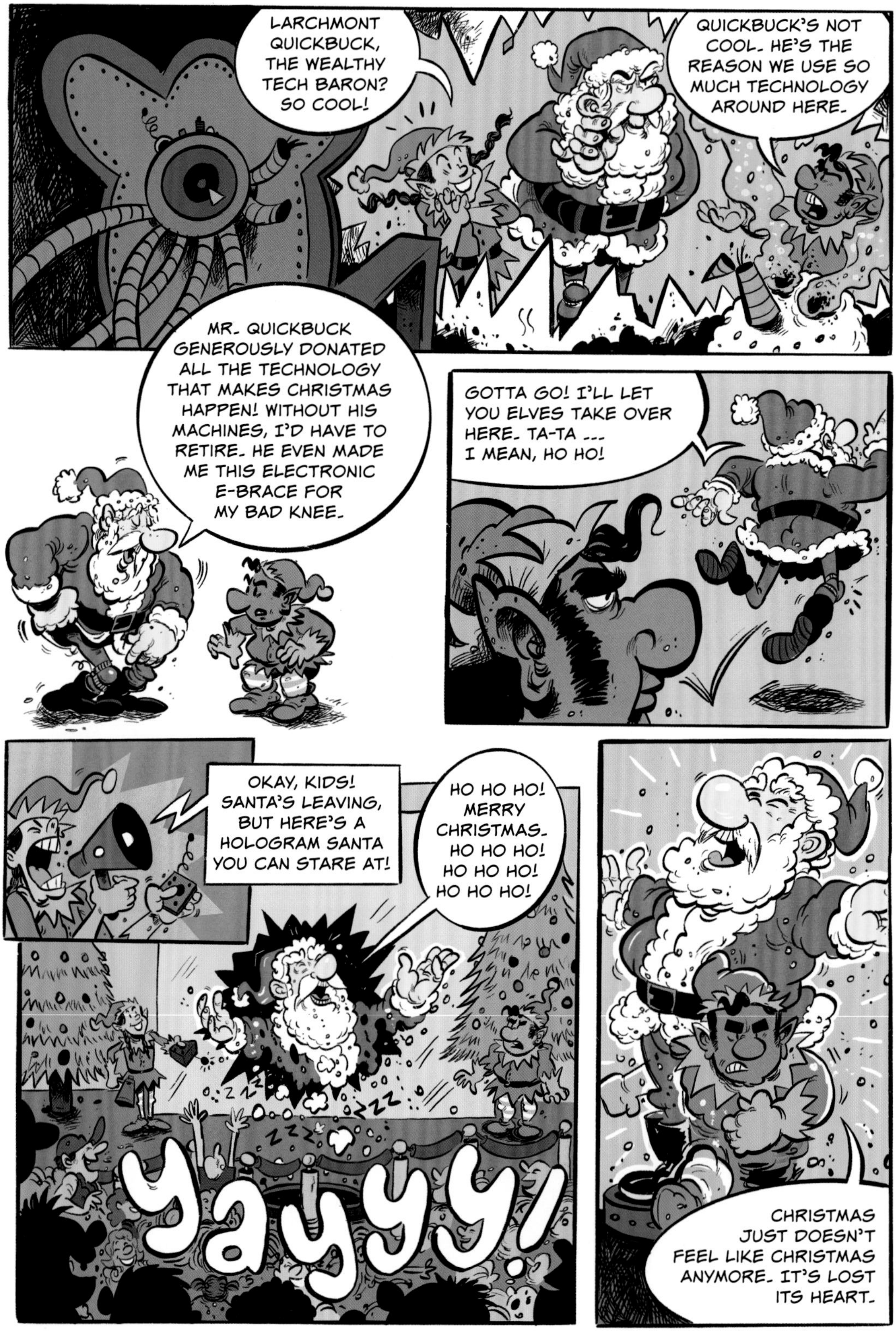
LARCHMONT QUICKBUCK, THE WEALTHY TECH BARON? SO COOL!
QUICKBUCK'S NOT COOL. HE'S THE REASON WE USE SO MUCH TECHNOLOGY AROUND HERE.
MR. QUICKBUCK GENEROUSLY DONATED ALL THE TECHNOLOGY THAT MAKES CHRISTMAS HAPPEN! WITHOUT HIS MACHINES, I'D HAVE TO RETIRE. HE EVEN MADE ME THIS ELECTRONIC E-BRACE FOR MY BAD KNEE.
GOTTA GO! I'LL LET YOU ELVES TAKE OVER HERE. TA-TA ... I MEAN, HO HO!
OKAY, KIDS! SANTA'S LEAVING, BUT HERE'S A HOLOGRAM SANTA YOU CAN STARE AT!
HO HO HO! MERRY CHRISTMAS. HO HO HO! HO HO HO! HO HO HO!
YAYYY!
CHRISTMAS JUST DOESN'T FEEL LIKE CHRISTMAS ANYMORE. IT'S LOST ITS HEART.

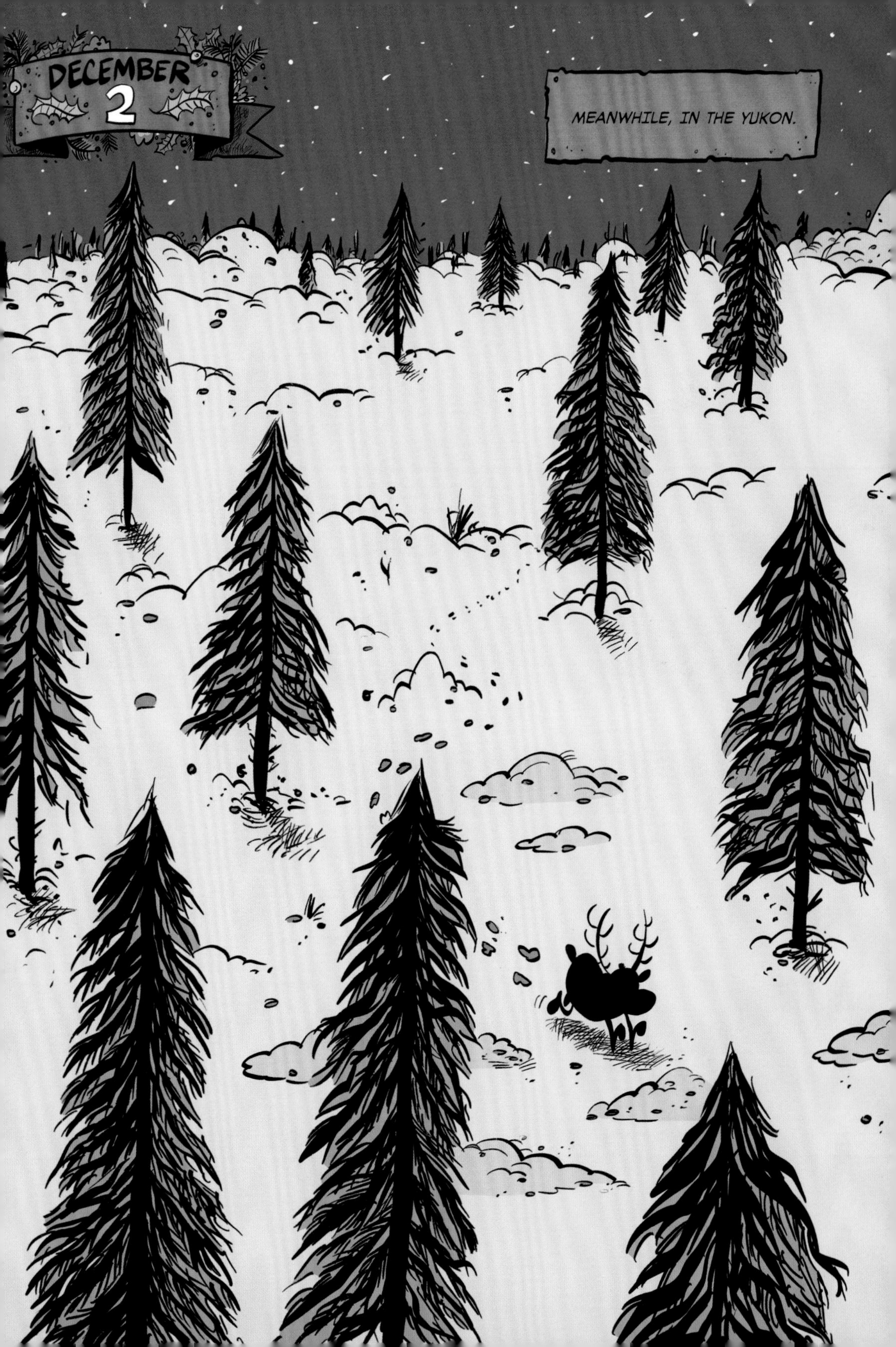
DECEMBER 2
MEANWHILE, IN THE YUKON.

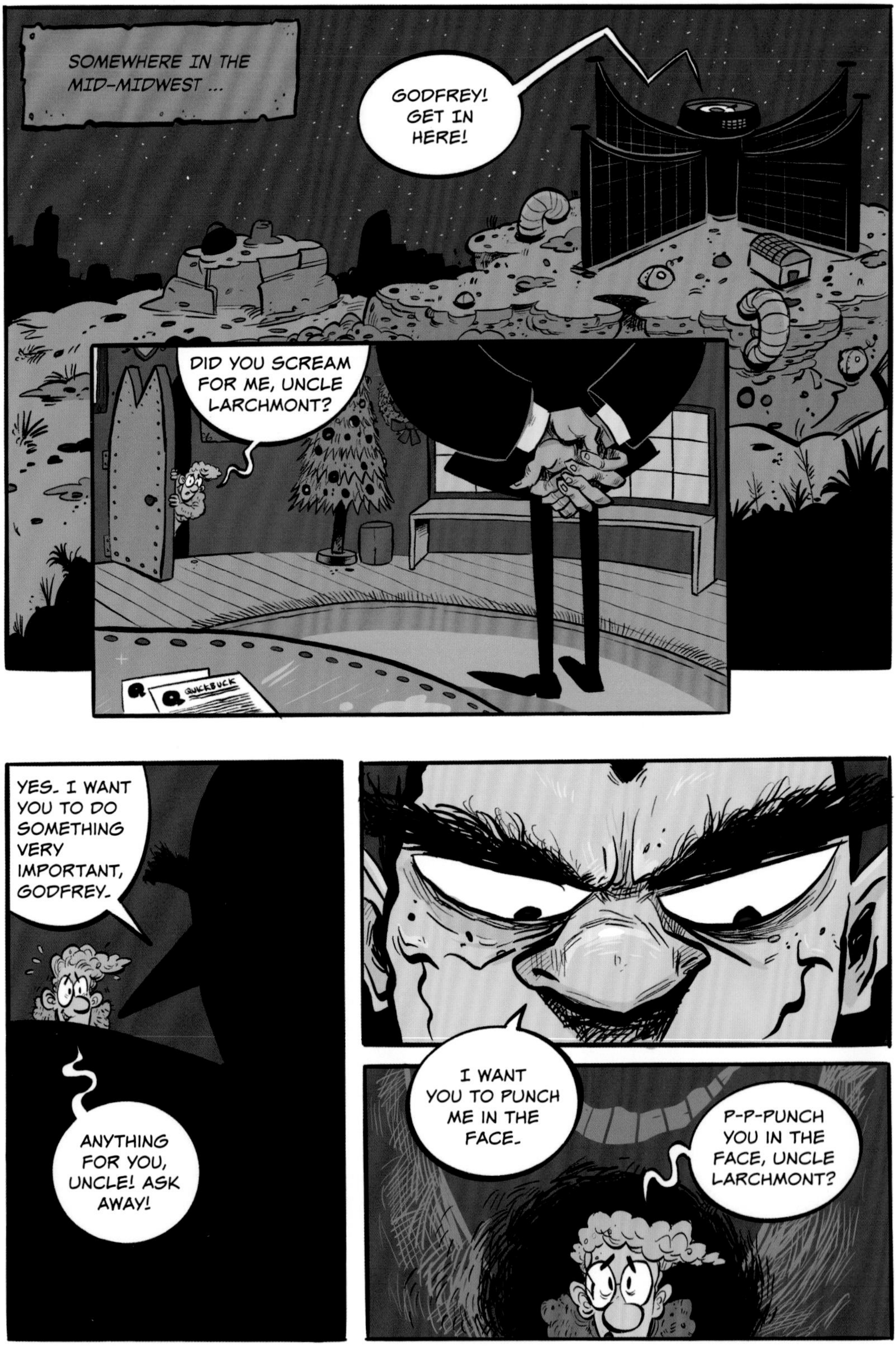
SOMEWHERE IN THE MID-MIDWEST ...
GODFREY! GET IN HERE!
DID YOU SCREAM FOR ME, UNCLE LARCHMONT?
YES. I WANT YOU TO DO SOMETHING VERY IMPORTANT, GODFREY.
ANYTHING FOR YOU, UNCLE! ASK AWAY!
I WANT YOU TO PUNCH ME IN THE FACE.
P-P-PUNCH YOU IN THE FACE, UNCLE LARCHMONT?

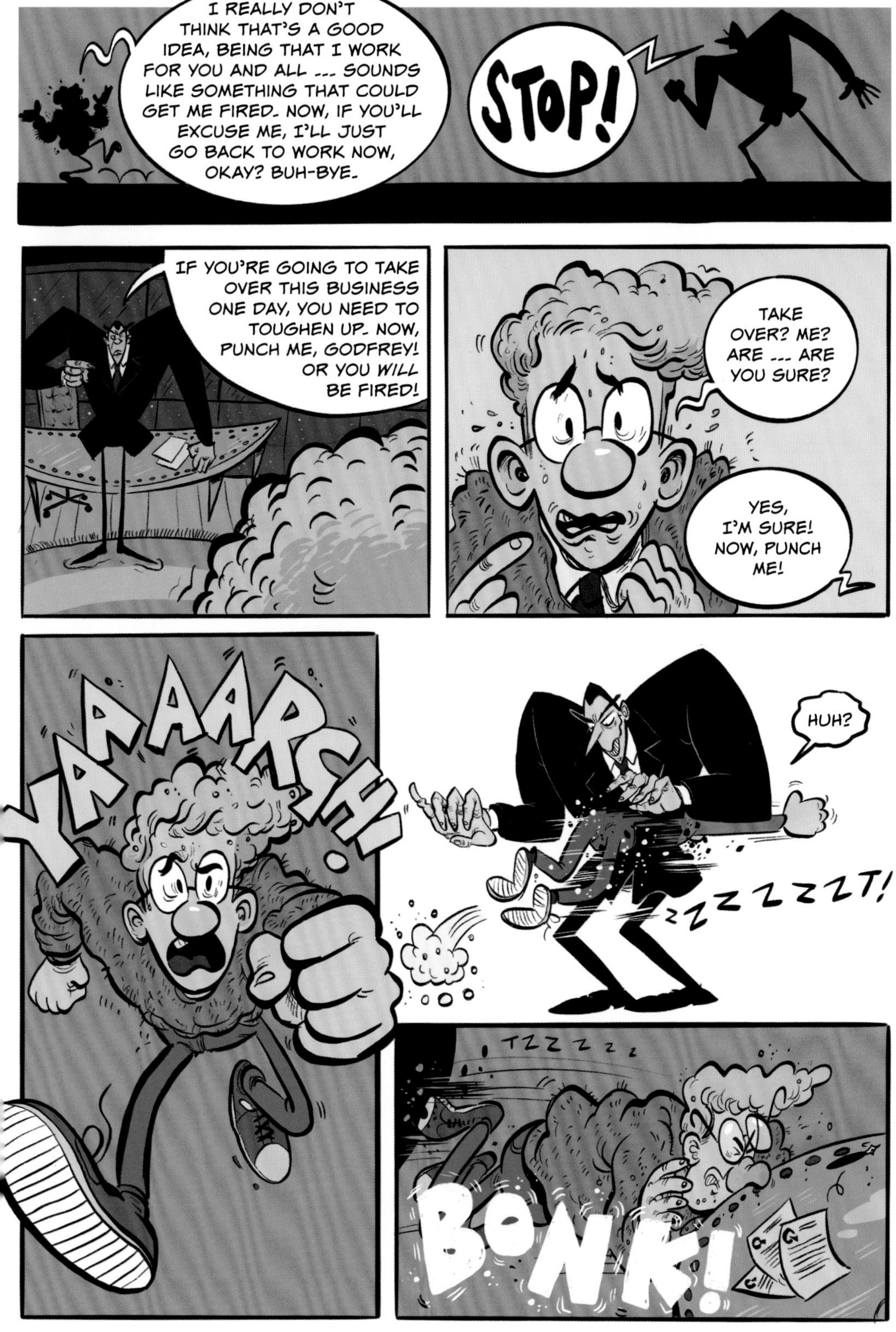
I REALLY DON'T THINK THAT'S A GOOD IDEA, BEING THAT I WORK FOR YOU AND ALL --- SOUNDS LIKE SOMETHING THAT COULD GET ME FIRED. NOW, IF YOU'LL EXCUSE ME, I'LL JUST GO BACK TO WORK NOW, OKAY? BUH-BYE.
STOP!
IF YOU'RE GOING TO TAKE OVER THIS BUSINESS ONE DAY, YOU NEED TO TOUGHEN UP. NOW, PUNCH ME, GODFREY! OR YOU *WILL* BE FIRED!
TAKE OVER? ME? ARE --- ARE YOU SURE?
YES, I'M SURE! NOW, PUNCH ME!
YAAARCH!
HUH?
ZZZZZZZT!
TZZZzzz
BONK!

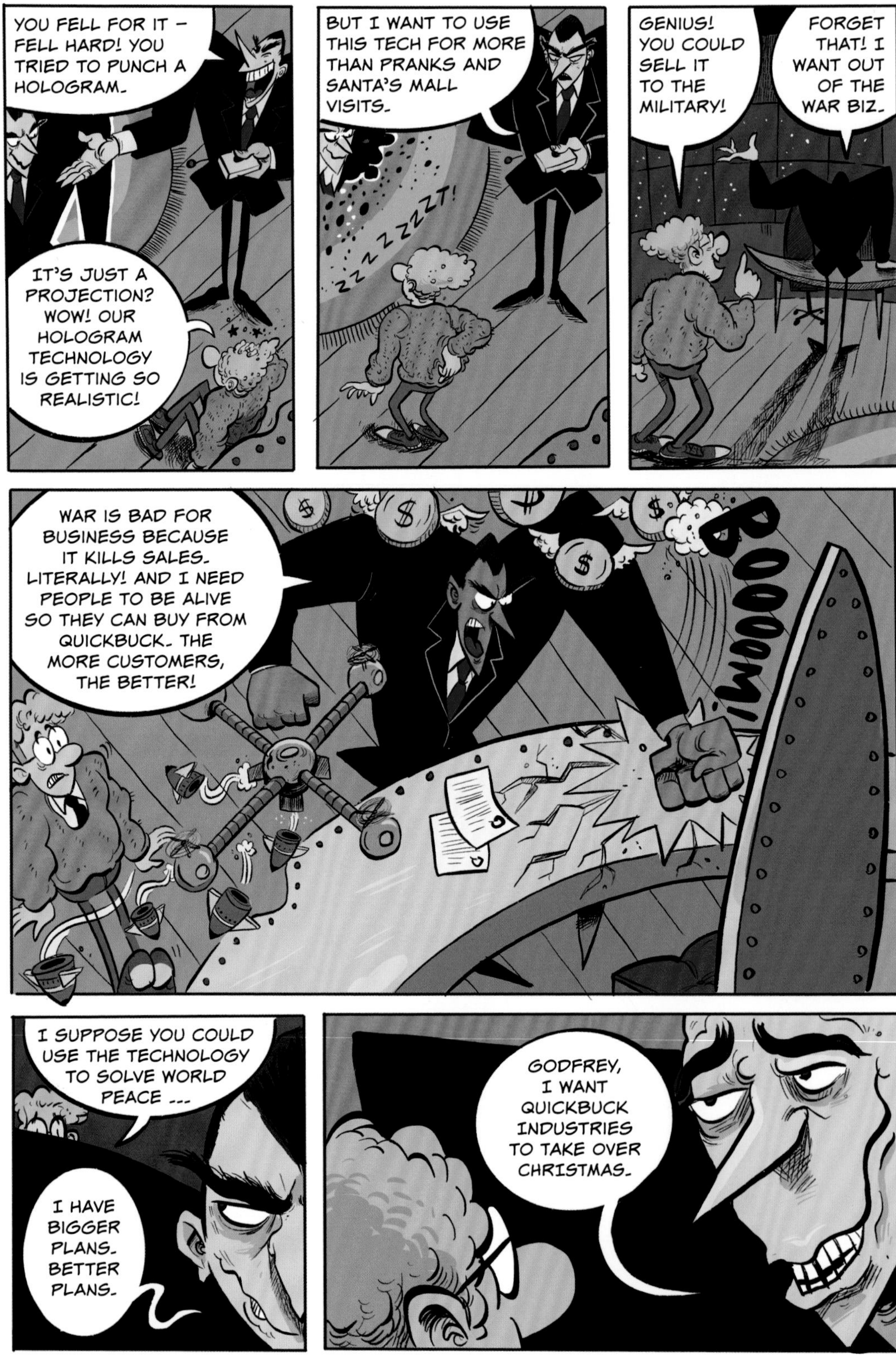
YOU FELL FOR IT — FELL HARD! YOU TRIED TO PUNCH A HOLOGRAM.
IT'S JUST A PROJECTION? WOW! OUR HOLOGRAM TECHNOLOGY IS GETTING SO REALISTIC!
BUT I WANT TO USE THIS TECH FOR MORE THAN PRANKS AND SANTA'S MALL VISITS.
ZZZZZZZZT!
GENIUS! YOU COULD SELL IT TO THE MILITARY!
FORGET THAT! I WANT OUT OF THE WAR BIZ.
WAR IS BAD FOR BUSINESS BECAUSE IT KILLS SALES. LITERALLY! AND I NEED PEOPLE TO BE ALIVE SO THEY CAN BUY FROM QUICKBUCK. THE MORE CUSTOMERS, THE BETTER!
BOOOOOM!
I SUPPOSE YOU COULD USE THE TECHNOLOGY TO SOLVE WORLD PEACE ...
I HAVE BIGGER PLANS. BETTER PLANS.
GODFREY, I WANT QUICKBUCK INDUSTRIES TO TAKE OVER CHRISTMAS.

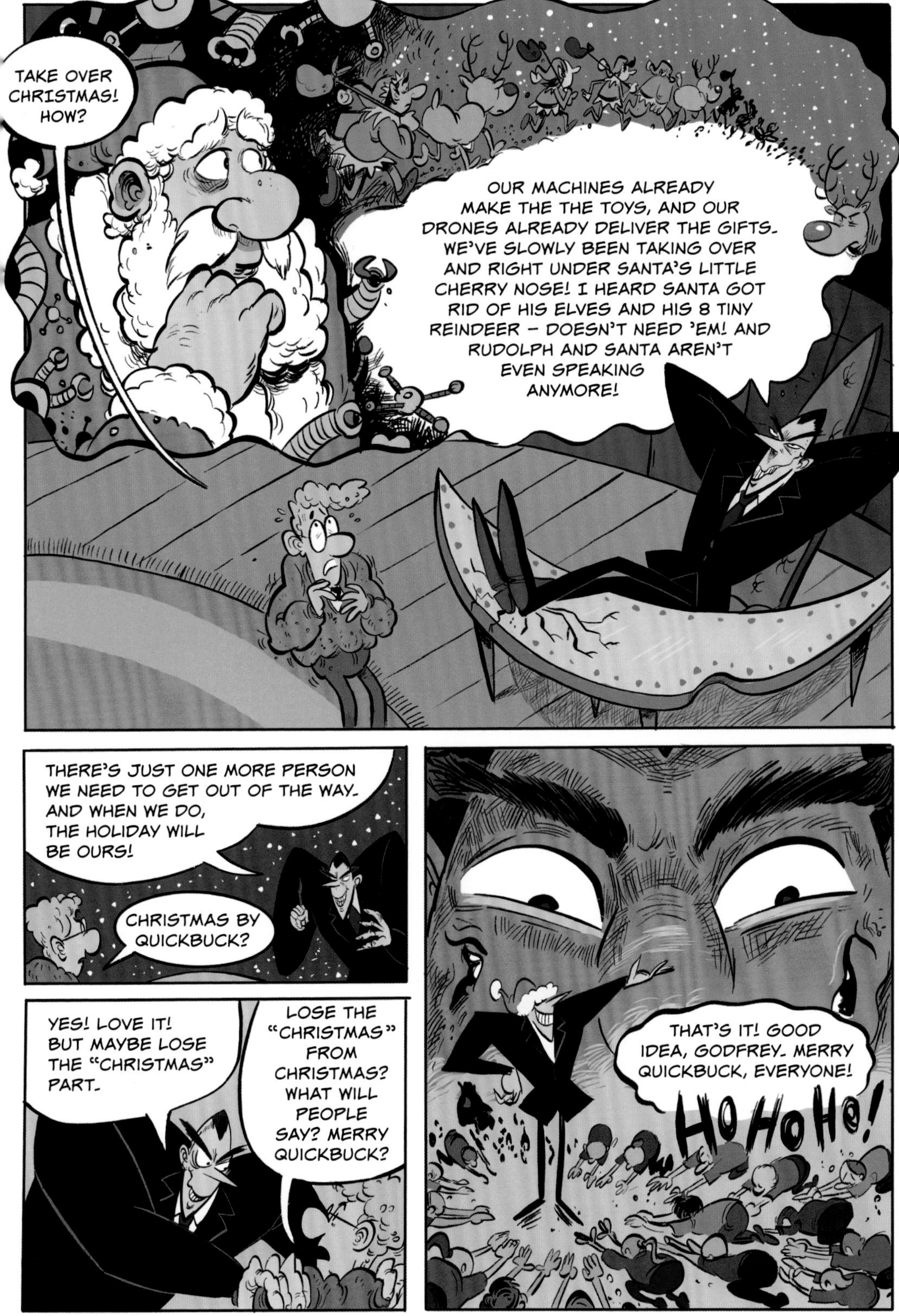
TAKE OVER CHRISTMAS! HOW?
OUR MACHINES ALREADY MAKE THE THE TOYS, AND OUR DRONES ALREADY DELIVER THE GIFTS. WE'VE SLOWLY BEEN TAKING OVER AND RIGHT UNDER SANTA'S LITTLE CHERRY NOSE! I HEARD SANTA GOT RID OF HIS ELVES AND HIS 8 TINY REINDEER – DOESN'T NEED 'EM! AND RUDOLPH AND SANTA AREN'T EVEN SPEAKING ANYMORE!
THERE'S JUST ONE MORE PERSON WE NEED TO GET OUT OF THE WAY. AND WHEN WE DO, THE HOLIDAY WILL BE OURS!
CHRISTMAS BY QUICKBUCK?
YES! LOVE IT! BUT MAYBE LOSE THE "CHRISTMAS" PART.
LOSE THE "CHRISTMAS" FROM CHRISTMAS? WHAT WILL PEOPLE SAY? MERRY QUICKBUCK?
THAT'S IT! GOOD IDEA, GODFREY. MERRY QUICKBUCK, EVERYONE!
HO HO HO!

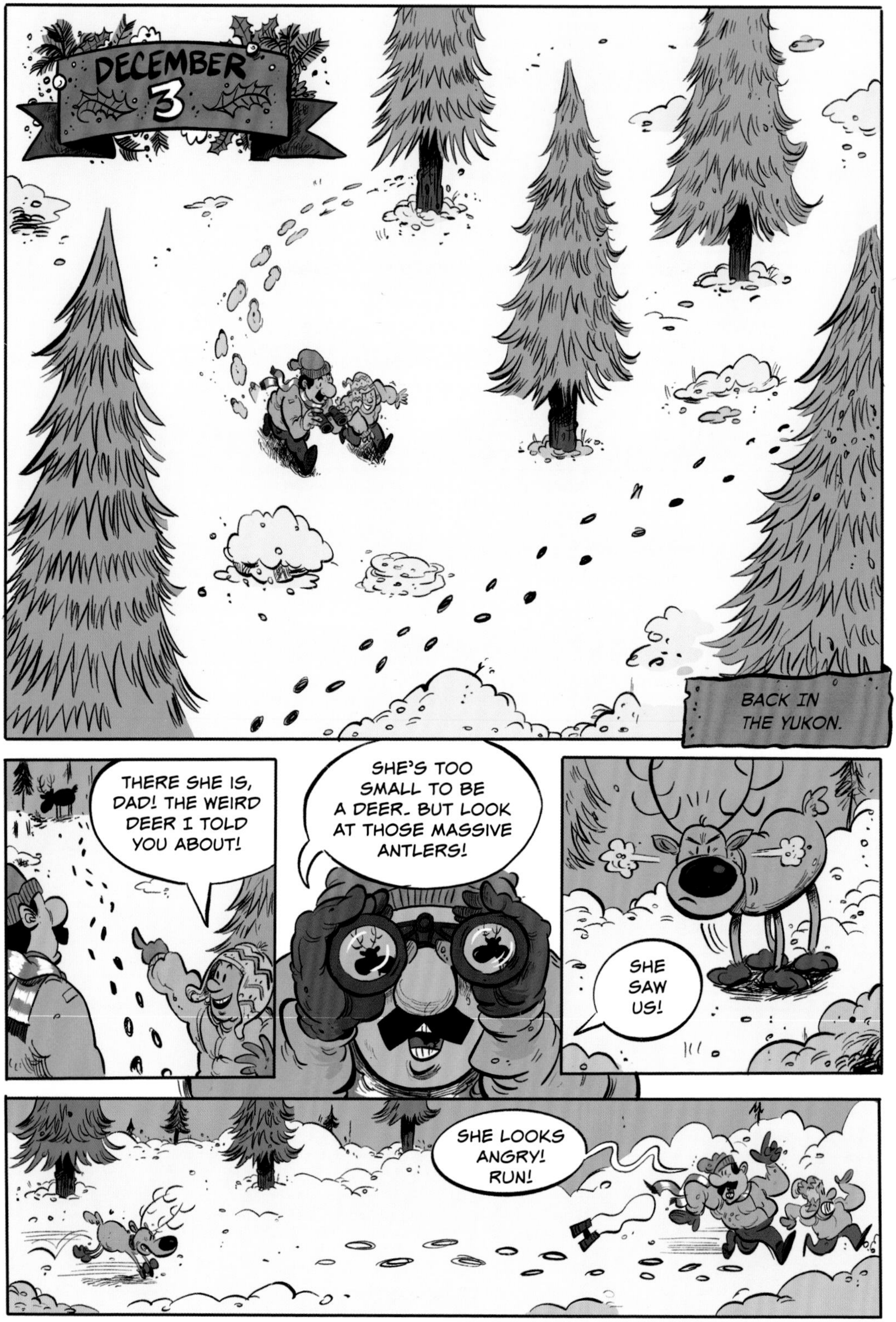
DECEMBER 3
BACK IN THE YUKON.
THERE SHE IS, DAD! THE WEIRD DEER I TOLD YOU ABOUT!
SHE'S TOO SMALL TO BE A DEER. BUT LOOK AT THOSE MASSIVE ANTLERS!
SHE SAW US!
SHE LOOKS ANGRY! RUN!

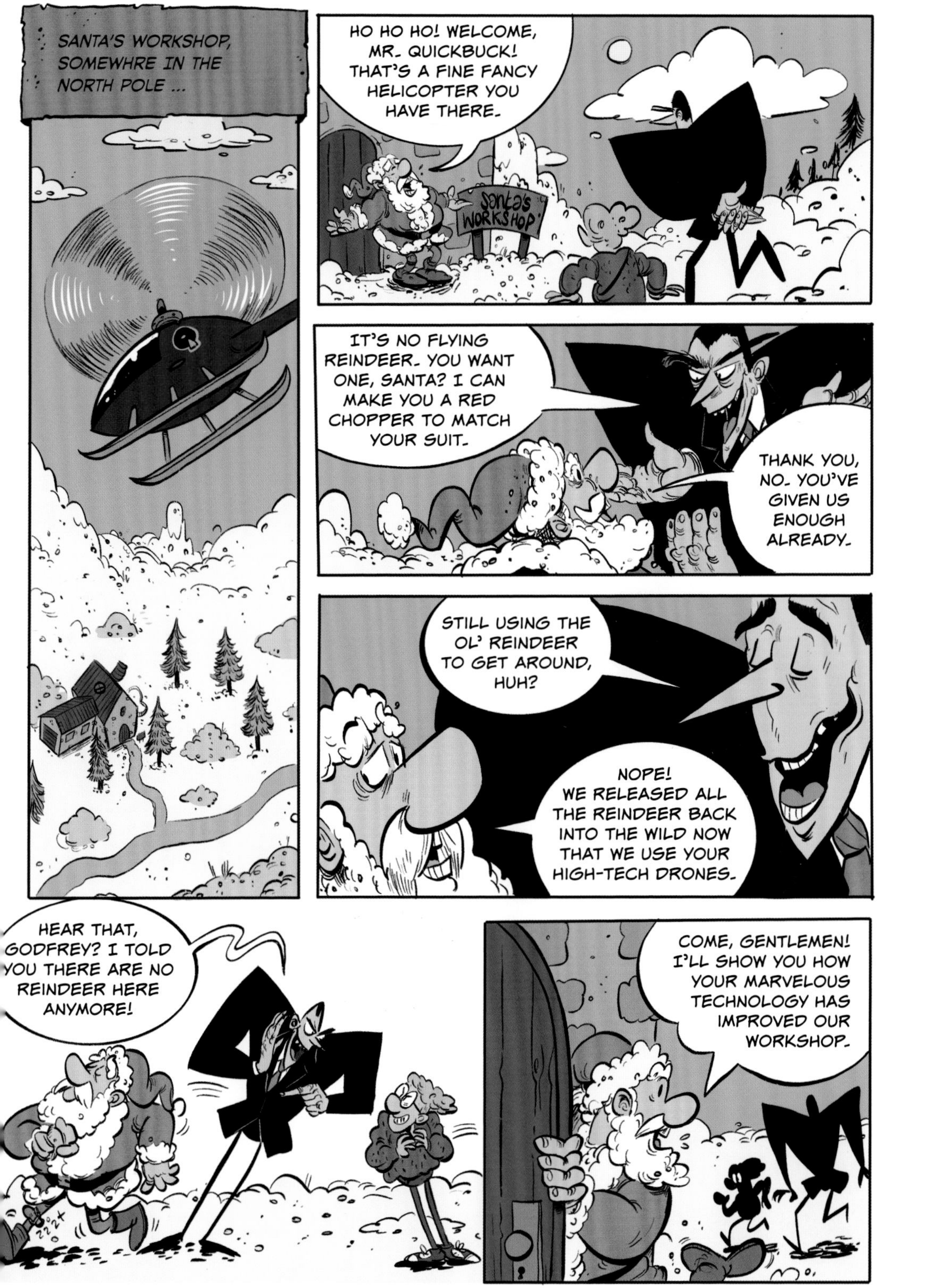

SANTA'S WORKSHOP, SOMEWHRE IN THE NORTH POLE ...
HO HO HO! WELCOME, MR. QUICKBUCK! THAT'S A FINE FANCY HELICOPTER YOU HAVE THERE.
SANTA'S WORKSHOP
IT'S NO FLYING REINDEER. YOU WANT ONE, SANTA? I CAN MAKE YOU A RED CHOPPER TO MATCH YOUR SUIT.
THANK YOU, NO. YOU'VE GIVEN US ENOUGH ALREADY.
STILL USING THE OL' REINDEER TO GET AROUND, HUH?
NOPE! WE RELEASED ALL THE REINDEER BACK INTO THE WILD NOW THAT WE USE YOUR HIGH-TECH DRONES.
HEAR THAT, GODFREY? I TOLD YOU THERE ARE NO REINDEER HERE ANYMORE!
COME, GENTLEMEN! I'LL SHOW YOU HOW YOUR MARVELOUS TECHNOLOGY HAS IMPROVED OUR WORKSHOP.

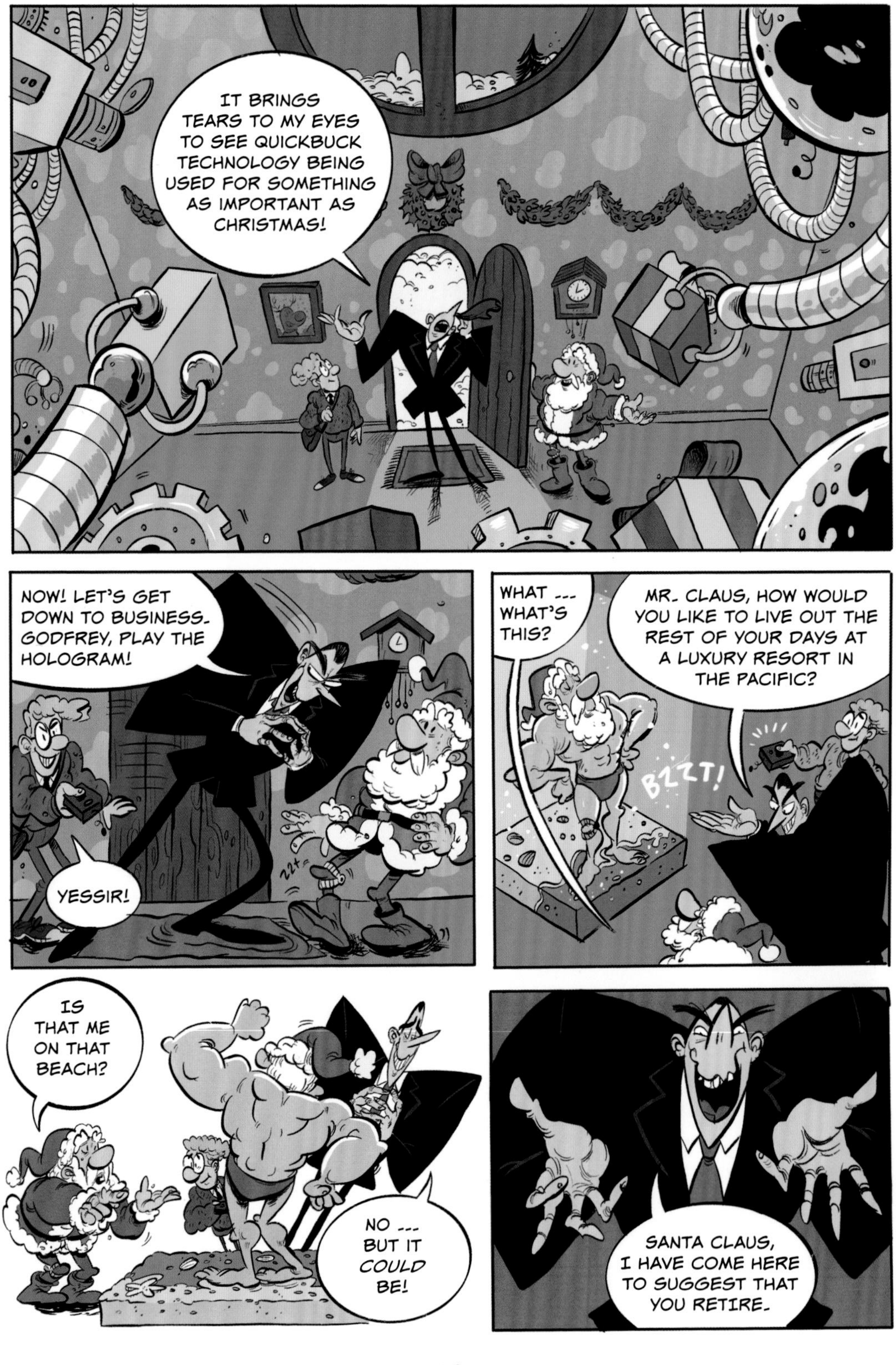
IT BRINGS TEARS TO MY EYES TO SEE QUICKBUCK TECHNOLOGY BEING USED FOR SOMETHING AS IMPORTANT AS CHRISTMAS!
NOW! LET'S GET DOWN TO BUSINESS. GODFREY, PLAY THE HOLOGRAM!
YESSIR!
WHAT ... WHAT'S THIS?
MR. CLAUS, HOW WOULD YOU LIKE TO LIVE OUT THE REST OF YOUR DAYS AT A LUXURY RESORT IN THE PACIFIC?
BZZT!
IS THAT ME ON THAT BEACH?
NO ... BUT IT COULD BE!
SANTA CLAUS, I HAVE COME HERE TO SUGGEST THAT YOU RETIRE.

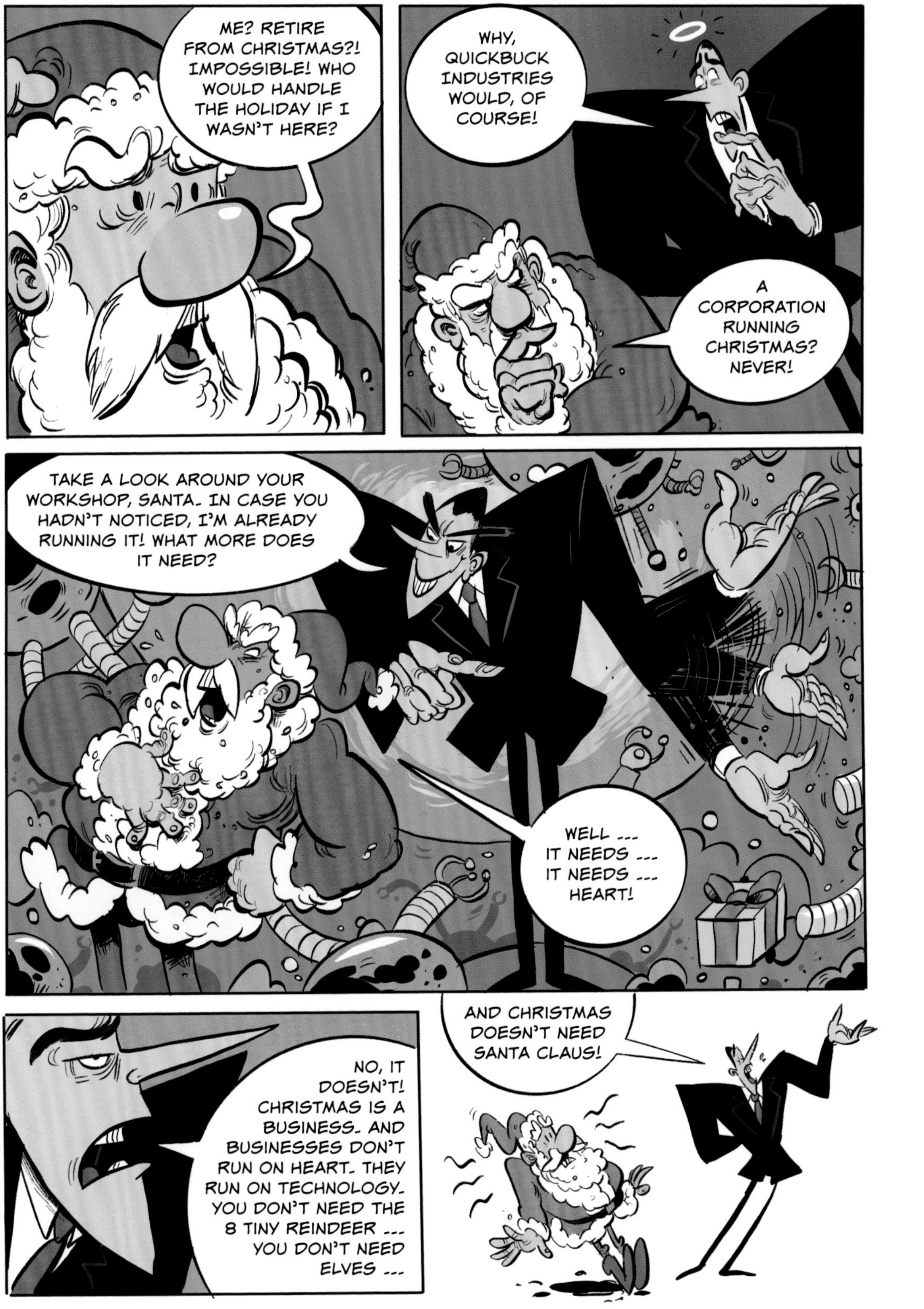

ME? RETIRE FROM CHRISTMAS?! IMPOSSIBLE! WHO WOULD HANDLE THE HOLIDAY IF I WASN'T HERE?
WHY, QUICKBUCK INDUSTRIES WOULD, OF COURSE!
A CORPORATION RUNNING CHRISTMAS? NEVER!
TAKE A LOOK AROUND YOUR WORKSHOP, SANTA. IN CASE YOU HADN'T NOTICED, I'M ALREADY RUNNING IT! WHAT MORE DOES IT NEED?
WELL ... IT NEEDS ... IT NEEDS ... HEART!
NO, IT DOESN'T! CHRISTMAS IS A BUSINESS. AND BUSINESSES DON'T RUN ON HEART. THEY RUN ON TECHNOLOGY. YOU DON'T NEED THE 8 TINY REINDEER ... YOU DON'T NEED ELVES ...
AND CHRISTMAS DOESN'T NEED SANTA CLAUS!

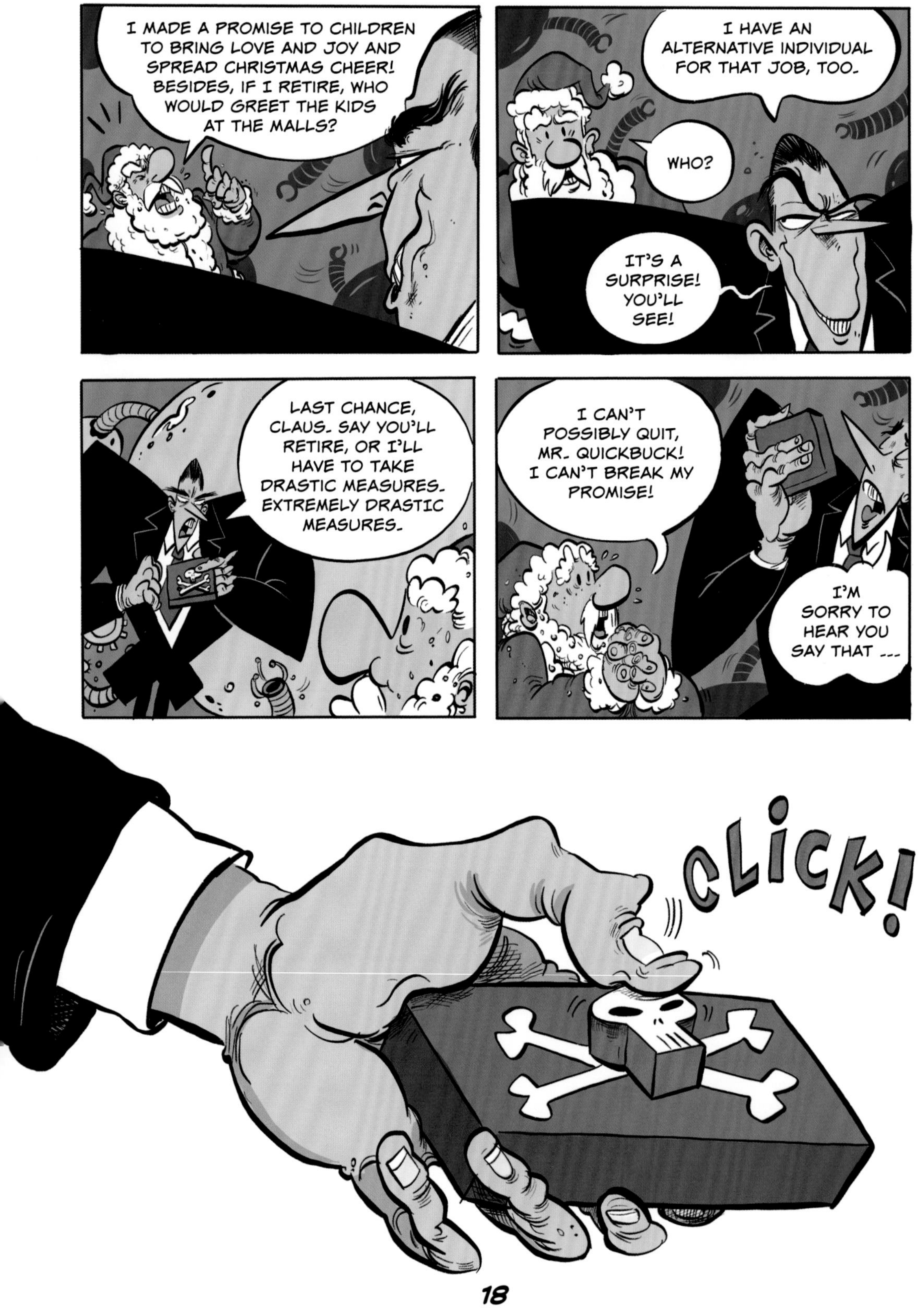
I MADE A PROMISE TO CHILDREN TO BRING LOVE AND JOY AND SPREAD CHRISTMAS CHEER! BESIDES, IF I RETIRE, WHO WOULD GREET THE KIDS AT THE MALLS?
I HAVE AN ALTERNATIVE INDIVIDUAL FOR THAT JOB, TOO.
WHO?
IT'S A SURPRISE! YOU'LL SEE!
LAST CHANCE, CLAUS. SAY YOU'LL RETIRE, OR I'LL HAVE TO TAKE DRASTIC MEASURES. EXTREMELY DRASTIC MEASURES.
I CAN'T POSSIBLY QUIT, MR. QUICKBUCK! I CAN'T BREAK MY PROMISE!
I'M SORRY TO HEAR YOU SAY THAT ...
CLICK!

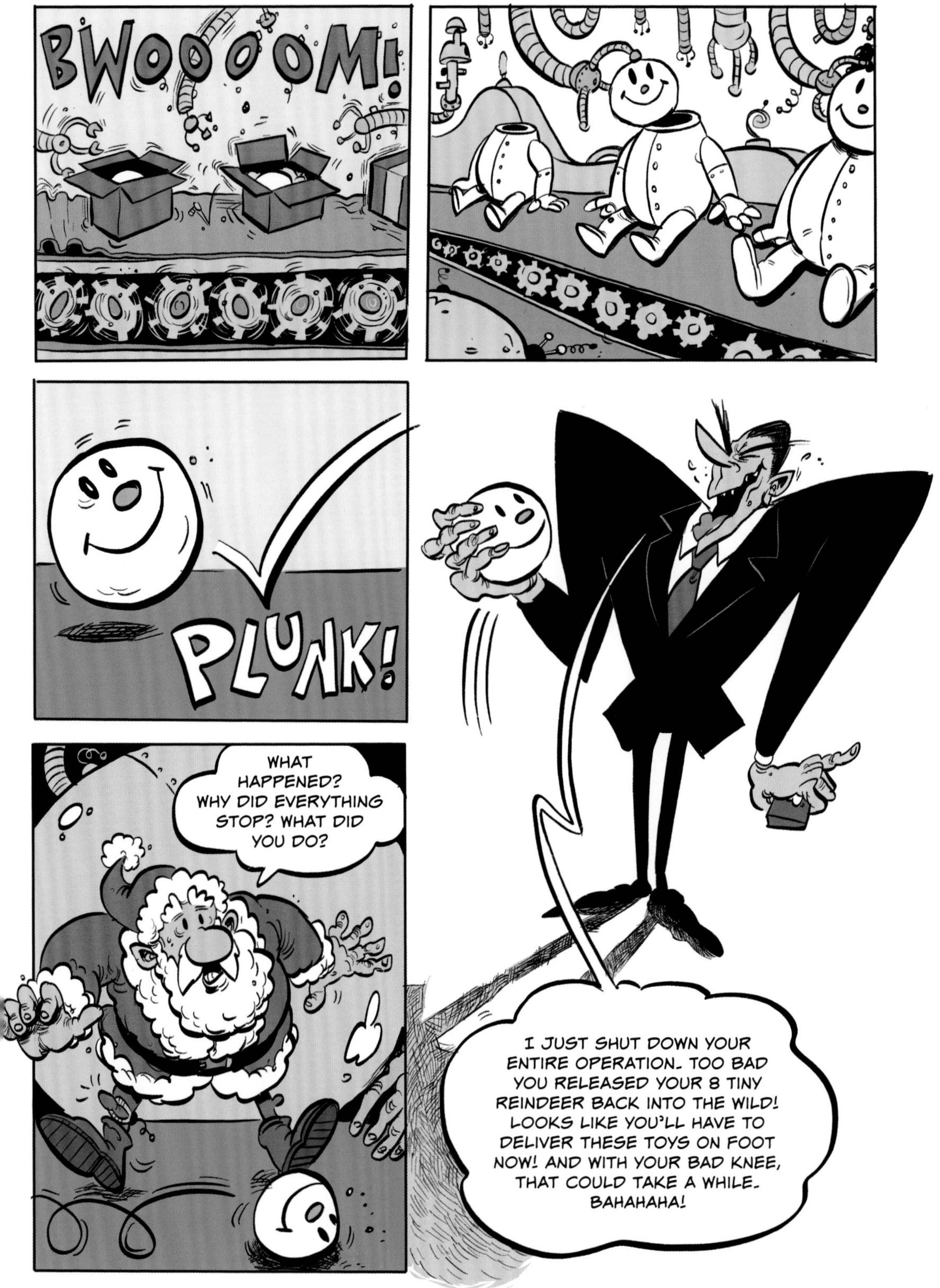
BWOOOOM!
PLUNK!
WHAT HAPPENED? WHY DID EVERYTHING STOP? WHAT DID YOU DO?
I JUST SHUT DOWN YOUR ENTIRE OPERATION. TOO BAD YOU RELEASED YOUR 8 TINY REINDEER BACK INTO THE WILD! LOOKS LIKE YOU'LL HAVE TO DELIVER THESE TOYS ON FOOT NOW! AND WITH YOUR BAD KNEE, THAT COULD TAKE A WHILE. BAHAHAHA!

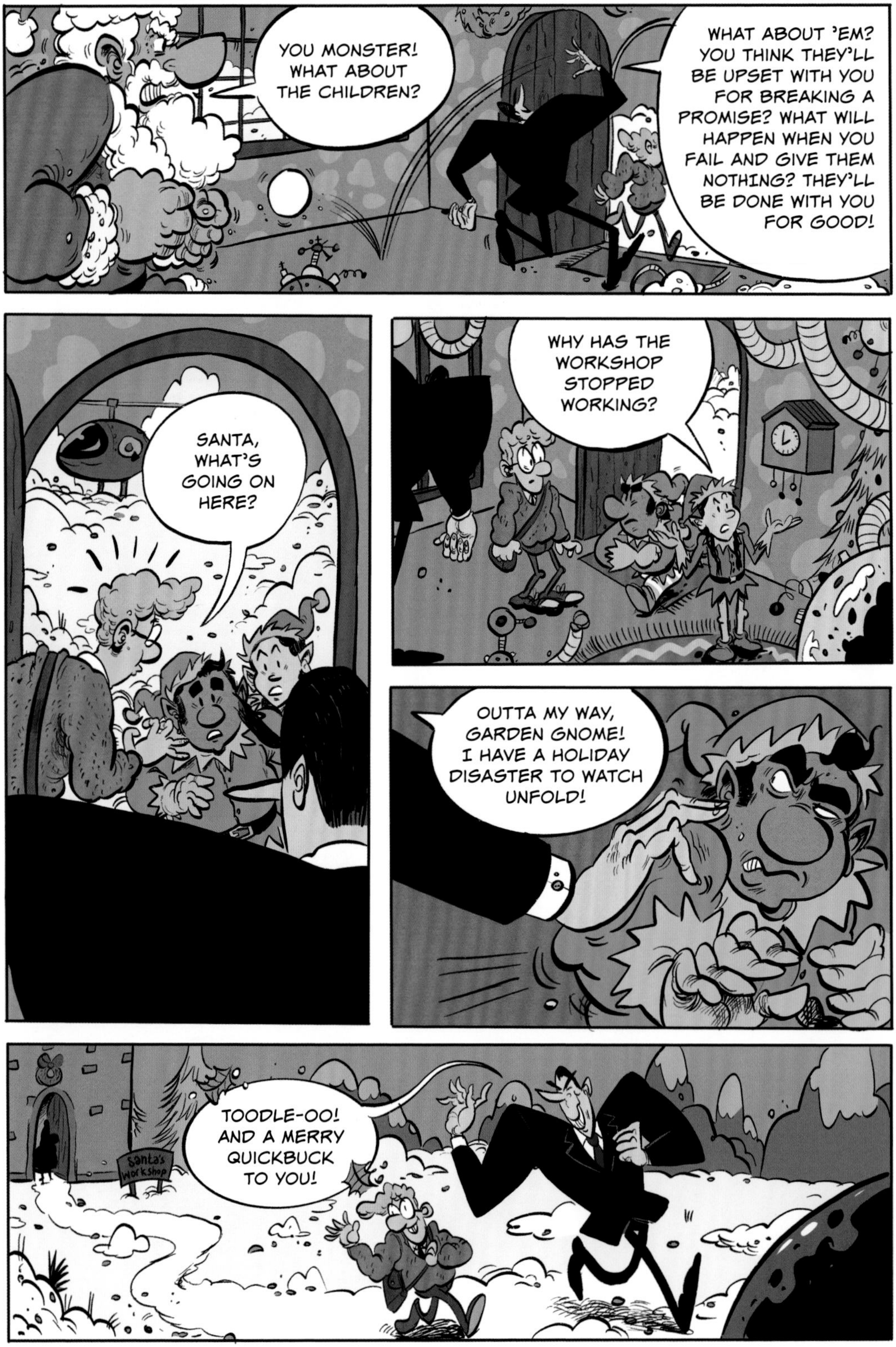
YOU MONSTER! WHAT ABOUT THE CHILDREN?
WHAT ABOUT 'EM? YOU THINK THEY'LL BE UPSET WITH YOU FOR BREAKING A PROMISE? WHAT WILL HAPPEN WHEN YOU FAIL AND GIVE THEM NOTHING? THEY'LL BE DONE WITH YOU FOR GOOD!
SANTA, WHAT'S GOING ON HERE?
WHY HAS THE WORKSHOP STOPPED WORKING?
OUTTA MY WAY, GARDEN GNOME! I HAVE A HOLIDAY DISASTER TO WATCH UNFOLD!
Santa's Workshop
TOODLE-OO! AND A MERRY QUICKBUCK TO YOU!

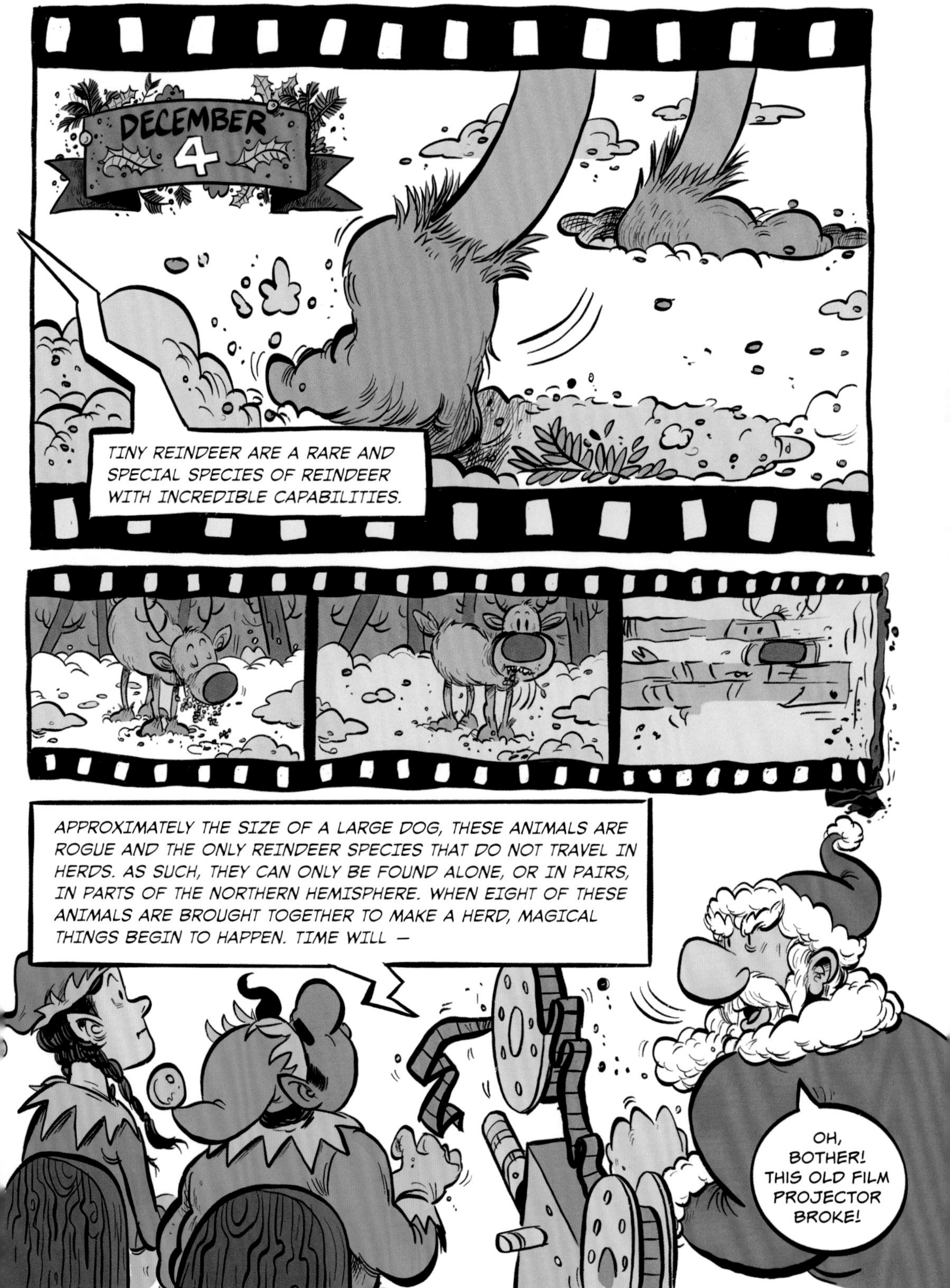
DECEMBER 4
TINY REINDEER ARE A RARE AND SPECIAL SPECIES OF REINDEER WITH INCREDIBLE CAPABILITIES.
APPROXIMATELY THE SIZE OF A LARGE DOG, THESE ANIMALS ARE ROGUE AND THE ONLY REINDEER SPECIES THAT DO NOT TRAVEL IN HERDS. AS SUCH, THEY CAN ONLY BE FOUND ALONE, OR IN PAIRS, IN PARTS OF THE NORTHERN HEMISPHERE. WHEN EIGHT OF THESE ANIMALS ARE BROUGHT TOGETHER TO MAKE A HERD, MAGICAL THINGS BEGIN TO HAPPEN. TIME WILL —
OH, BOTHER! THIS OLD FILM PROJECTOR BROKE!

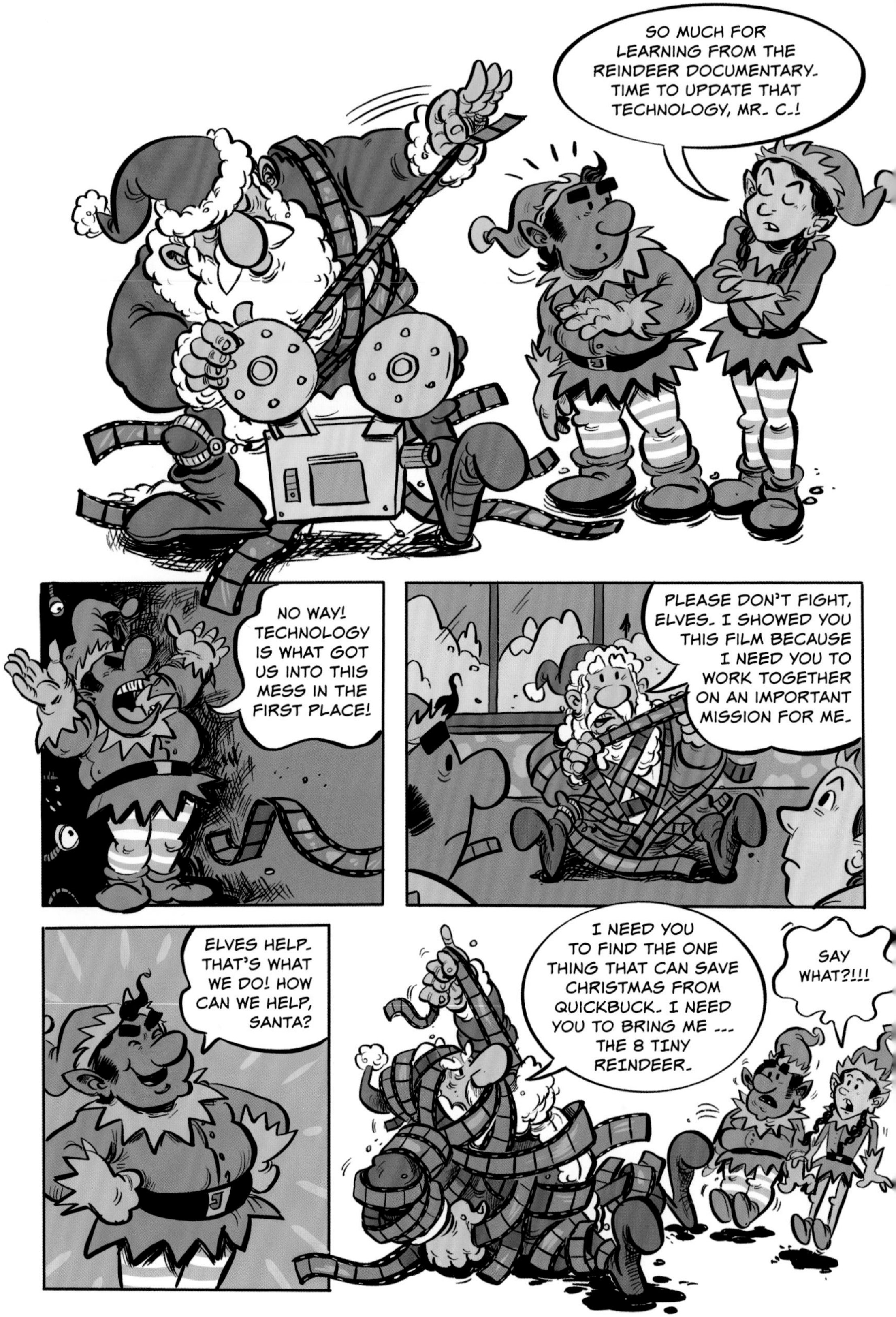
SO MUCH FOR LEARNING FROM THE REINDEER DOCUMENTARY. TIME TO UPDATE THAT TECHNOLOGY, MR. C.!
NO WAY! TECHNOLOGY IS WHAT GOT US INTO THIS MESS IN THE FIRST PLACE!
PLEASE DON'T FIGHT, ELVES. I SHOWED YOU THIS FILM BECAUSE I NEED YOU TO WORK TOGETHER ON AN IMPORTANT MISSION FOR ME.
ELVES HELP. THAT'S WHAT WE DO! HOW CAN WE HELP, SANTA?
I NEED YOU TO FIND THE ONE THING THAT CAN SAVE CHRISTMAS FROM QUICKBUCK. I NEED YOU TO BRING ME ... THE 8 TINY REINDEER.
SAY WHAT?!!!

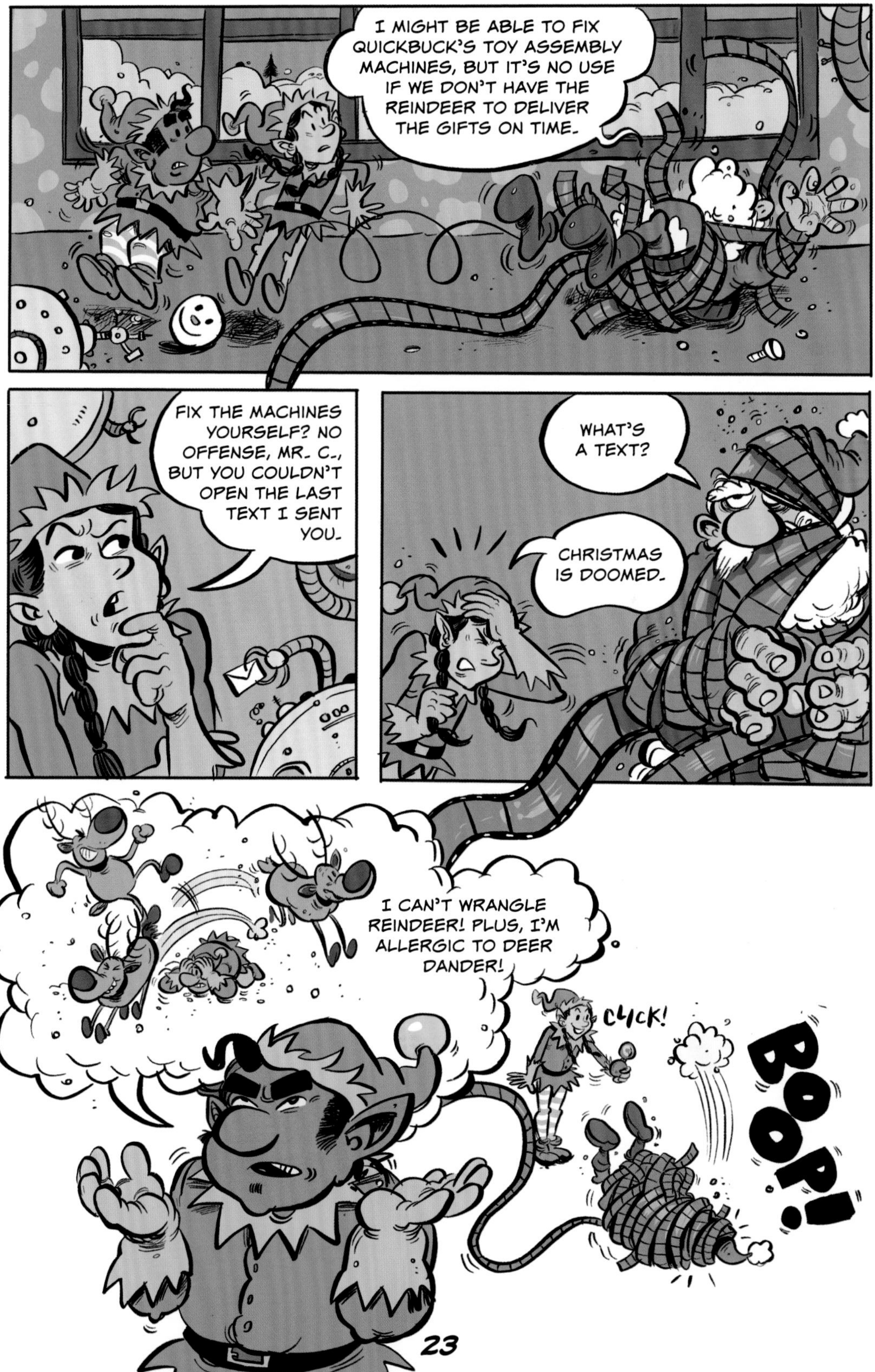
I MIGHT BE ABLE TO FIX QUICKBUCK'S TOY ASSEMBLY MACHINES, BUT IT'S NO USE IF WE DON'T HAVE THE REINDEER TO DELIVER THE GIFTS ON TIME.
FIX THE MACHINES YOURSELF? NO OFFENSE, MR. C., BUT YOU COULDN'T OPEN THE LAST TEXT I SENT YOU.
WHAT'S A TEXT?
CHRISTMAS IS DOOMED.
I CAN'T WRANGLE REINDEER! PLUS, I'M ALLERGIC TO DEER DANDER!
CLICK!
BOOP!

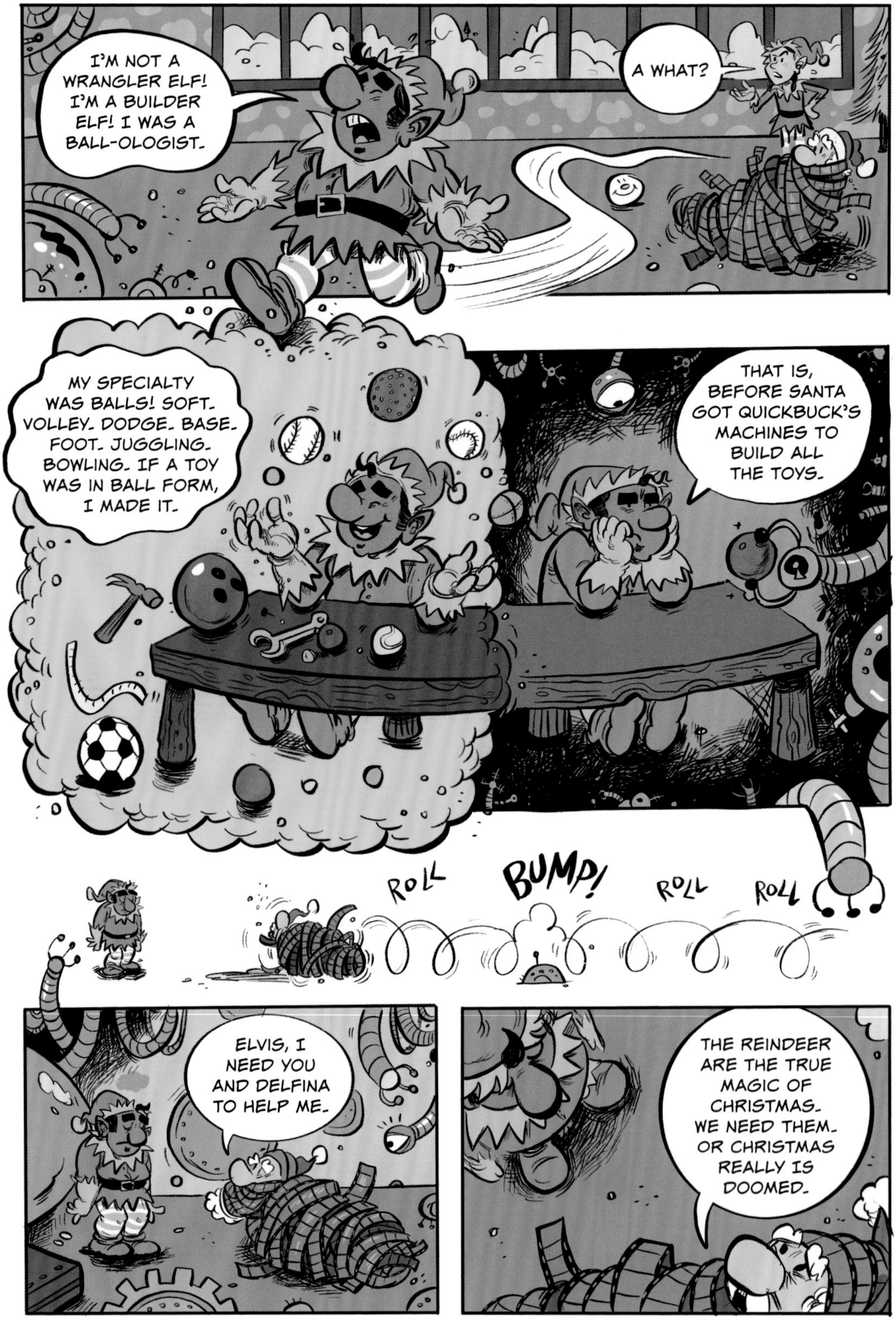
I'M NOT A WRANGLER ELF! I'M A BUILDER ELF! I WAS A BALL-OLOGIST.
A WHAT?
MY SPECIALTY WAS BALLS! SOFT. VOLLEY. DODGE. BASE. FOOT. JUGGLING. BOWLING. IF A TOY WAS IN BALL FORM, I MADE IT.
THAT IS, BEFORE SANTA GOT QUICKBUCK'S MACHINES TO BUILD ALL THE TOYS.
ROLL
BUMP!
ROLL
ROLL
ELVIS, I NEED YOU AND DELFINA TO HELP ME.
THE REINDEER ARE THE TRUE MAGIC OF CHRISTMAS. WE NEED THEM. OR CHRISTMAS REALLY IS DOOMED.

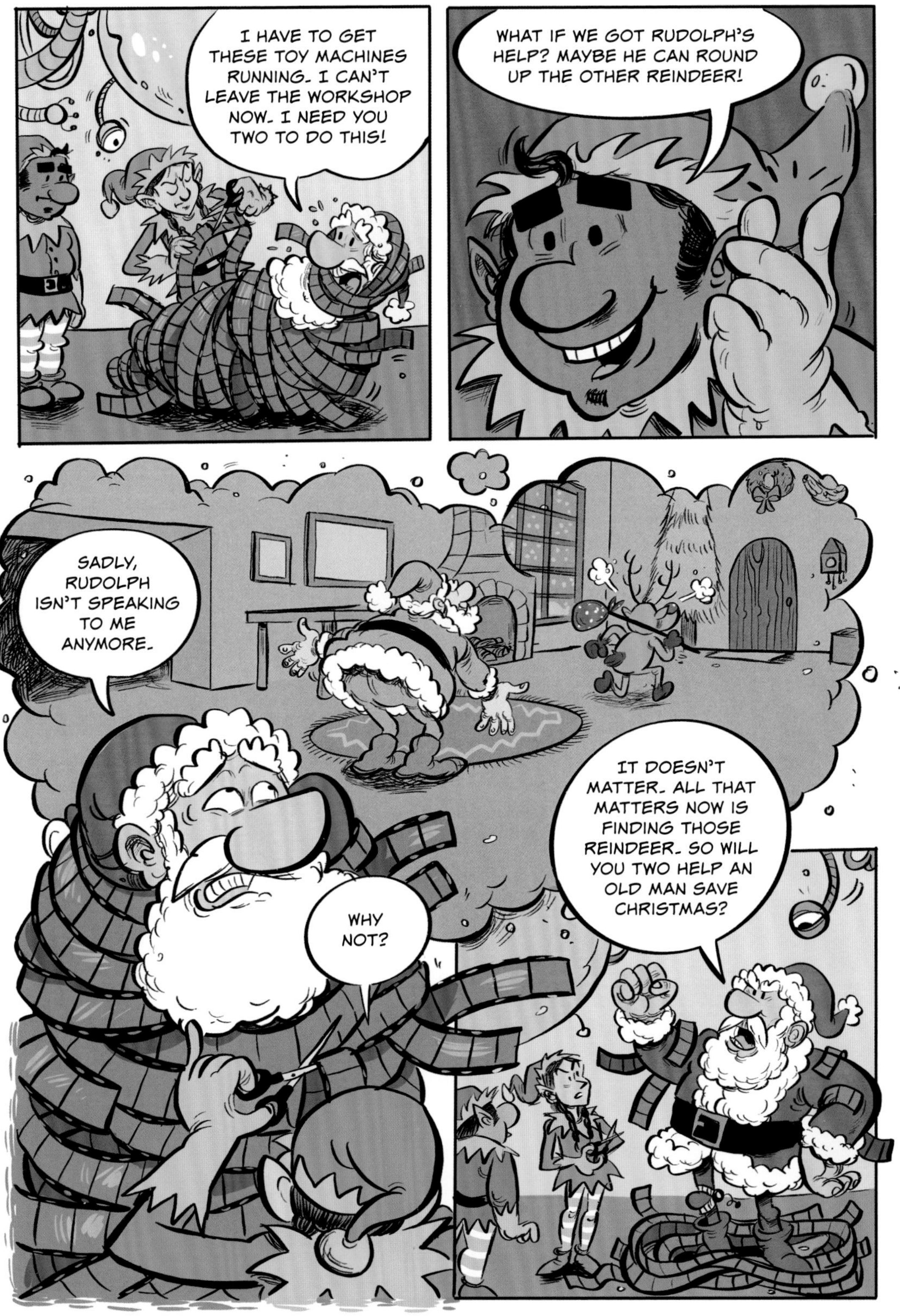
I HAVE TO GET THESE TOY MACHINES RUNNING. I CAN'T LEAVE THE WORKSHOP NOW. I NEED YOU TWO TO DO THIS!
WHAT IF WE GOT RUDOLPH'S HELP? MAYBE HE CAN ROUND UP THE OTHER REINDEER!
SADLY, RUDOLPH ISN'T SPEAKING TO ME ANYMORE.
WHY NOT?
IT DOESN'T MATTER. ALL THAT MATTERS NOW IS FINDING THOSE REINDEER. SO WILL YOU TWO HELP AN OLD MAN SAVE CHRISTMAS?

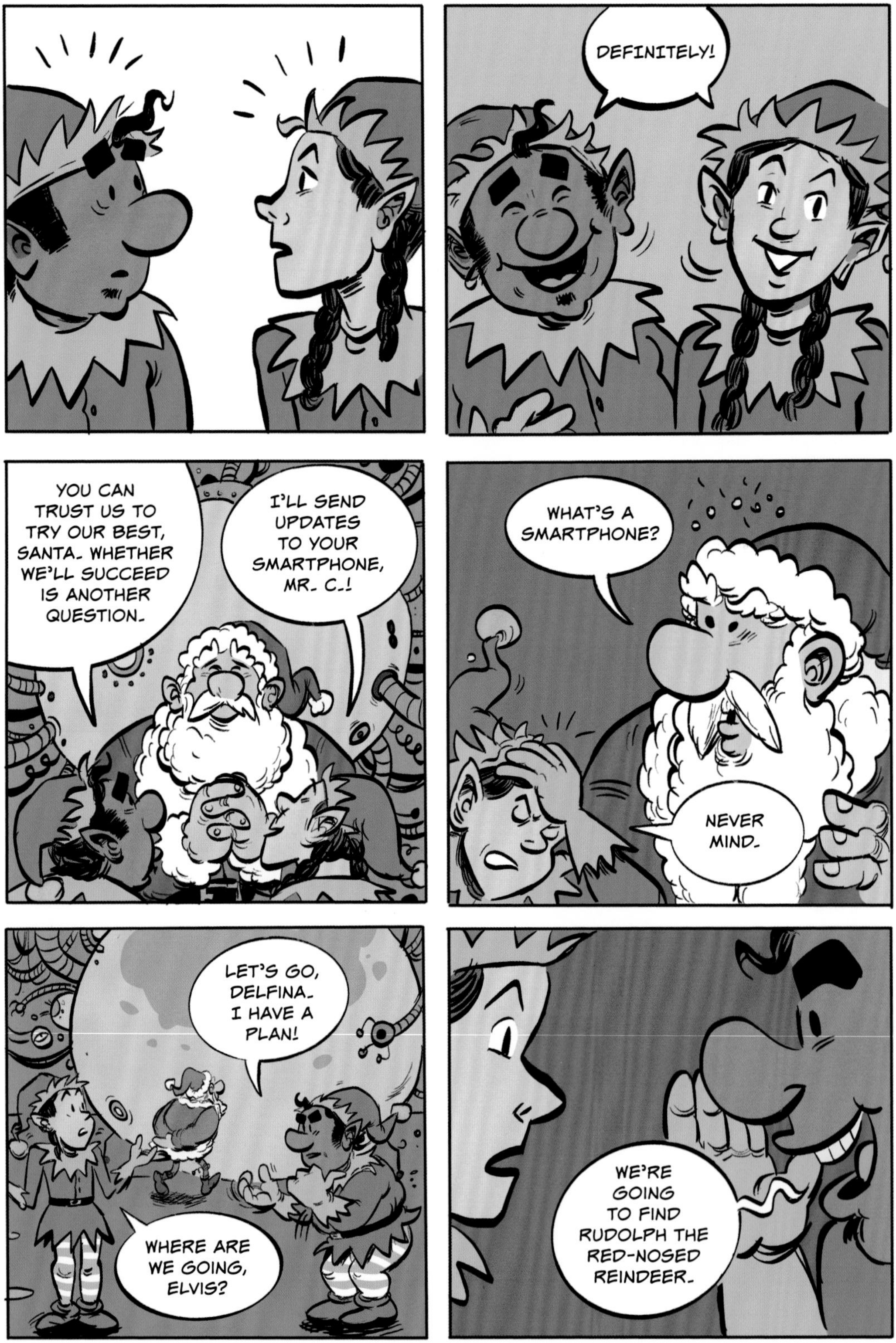
DEFINITELY!
YOU CAN TRUST US TO TRY OUR BEST, SANTA. WHETHER WE'LL SUCCEED IS ANOTHER QUESTION.
I'LL SEND UPDATES TO YOUR SMARTPHONE, MR. C.!
WHAT'S A SMARTPHONE?
NEVER MIND.
LET'S GO, DELFINA. I HAVE A PLAN!
WHERE ARE WE GOING, ELVIS?
WE'RE GOING TO FIND RUDOLPH THE RED-NOSED REINDEER.

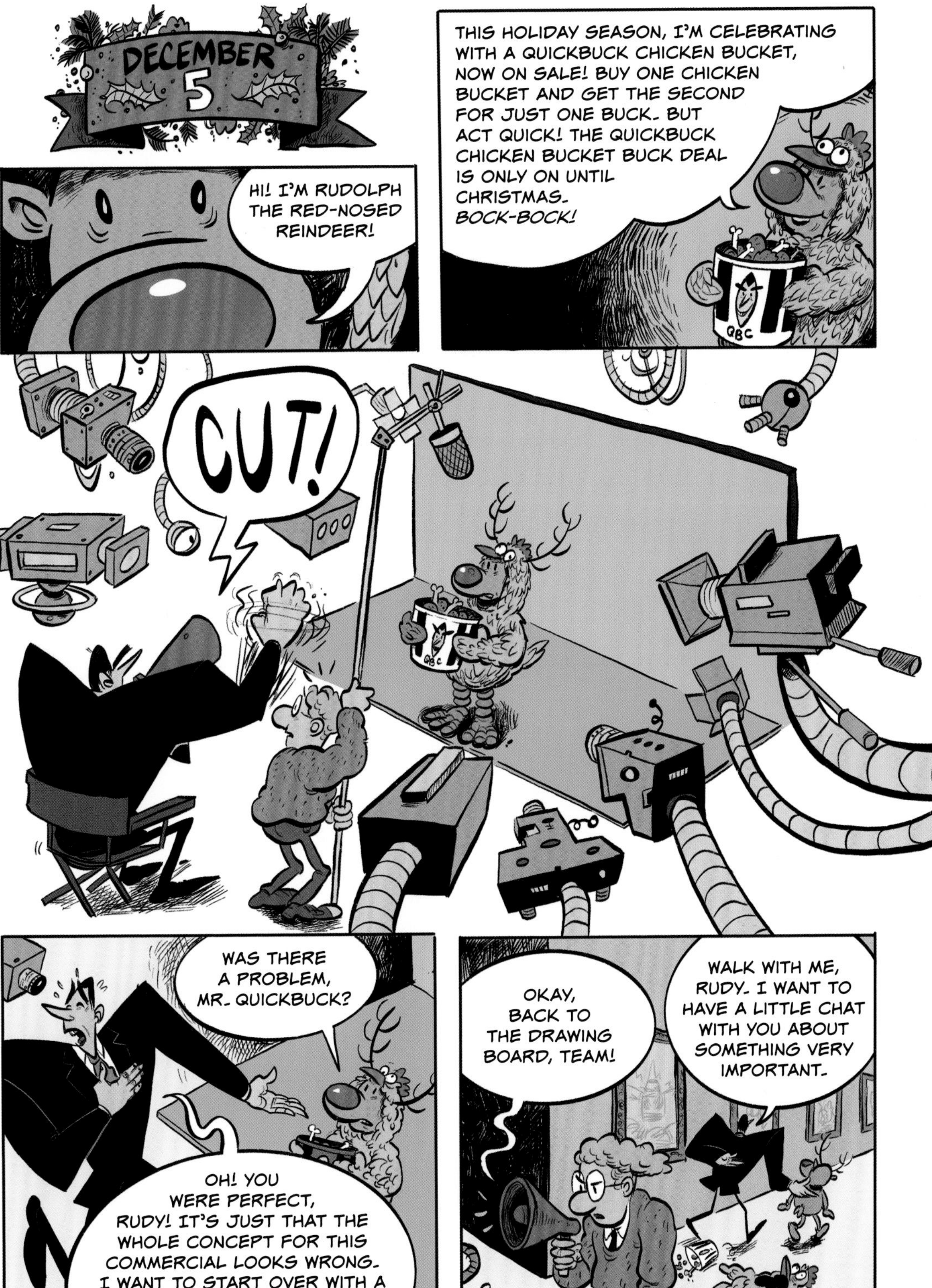
DECEMBER 5
HI! I'M RUDOLPH THE RED-NOSED REINDEER!
THIS HOLIDAY SEASON, I'M CELEBRATING WITH A QUICKBUCK CHICKEN BUCKET, NOW ON SALE! BUY ONE CHICKEN BUCKET AND GET THE SECOND FOR JUST ONE BUCK. BUT ACT QUICK! THE QUICKBUCK CHICKEN BUCKET BUCK DEAL IS ONLY ON UNTIL CHRISTMAS. BOCK-BOCK!
QBC
CUT!
QBC
WAS THERE A PROBLEM, MR. QUICKBUCK?
OH! YOU WERE PERFECT, RUDY! IT'S JUST THAT THE WHOLE CONCEPT FOR THIS COMMERCIAL LOOKS WRONG. I WANT TO START OVER WITH A BETTER QUICKBUCK CONCEPT.
WALK WITH ME, RUDY. I WANT TO HAVE A LITTLE CHAT WITH YOU ABOUT SOMETHING VERY IMPORTANT.
OKAY, BACK TO THE DRAWING BOARD, TEAM!

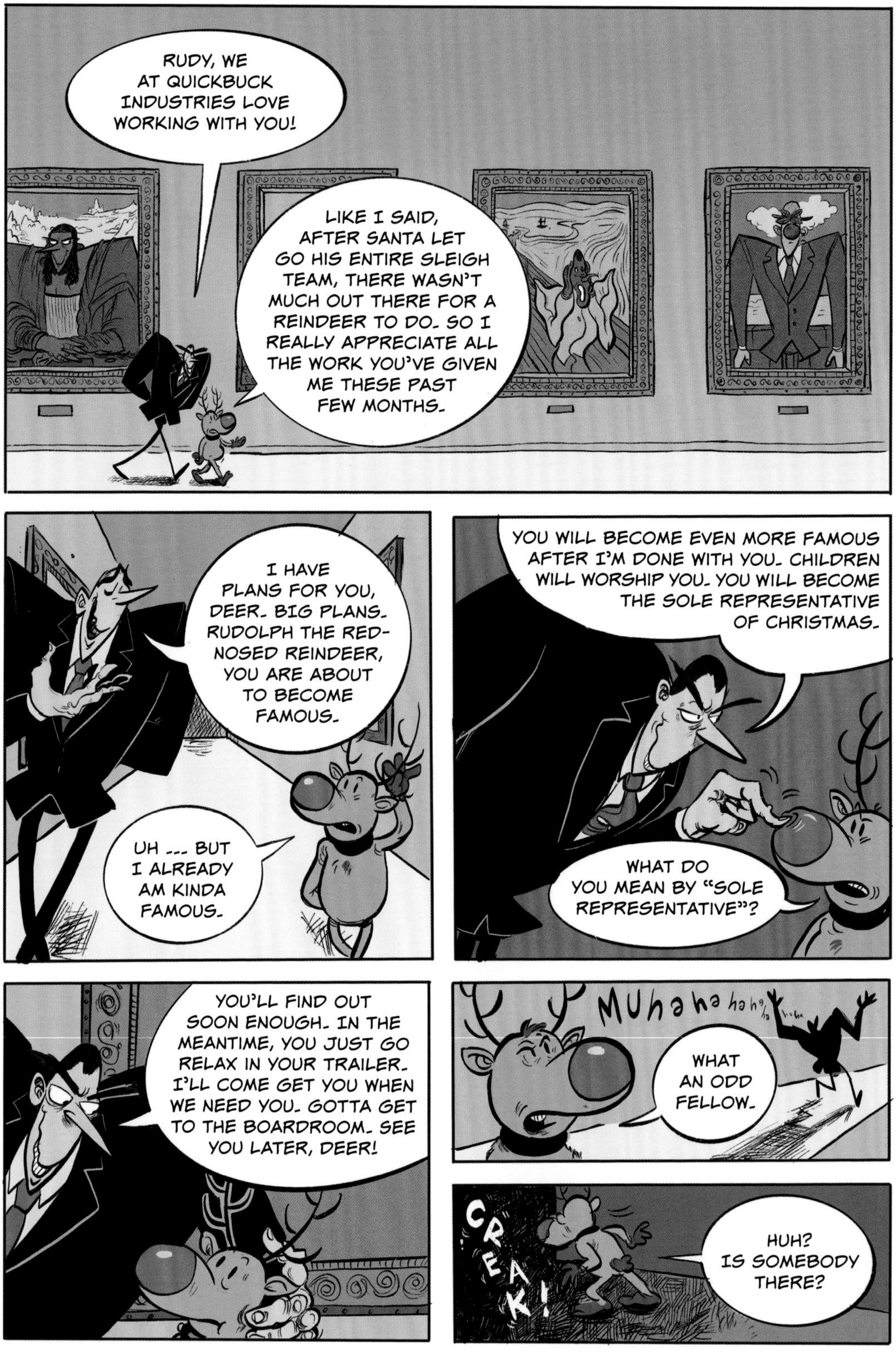
RUDY, WE AT QUICKBUCK INDUSTRIES LOVE WORKING WITH YOU!
LIKE I SAID, AFTER SANTA LET GO HIS ENTIRE SLEIGH TEAM, THERE WASN'T MUCH OUT THERE FOR A REINDEER TO DO. SO I REALLY APPRECIATE ALL THE WORK YOU'VE GIVEN ME THESE PAST FEW MONTHS.
I HAVE PLANS FOR YOU, DEER. BIG PLANS. RUDOLPH THE RED-NOSED REINDEER, YOU ARE ABOUT TO BECOME FAMOUS.
UH ... BUT I ALREADY AM KINDA FAMOUS.
YOU WILL BECOME EVEN MORE FAMOUS AFTER I'M DONE WITH YOU. CHILDREN WILL WORSHIP YOU. YOU WILL BECOME THE SOLE REPRESENTATIVE OF CHRISTMAS.
WHAT DO YOU MEAN BY "SOLE REPRESENTATIVE"?
YOU'LL FIND OUT SOON ENOUGH. IN THE MEANTIME, YOU JUST GO RELAX IN YOUR TRAILER. I'LL COME GET YOU WHEN WE NEED YOU. GOTTA GET TO THE BOARDROOM. SEE YOU LATER, DEER!
MUhahahahaha
WHAT AN ODD FELLOW.
CREAK!
HUH? IS SOMEBODY THERE?

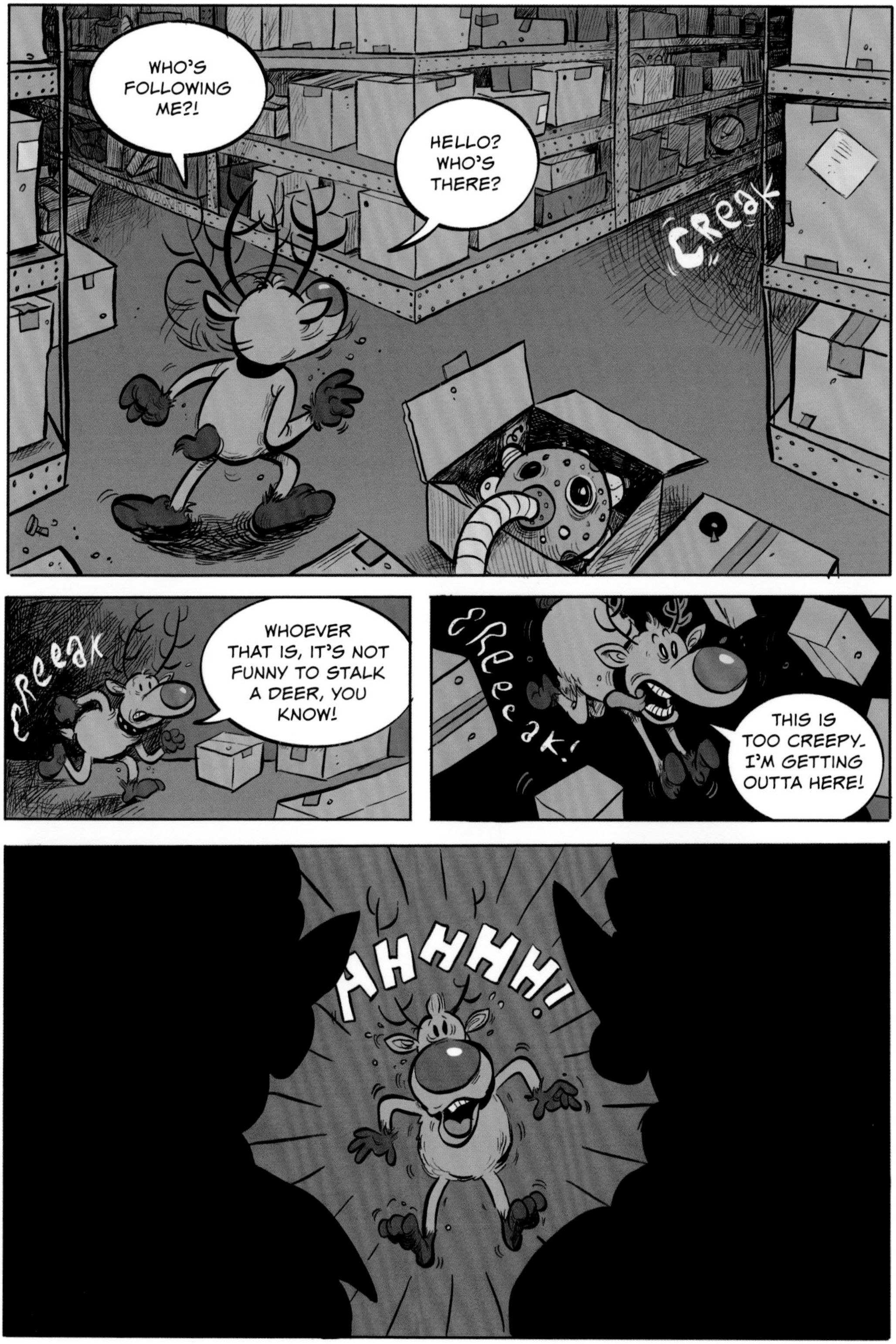
WHO'S FOLLOWING ME?!
HELLO? WHO'S THERE?
CREAK
CREEAK
WHOEVER THAT IS, IT'S NOT FUNNY TO STALK A DEER, YOU KNOW!
CREEEAK!
THIS IS TOO CREEPY. I'M GETTING OUTTA HERE!
AHHHH!

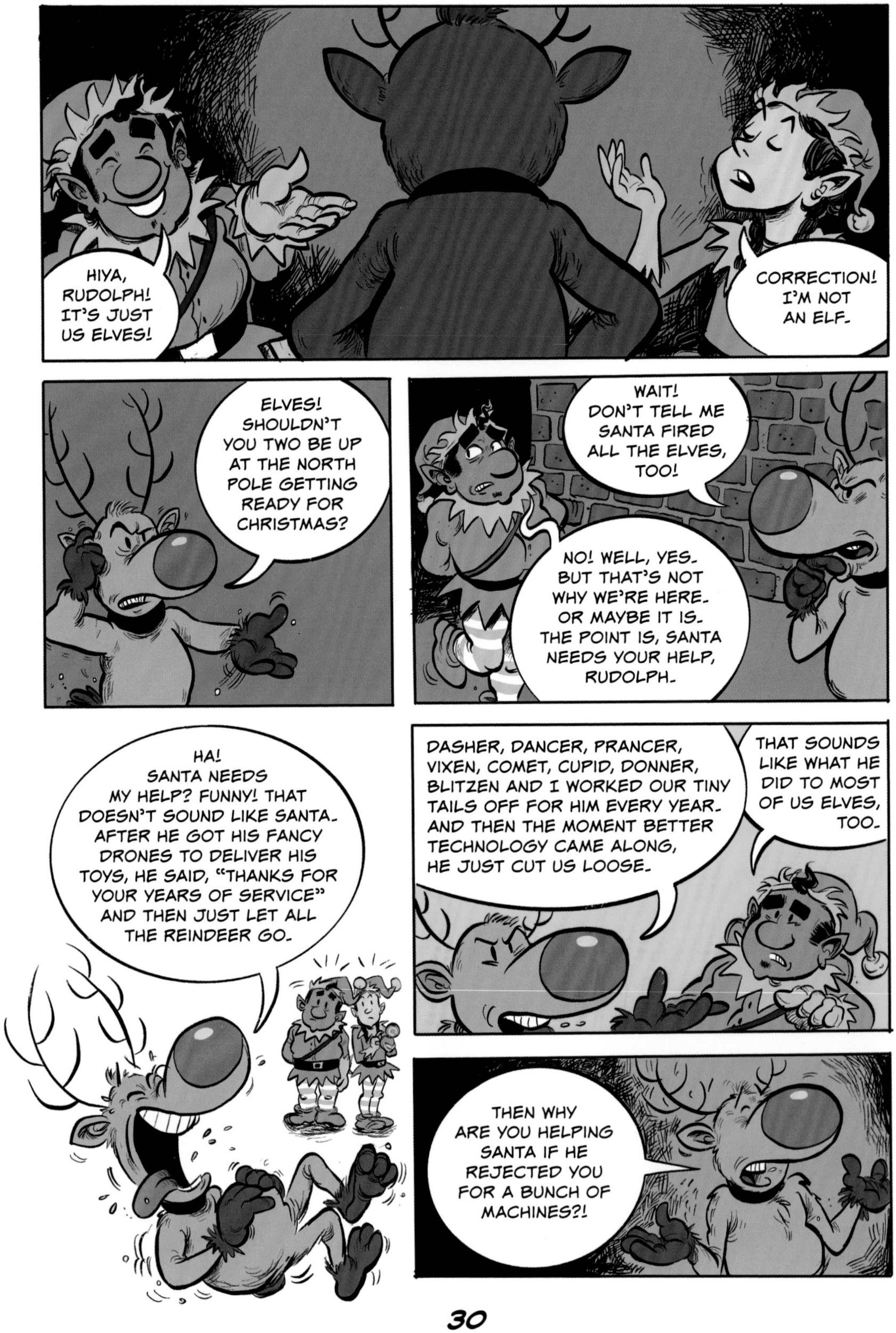
HIYA, RUDOLPH! IT'S JUST US ELVES!
CORRECTION! I'M NOT AN ELF.
ELVES! SHOULDN'T YOU TWO BE UP AT THE NORTH POLE GETTING READY FOR CHRISTMAS?
WAIT! DON'T TELL ME SANTA FIRED ALL THE ELVES, TOO!
NO! WELL, YES. BUT THAT'S NOT WHY WE'RE HERE. OR MAYBE IT IS. THE POINT IS, SANTA NEEDS YOUR HELP, RUDOLPH.
HA! SANTA NEEDS MY HELP? FUNNY! THAT DOESN'T SOUND LIKE SANTA. AFTER HE GOT HIS FANCY DRONES TO DELIVER HIS TOYS, HE SAID, "THANKS FOR YOUR YEARS OF SERVICE" AND THEN JUST LET ALL THE REINDEER GO.
DASHER, DANCER, PRANCER, VIXEN, COMET, CUPID, DONNER, BLITZEN AND I WORKED OUR TINY TAILS OFF FOR HIM EVERY YEAR. AND THEN THE MOMENT BETTER TECHNOLOGY CAME ALONG, HE JUST CUT US LOOSE.
THAT SOUNDS LIKE WHAT HE DID TO MOST OF US ELVES, TOO.
THEN WHY ARE YOU HELPING SANTA IF HE REJECTED YOU FOR A BUNCH OF MACHINES?!

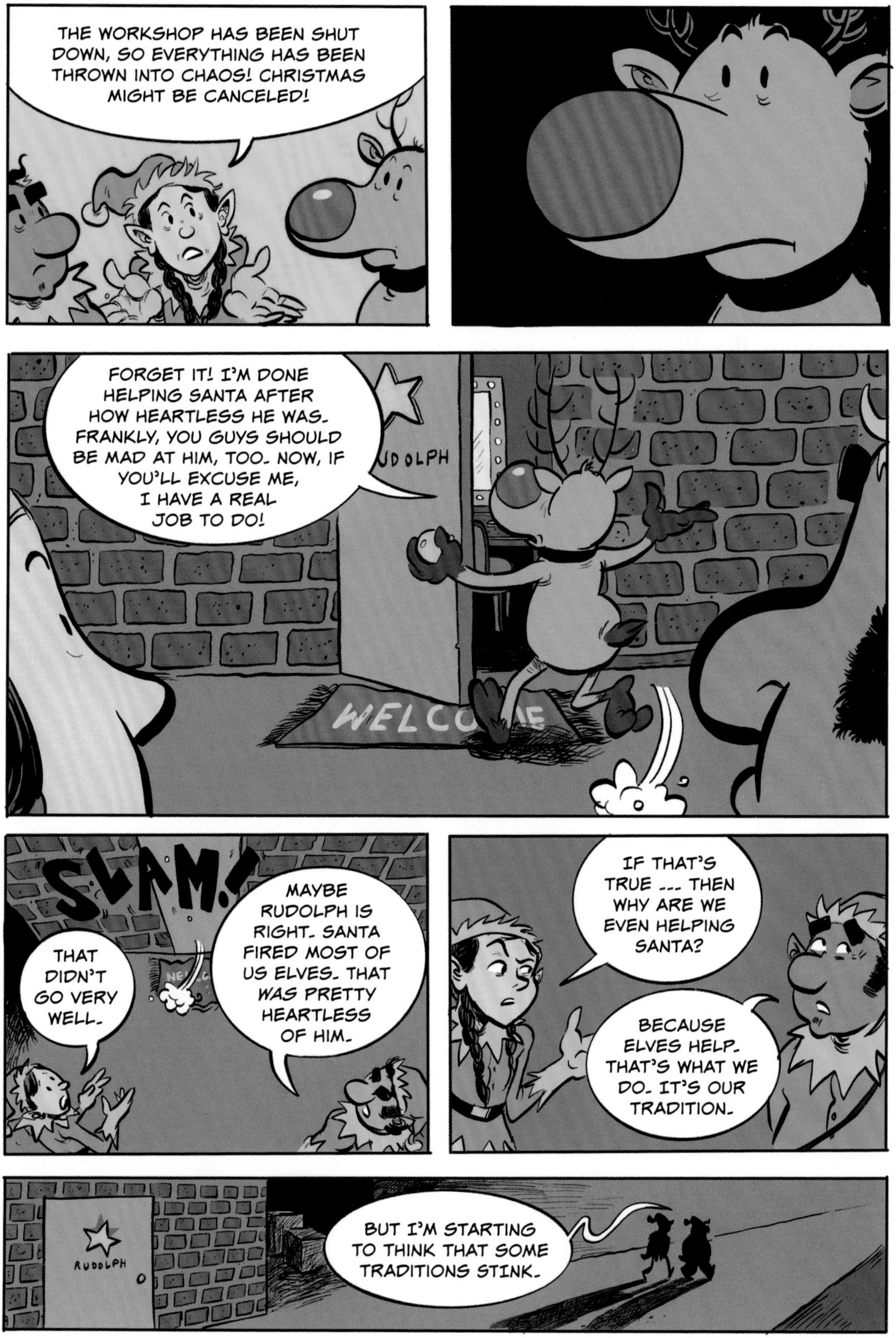
THE WORKSHOP HAS BEEN SHUT DOWN, SO EVERYTHING HAS BEEN THROWN INTO CHAOS! CHRISTMAS MIGHT BE CANCELED!
FORGET IT! I'M DONE HELPING SANTA AFTER HOW HEARTLESS HE WAS. FRANKLY, YOU GUYS SHOULD BE MAD AT HIM, TOO. NOW, IF YOU'LL EXCUSE ME, I HAVE A REAL JOB TO DO!
UDOLPH
WELCOME
SLAM!
THAT DIDN'T GO VERY WELL.
MAYBE RUDOLPH IS RIGHT. SANTA FIRED MOST OF US ELVES. THAT WAS PRETTY HEARTLESS OF HIM.
IF THAT'S TRUE ... THEN WHY ARE WE EVEN HELPING SANTA?
BECAUSE ELVES HELP. THAT'S WHAT WE DO. IT'S OUR TRADITION.
RUDOLPH
BUT I'M STARTING TO THINK THAT SOME TRADITIONS STINK.

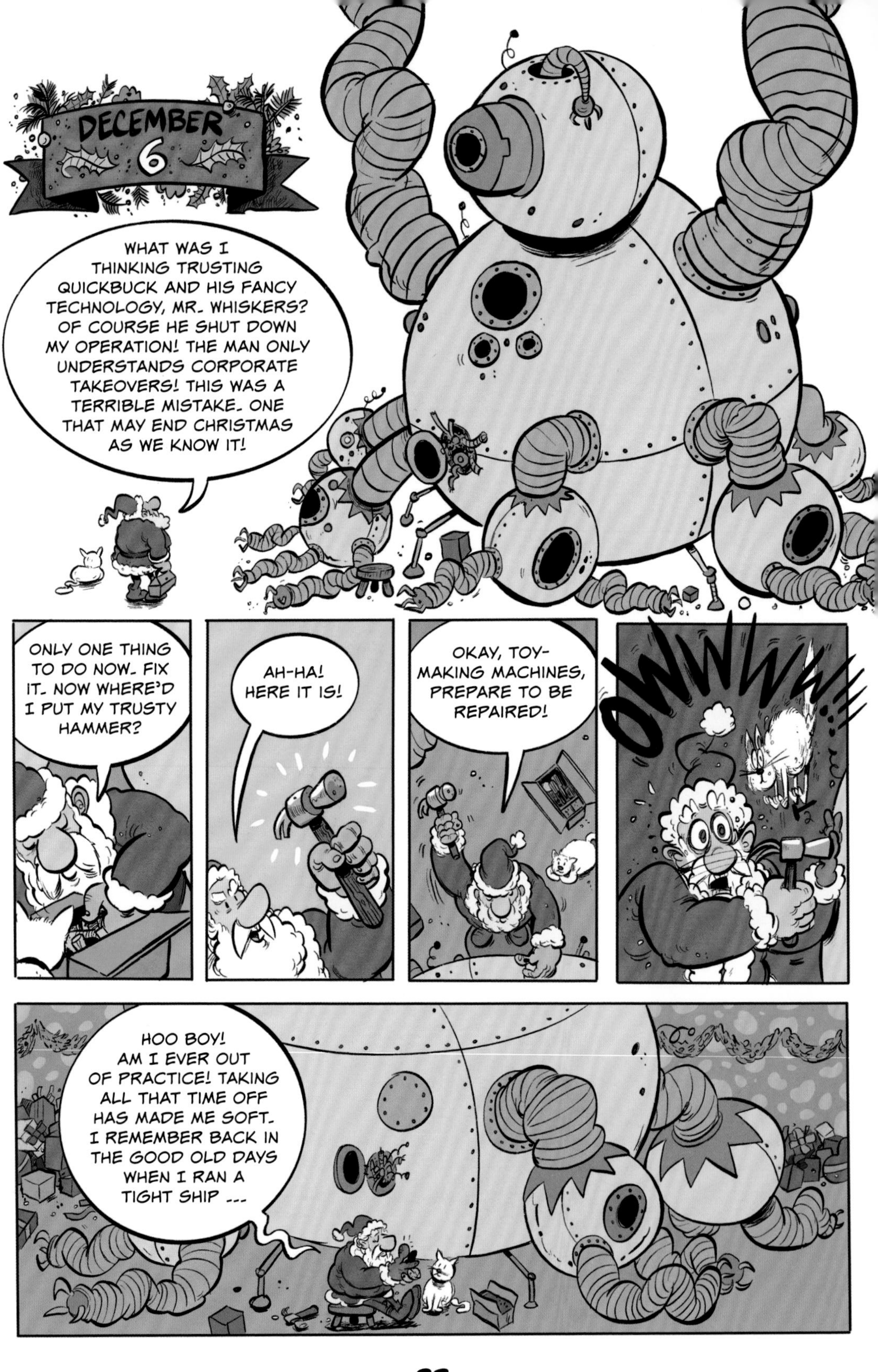
DECEMBER 6
WHAT WAS I THINKING TRUSTING QUICKBUCK AND HIS FANCY TECHNOLOGY, MR. WHISKERS? OF COURSE HE SHUT DOWN MY OPERATION! THE MAN ONLY UNDERSTANDS CORPORATE TAKEOVERS! THIS WAS A TERRIBLE MISTAKE. ONE THAT MAY END CHRISTMAS AS WE KNOW IT!
ONLY ONE THING TO DO NOW. FIX IT. NOW WHERE'D I PUT MY TRUSTY HAMMER?
AH-HA! HERE IT IS!
OKAY, TOY-MAKING MACHINES, PREPARE TO BE REPAIRED!
OWWWW!!
HOO BOY! AM I EVER OUT OF PRACTICE! TAKING ALL THAT TIME OFF HAS MADE ME SOFT. I REMEMBER BACK IN THE GOOD OLD DAYS WHEN I RAN A TIGHT SHIP ...

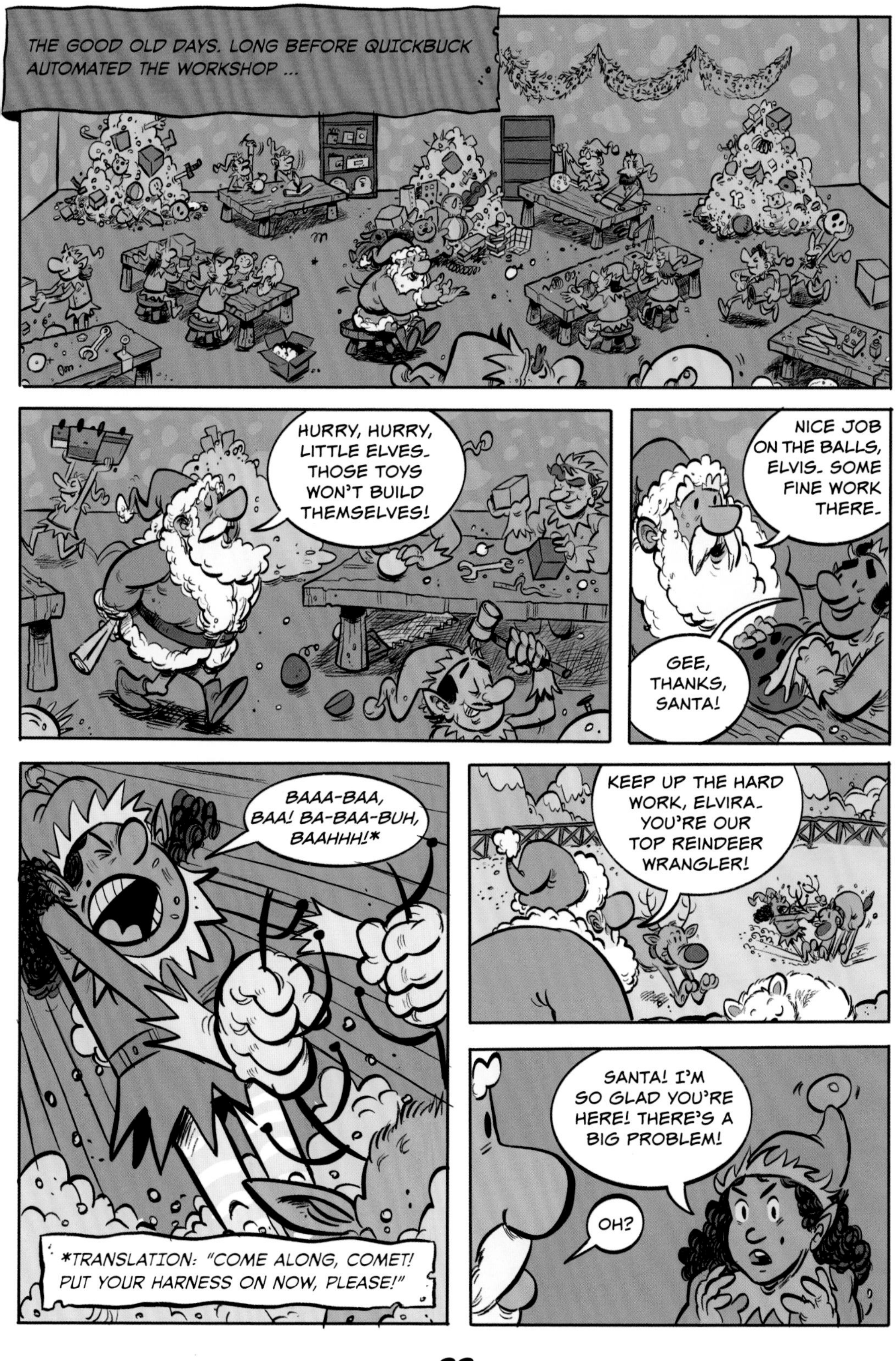
THE GOOD OLD DAYS. LONG BEFORE QUICKBUCK AUTOMATED THE WORKSHOP ...
HURRY, HURRY, LITTLE ELVES. THOSE TOYS WON'T BUILD THEMSELVES!
NICE JOB ON THE BALLS, ELVIS. SOME FINE WORK THERE.
GEE, THANKS, SANTA!
BAAA-BAA, BAA! BA-BAA-BUH, BAAHHH!*
*TRANSLATION: "COME ALONG, COMET! PUT YOUR HARNESS ON NOW, PLEASE!"
KEEP UP THE HARD WORK, ELVIRA. YOU'RE OUR TOP REINDEER WRANGLER!
SANTA! I'M SO GLAD YOU'RE HERE! THERE'S A BIG PROBLEM!
OH?

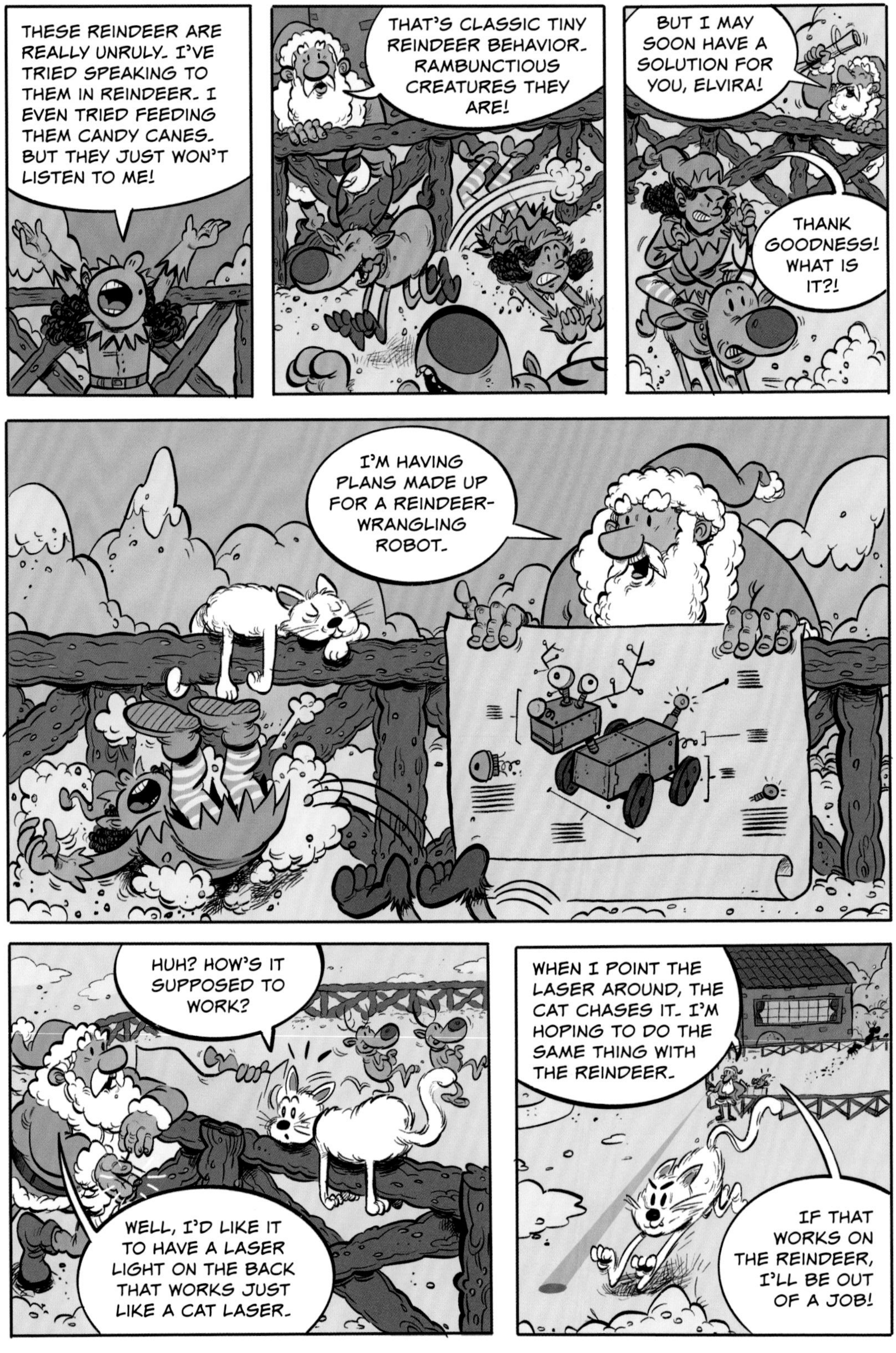

THESE REINDEER ARE REALLY UNRULY. I'VE TRIED SPEAKING TO THEM IN REINDEER. I EVEN TRIED FEEDING THEM CANDY CANES. BUT THEY JUST WON'T LISTEN TO ME!
THAT'S CLASSIC TINY REINDEER BEHAVIOR. RAMBUNCTIOUS CREATURES THEY ARE!
BUT I MAY SOON HAVE A SOLUTION FOR YOU, ELVIRA!
THANK GOODNESS! WHAT IS IT?!
I'M HAVING PLANS MADE UP FOR A REINDEER-WRANGLING ROBOT.
HUH? HOW'S IT SUPPOSED TO WORK?
WELL, I'D LIKE IT TO HAVE A LASER LIGHT ON THE BACK THAT WORKS JUST LIKE A CAT LASER.
WHEN I POINT THE LASER AROUND, THE CAT CHASES IT. I'M HOPING TO DO THE SAME THING WITH THE REINDEER.
IF THAT WORKS ON THE REINDEER, I'LL BE OUT OF A JOB!

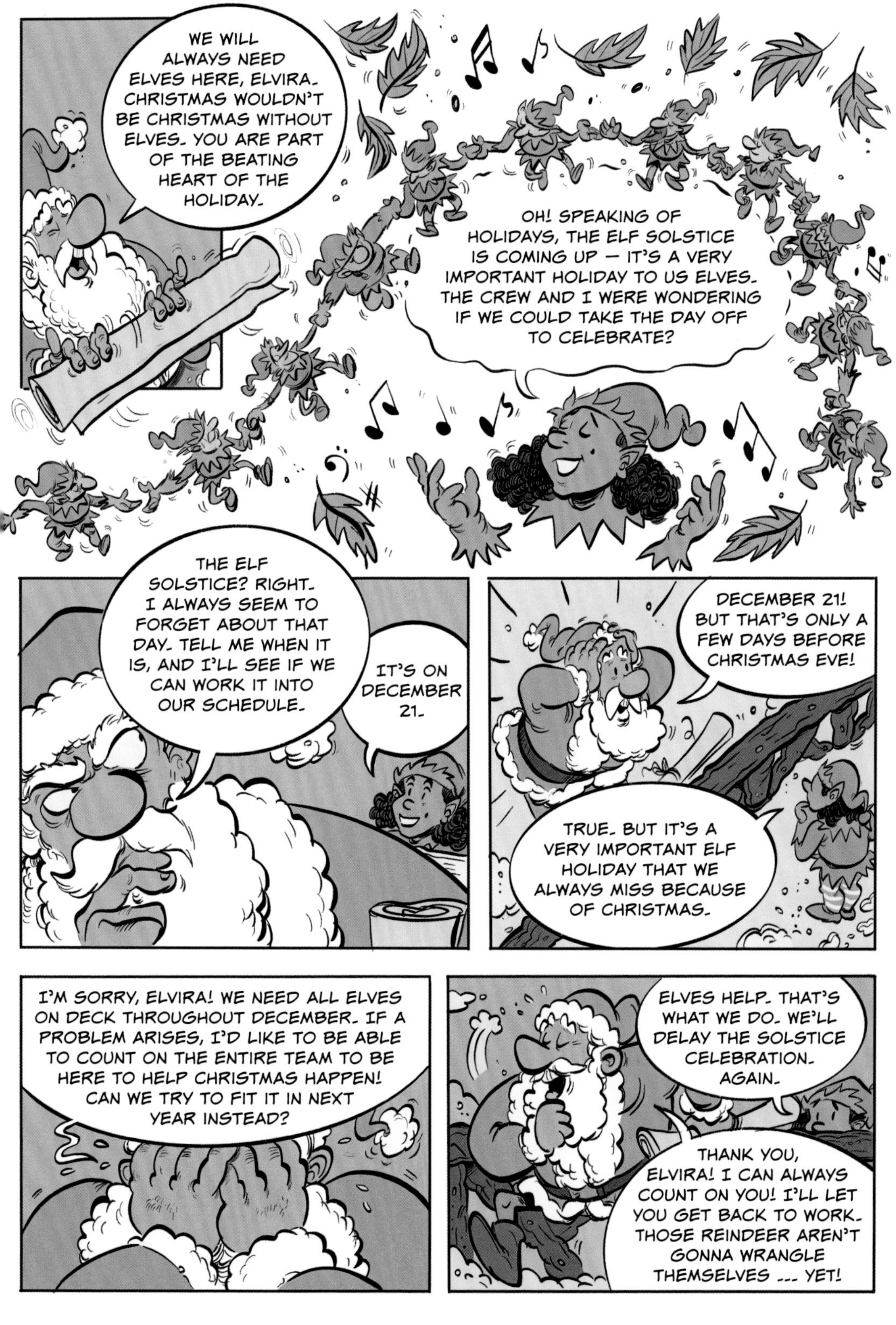
WE WILL ALWAYS NEED ELVES HERE, ELVIRA. CHRISTMAS WOULDN'T BE CHRISTMAS WITHOUT ELVES. YOU ARE PART OF THE BEATING HEART OF THE HOLIDAY.
OH! SPEAKING OF HOLIDAYS, THE ELF SOLSTICE IS COMING UP — IT'S A VERY IMPORTANT HOLIDAY TO US ELVES. THE CREW AND I WERE WONDERING IF WE COULD TAKE THE DAY OFF TO CELEBRATE?
THE ELF SOLSTICE? RIGHT. I ALWAYS SEEM TO FORGET ABOUT THAT DAY. TELL ME WHEN IT IS, AND I'LL SEE IF WE CAN WORK IT INTO OUR SCHEDULE.
IT'S ON DECEMBER 21.
DECEMBER 21! BUT THAT'S ONLY A FEW DAYS BEFORE CHRISTMAS EVE!
TRUE. BUT IT'S A VERY IMPORTANT ELF HOLIDAY THAT WE ALWAYS MISS BECAUSE OF CHRISTMAS.
I'M SORRY, ELVIRA! WE NEED ALL ELVES ON DECK THROUGHOUT DECEMBER. IF A PROBLEM ARISES, I'D LIKE TO BE ABLE TO COUNT ON THE ENTIRE TEAM TO BE HERE TO HELP CHRISTMAS HAPPEN! CAN WE TRY TO FIT IT IN NEXT YEAR INSTEAD?
ELVES HELP. THAT'S WHAT WE DO. WE'LL DELAY THE SOLSTICE CELEBRATION. AGAIN.
THANK YOU, ELVIRA! I CAN ALWAYS COUNT ON YOU! I'LL LET YOU GET BACK TO WORK. THOSE REINDEER AREN'T GONNA WRANGLE THEMSELVES ... YET!

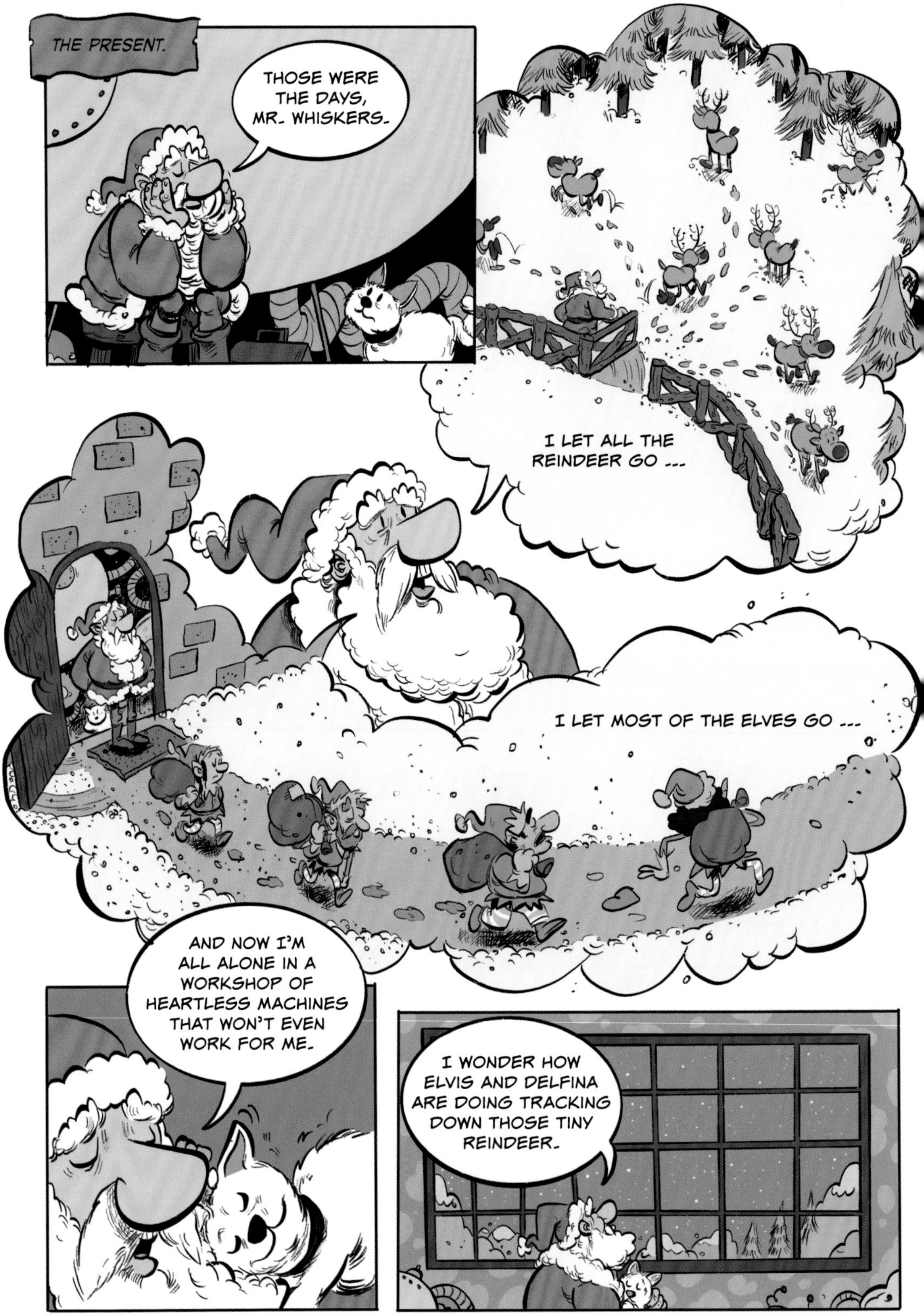
THE PRESENT.
THOSE WERE THE DAYS, MR. WHISKERS.
I LET ALL THE REINDEER GO ...
I LET MOST OF THE ELVES GO ...
AND NOW I'M ALL ALONE IN A WORKSHOP OF HEARTLESS MACHINES THAT WON'T EVEN WORK FOR ME.
I WONDER HOW ELVIS AND DELFINA ARE DOING TRACKING DOWN THOSE TINY REINDEER.

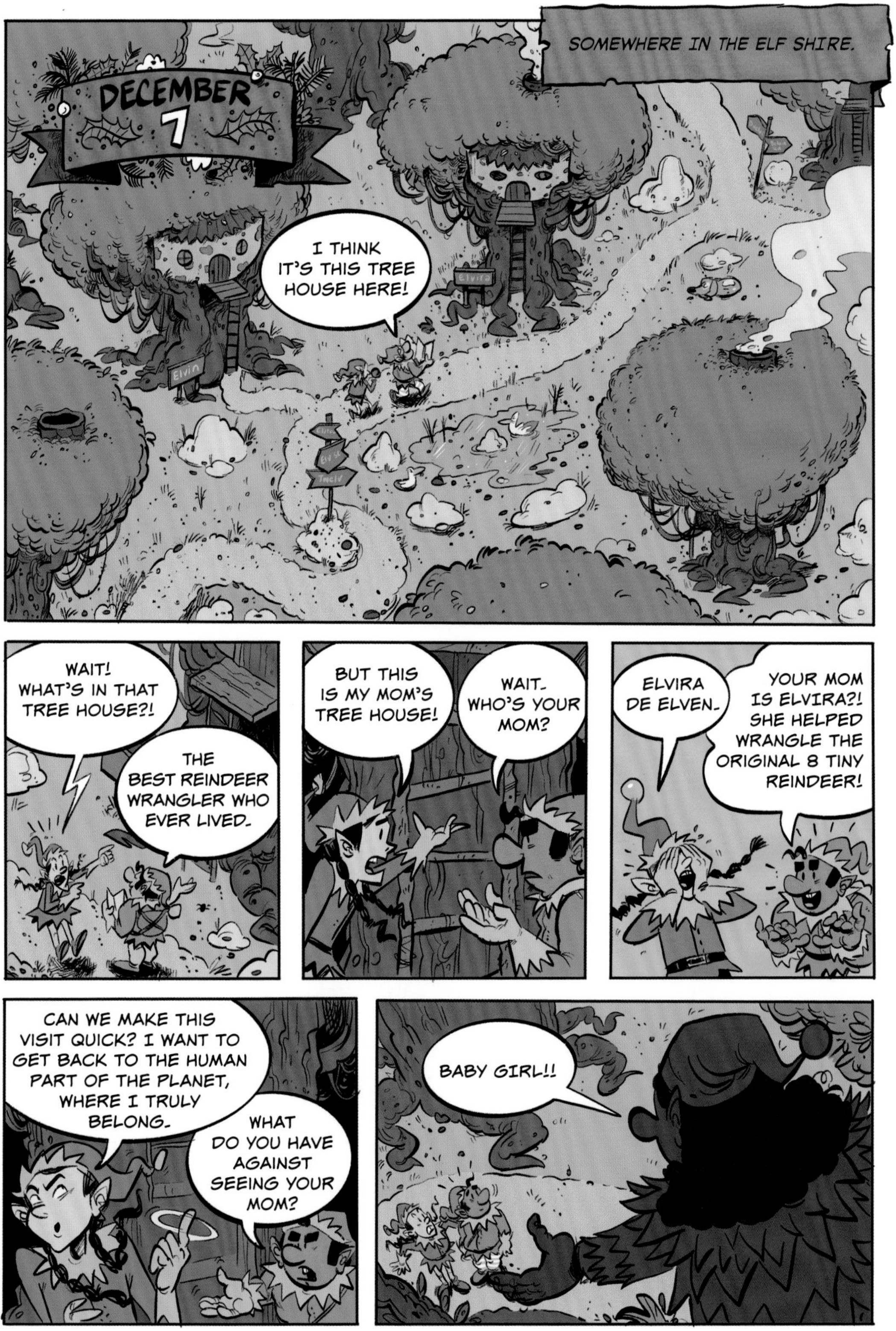
DECEMBER 7
SOMEWHERE IN THE ELF SHIRE.
I THINK IT'S THIS TREE HOUSE HERE!
Elvira
Elvin
WAIT! WHAT'S IN THAT TREE HOUSE?!
THE BEST REINDEER WRANGLER WHO EVER LIVED.
BUT THIS IS MY MOM'S TREE HOUSE!
WAIT. WHO'S YOUR MOM?
ELVIRA DE ELVEN.
YOUR MOM IS ELVIRA?! SHE HELPED WRANGLE THE ORIGINAL 8 TINY REINDEER!
CAN WE MAKE THIS VISIT QUICK? I WANT TO GET BACK TO THE HUMAN PART OF THE PLANET, WHERE I TRULY BELONG.
WHAT DO YOU HAVE AGAINST SEEING YOUR MOM?
BABY GIRL!!

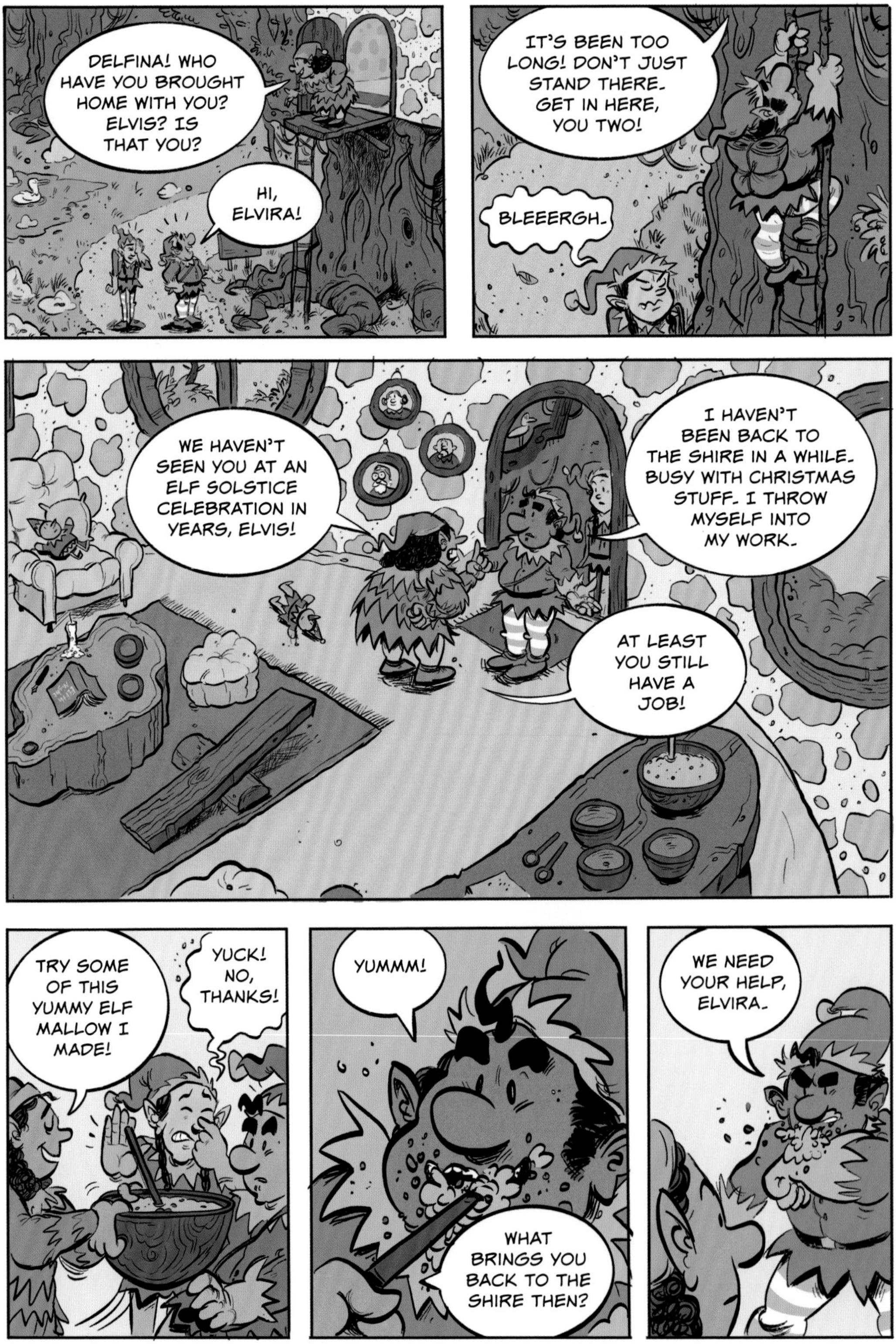

DELFINA! WHO HAVE YOU BROUGHT HOME WITH YOU? ELVIS? IS THAT YOU?
HI, ELVIRA!
IT'S BEEN TOO LONG! DON'T JUST STAND THERE. GET IN HERE, YOU TWO!
BLEEERGH.
WE HAVEN'T SEEN YOU AT AN ELF SOLSTICE CELEBRATION IN YEARS, ELVIS!
I HAVEN'T BEEN BACK TO THE SHIRE IN A WHILE. BUSY WITH CHRISTMAS STUFF. I THROW MYSELF INTO MY WORK.
AT LEAST YOU STILL HAVE A JOB!
TRY SOME OF THIS YUMMY ELF MALLOW I MADE!
YUCK! NO, THANKS!
YUMMM!
WHAT BRINGS YOU BACK TO THE SHIRE THEN?
WE NEED YOUR HELP, ELVIRA.

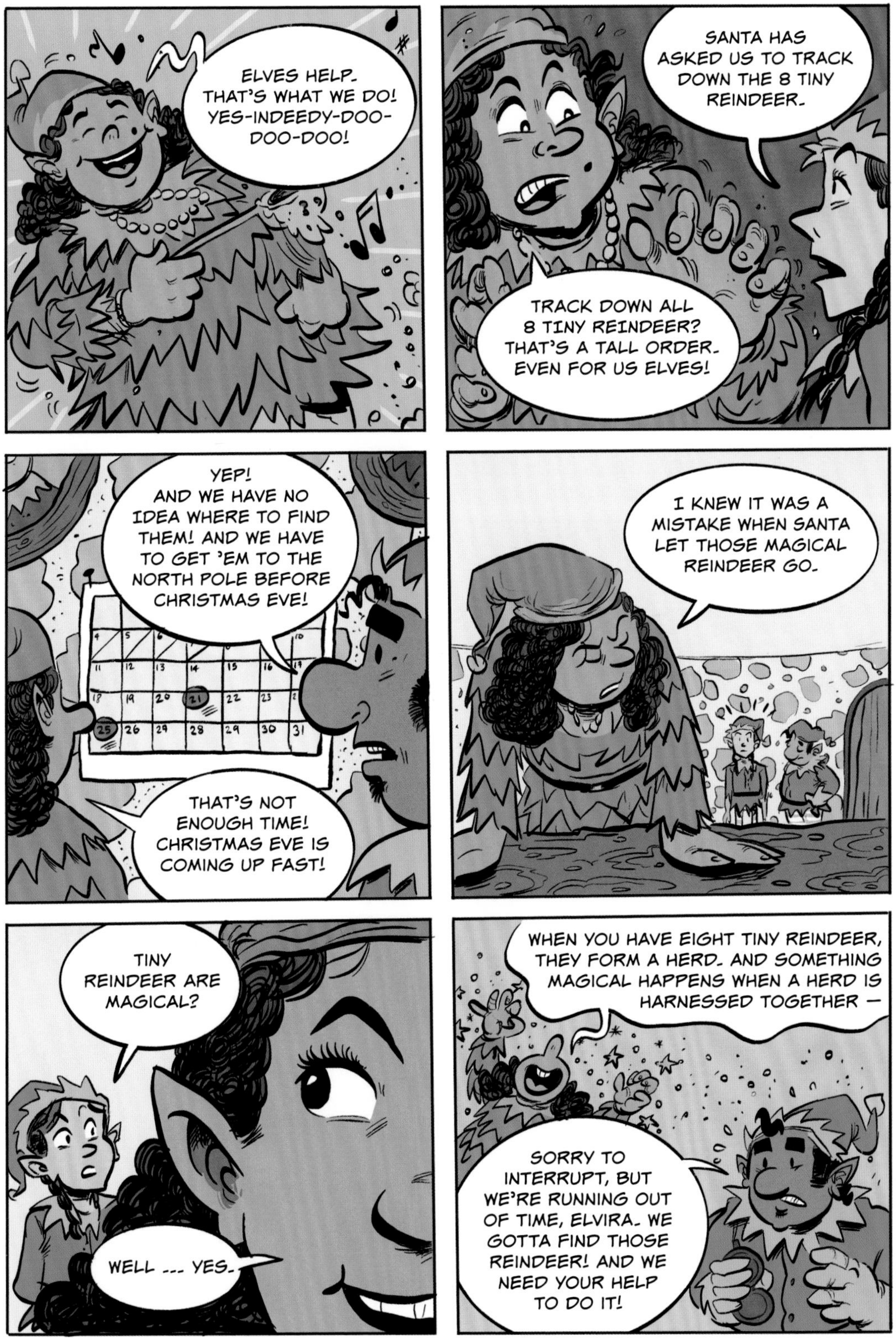
ELVES HELP. THAT'S WHAT WE DO! YES-INDEEDY-DOO-DOO-DOO!
SANTA HAS ASKED US TO TRACK DOWN THE 8 TINY REINDEER.
TRACK DOWN ALL 8 TINY REINDEER? THAT'S A TALL ORDER. EVEN FOR US ELVES!
YEP! AND WE HAVE NO IDEA WHERE TO FIND THEM! AND WE HAVE TO GET 'EM TO THE NORTH POLE BEFORE CHRISTMAS EVE!
THAT'S NOT ENOUGH TIME! CHRISTMAS EVE IS COMING UP FAST!
I KNEW IT WAS A MISTAKE WHEN SANTA LET THOSE MAGICAL REINDEER GO.
TINY REINDEER ARE MAGICAL?
WELL ... YES.
WHEN YOU HAVE EIGHT TINY REINDEER, THEY FORM A HERD. AND SOMETHING MAGICAL HAPPENS WHEN A HERD IS HARNESSED TOGETHER —
SORRY TO INTERRUPT, BUT WE'RE RUNNING OUT OF TIME, ELVIRA. WE GOTTA FIND THOSE REINDEER! AND WE NEED YOUR HELP TO DO IT!

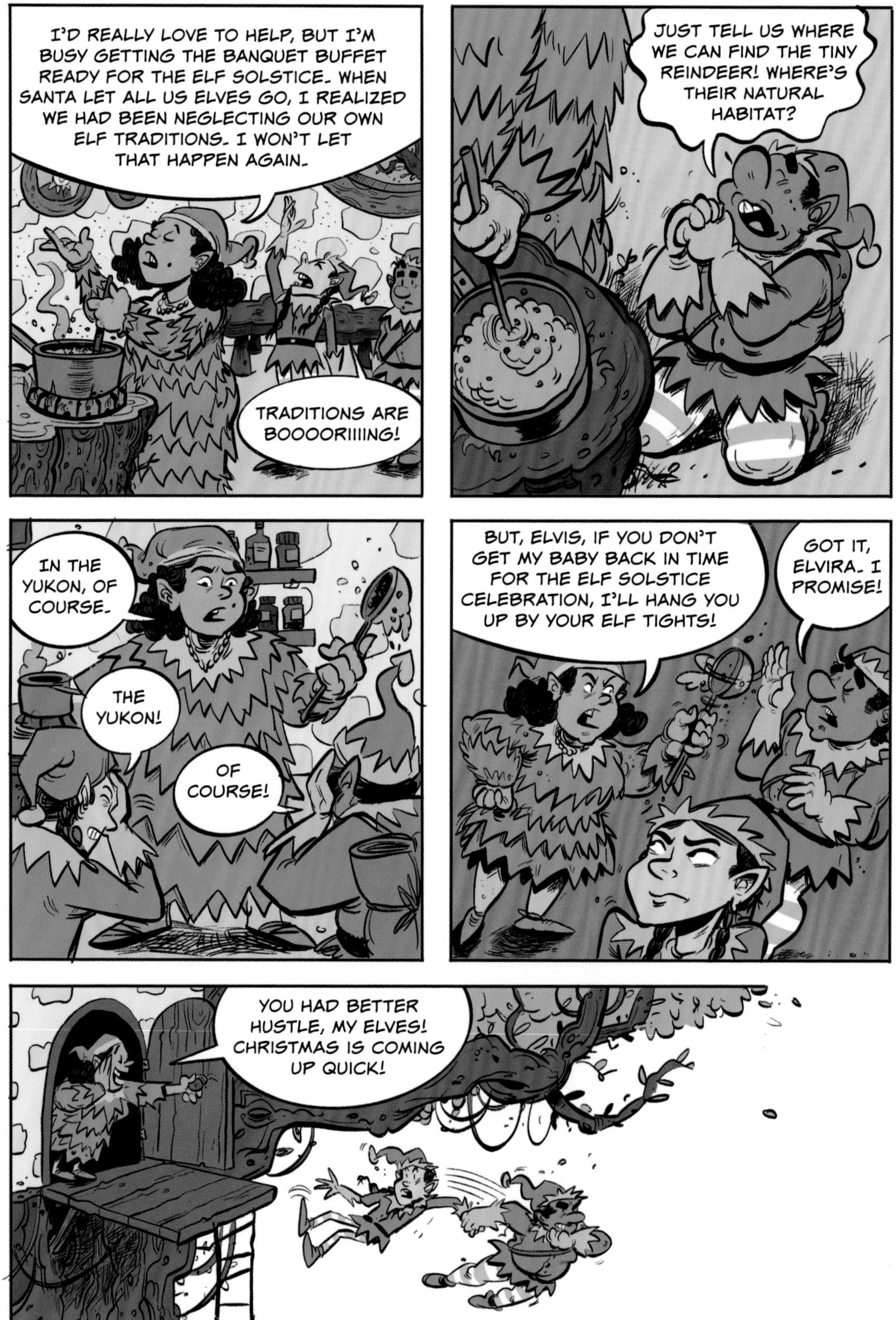
I'D REALLY LOVE TO HELP, BUT I'M BUSY GETTING THE BANQUET BUFFET READY FOR THE ELF SOLSTICE. WHEN SANTA LET ALL US ELVES GO, I REALIZED WE HAD BEEN NEGLECTING OUR OWN ELF TRADITIONS. I WON'T LET THAT HAPPEN AGAIN.
TRADITIONS ARE BOOOORIIIING!
JUST TELL US WHERE WE CAN FIND THE TINY REINDEER! WHERE'S THEIR NATURAL HABITAT?
IN THE YUKON, OF COURSE.
THE YUKON!
OF COURSE!
BUT, ELVIS, IF YOU DON'T GET MY BABY BACK IN TIME FOR THE ELF SOLSTICE CELEBRATION, I'LL HANG YOU UP BY YOUR ELF TIGHTS!
GOT IT, ELVIRA. I PROMISE!
YOU HAD BETTER HUSTLE, MY ELVES! CHRISTMAS IS COMING UP QUICK!

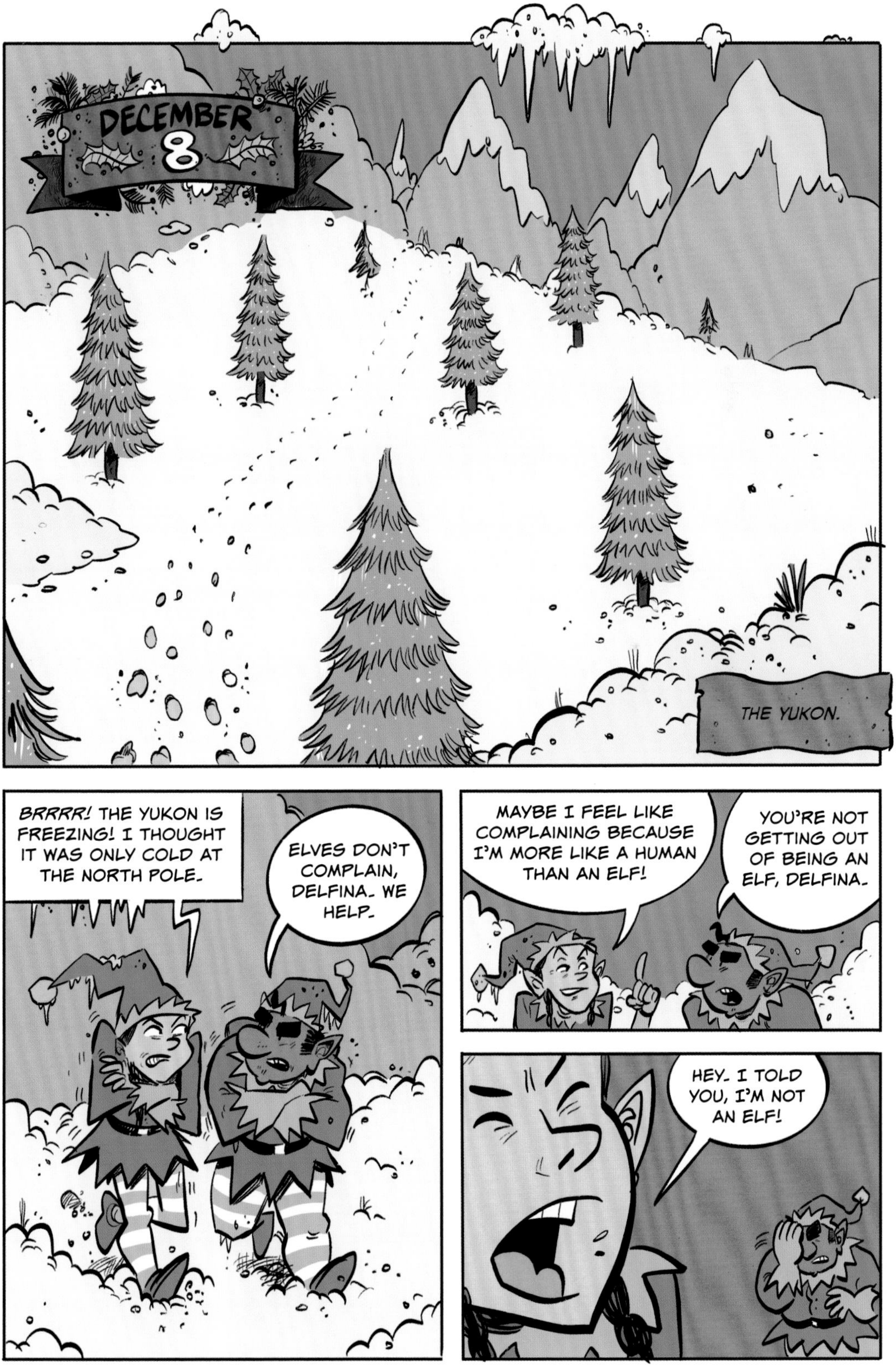
DECEMBER 8
THE YUKON.
BRRRR! THE YUKON IS FREEZING! I THOUGHT IT WAS ONLY COLD AT THE NORTH POLE.
ELVES DON'T COMPLAIN, DELFINA. WE HELP.
MAYBE I FEEL LIKE COMPLAINING BECAUSE I'M MORE LIKE A HUMAN THAN AN ELF!
YOU'RE NOT GETTING OUT OF BEING AN ELF, DELFINA.
HEY. I TOLD YOU, I'M NOT AN ELF!

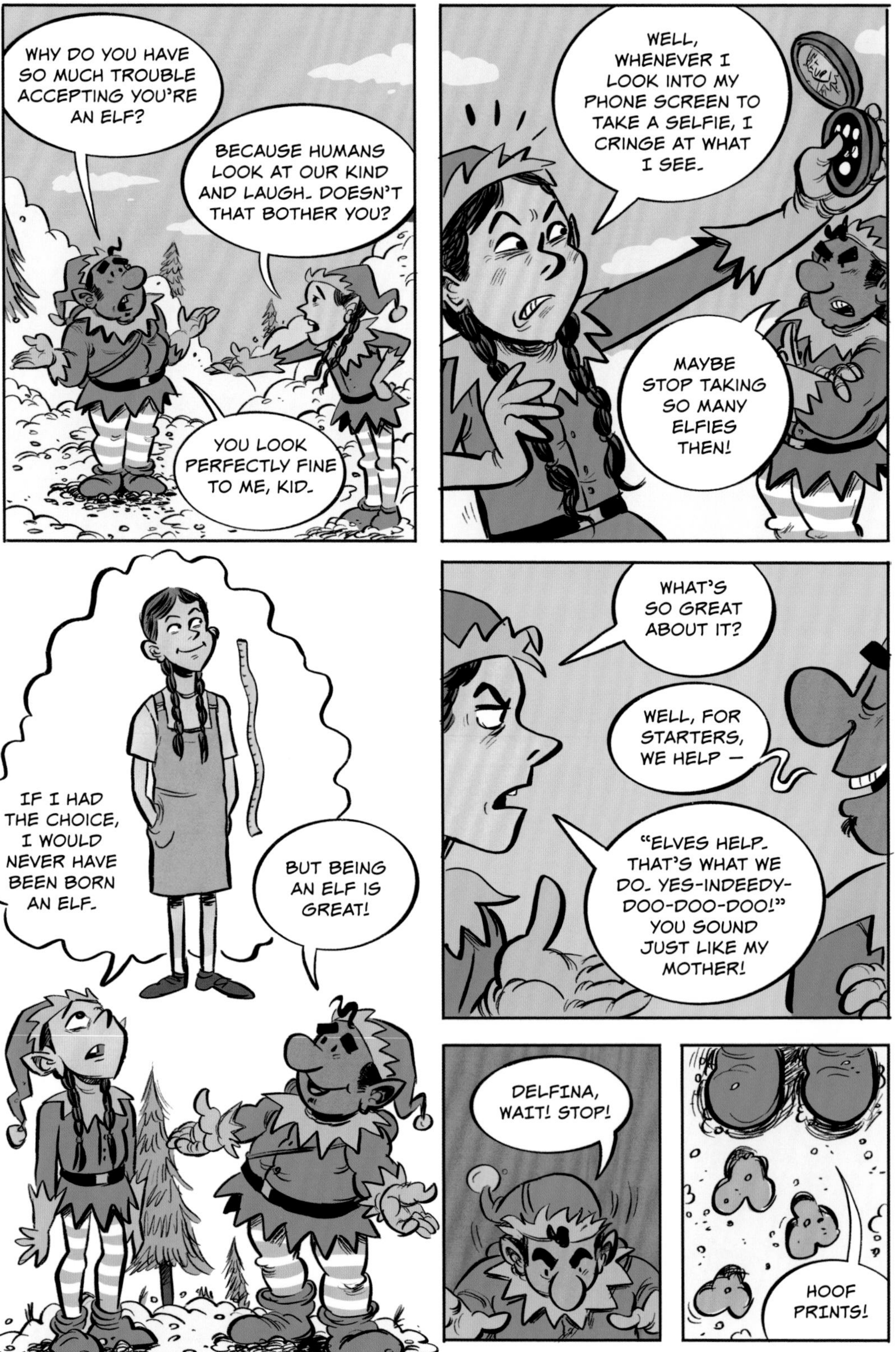
WHY DO YOU HAVE SO MUCH TROUBLE ACCEPTING YOU'RE AN ELF?
BECAUSE HUMANS LOOK AT OUR KIND AND LAUGH. DOESN'T THAT BOTHER YOU?
YOU LOOK PERFECTLY FINE TO ME, KID.
WELL, WHENEVER I LOOK INTO MY PHONE SCREEN TO TAKE A SELFIE, I CRINGE AT WHAT I SEE.
MAYBE STOP TAKING SO MANY ELFIES THEN!
IF I HAD THE CHOICE, I WOULD NEVER HAVE BEEN BORN AN ELF.
BUT BEING AN ELF IS GREAT!
WHAT'S SO GREAT ABOUT IT?
WELL, FOR STARTERS, WE HELP —
"ELVES HELP. THAT'S WHAT WE DO. YES-INDEEDY-DOO-DOO-DOO!" YOU SOUND JUST LIKE MY MOTHER!
DELFINA, WAIT! STOP!
HOOF PRINTS!

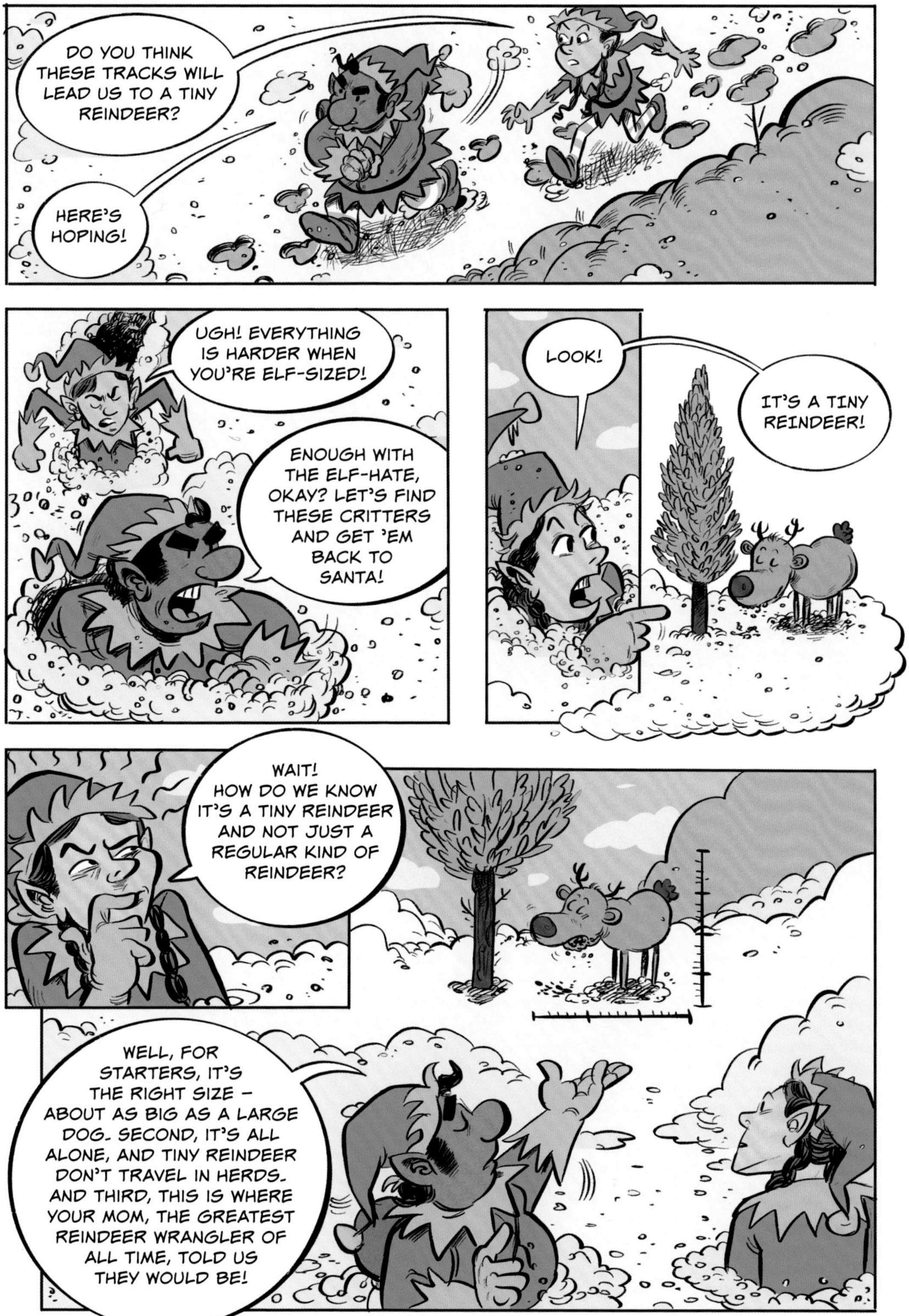
DO YOU THINK THESE TRACKS WILL LEAD US TO A TINY REINDEER?
HERE'S HOPING!
UGH! EVERYTHING IS HARDER WHEN YOU'RE ELF-SIZED!
ENOUGH WITH THE ELF-HATE, OKAY? LET'S FIND THESE CRITTERS AND GET 'EM BACK TO SANTA!
LOOK!
IT'S A TINY REINDEER!
WAIT! HOW DO WE KNOW IT'S A TINY REINDEER AND NOT JUST A REGULAR KIND OF REINDEER?
WELL, FOR STARTERS, IT'S THE RIGHT SIZE – ABOUT AS BIG AS A LARGE DOG. SECOND, IT'S ALL ALONE, AND TINY REINDEER DON'T TRAVEL IN HERDS. AND THIRD, THIS IS WHERE YOUR MOM, THE GREATEST REINDEER WRANGLER OF ALL TIME, TOLD US THEY WOULD BE!

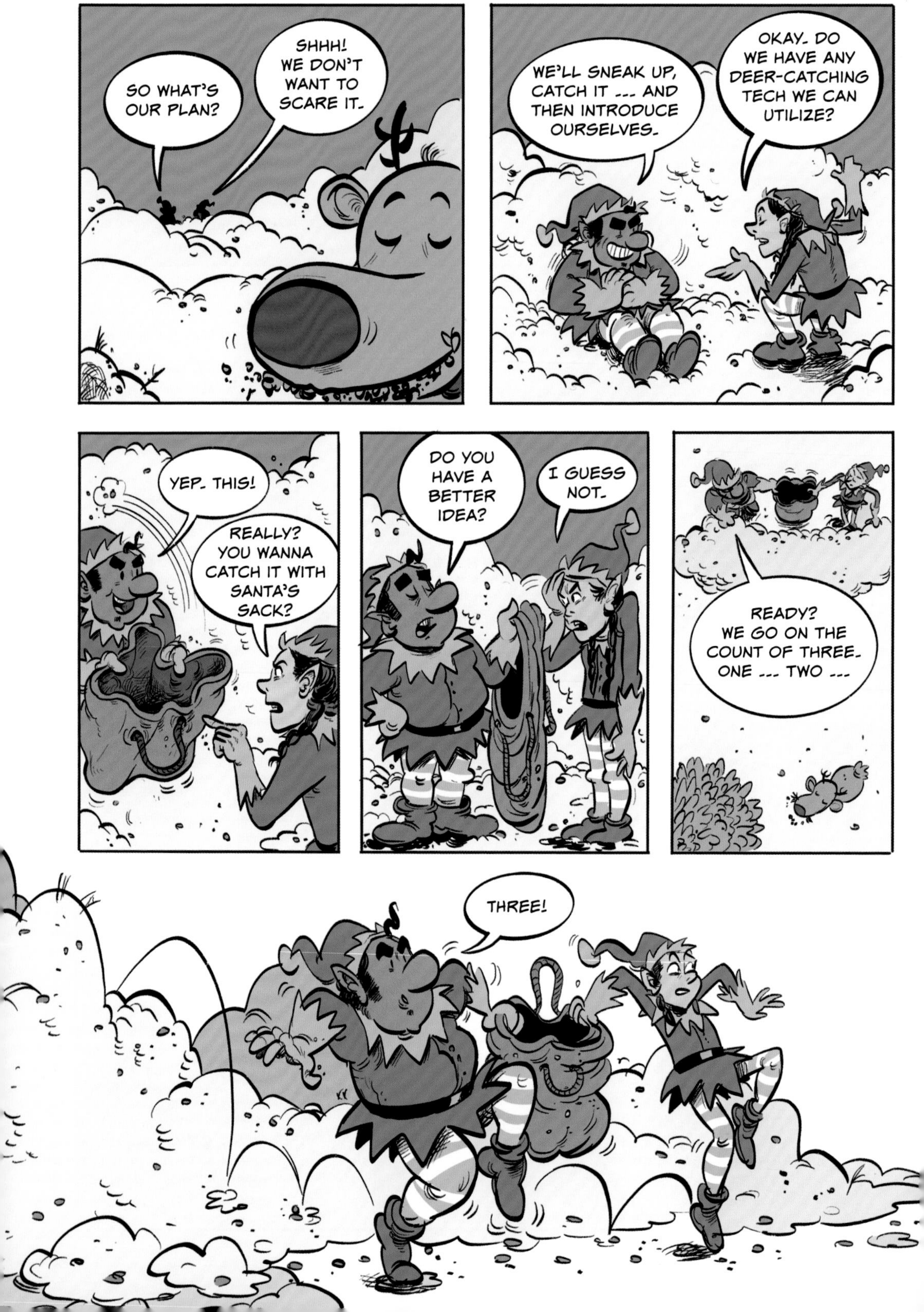
SO WHAT'S OUR PLAN?
SHHH! WE DON'T WANT TO SCARE IT.
WE'LL SNEAK UP, CATCH IT ... AND THEN INTRODUCE OURSELVES.
OKAY. DO WE HAVE ANY DEER-CATCHING TECH WE CAN UTILIZE?
YEP. THIS!
REALLY? YOU WANNA CATCH IT WITH SANTA'S SACK?
DO YOU HAVE A BETTER IDEA?
I GUESS NOT.
READY? WE GO ON THE COUNT OF THREE. ONE ... TWO ...
THREE!

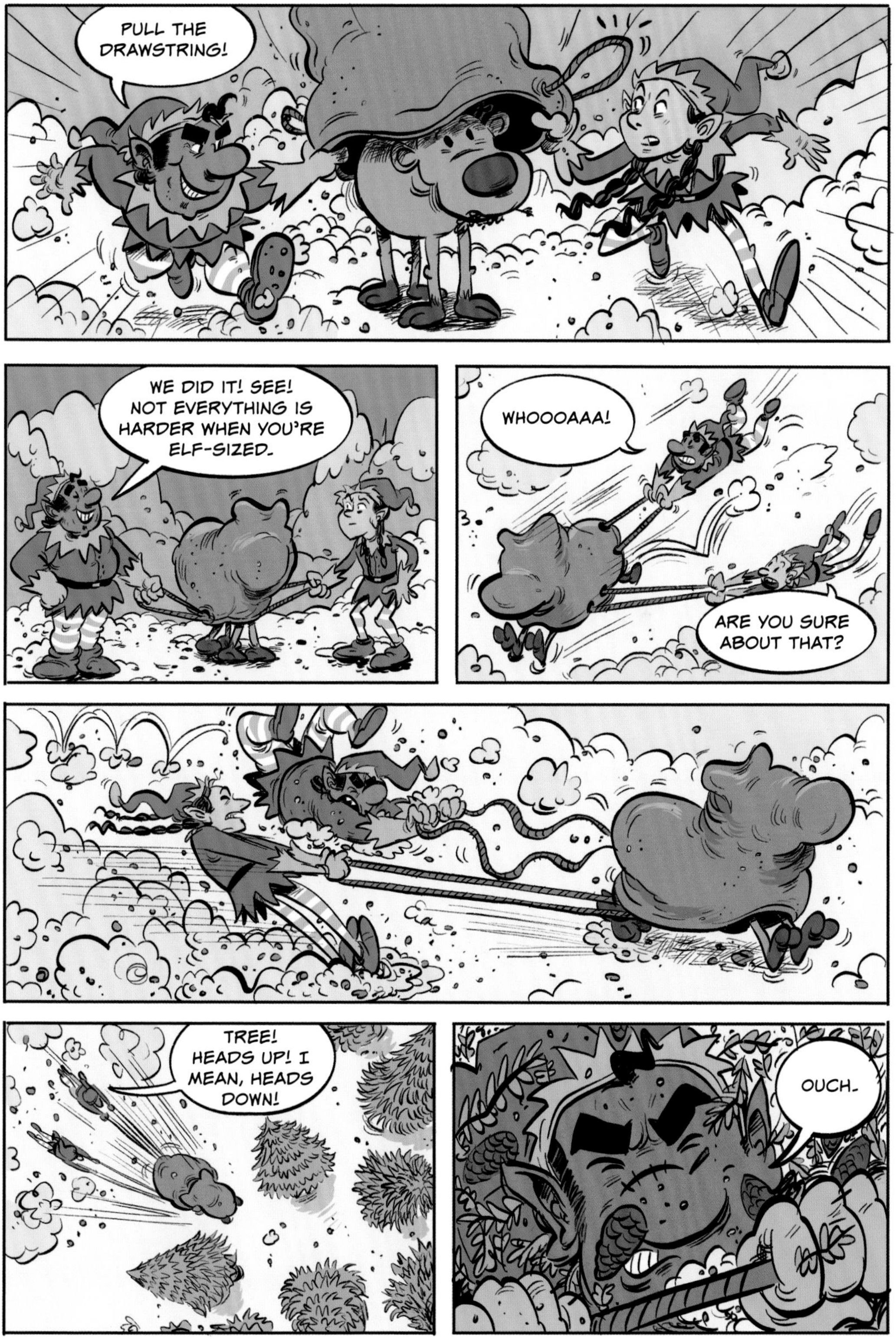
PULL THE DRAWSTRING!
WE DID IT! SEE! NOT EVERYTHING IS HARDER WHEN YOU'RE ELF-SIZED.
WHOOOAAA!
ARE YOU SURE ABOUT THAT?
TREE! HEADS UP! I MEAN, HEADS DOWN!
OUCH.

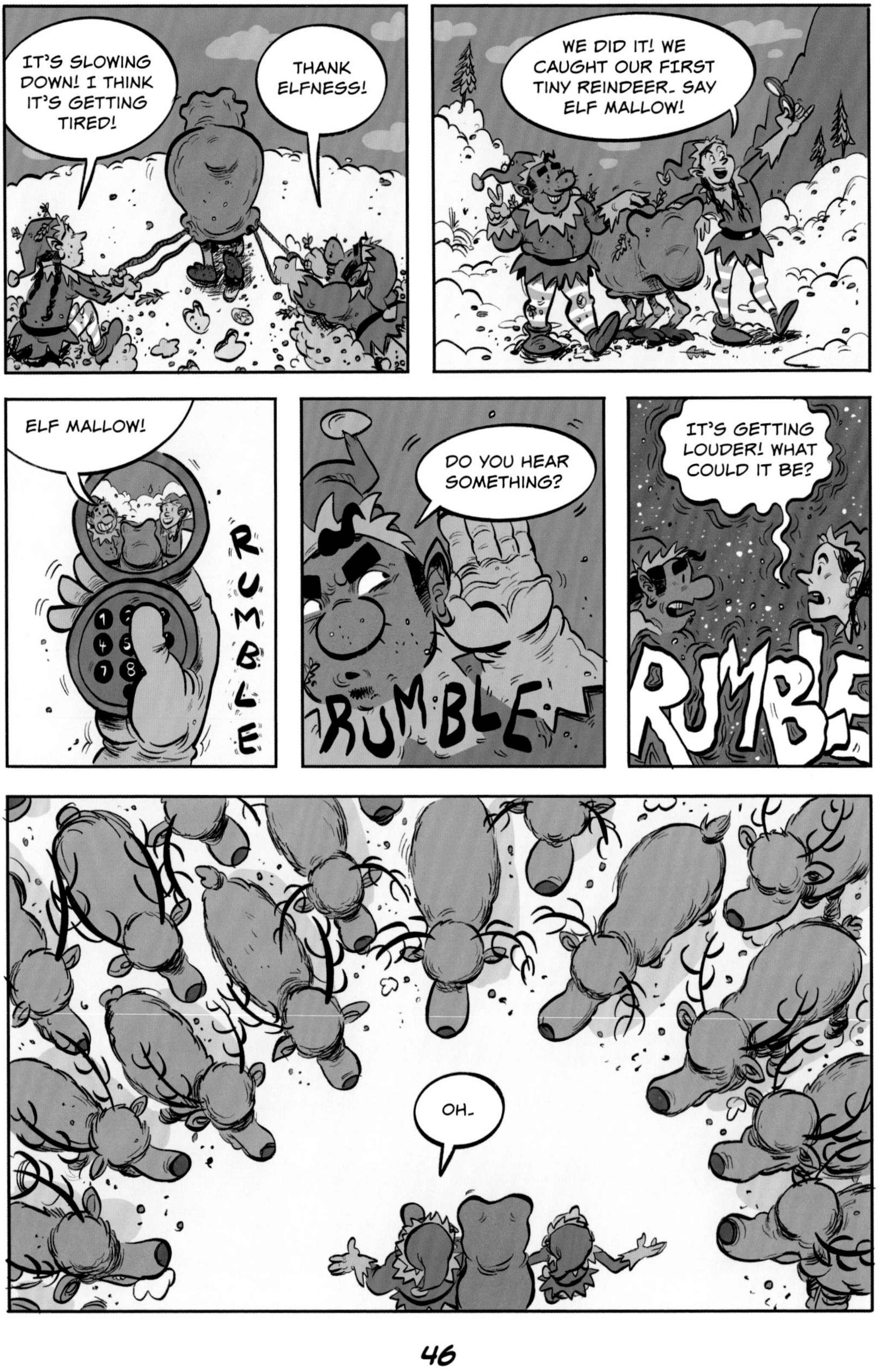
IT'S SLOWING DOWN! I THINK IT'S GETTING TIRED!
THANK ELFNESS!
WE DID IT! WE CAUGHT OUR FIRST TINY REINDEER. SAY ELF MALLOW!
ELF MALLOW!
RUMBLE
DO YOU HEAR SOMETHING?
RUMBLE
IT'S GETTING LOUDER! WHAT COULD IT BE?
RUMBLE
OH.

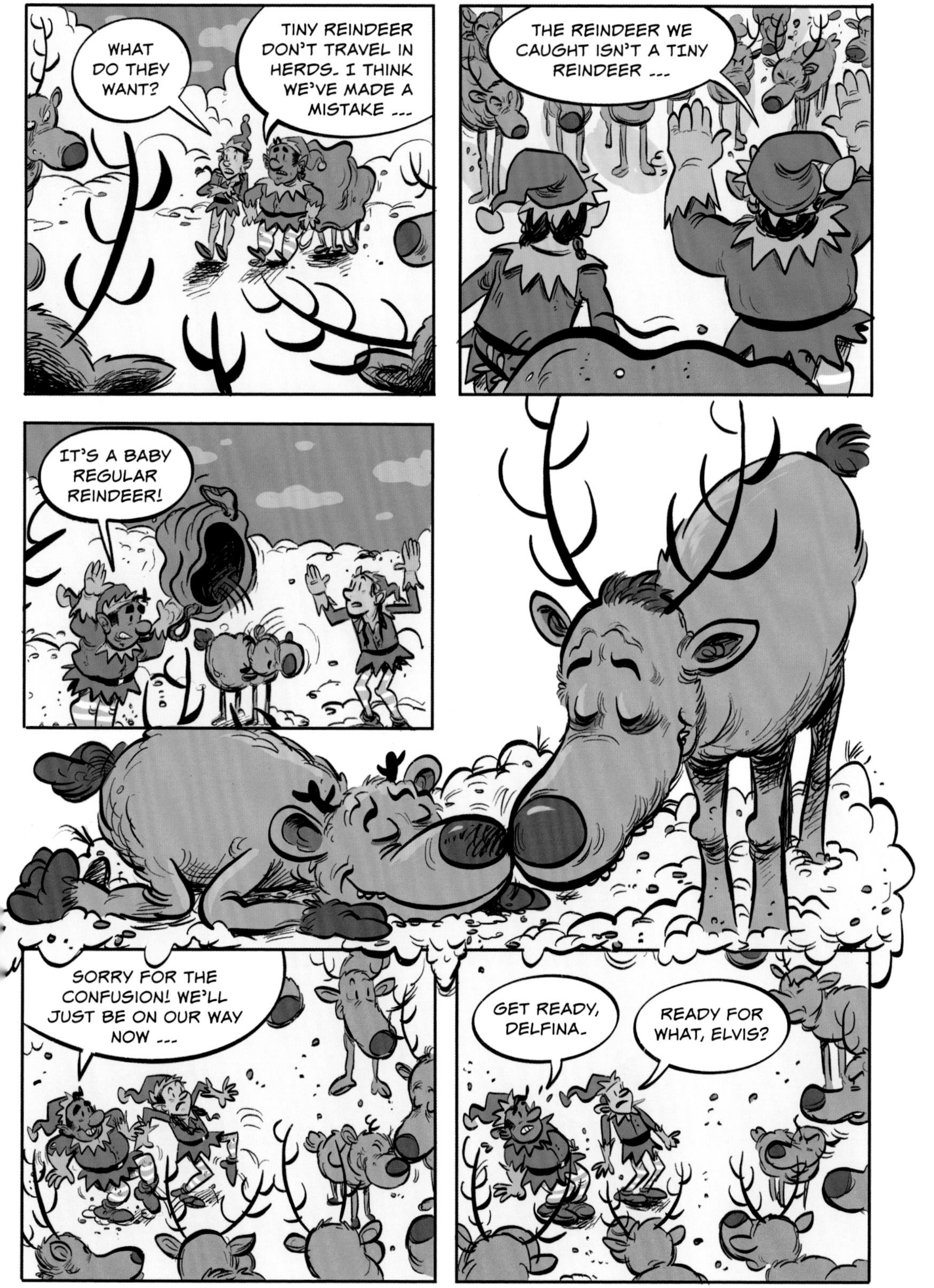
WHAT DO THEY WANT?
TINY REINDEER DON'T TRAVEL IN HERDS. I THINK WE'VE MADE A MISTAKE ...
THE REINDEER WE CAUGHT ISN'T A TINY REINDEER ...
IT'S A BABY REGULAR REINDEER!
SORRY FOR THE CONFUSION! WE'LL JUST BE ON OUR WAY NOW ...
GET READY, DELFINA.
READY FOR WHAT, ELVIS?

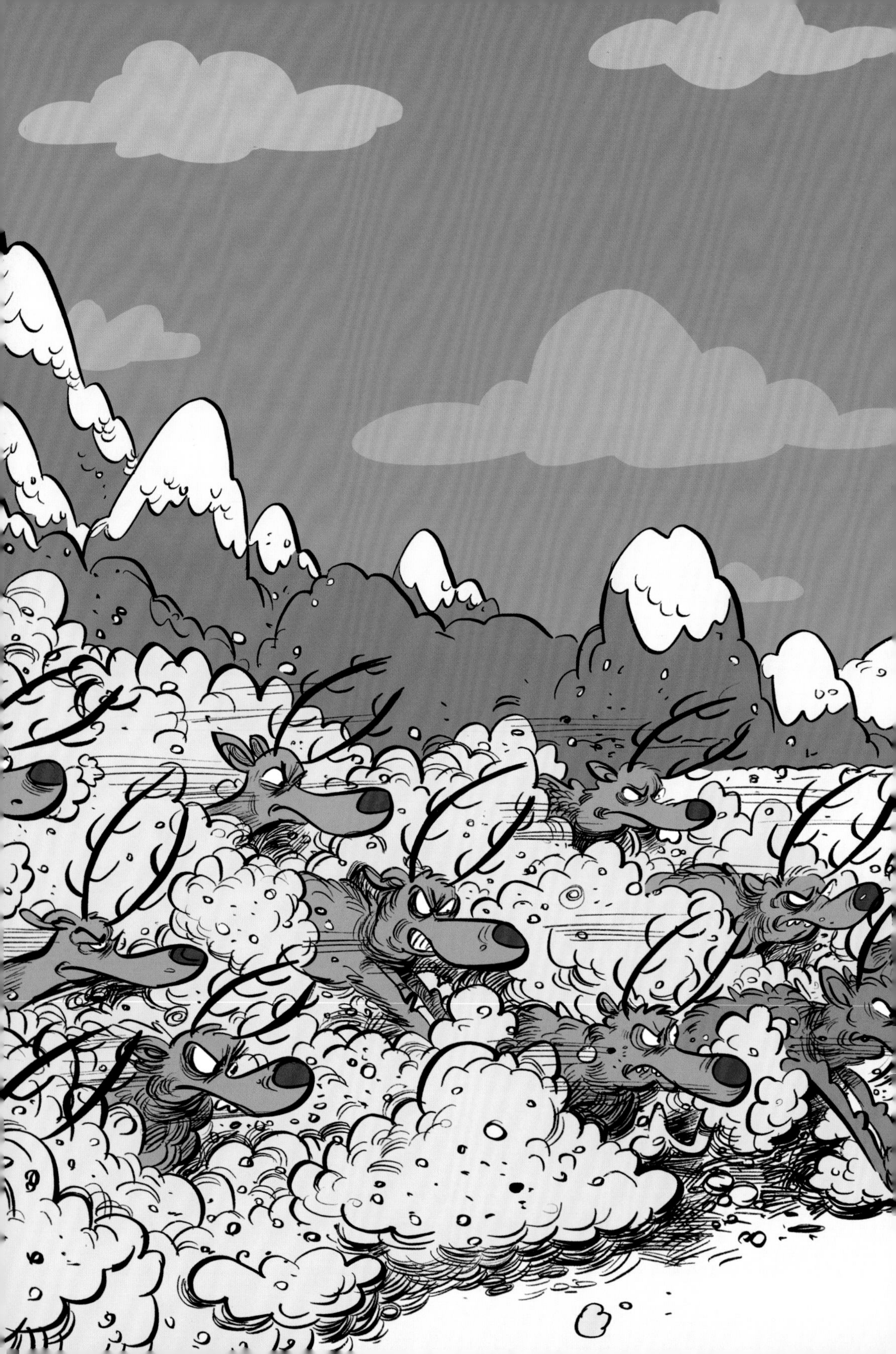

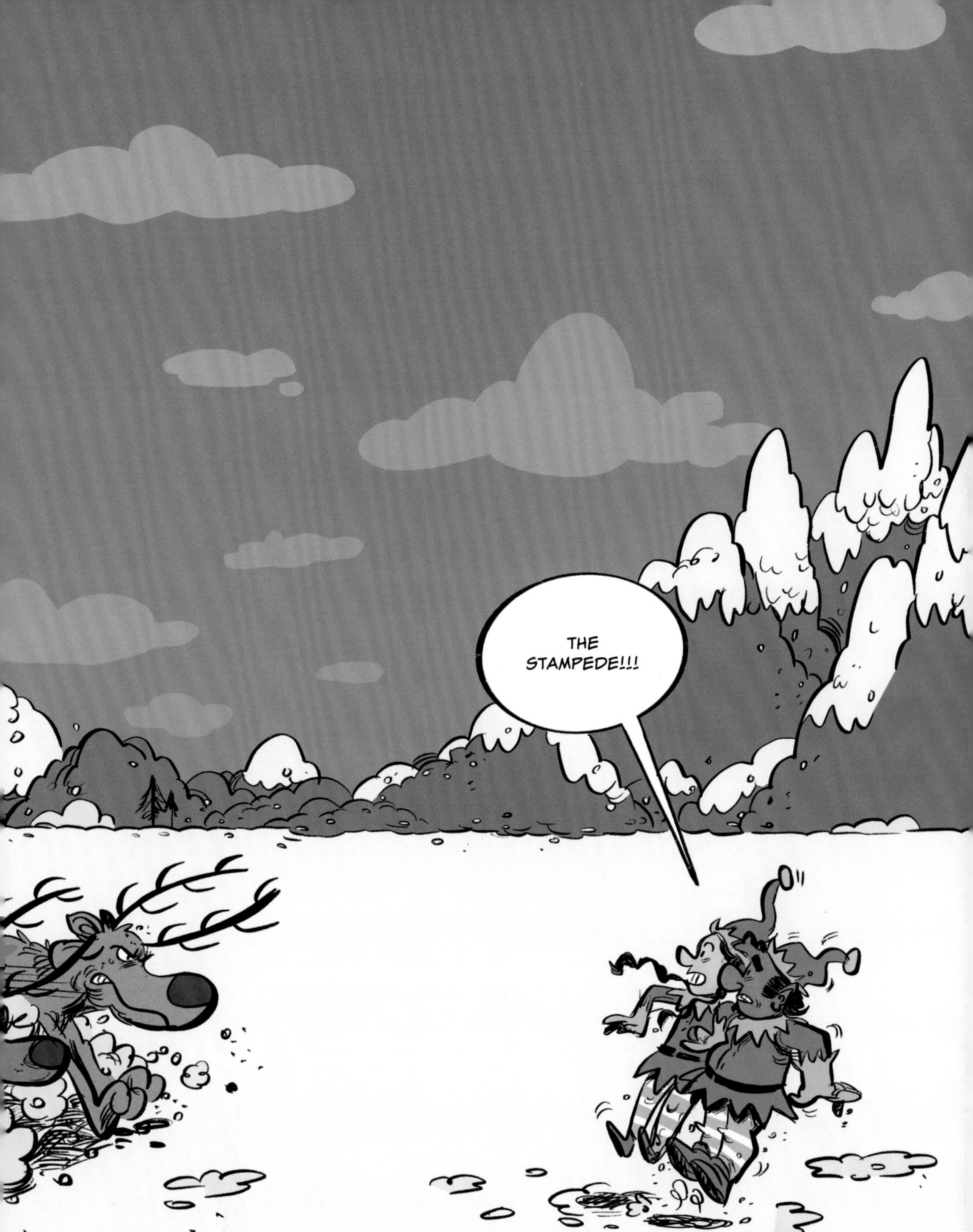
THE STAMPEDE!!!

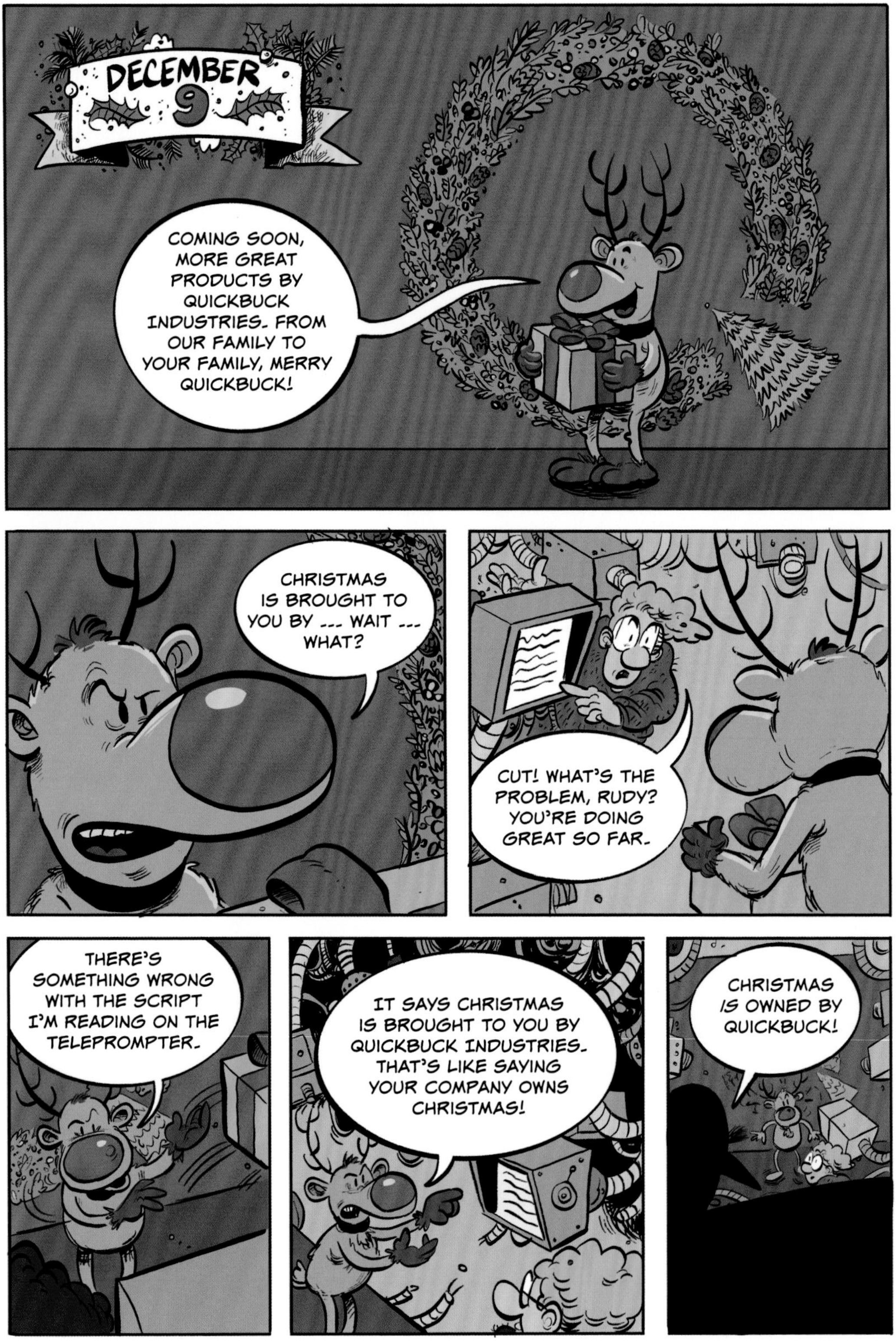
DECEMBER 9
COMING SOON, MORE GREAT PRODUCTS BY QUICKBUCK INDUSTRIES. FROM OUR FAMILY TO YOUR FAMILY, MERRY QUICKBUCK!
CHRISTMAS IS BROUGHT TO YOU BY --- WAIT --- WHAT?
CUT! WHAT'S THE PROBLEM, RUDY? YOU'RE DOING GREAT SO FAR.
THERE'S SOMETHING WRONG WITH THE SCRIPT I'M READING ON THE TELEPROMPTER.
IT SAYS CHRISTMAS IS BROUGHT TO YOU BY QUICKBUCK INDUSTRIES. THAT'S LIKE SAYING YOUR COMPANY OWNS CHRISTMAS!
CHRISTMAS IS OWNED BY QUICKBUCK!

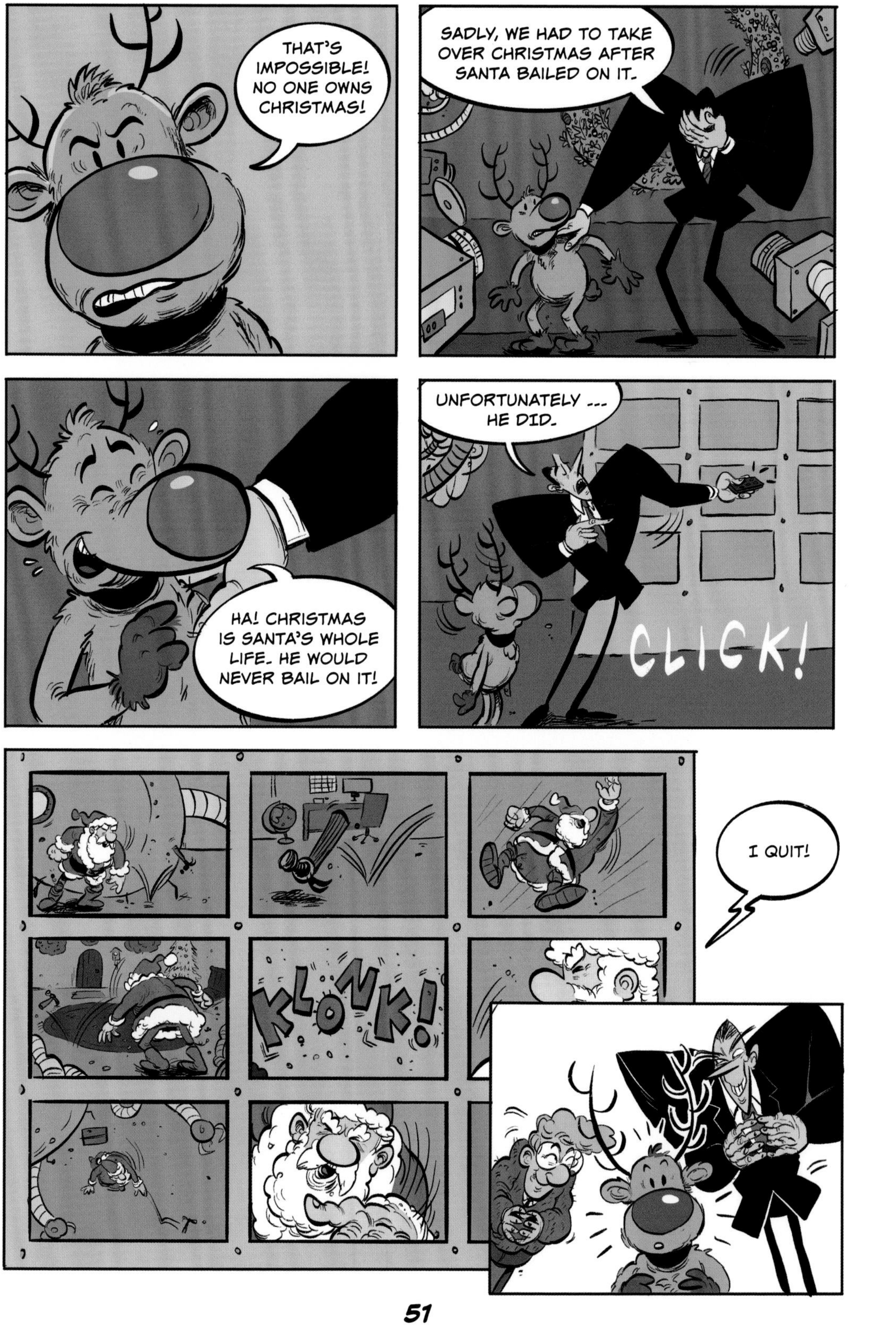
THAT'S IMPOSSIBLE! NO ONE OWNS CHRISTMAS!
SADLY, WE HAD TO TAKE OVER CHRISTMAS AFTER SANTA BAILED ON IT.
HA! CHRISTMAS IS SANTA'S WHOLE LIFE. HE WOULD NEVER BAIL ON IT!
UNFORTUNATELY ... HE DID.
CLICK!
KLONK!
I QUIT!

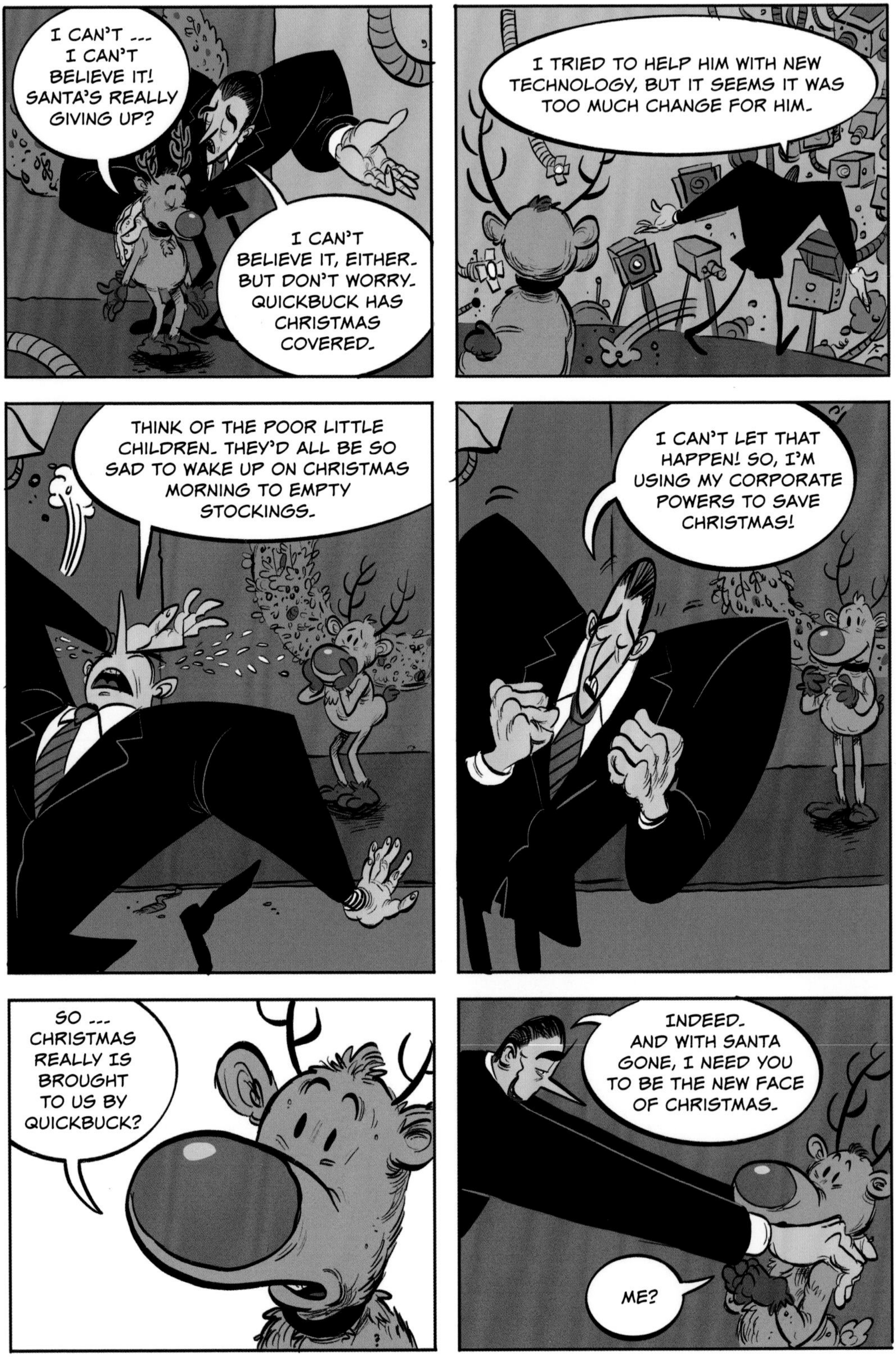
I CAN'T ... I CAN'T BELIEVE IT! SANTA'S REALLY GIVING UP?
I CAN'T BELIEVE IT, EITHER. BUT DON'T WORRY. QUICKBUCK HAS CHRISTMAS COVERED.
I TRIED TO HELP HIM WITH NEW TECHNOLOGY, BUT IT SEEMS IT WAS TOO MUCH CHANGE FOR HIM.
THINK OF THE POOR LITTLE CHILDREN. THEY'D ALL BE SO SAD TO WAKE UP ON CHRISTMAS MORNING TO EMPTY STOCKINGS.
I CAN'T LET THAT HAPPEN! SO, I'M USING MY CORPORATE POWERS TO SAVE CHRISTMAS!
SO ... CHRISTMAS REALLY IS BROUGHT TO US BY QUICKBUCK?
INDEED. AND WITH SANTA GONE, I NEED YOU TO BE THE NEW FACE OF CHRISTMAS.
ME?

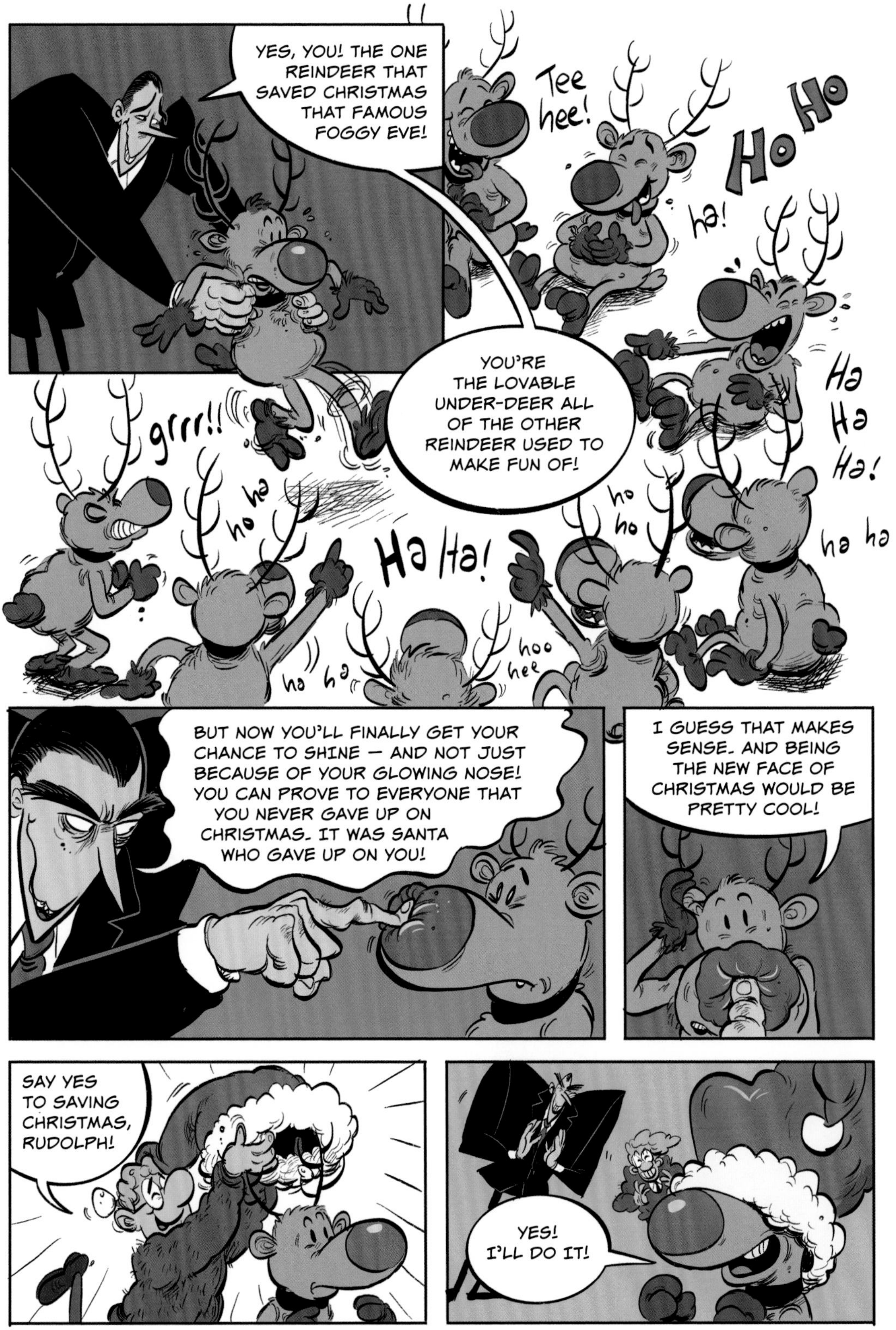
YES, YOU! THE ONE REINDEER THAT SAVED CHRISTMAS THAT FAMOUS FOGGY EVE!
Tee hee!
Ho Ho
Ho
ha!
YOU'RE THE LOVABLE UNDER-DEER ALL OF THE OTHER REINDEER USED TO MAKE FUN OF!
grrr!!
ho ha
Ha Ha!
ho ho
Ha Ha Ha!
ha ha
ha ha
hoo hee
BUT NOW YOU'LL FINALLY GET YOUR CHANCE TO SHINE — AND NOT JUST BECAUSE OF YOUR GLOWING NOSE! YOU CAN PROVE TO EVERYONE THAT YOU NEVER GAVE UP ON CHRISTMAS. IT WAS SANTA WHO GAVE UP ON YOU!
I GUESS THAT MAKES SENSE. AND BEING THE NEW FACE OF CHRISTMAS WOULD BE PRETTY COOL!
SAY YES TO SAVING CHRISTMAS, RUDOLPH!
YES! I'LL DO IT!

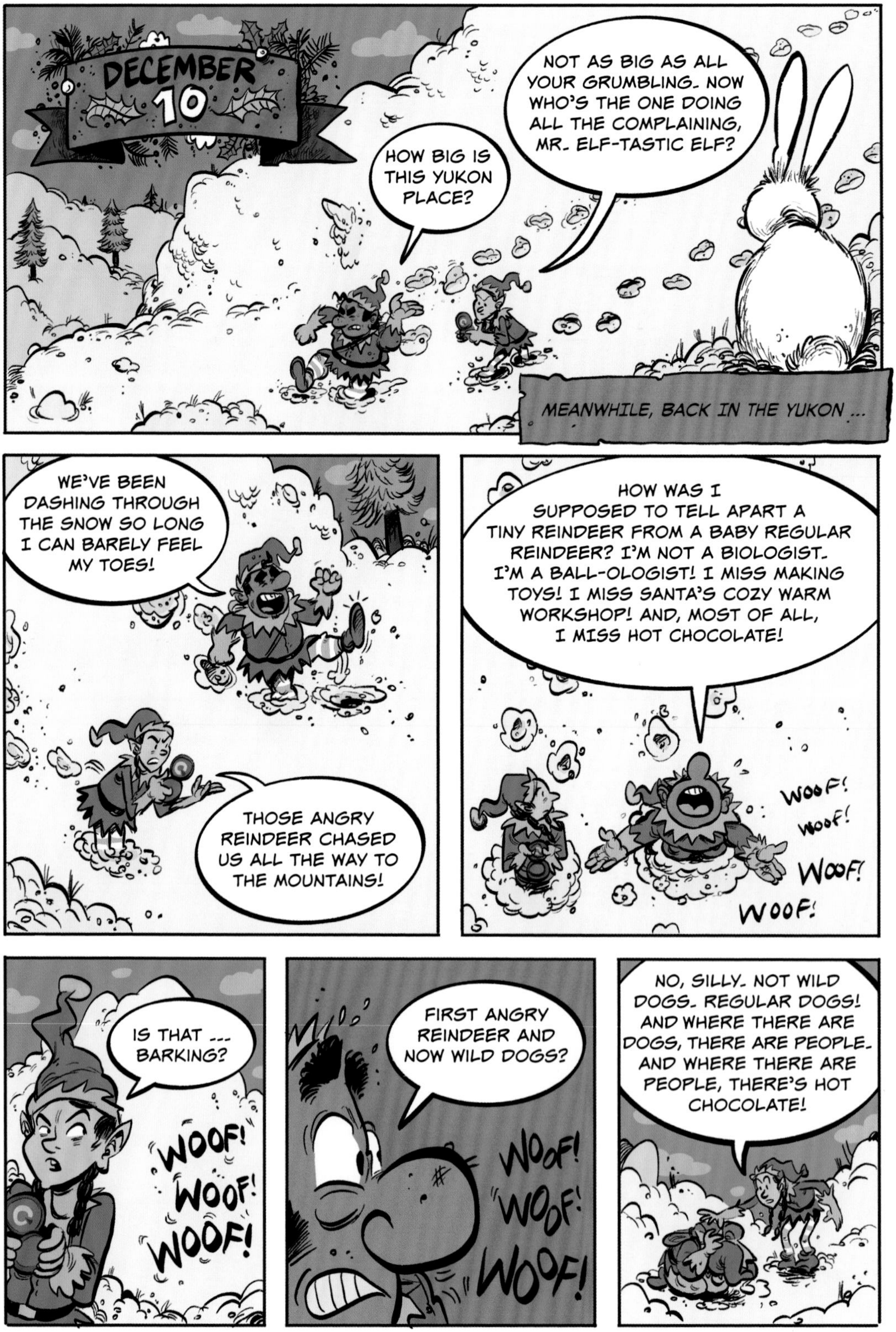
DECEMBER 10
MEANWHILE, BACK IN THE YUKON ...
HOW BIG IS THIS YUKON PLACE?
NOT AS BIG AS ALL YOUR GRUMBLING. NOW WHO'S THE ONE DOING ALL THE COMPLAINING, MR. ELF-TASTIC ELF?
WE'VE BEEN DASHING THROUGH THE SNOW SO LONG I CAN BARELY FEEL MY TOES!
THOSE ANGRY REINDEER CHASED US ALL THE WAY TO THE MOUNTAINS!
HOW WAS I SUPPOSED TO TELL APART A TINY REINDEER FROM A BABY REGULAR REINDEER? I'M NOT A BIOLOGIST. I'M A BALL-OLOGIST! I MISS MAKING TOYS! I MISS SANTA'S COZY WARM WORKSHOP! AND, MOST OF ALL, I MISS HOT CHOCOLATE!
WOOF!
WOOF!
WOOF!
WOOF!
IS THAT ... BARKING?
WOOF!
WOOF!
WOOF!
FIRST ANGRY REINDEER AND NOW WILD DOGS?
WOOF!
WOOF!
WOOF!
NO, SILLY. NOT WILD DOGS. REGULAR DOGS! AND WHERE THERE ARE DOGS, THERE ARE PEOPLE. AND WHERE THERE ARE PEOPLE, THERE'S HOT CHOCOLATE!

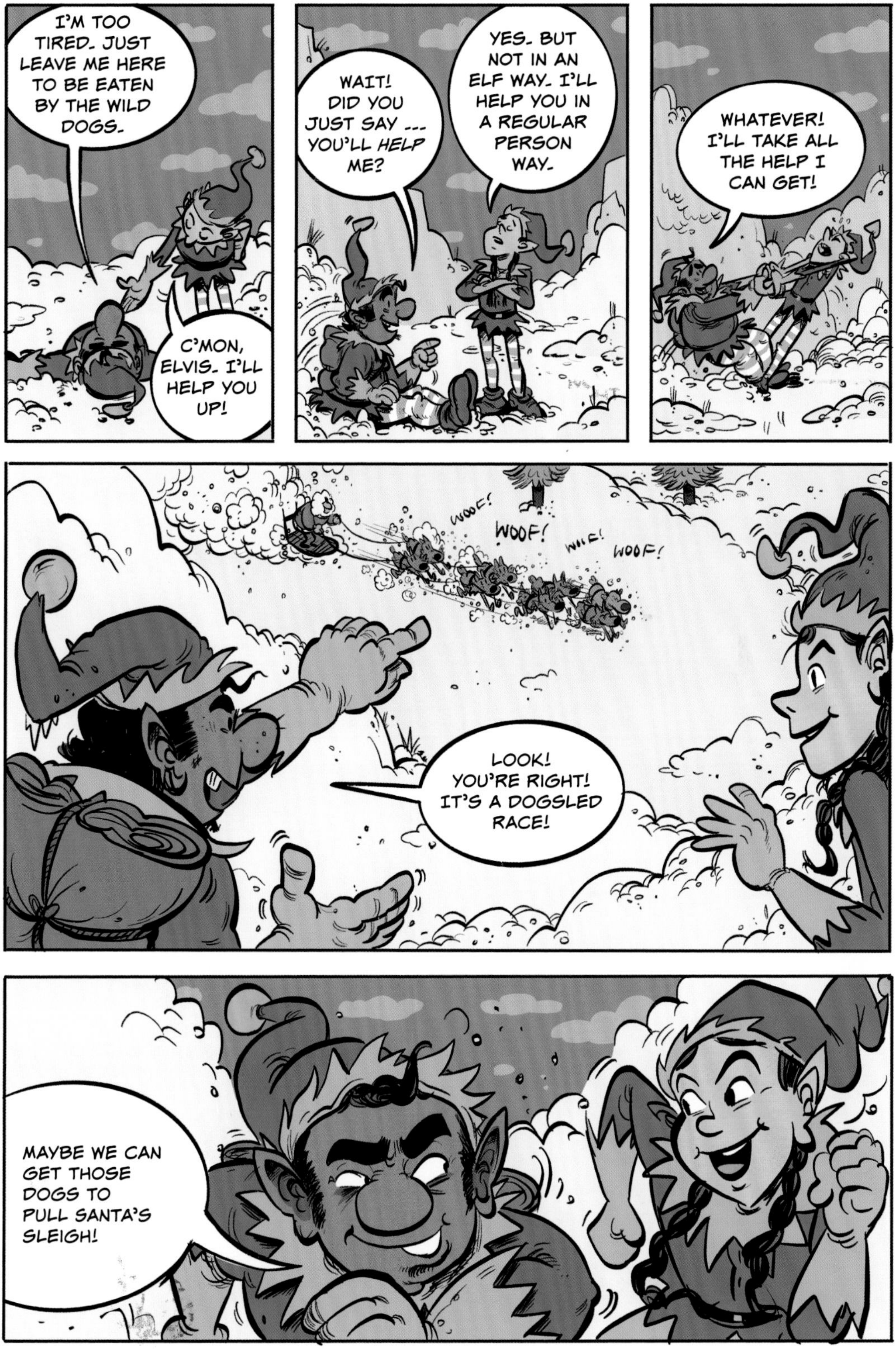
I'M TOO TIRED. JUST LEAVE ME HERE TO BE EATEN BY THE WILD DOGS.
C'MON, ELVIS. I'LL HELP YOU UP!
WAIT! DID YOU JUST SAY ... YOU'LL HELP ME?
YES. BUT NOT IN AN ELF WAY. I'LL HELP YOU IN A REGULAR PERSON WAY.
WHATEVER! I'LL TAKE ALL THE HELP I CAN GET!
WOOF!
WOOF!
WOOF!
WOOF!
LOOK! YOU'RE RIGHT! IT'S A DOGSLED RACE!
MAYBE WE CAN GET THOSE DOGS TO PULL SANTA'S SLEIGH!

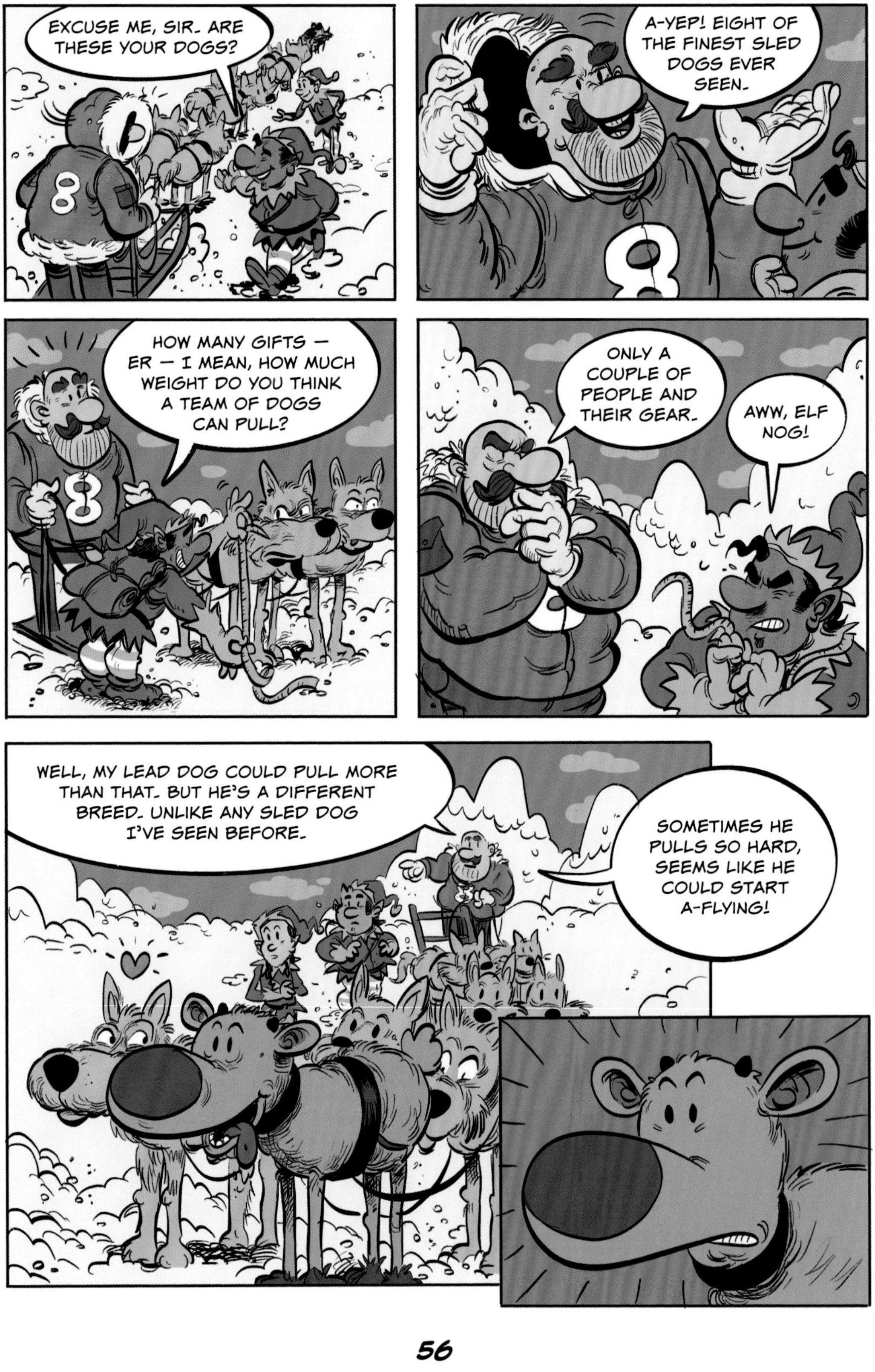
EXCUSE ME, SIR. ARE THESE YOUR DOGS?
A-YEP! EIGHT OF THE FINEST SLED DOGS EVER SEEN.
HOW MANY GIFTS — ER — I MEAN, HOW MUCH WEIGHT DO YOU THINK A TEAM OF DOGS CAN PULL?
ONLY A COUPLE OF PEOPLE AND THEIR GEAR.
AWW, ELF NOG!
WELL, MY LEAD DOG COULD PULL MORE THAN THAT. BUT HE'S A DIFFERENT BREED. UNLIKE ANY SLED DOG I'VE SEEN BEFORE.
SOMETIMES HE PULLS SO HARD, SEEMS LIKE HE COULD START A-FLYING!

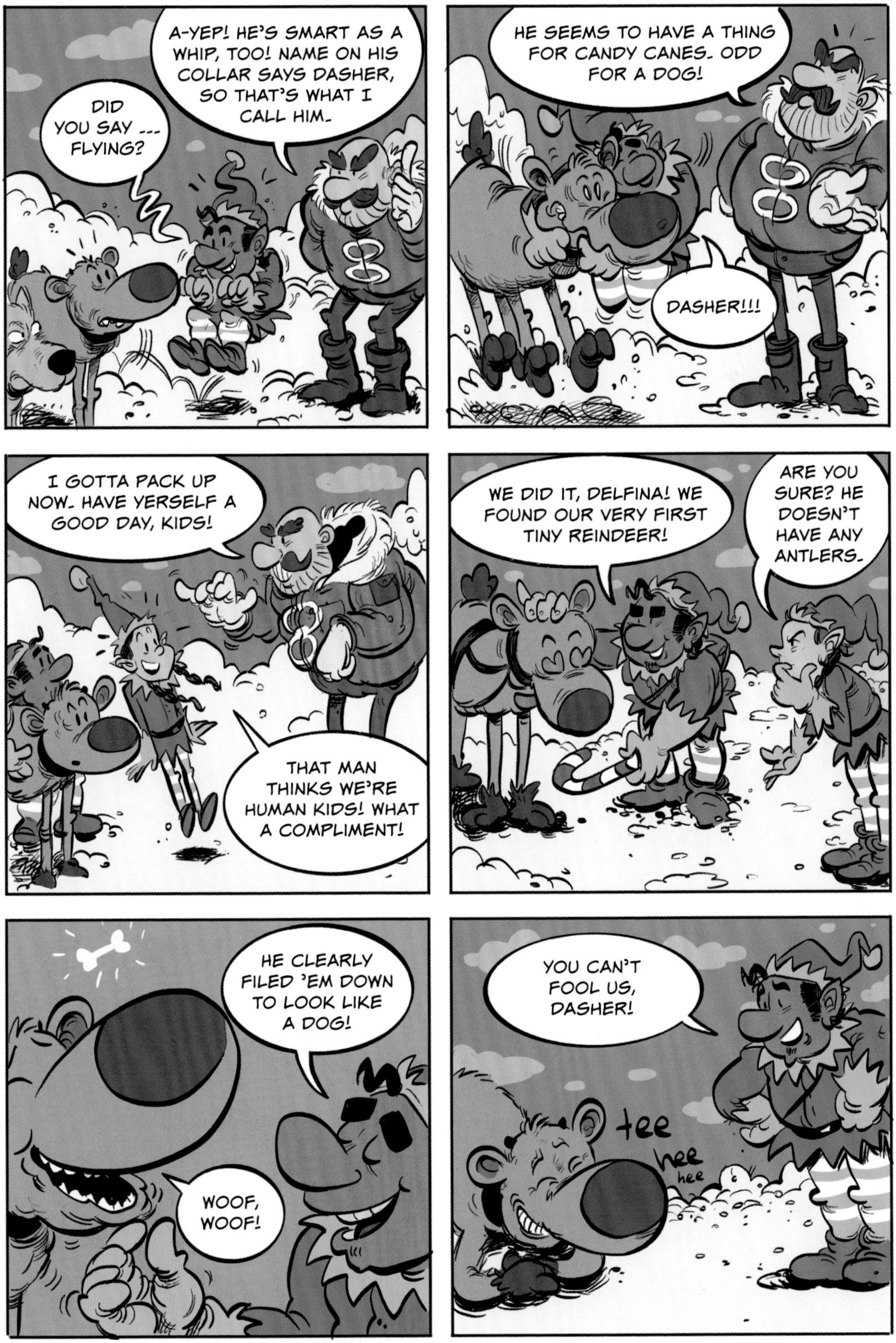
A-YEP! HE'S SMART AS A WHIP, TOO! NAME ON HIS COLLAR SAYS DASHER, SO THAT'S WHAT I CALL HIM.
DID YOU SAY ... FLYING?
HE SEEMS TO HAVE A THING FOR CANDY CANES. ODD FOR A DOG!
DASHER!!!
I GOTTA PACK UP NOW. HAVE YERSELF A GOOD DAY, KIDS!
THAT MAN THINKS WE'RE HUMAN KIDS! WHAT A COMPLIMENT!
WE DID IT, DELFINA! WE FOUND OUR VERY FIRST TINY REINDEER!
ARE YOU SURE? HE DOESN'T HAVE ANY ANTLERS.
HE CLEARLY FILED 'EM DOWN TO LOOK LIKE A DOG!
WOOF, WOOF!
YOU CAN'T FOOL US, DASHER!
tee
hee
hee

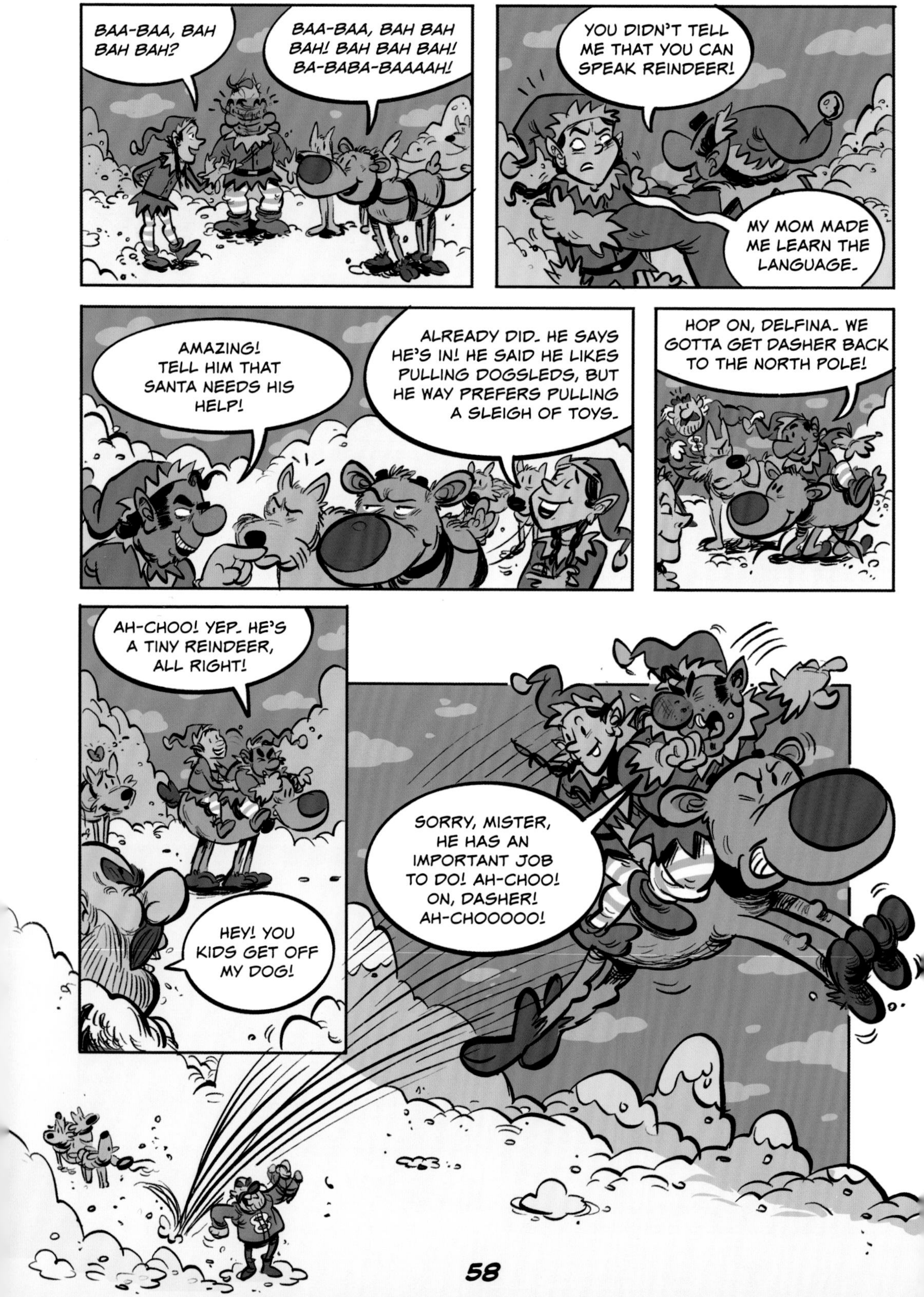
BAA-BAA, BAH BAH BAH?
BAA-BAA, BAH BAH BAH! BAH BAH BAH! BA-BABA-BAAAAH!
YOU DIDN'T TELL ME THAT YOU CAN SPEAK REINDEER!
MY MOM MADE ME LEARN THE LANGUAGE.
AMAZING! TELL HIM THAT SANTA NEEDS HIS HELP!
ALREADY DID. HE SAYS HE'S IN! HE SAID HE LIKES PULLING DOGSLEDS, BUT HE WAY PREFERS PULLING A SLEIGH OF TOYS.
HOP ON, DELFINA. WE GOTTA GET DASHER BACK TO THE NORTH POLE!
AH-CHOO! YEP. HE'S A TINY REINDEER, ALL RIGHT!
HEY! YOU KIDS GET OFF MY DOG!
SORRY, MISTER, HE HAS AN IMPORTANT JOB TO DO! AH-CHOO! ON, DASHER! AH-CHOOOOO!

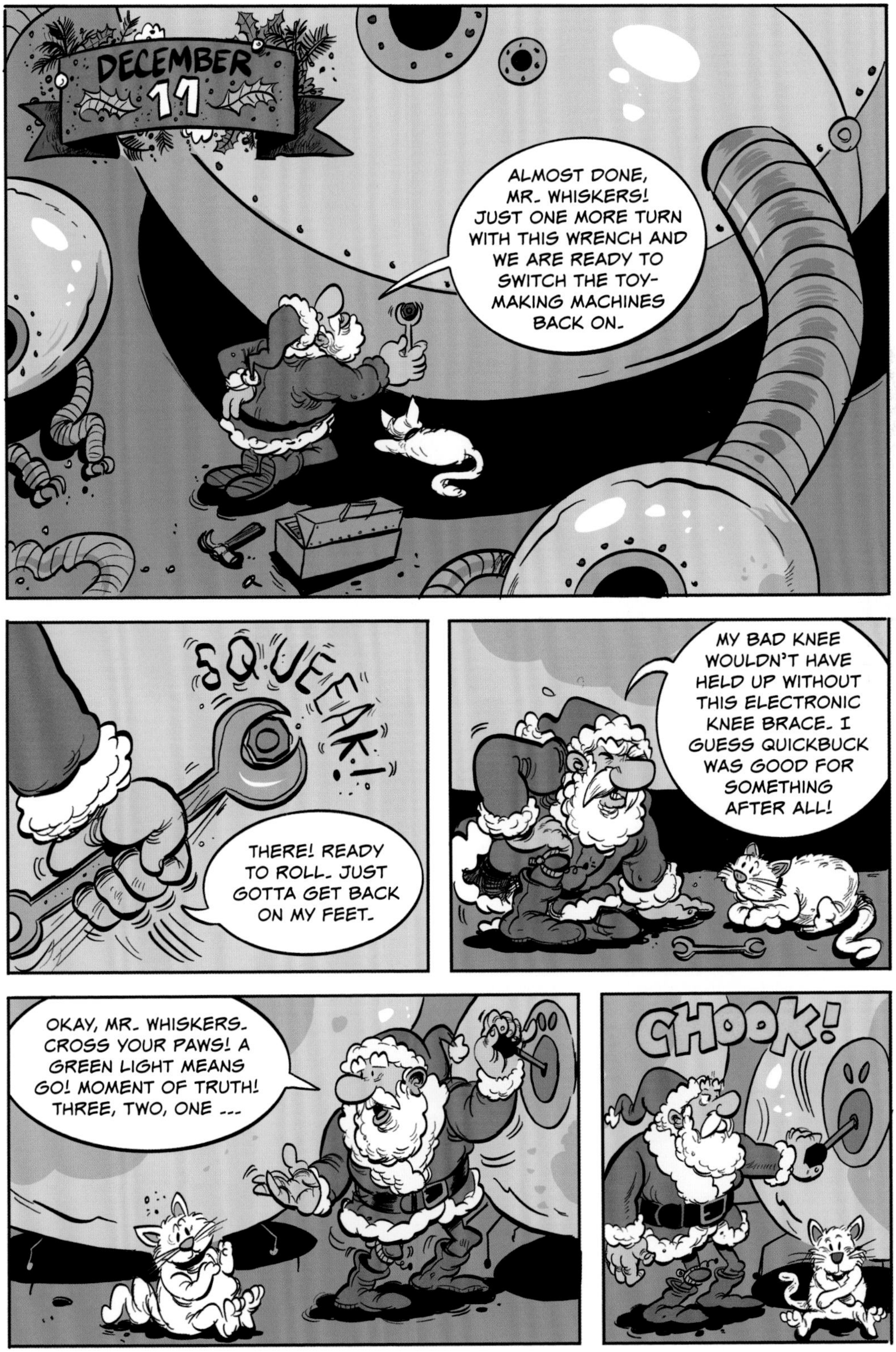
DECEMBER 11
ALMOST DONE, MR. WHISKERS! JUST ONE MORE TURN WITH THIS WRENCH AND WE ARE READY TO SWITCH THE TOY-MAKING MACHINES BACK ON.
SQUEEAK!
THERE! READY TO ROLL. JUST GOTTA GET BACK ON MY FEET.
MY BAD KNEE WOULDN'T HAVE HELD UP WITHOUT THIS ELECTRONIC KNEE BRACE. I GUESS QUICKBUCK WAS GOOD FOR SOMETHING AFTER ALL!
OKAY, MR. WHISKERS. CROSS YOUR PAWS! A GREEN LIGHT MEANS GO! MOMENT OF TRUTH! THREE, TWO, ONE ...
CHOOK!

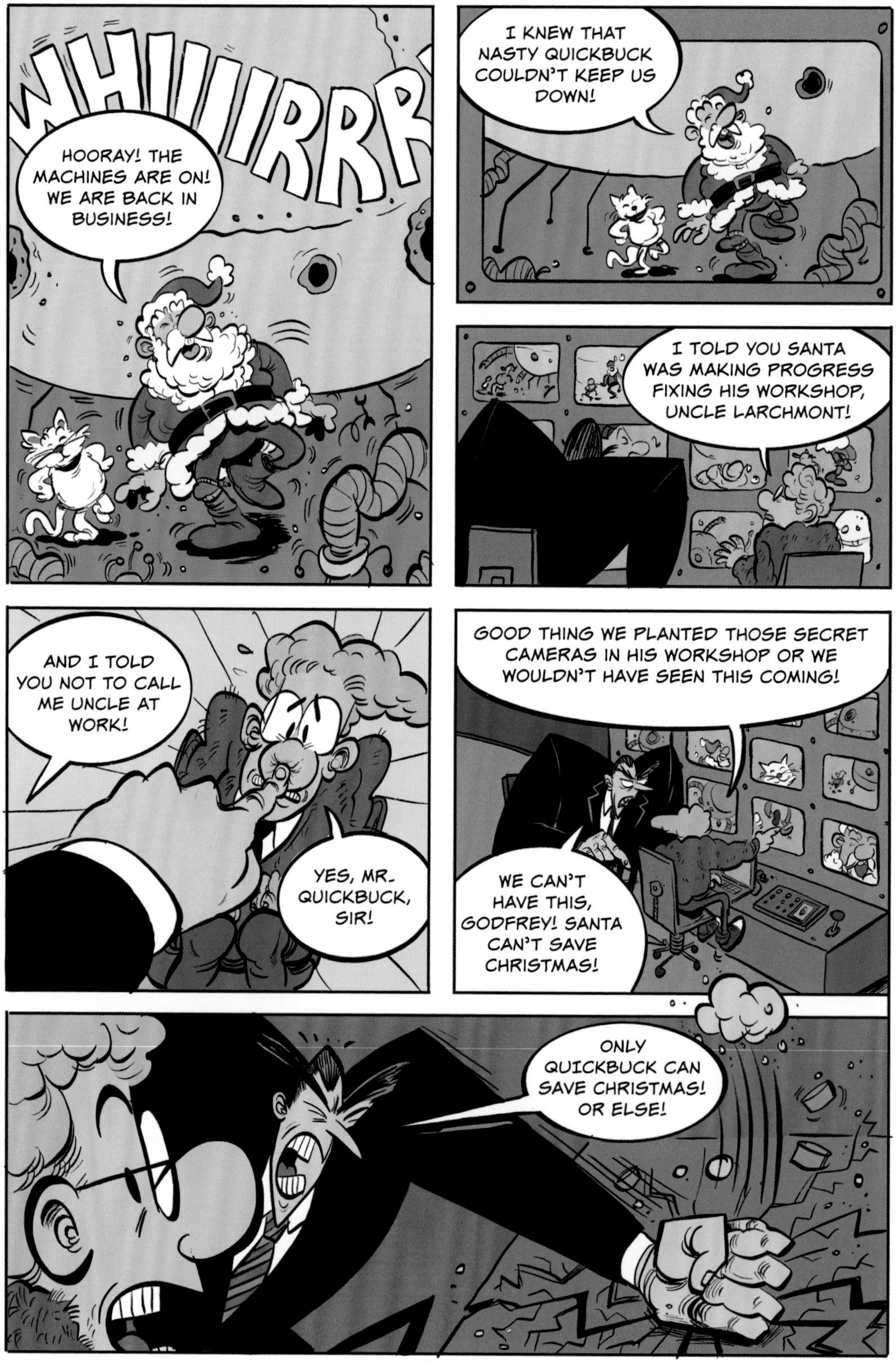
WHIIIRRR
HOORAY! THE MACHINES ARE ON! WE ARE BACK IN BUSINESS!
I KNEW THAT NASTY QUICKBUCK COULDN'T KEEP US DOWN!
I TOLD YOU SANTA WAS MAKING PROGRESS FIXING HIS WORKSHOP, UNCLE LARCHMONT!
AND I TOLD YOU NOT TO CALL ME UNCLE AT WORK!
YES, MR. QUICKBUCK, SIR!
GOOD THING WE PLANTED THOSE SECRET CAMERAS IN HIS WORKSHOP OR WE WOULDN'T HAVE SEEN THIS COMING!
WE CAN'T HAVE THIS, GODFREY! SANTA CAN'T SAVE CHRISTMAS!
ONLY QUICKBUCK CAN SAVE CHRISTMAS! OR ELSE!

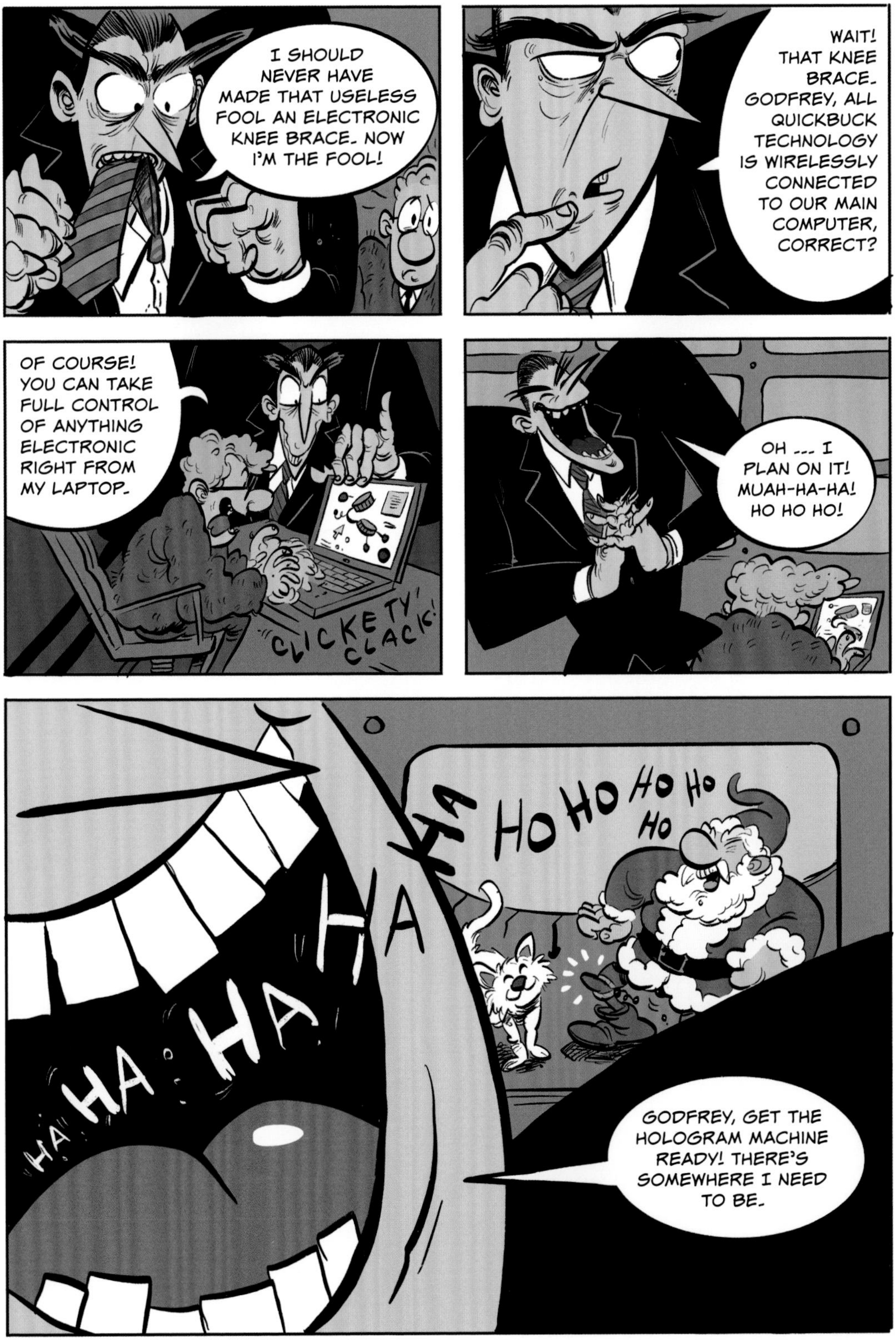
I SHOULD NEVER HAVE MADE THAT USELESS FOOL AN ELECTRONIC KNEE BRACE. NOW I'M THE FOOL!
WAIT! THAT KNEE BRACE. GODFREY, ALL QUICKBUCK TECHNOLOGY IS WIRELESSLY CONNECTED TO OUR MAIN COMPUTER, CORRECT?
OF COURSE! YOU CAN TAKE FULL CONTROL OF ANYTHING ELECTRONIC RIGHT FROM MY LAPTOP.
CLICKETY CLACK!
OH ... I PLAN ON IT! MUAH-HA-HA! HO HO HO!
HA HA HA HA HA HA
HO HO HO HO HO HO
GODFREY, GET THE HOLOGRAM MACHINE READY! THERE'S SOMEWHERE I NEED TO BE.

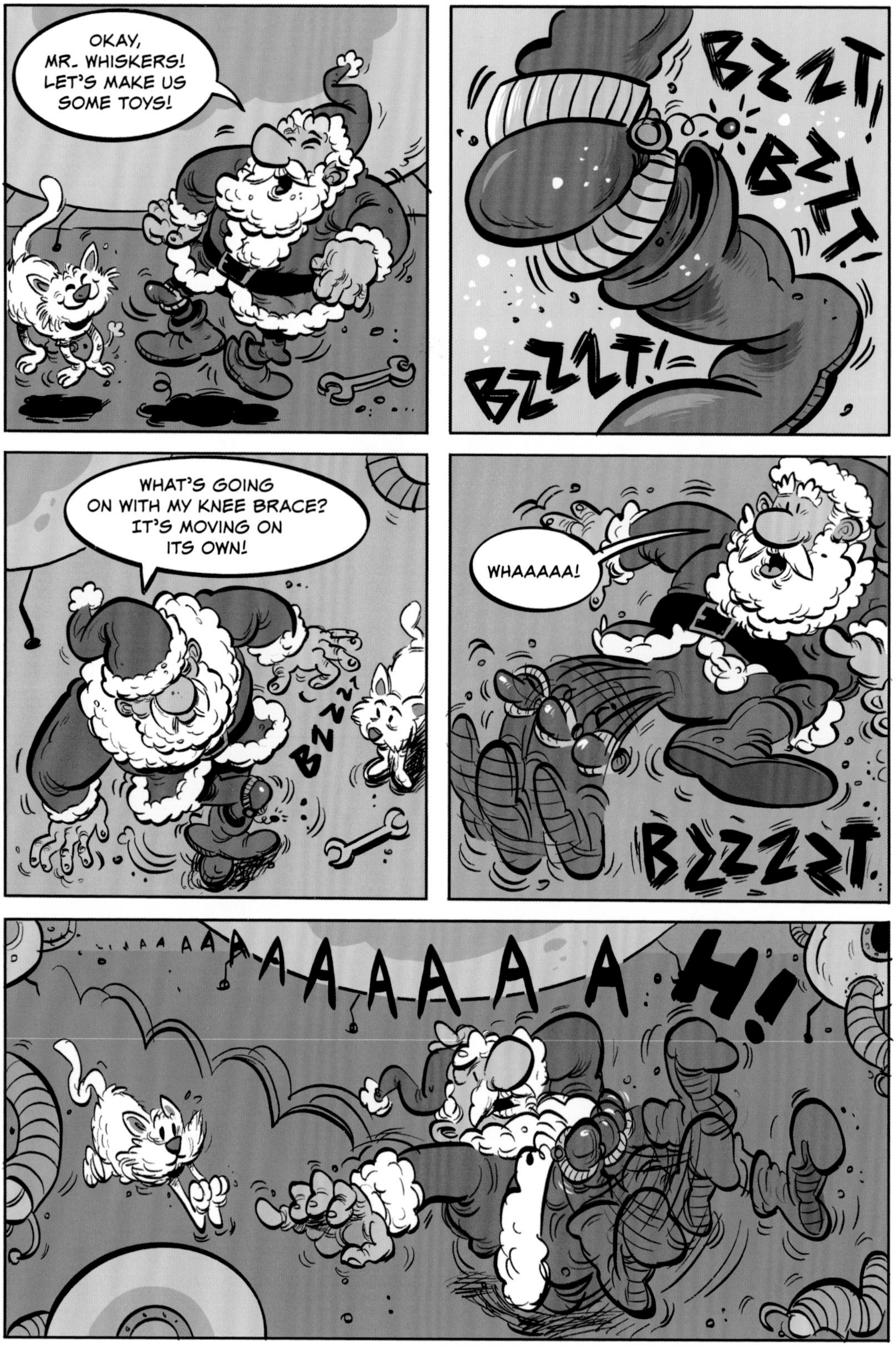
OKAY, MR. WHISKERS! LET'S MAKE US SOME TOYS!
BZZT!
BZZT!
BZZZT!
WHAT'S GOING ON WITH MY KNEE BRACE? IT'S MOVING ON ITS OWN!
BZZZ
WHAAAAA!
BZZZZT.
AAAAAAAAAAAAAH!

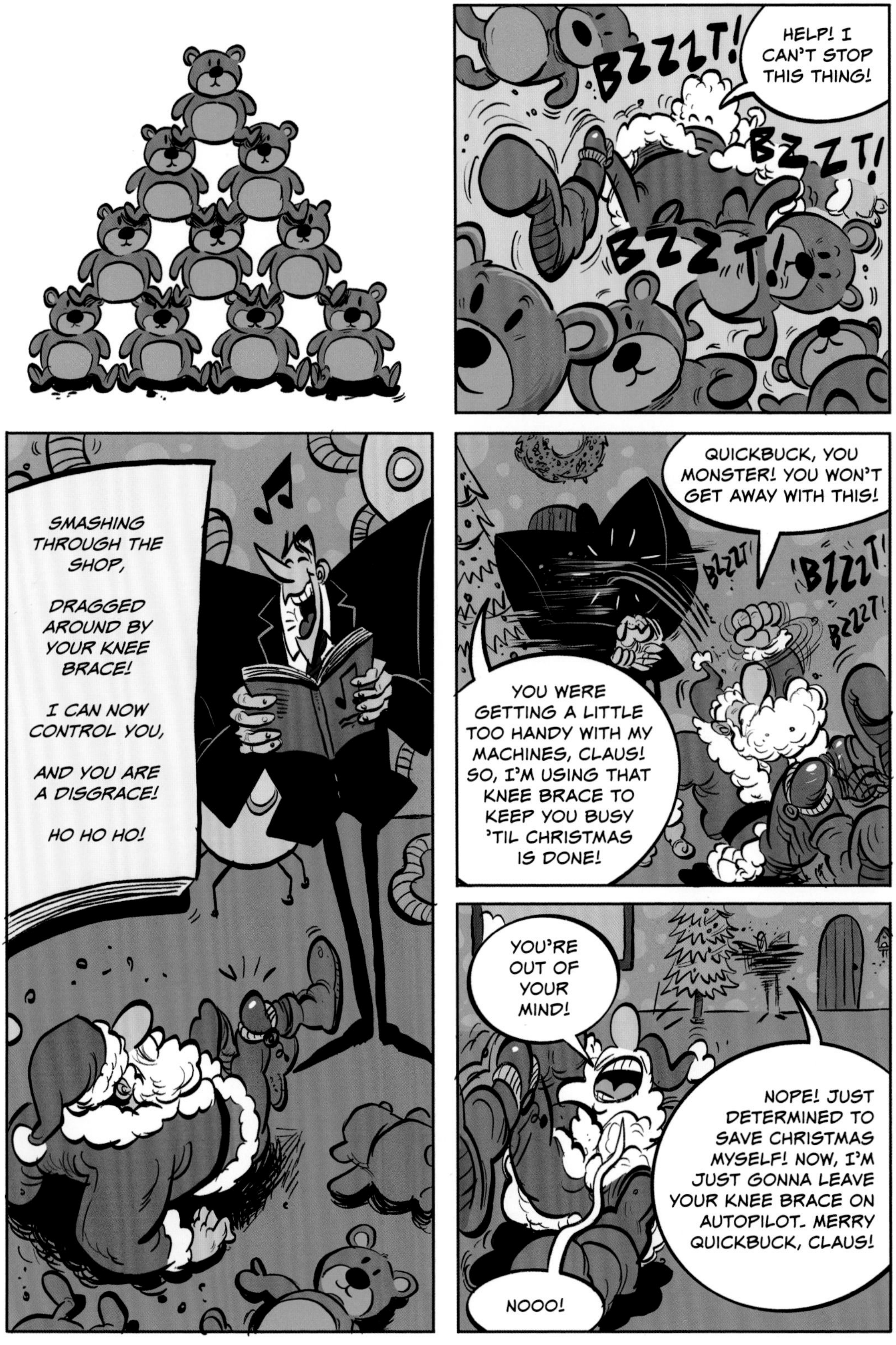
BZZZT!
HELP! I CAN'T STOP THIS THING!
BZZZT!
BZZZT!
SMASHING THROUGH THE SHOP,
DRAGGED AROUND BY YOUR KNEE BRACE!
I CAN NOW CONTROL YOU,
AND YOU ARE A DISGRACE!
HO HO HO!
QUICKBUCK, YOU MONSTER! YOU WON'T GET AWAY WITH THIS!
BZZZT!
BZZZT!
BZZZT!
YOU WERE GETTING A LITTLE TOO HANDY WITH MY MACHINES, CLAUS! SO, I'M USING THAT KNEE BRACE TO KEEP YOU BUSY 'TIL CHRISTMAS IS DONE!
YOU'RE OUT OF YOUR MIND!
NOPE! JUST DETERMINED TO SAVE CHRISTMAS MYSELF! NOW, I'M JUST GONNA LEAVE YOUR KNEE BRACE ON AUTOPILOT. MERRY QUICKBUCK, CLAUS!
NOOO!

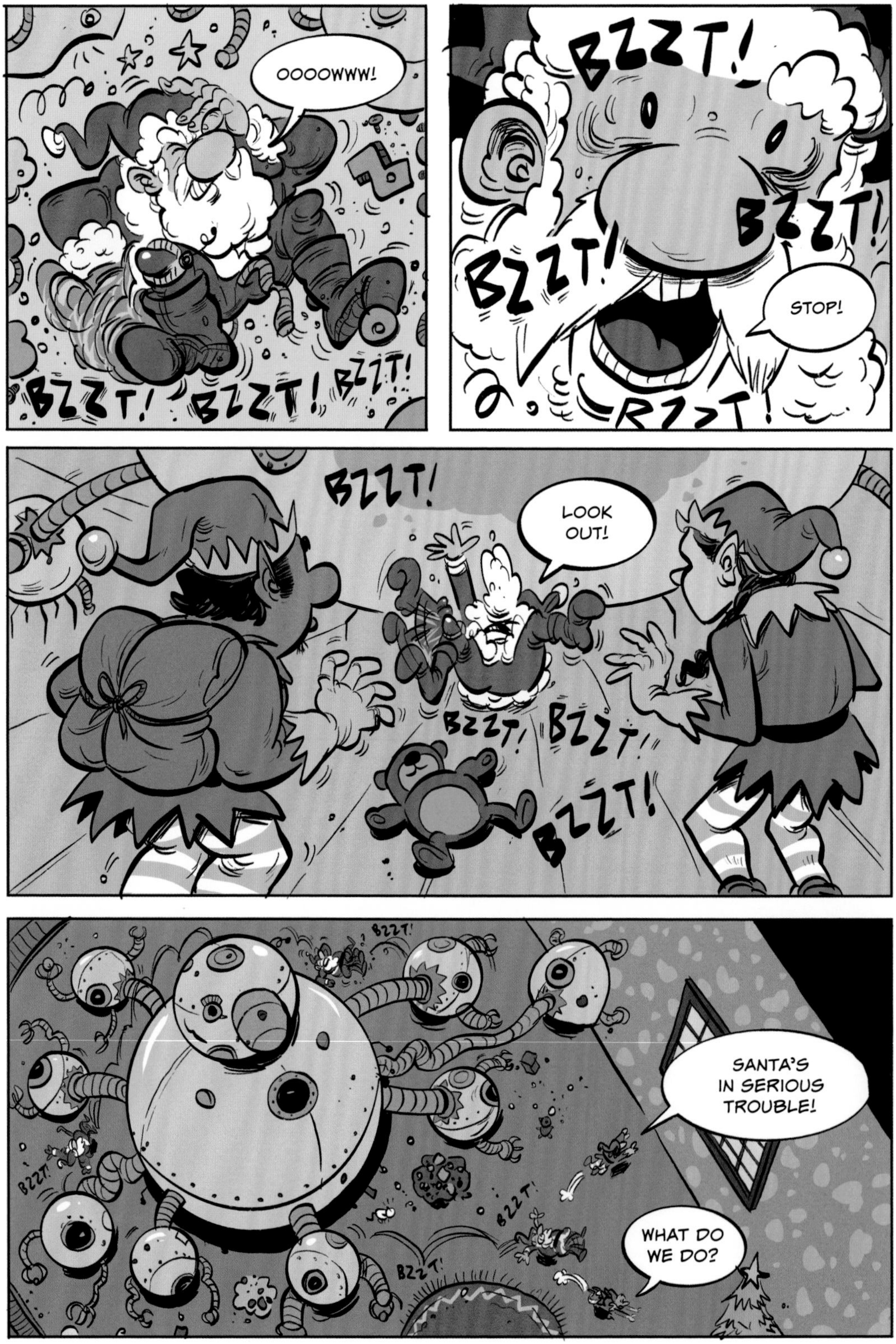
OOOOWWW!
BZZT! BZZT! BZZT!
BZZT!
BZZT!
BZZT!
STOP!
RZZT!
BZZT!
LOOK OUT!
BZZT! BZZT!
BZZT!
SANTA'S IN SERIOUS TROUBLE!
WHAT DO WE DO?

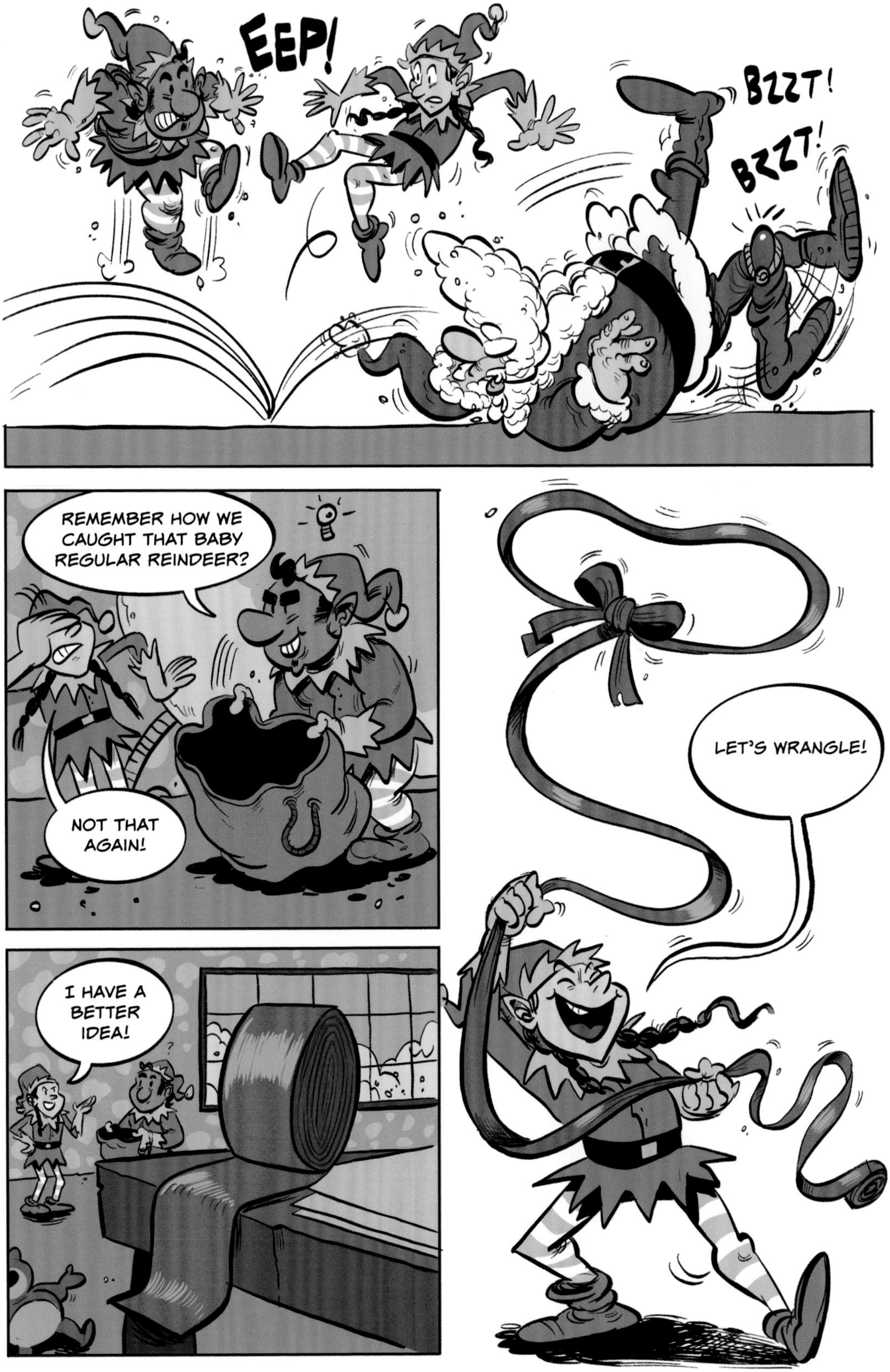
EEP!
BZZT!
BZZT!
REMEMBER HOW WE CAUGHT THAT BABY REGULAR REINDEER?
NOT THAT AGAIN!
I HAVE A BETTER IDEA!
LET'S WRANGLE!

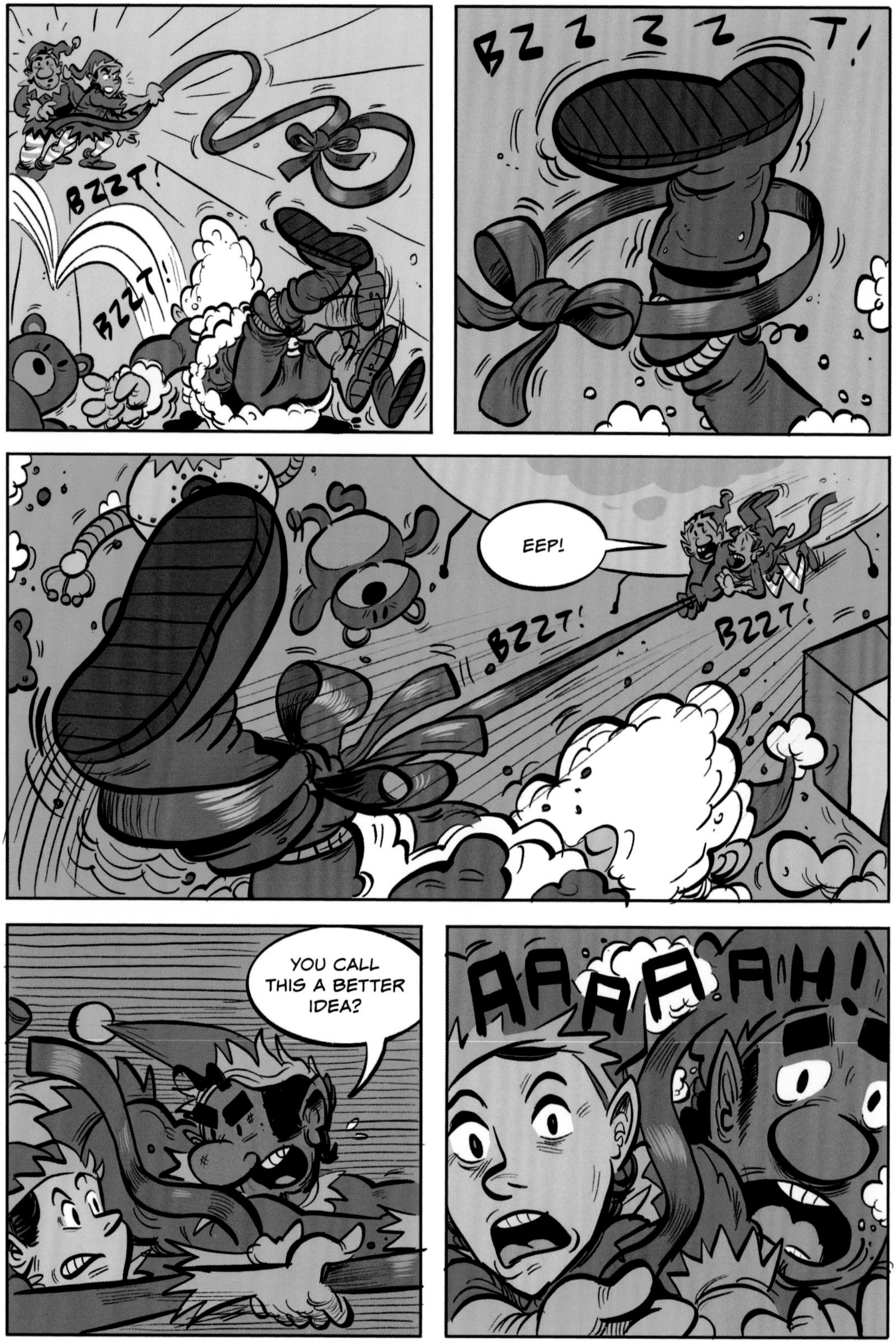
BZZT!
BZZT!
BZZZZZT!
EEP!
BZZT!
BZZT!
YOU CALL THIS A BETTER IDEA?
AAAAAH!

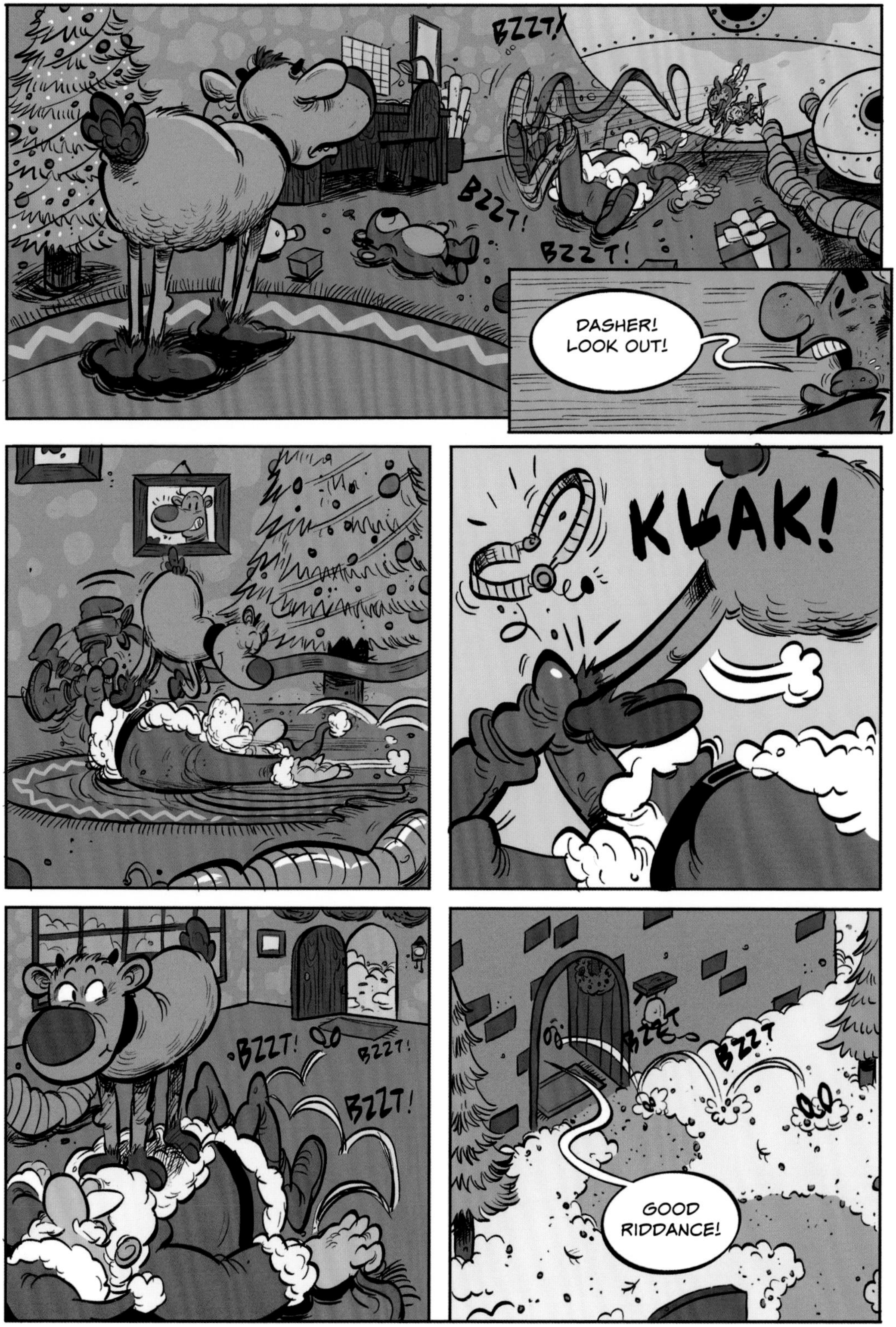
BZZT!
BZZT!
BZZT!
DASHER! LOOK OUT!
KLAK!
BZZT!
BZZT!
BZZT!
BZZT
BZZT
GOOD RIDDANCE!

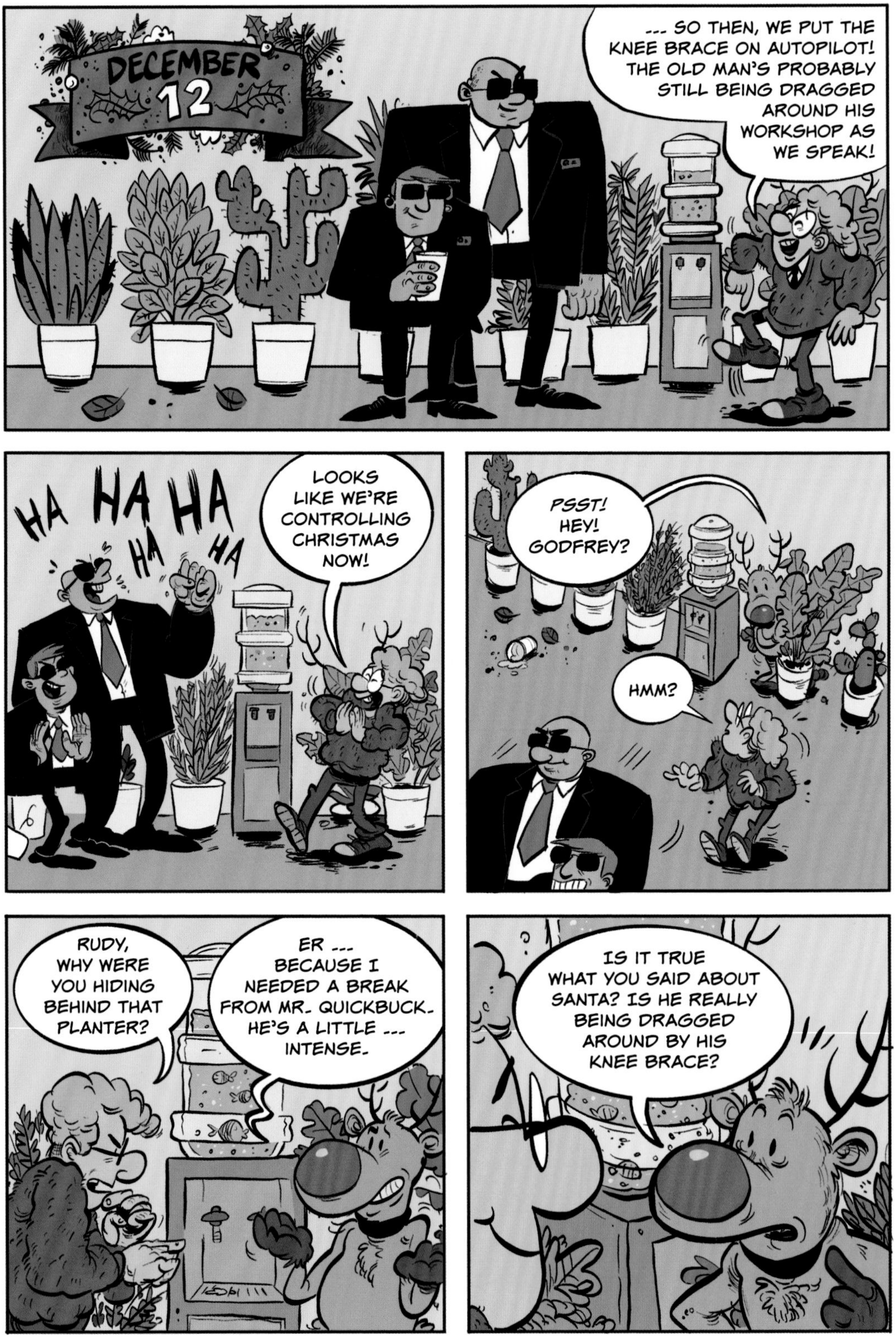
DECEMBER 12
... SO THEN, WE PUT THE KNEE BRACE ON AUTOPILOT! THE OLD MAN'S PROBABLY STILL BEING DRAGGED AROUND HIS WORKSHOP AS WE SPEAK!
HA HA HA HA HA HA
LOOKS LIKE WE'RE CONTROLLING CHRISTMAS NOW!
PSST! HEY! GODFREY?
HMM?
RUDY, WHY WERE YOU HIDING BEHIND THAT PLANTER?
ER ... BECAUSE I NEEDED A BREAK FROM MR. QUICKBUCK. HE'S A LITTLE ... INTENSE.
IS IT TRUE WHAT YOU SAID ABOUT SANTA? IS HE REALLY BEING DRAGGED AROUND BY HIS KNEE BRACE?

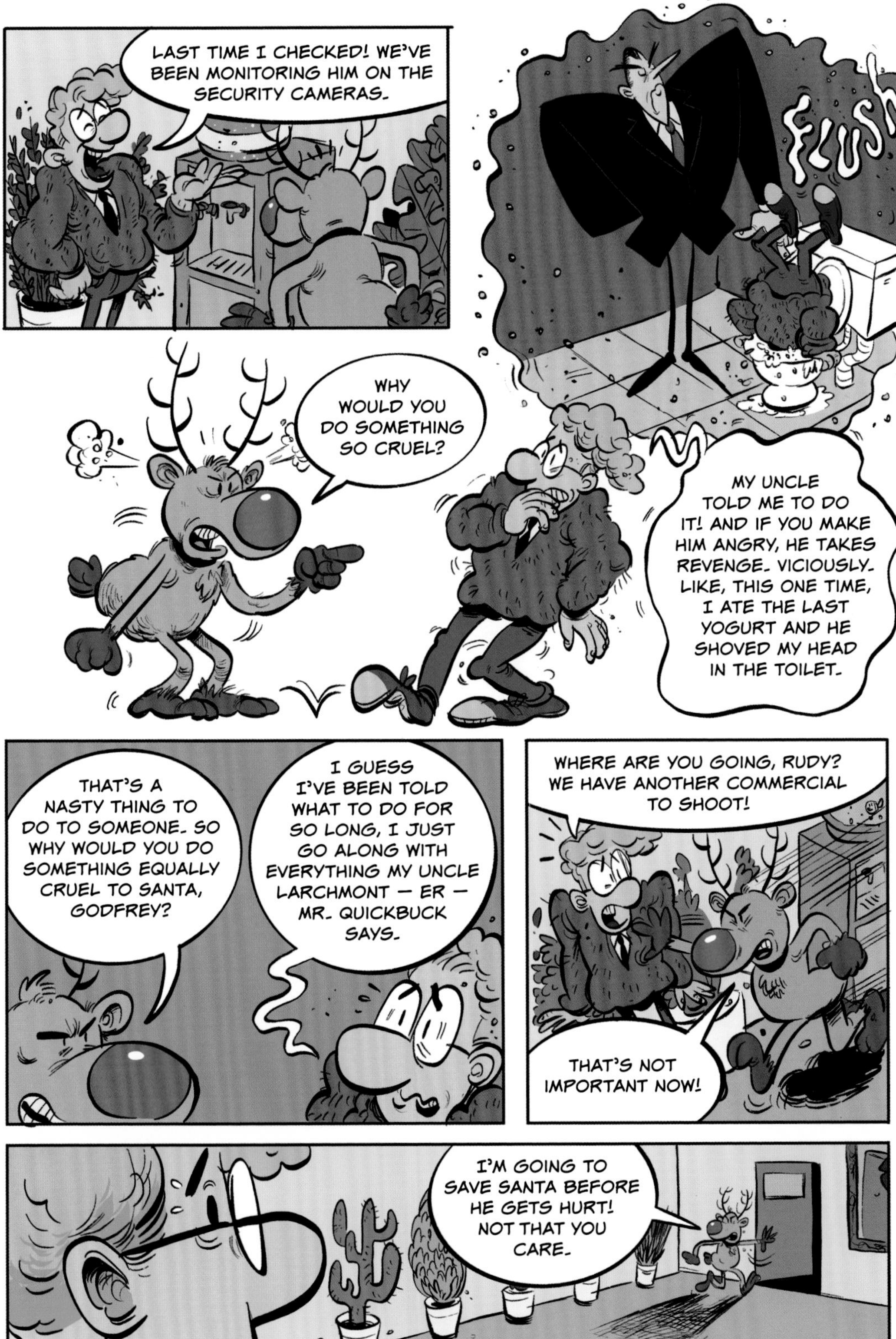
LAST TIME I CHECKED! WE'VE BEEN MONITORING HIM ON THE SECURITY CAMERAS.
FLUSH
WHY WOULD YOU DO SOMETHING SO CRUEL?
MY UNCLE TOLD ME TO DO IT! AND IF YOU MAKE HIM ANGRY, HE TAKES REVENGE. VICIOUSLY. LIKE, THIS ONE TIME, I ATE THE LAST YOGURT AND HE SHOVED MY HEAD IN THE TOILET.
THAT'S A NASTY THING TO DO TO SOMEONE. SO WHY WOULD YOU DO SOMETHING EQUALLY CRUEL TO SANTA, GODFREY?
I GUESS I'VE BEEN TOLD WHAT TO DO FOR SO LONG, I JUST GO ALONG WITH EVERYTHING MY UNCLE LARCHMONT — ER — MR. QUICKBUCK SAYS.
WHERE ARE YOU GOING, RUDY? WE HAVE ANOTHER COMMERCIAL TO SHOOT!
THAT'S NOT IMPORTANT NOW!
I'M GOING TO SAVE SANTA BEFORE HE GETS HURT! NOT THAT YOU CARE.

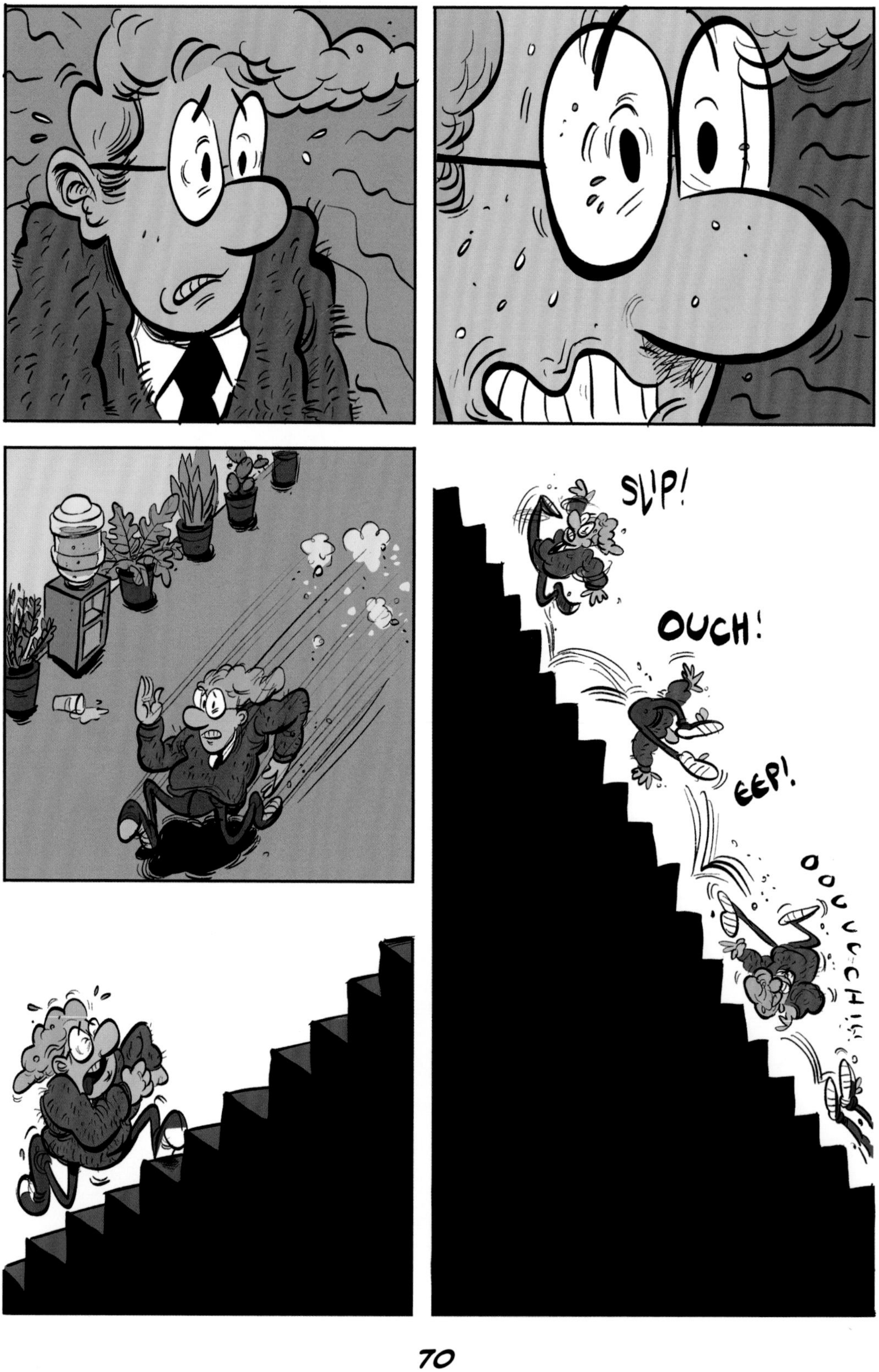
SLIP!
OUCH!
EEP!
OOUUCCH!!!

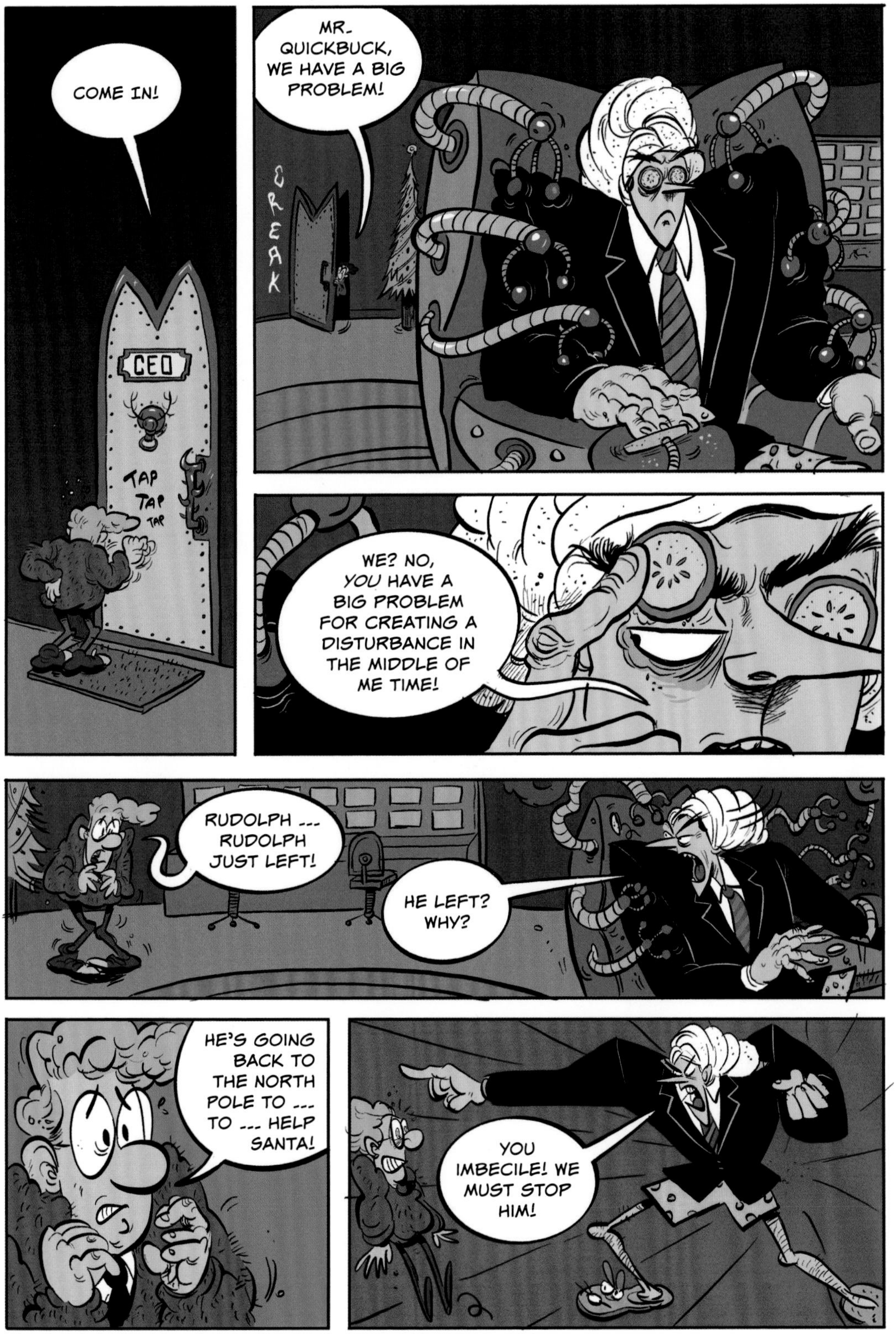
COME IN!
TAP TAP TAP
CEO
MR. QUICKBUCK, WE HAVE A BIG PROBLEM!
CREAK
WE? NO, *YOU* HAVE A BIG PROBLEM FOR CREATING A DISTURBANCE IN THE MIDDLE OF ME TIME!
RUDOLPH --- RUDOLPH JUST LEFT!
HE LEFT? WHY?
HE'S GOING BACK TO THE NORTH POLE TO --- TO --- HELP SANTA!
YOU IMBECILE! WE MUST STOP HIM!

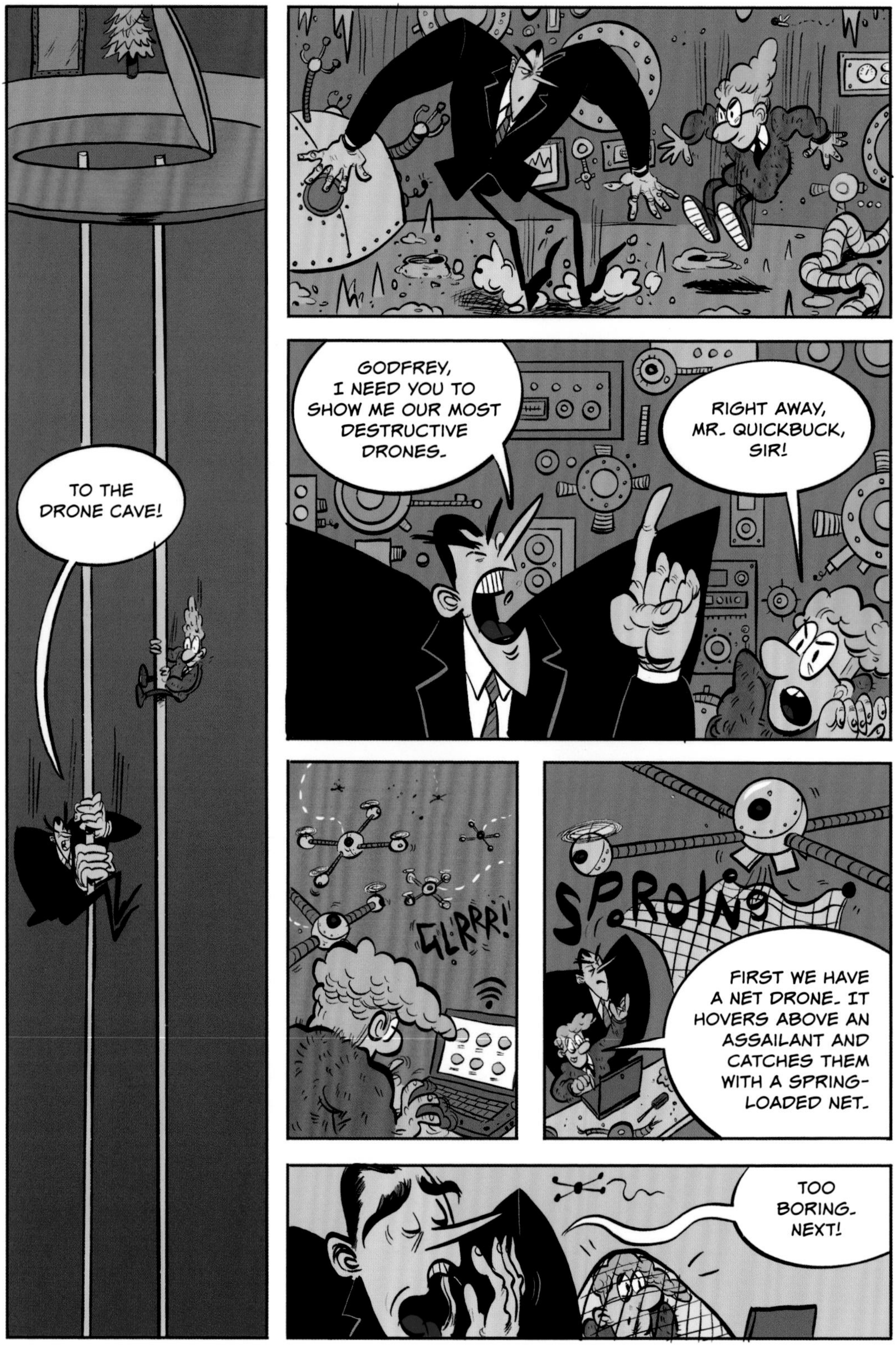
TO THE DRONE CAVE!
GODFREY, I NEED YOU TO SHOW ME OUR MOST DESTRUCTIVE DRONES.
RIGHT AWAY, MR. QUICKBUCK, SIR!
GLRRR!
SPROING
FIRST WE HAVE A NET DRONE. IT HOVERS ABOVE AN ASSAILANT AND CATCHES THEM WITH A SPRING-LOADED NET.
TOO BORING. NEXT!

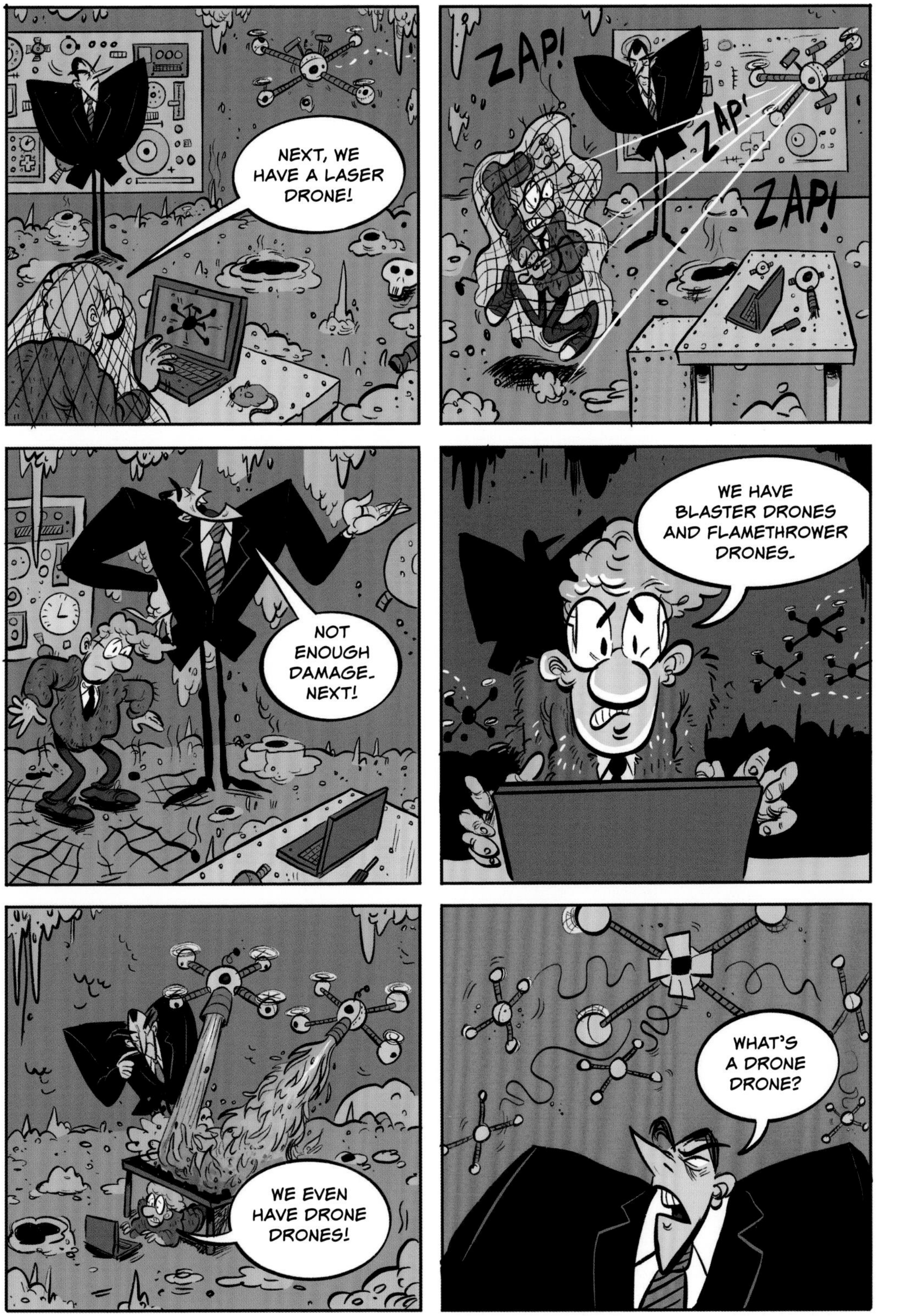
NEXT, WE HAVE A LASER DRONE!
ZAP!
ZAP!
ZAP!
NOT ENOUGH DAMAGE. NEXT!
WE HAVE BLASTER DRONES AND FLAMETHROWER DRONES.
WE EVEN HAVE DRONE DRONES!
WHAT'S A DRONE DRONE?

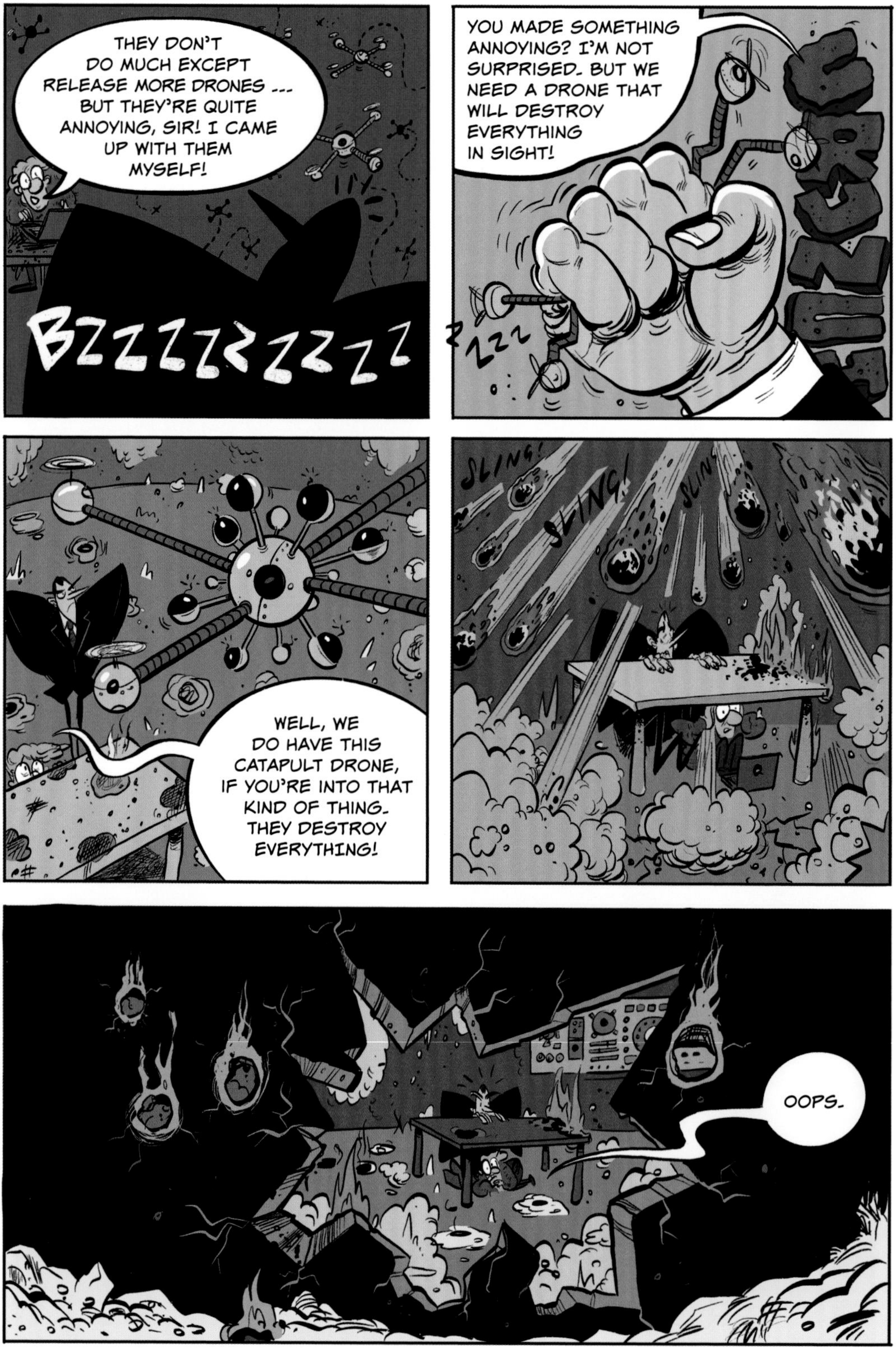
THEY DON'T DO MUCH EXCEPT RELEASE MORE DRONES ... BUT THEY'RE QUITE ANNOYING, SIR! I CAME UP WITH THEM MYSELF!
YOU MADE SOMETHING ANNOYING? I'M NOT SURPRISED. BUT WE NEED A DRONE THAT WILL DESTROY EVERYTHING IN SIGHT!
WELL, WE DO HAVE THIS CATAPULT DRONE, IF YOU'RE INTO THAT KIND OF THING. THEY DESTROY EVERYTHING!
SLING!
SLING!
SLING!
OOPS.

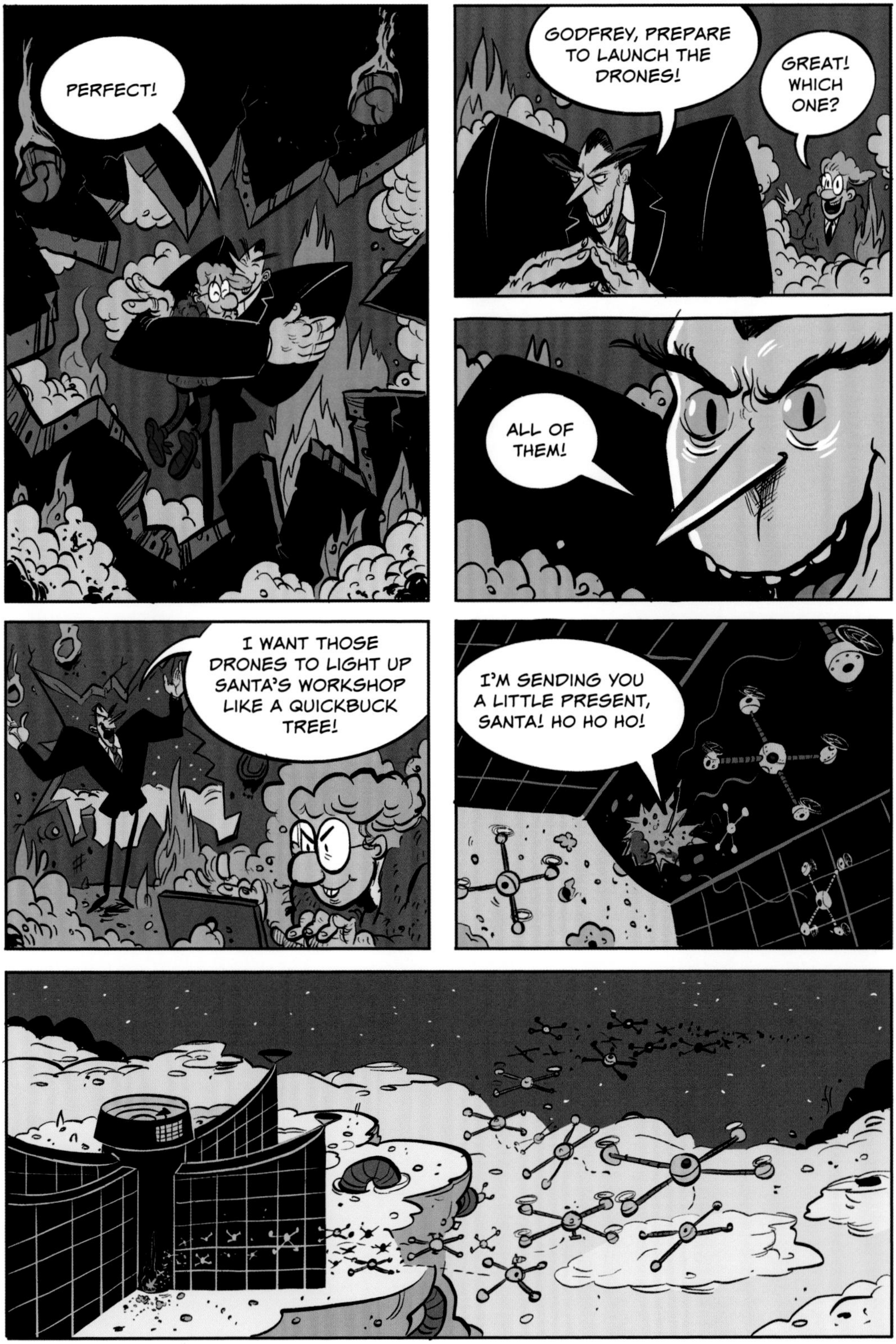
PERFECT!
GODFREY, PREPARE TO LAUNCH THE DRONES!
GREAT! WHICH ONE?
ALL OF THEM!
I WANT THOSE DRONES TO LIGHT UP SANTA'S WORKSHOP LIKE A QUICKBUCK TREE!
I'M SENDING YOU A LITTLE PRESENT, SANTA! HO HO HO!

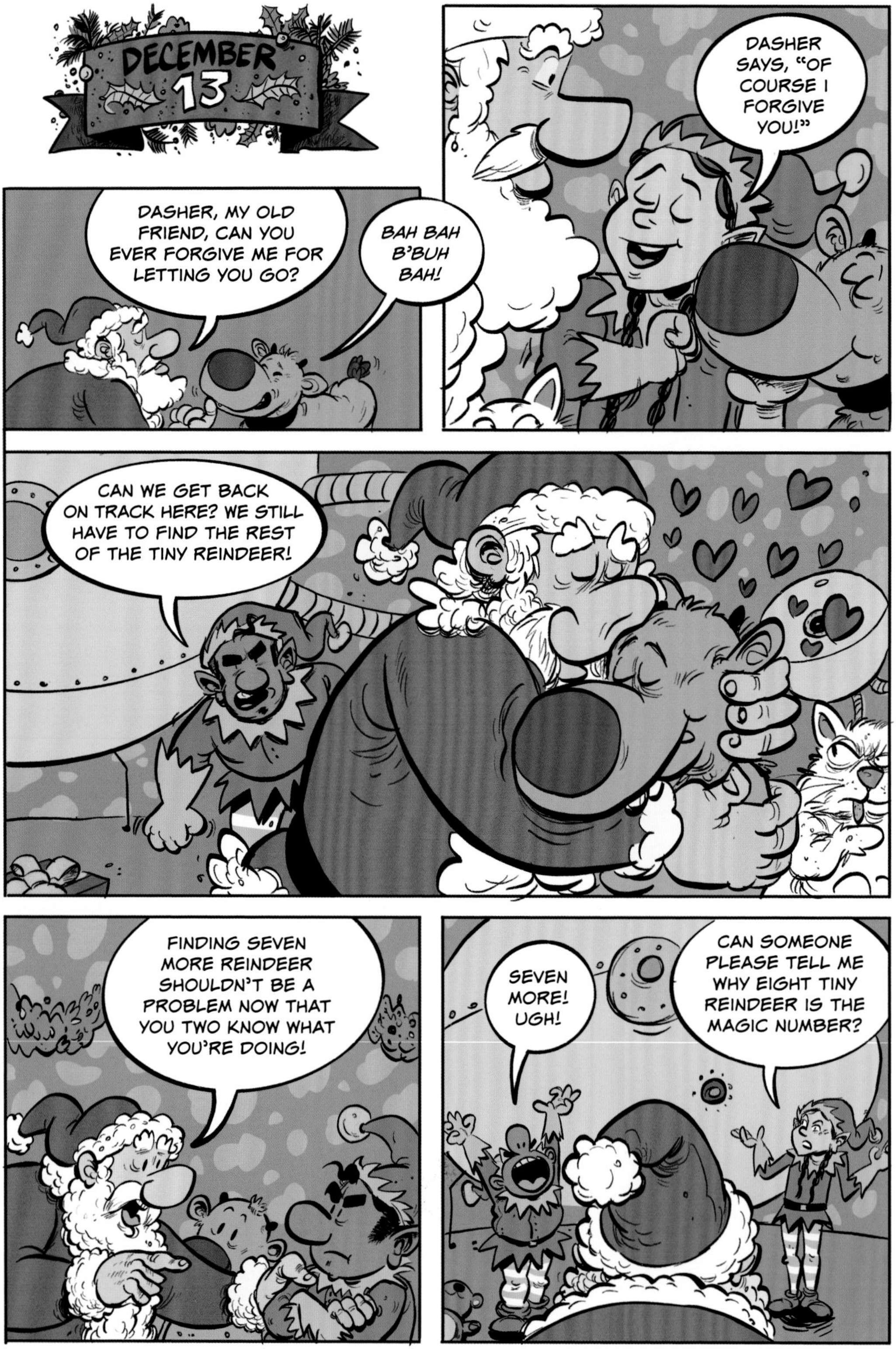
DECEMBER 13
DASHER, MY OLD FRIEND, CAN YOU EVER FORGIVE ME FOR LETTING YOU GO?
BAH BAH B'BUH BAH!
DASHER SAYS, "OF COURSE I FORGIVE YOU!"
CAN WE GET BACK ON TRACK HERE? WE STILL HAVE TO FIND THE REST OF THE TINY REINDEER!
FINDING SEVEN MORE REINDEER SHOULDN'T BE A PROBLEM NOW THAT YOU TWO KNOW WHAT YOU'RE DOING!
SEVEN MORE! UGH!
CAN SOMEONE PLEASE TELL ME WHY EIGHT TINY REINDEER IS THE MAGIC NUMBER?

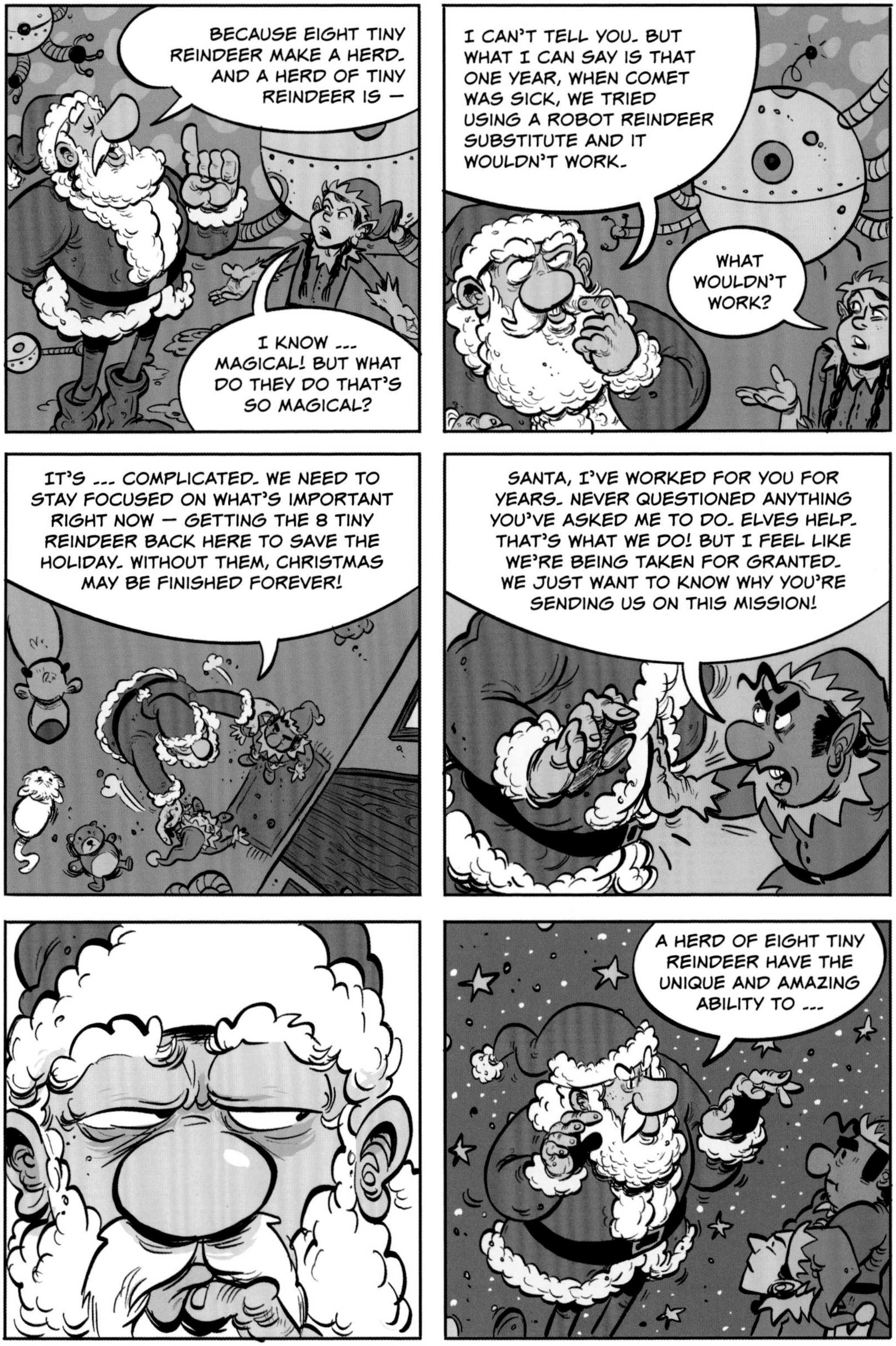
BECAUSE EIGHT TINY REINDEER MAKE A HERD. AND A HERD OF TINY REINDEER IS —
I KNOW ... MAGICAL! BUT WHAT DO THEY DO THAT'S SO MAGICAL?
I CAN'T TELL YOU. BUT WHAT I CAN SAY IS THAT ONE YEAR, WHEN COMET WAS SICK, WE TRIED USING A ROBOT REINDEER SUBSTITUTE AND IT WOULDN'T WORK.
WHAT WOULDN'T WORK?
IT'S ... COMPLICATED. WE NEED TO STAY FOCUSED ON WHAT'S IMPORTANT RIGHT NOW — GETTING THE 8 TINY REINDEER BACK HERE TO SAVE THE HOLIDAY. WITHOUT THEM, CHRISTMAS MAY BE FINISHED FOREVER!
SANTA, I'VE WORKED FOR YOU FOR YEARS. NEVER QUESTIONED ANYTHING YOU'VE ASKED ME TO DO. ELVES HELP. THAT'S WHAT WE DO! BUT I FEEL LIKE WE'RE BEING TAKEN FOR GRANTED. WE JUST WANT TO KNOW WHY YOU'RE SENDING US ON THIS MISSION!
A HERD OF EIGHT TINY REINDEER HAVE THE UNIQUE AND AMAZING ABILITY TO ...

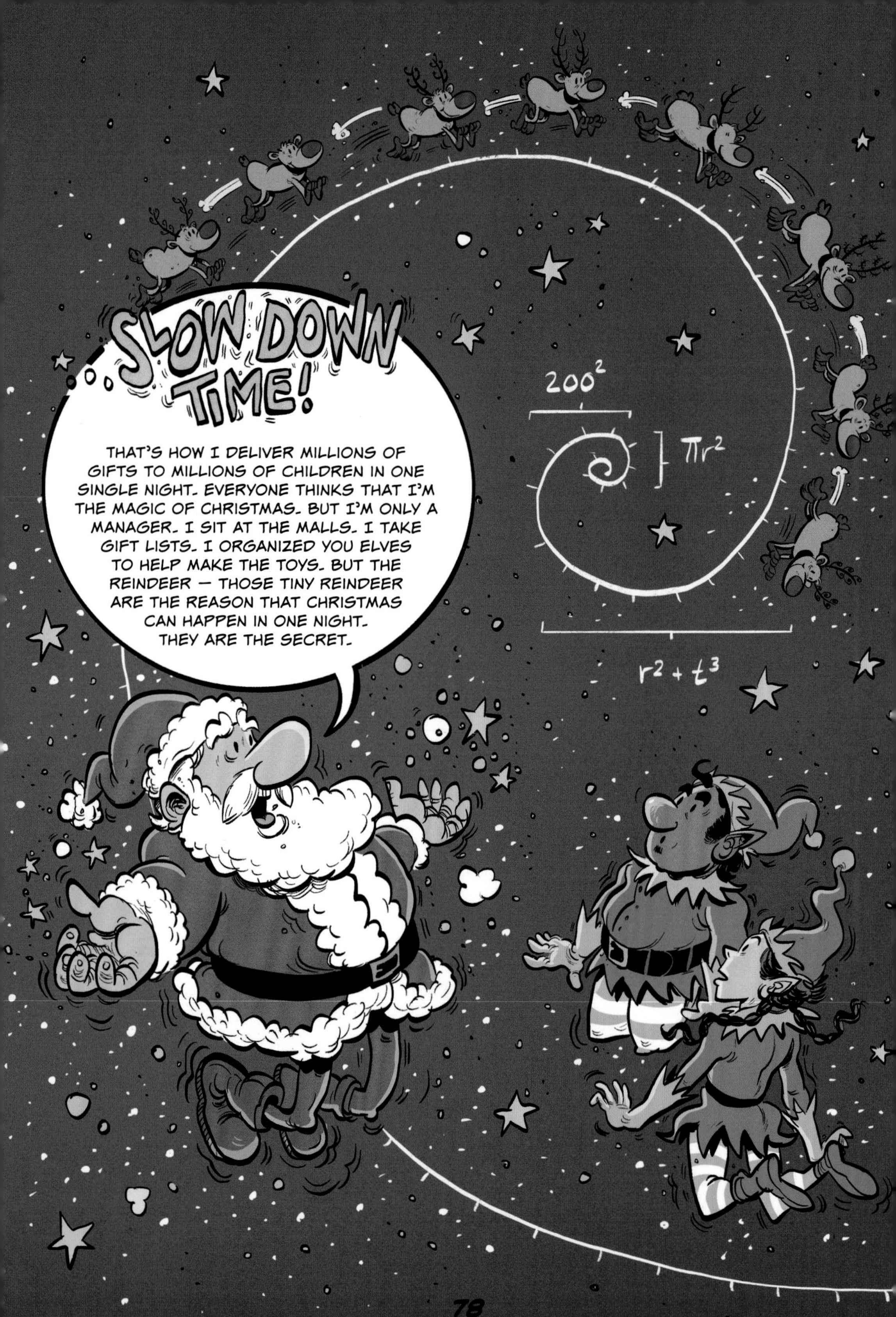
SLOW DOWN TIME!
THAT'S HOW I DELIVER MILLIONS OF GIFTS TO MILLIONS OF CHILDREN IN ONE SINGLE NIGHT. EVERYONE THINKS THAT I'M THE MAGIC OF CHRISTMAS. BUT I'M ONLY A MANAGER. I SIT AT THE MALLS. I TAKE GIFT LISTS. I ORGANIZED YOU ELVES TO HELP MAKE THE TOYS. BUT THE REINDEER — THOSE TINY REINDEER ARE THE REASON THAT CHRISTMAS CAN HAPPEN IN ONE NIGHT. THEY ARE THE SECRET.
200^2
πr^2
$r^2 + t^3$

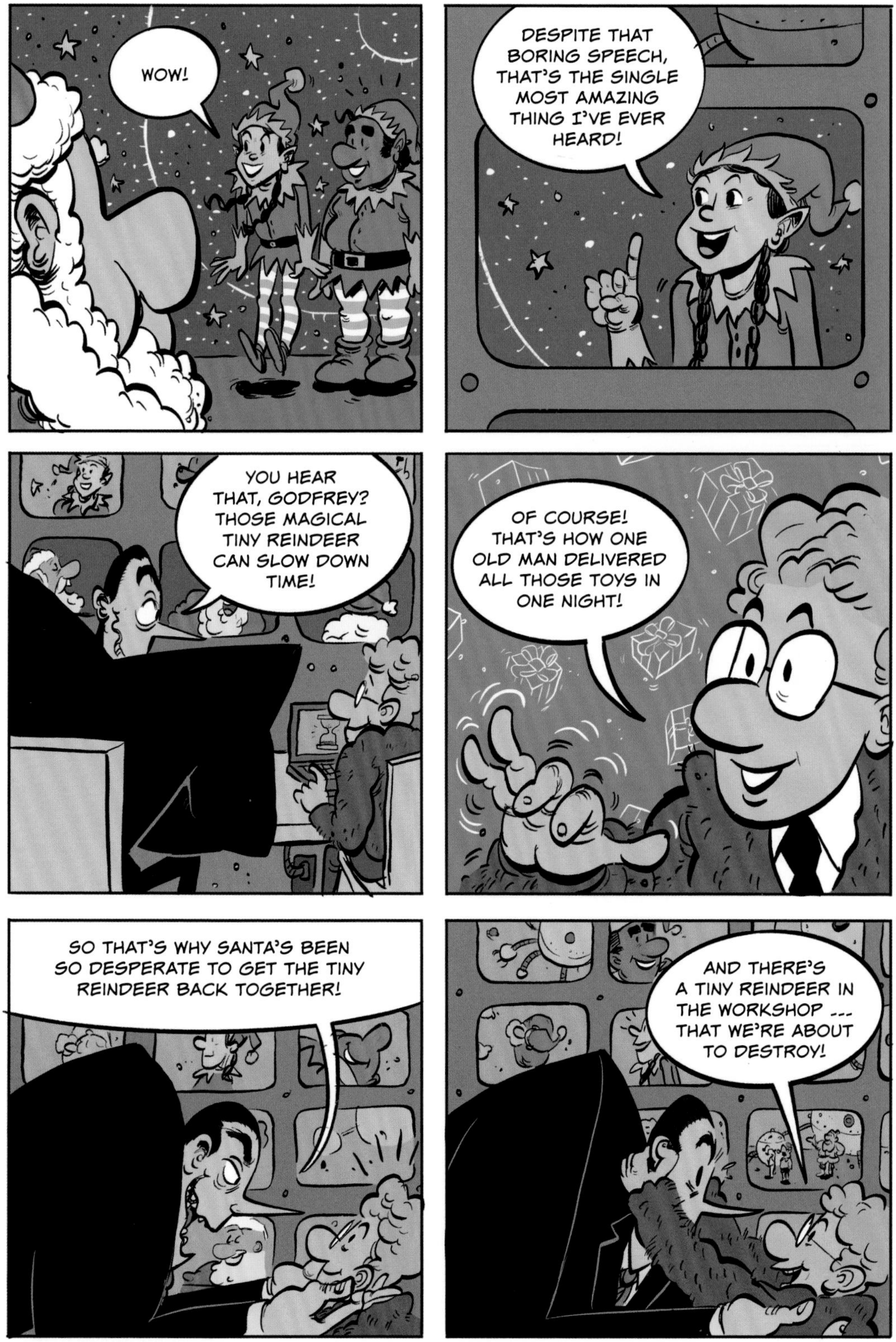
WOW!
DESPITE THAT BORING SPEECH, THAT'S THE SINGLE MOST AMAZING THING I'VE EVER HEARD!
YOU HEAR THAT, GODFREY? THOSE MAGICAL TINY REINDEER CAN SLOW DOWN TIME!
OF COURSE! THAT'S HOW ONE OLD MAN DELIVERED ALL THOSE TOYS IN ONE NIGHT!
SO THAT'S WHY SANTA'S BEEN SO DESPERATE TO GET THE TINY REINDEER BACK TOGETHER!
AND THERE'S A TINY REINDEER IN THE WORKSHOP --- THAT WE'RE ABOUT TO DESTROY!

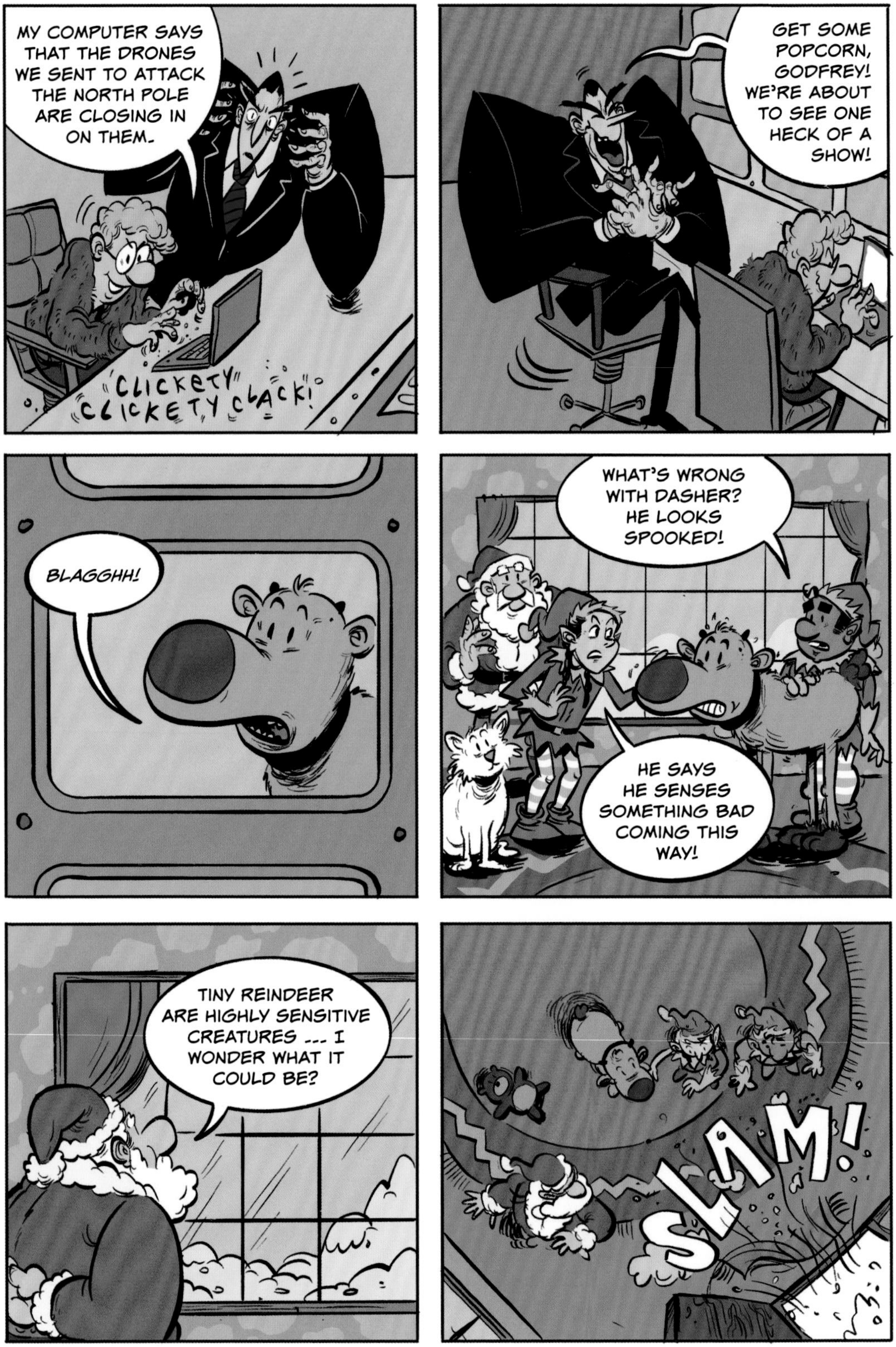
MY COMPUTER SAYS THAT THE DRONES WE SENT TO ATTACK THE NORTH POLE ARE CLOSING IN ON THEM.
CLICKETY CLICKETY CLACK!
GET SOME POPCORN, GODFREY! WE'RE ABOUT TO SEE ONE HECK OF A SHOW!
BLAGGHH!
WHAT'S WRONG WITH DASHER? HE LOOKS SPOOKED!
HE SAYS HE SENSES SOMETHING BAD COMING THIS WAY!
TINY REINDEER ARE HIGHLY SENSITIVE CREATURES --- I WONDER WHAT IT COULD BE?
SLAM!

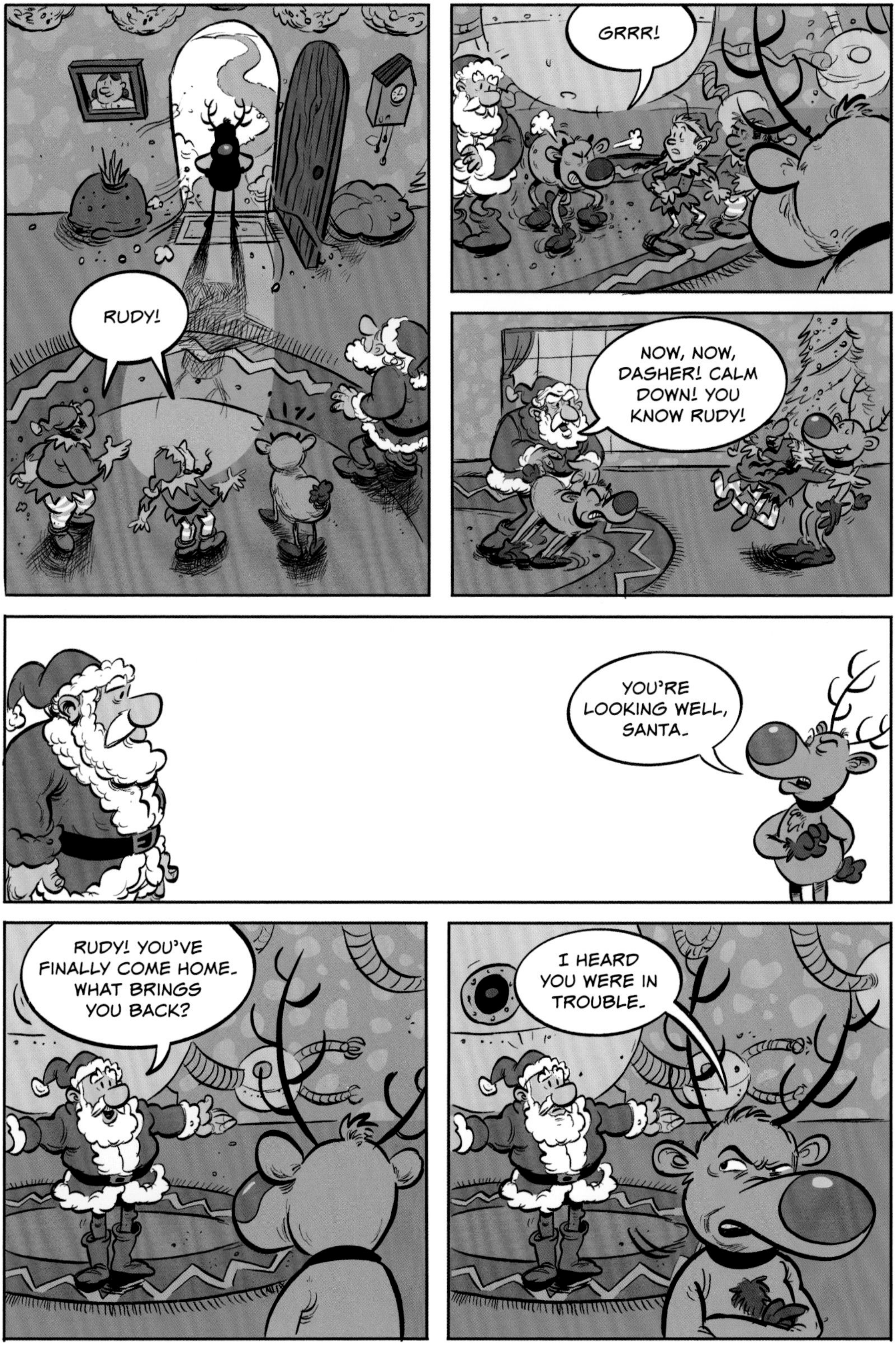
RUDY!
GRRR!
NOW, NOW, DASHER! CALM DOWN! YOU KNOW RUDY!
YOU'RE LOOKING WELL, SANTA.
RUDY! YOU'VE FINALLY COME HOME. WHAT BRINGS YOU BACK?
I HEARD YOU WERE IN TROUBLE.

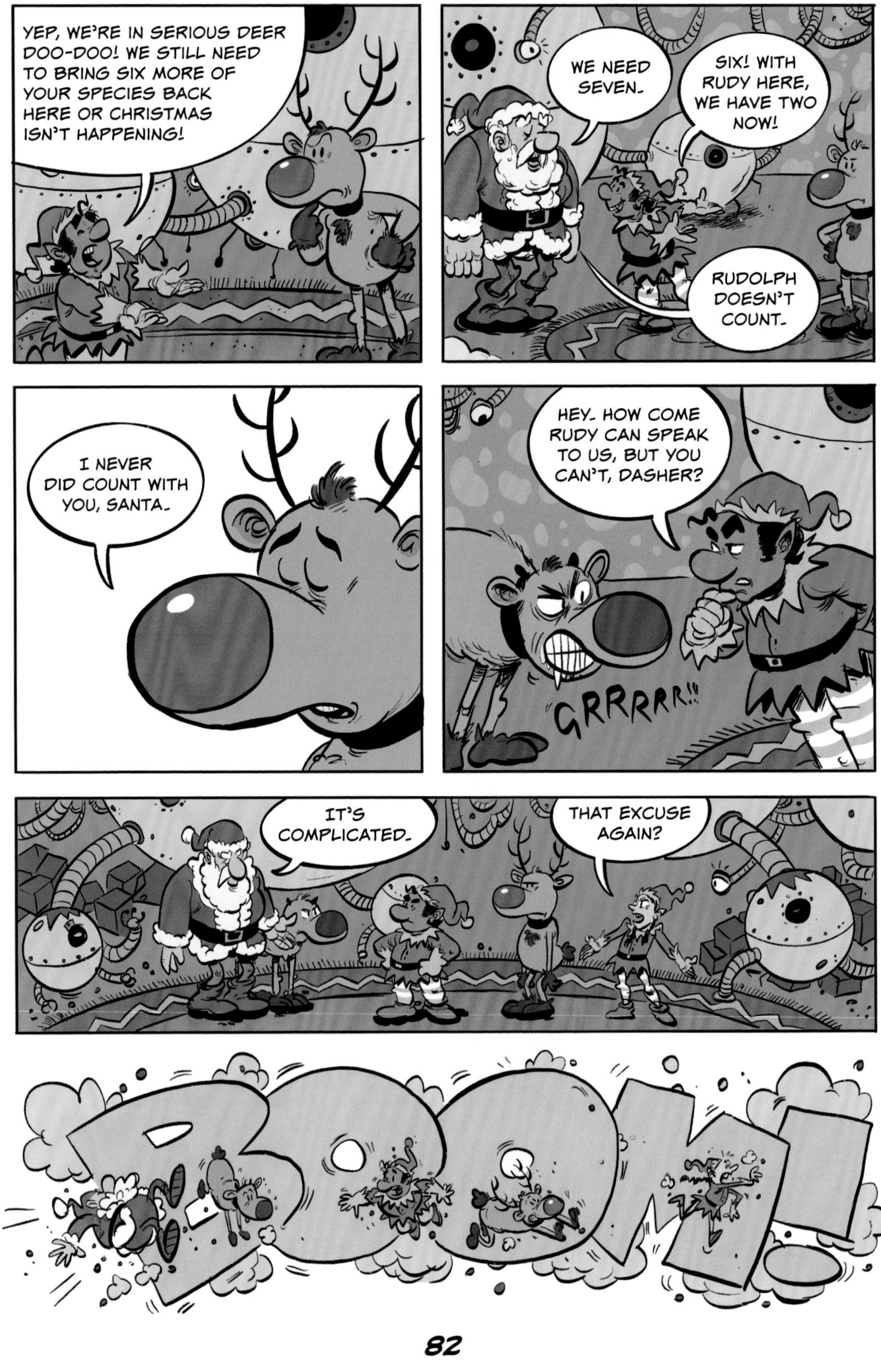
YEP, WE'RE IN SERIOUS DEER DOO-DOO! WE STILL NEED TO BRING SIX MORE OF YOUR SPECIES BACK HERE OR CHRISTMAS ISN'T HAPPENING!
WE NEED SEVEN.
SIX! WITH RUDY HERE, WE HAVE TWO NOW!
RUDOLPH DOESN'T COUNT.
I NEVER DID COUNT WITH YOU, SANTA.
HEY. HOW COME RUDY CAN SPEAK TO US, BUT YOU CAN'T, DASHER?
GRRRRRR!!
IT'S COMPLICATED.
THAT EXCUSE AGAIN?
BOOM!

WHAT WAS THAT?

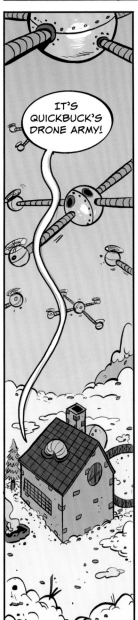

IT'S QUICKBUCK'S DRONE ARMY!

DID YOU SAY ... DRONE ARMY?!?!

YES. QUICKBUCK'S BEEN MONITORING YOU ON THE SECURITY CAMERAS! HE KNOWS EVERYTHING YOU'RE UP TO, AND NOW HE'S SENDING IN REINFORCEMENTS.

I REALLY, REALLY, REALLY, REEEEALLY DON'T LIKE THAT GUY!

THIS IS ABOUT TO GET UGLY. I'LL GO DISTRACT THE DRONES! YOU GUYS GET SANTA AND DASHER TO SAFETY! CHRISTMAS CAN'T HAPPEN WITHOUT THEM!

RUDOLPH, WAIT! I HAVE SOMETHING I NEED TO TELL YOU!

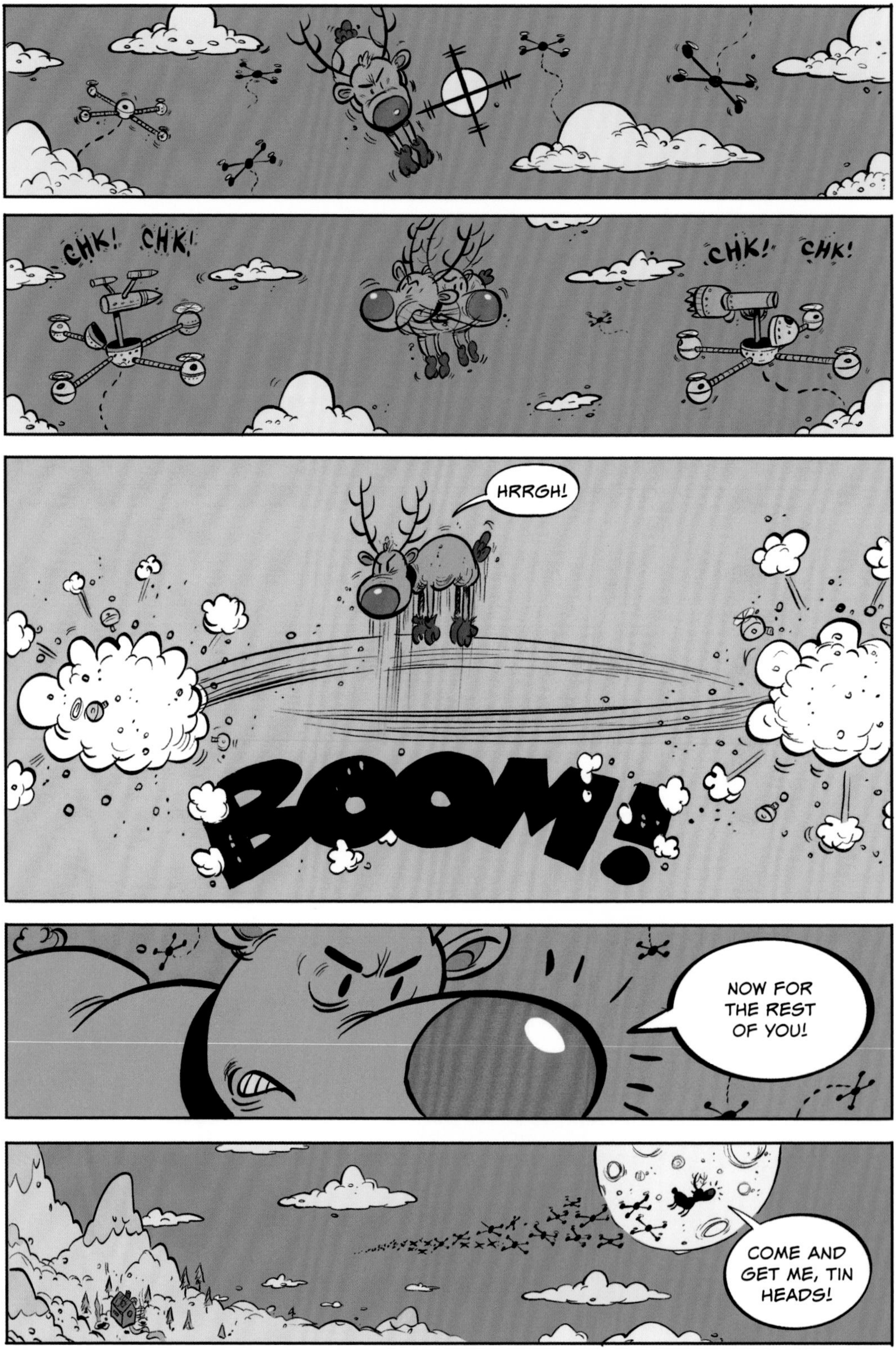
CHK! CHK!
CHK! CHK!
HRRGH!
BOOM!
NOW FOR THE REST OF YOU!
COME AND GET ME, TIN HEADS!

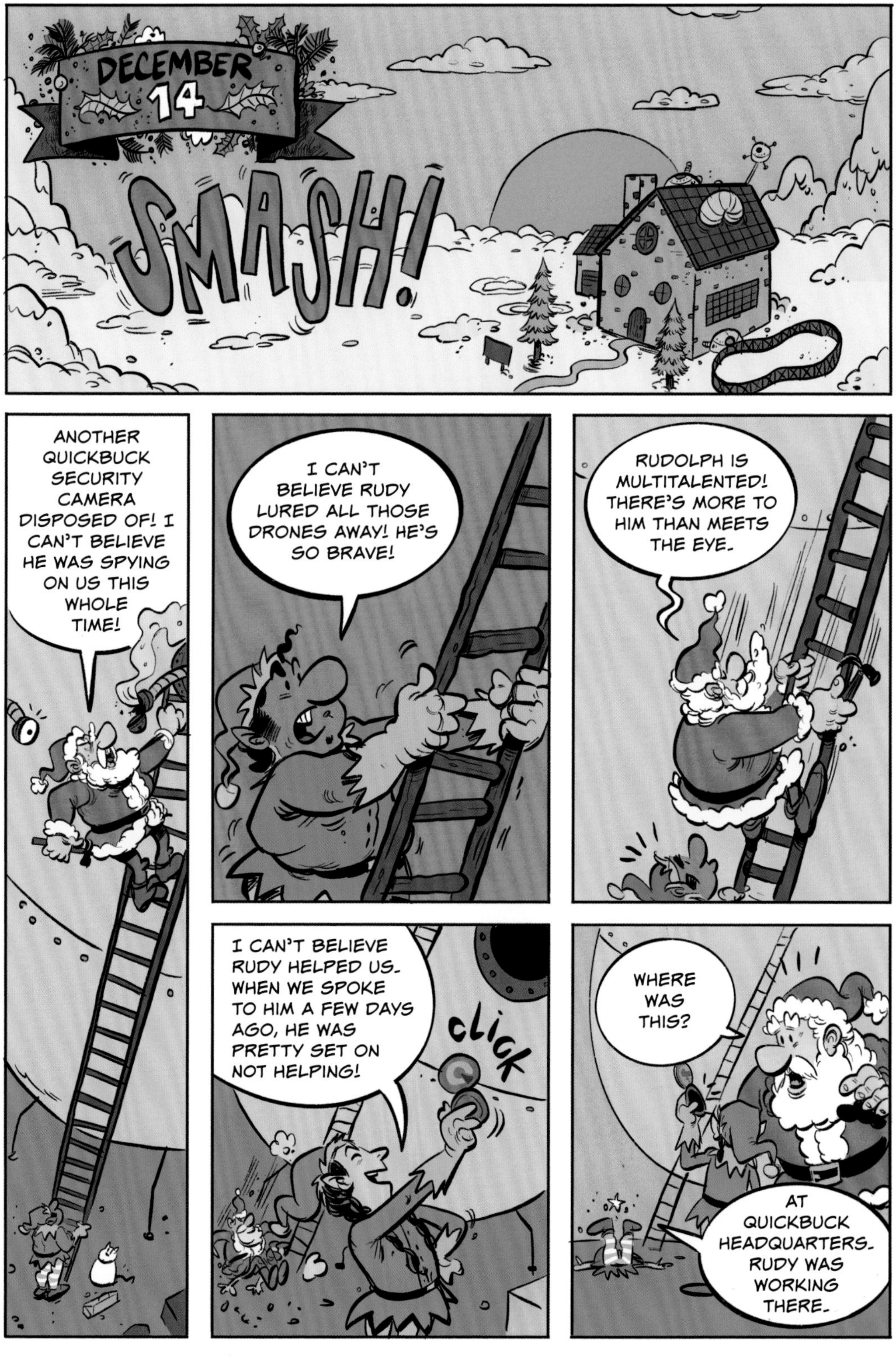
DECEMBER 14
SMASH!
ANOTHER QUICKBUCK SECURITY CAMERA DISPOSED OF! I CAN'T BELIEVE HE WAS SPYING ON US THIS WHOLE TIME!
I CAN'T BELIEVE RUDY LURED ALL THOSE DRONES AWAY! HE'S SO BRAVE!
RUDOLPH IS MULTITALENTED! THERE'S MORE TO HIM THAN MEETS THE EYE.
I CAN'T BELIEVE RUDY HELPED US. WHEN WE SPOKE TO HIM A FEW DAYS AGO, HE WAS PRETTY SET ON NOT HELPING!
CLICK
WHERE WAS THIS?
AT QUICKBUCK HEADQUARTERS. RUDY WAS WORKING THERE.

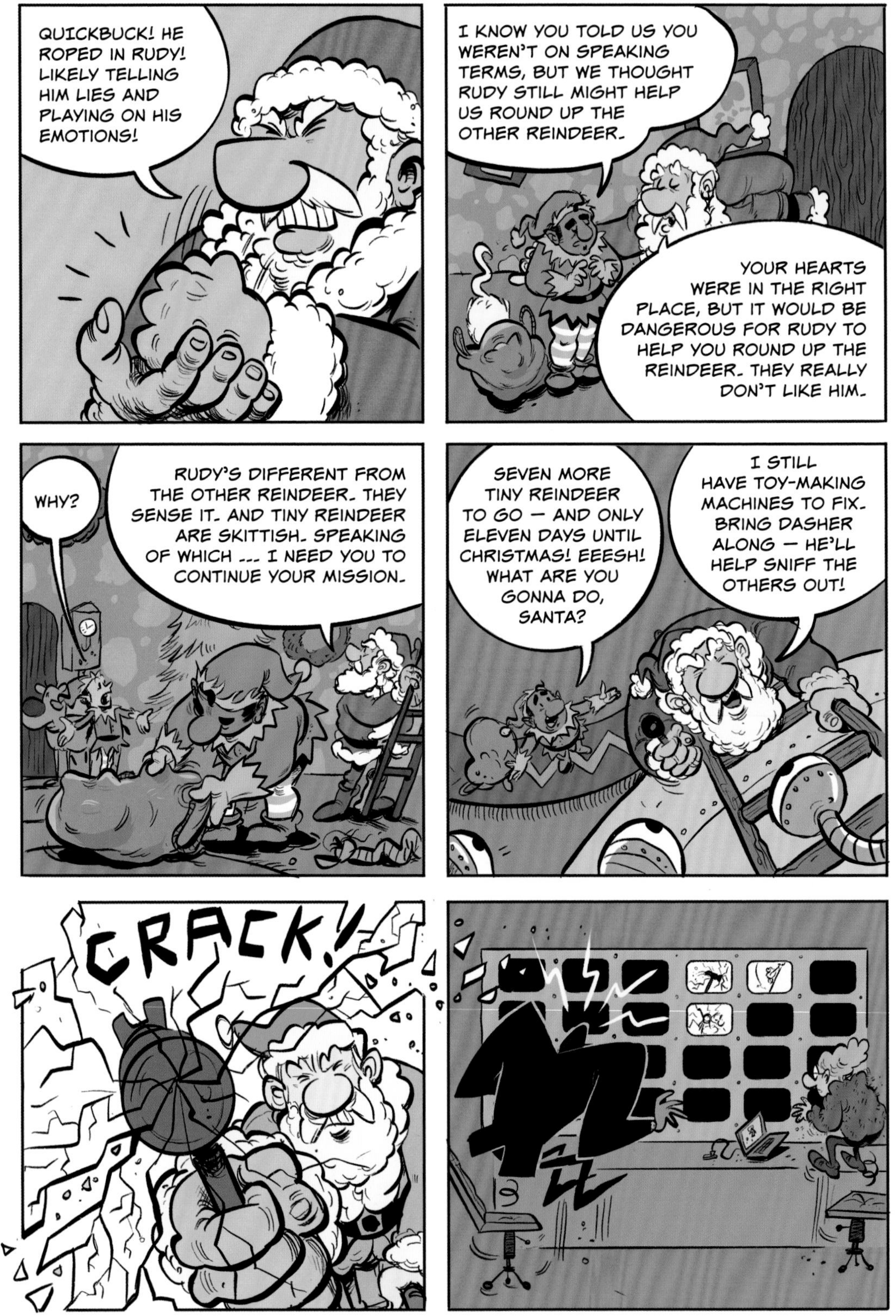
QUICKBUCK! HE ROPED IN RUDY! LIKELY TELLING HIM LIES AND PLAYING ON HIS EMOTIONS!
I KNOW YOU TOLD US YOU WEREN'T ON SPEAKING TERMS, BUT WE THOUGHT RUDY STILL MIGHT HELP US ROUND UP THE OTHER REINDEER.
YOUR HEARTS WERE IN THE RIGHT PLACE, BUT IT WOULD BE DANGEROUS FOR RUDY TO HELP YOU ROUND UP THE REINDEER. THEY REALLY DON'T LIKE HIM.
WHY?
RUDY'S DIFFERENT FROM THE OTHER REINDEER. THEY SENSE IT. AND TINY REINDEER ARE SKITTISH. SPEAKING OF WHICH ... I NEED YOU TO CONTINUE YOUR MISSION.
SEVEN MORE TINY REINDEER TO GO — AND ONLY ELEVEN DAYS UNTIL CHRISTMAS! EEESH! WHAT ARE YOU GONNA DO, SANTA?
I STILL HAVE TOY-MAKING MACHINES TO FIX. BRING DASHER ALONG — HE'LL HELP SNIFF THE OTHERS OUT!
CRACK!

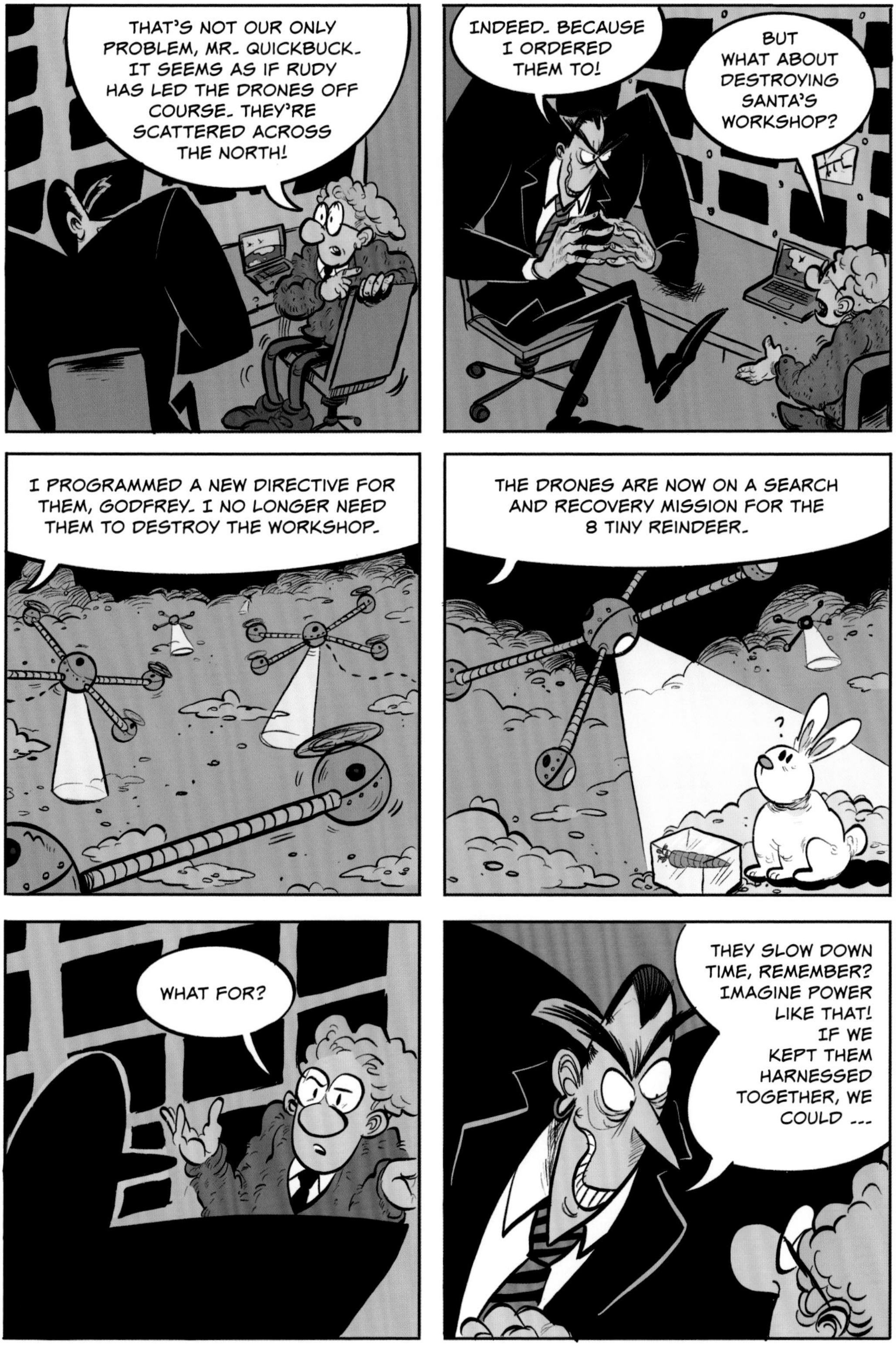
THAT'S NOT OUR ONLY PROBLEM, MR. QUICKBUCK. IT SEEMS AS IF RUDY HAS LED THE DRONES OFF COURSE. THEY'RE SCATTERED ACROSS THE NORTH!
INDEED. BECAUSE I ORDERED THEM TO!
BUT WHAT ABOUT DESTROYING SANTA'S WORKSHOP?
I PROGRAMMED A NEW DIRECTIVE FOR THEM, GODFREY. I NO LONGER NEED THEM TO DESTROY THE WORKSHOP.
THE DRONES ARE NOW ON A SEARCH AND RECOVERY MISSION FOR THE 8 TINY REINDEER.
?
WHAT FOR?
THEY SLOW DOWN TIME, REMEMBER? IMAGINE POWER LIKE THAT! IF WE KEPT THEM HARNESSED TOGETHER, WE COULD ...

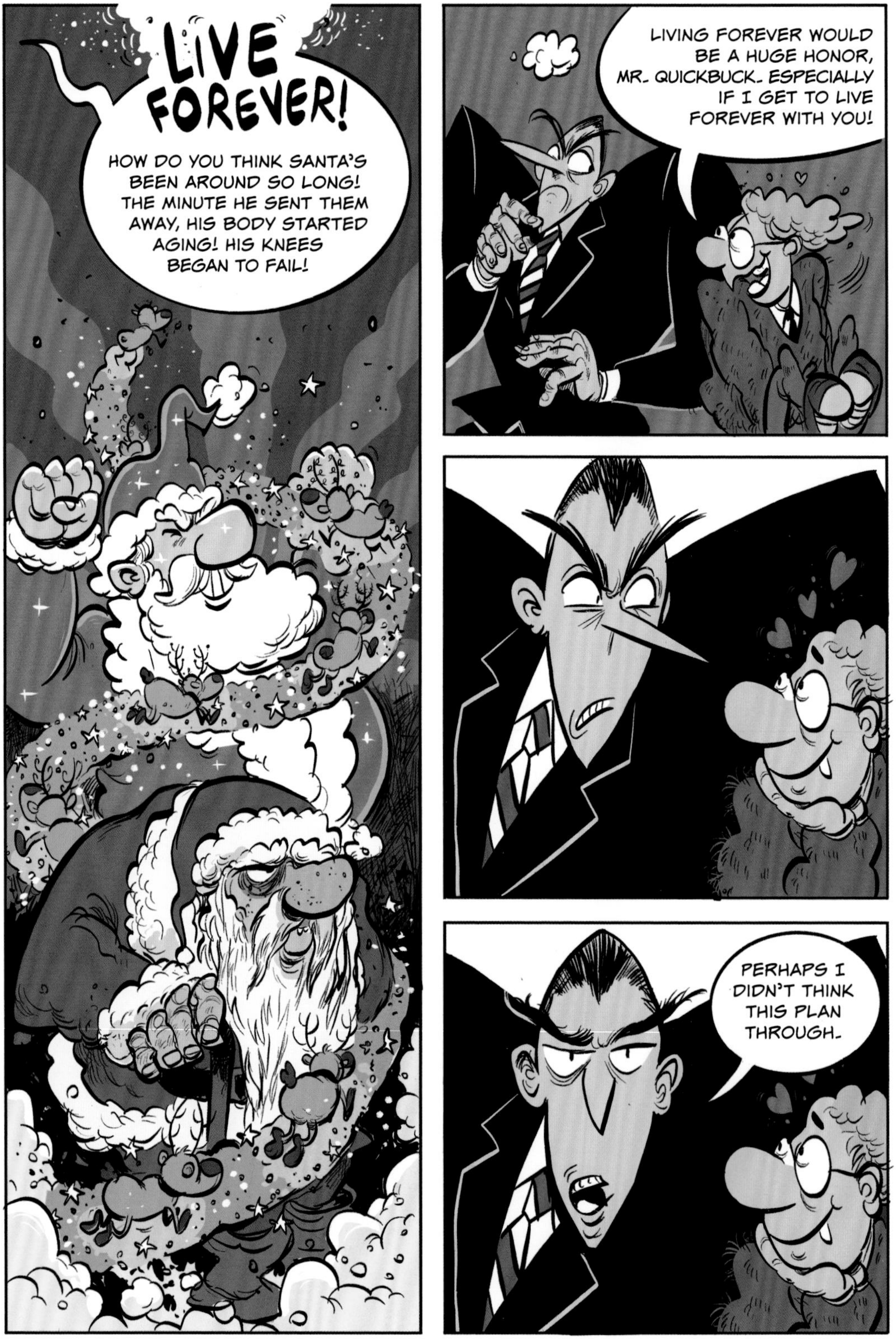
LIVE FOREVER!
HOW DO YOU THINK SANTA'S BEEN AROUND SO LONG! THE MINUTE HE SENT THEM AWAY, HIS BODY STARTED AGING! HIS KNEES BEGAN TO FAIL!
LIVING FOREVER WOULD BE A HUGE HONOR, MR. QUICKBUCK. ESPECIALLY IF I GET TO LIVE FOREVER WITH YOU!
PERHAPS I DIDN'T THINK THIS PLAN THROUGH.

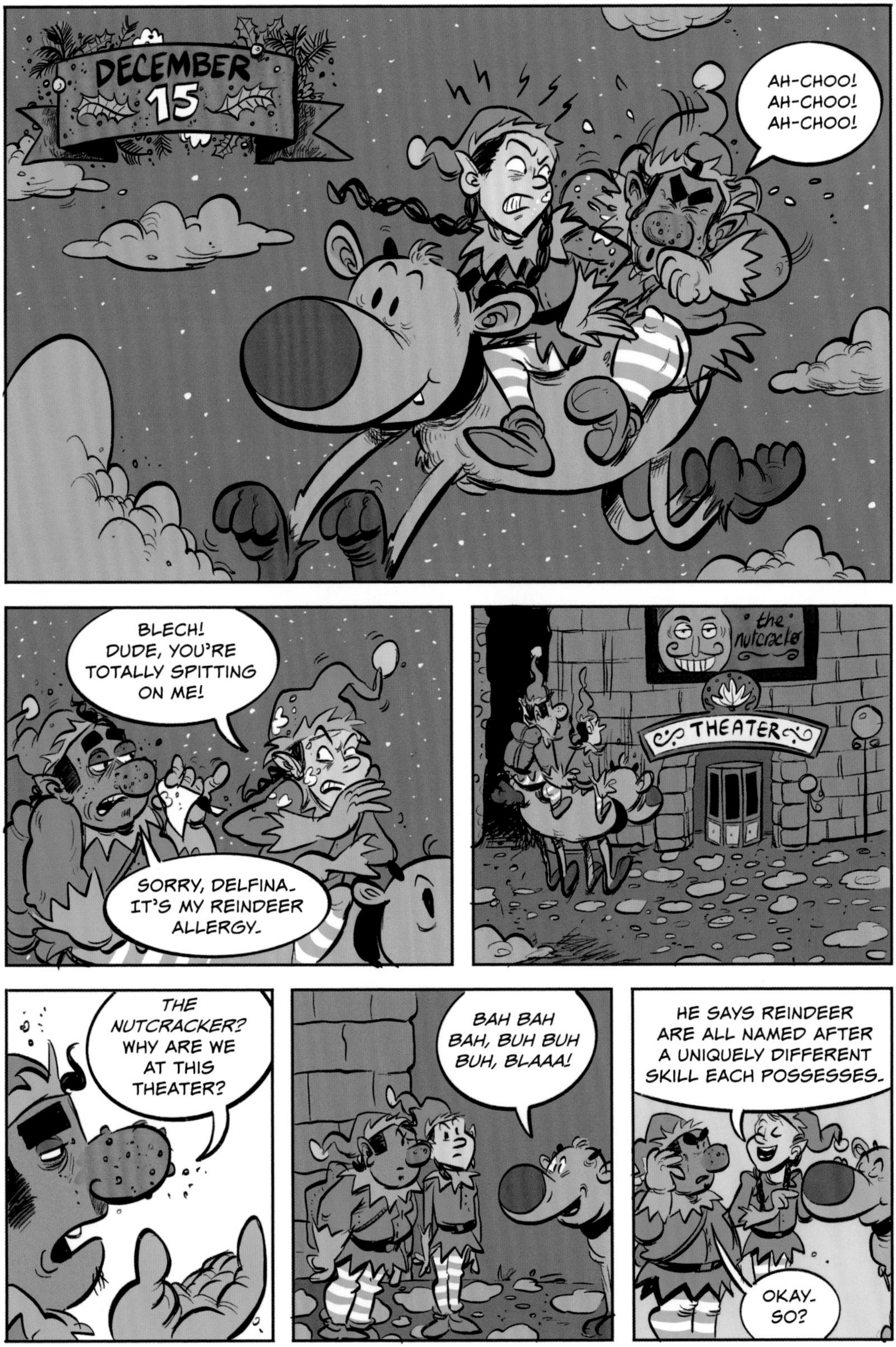
DECEMBER 15
AH-CHOO! AH-CHOO! AH-CHOO!
BLECH! DUDE, YOU'RE TOTALLY SPITTING ON ME!
SORRY, DELFINA. IT'S MY REINDEER ALLERGY.
the nutcracker
THEATER
THE NUTCRACKER? WHY ARE WE AT THIS THEATER?
BAH BAH BAH, BUH BUH BUH, BLAAA!
HE SAYS REINDEER ARE ALL NAMED AFTER A UNIQUELY DIFFERENT SKILL EACH POSSESSES.
OKAY. SO?

SO, WE FOUND DASHER DASHING IN A DOGSLED RACE, AND NOW HE SAYS WE'RE GOING TO FIND DANCER HERE.

LEMME GUESS. WE'RE GONNA FIND DANCER DANCING? HAH! HILARIOUS. REINDEER DON'T DANCE! HAHA!

ACCORDING TO DASHER, DANCER DOES DANCE, AND HE'S INSIDE THIS THEATER.

SO, DANCER IS HIDING IN PLAIN SIGHT LIKE YOU, EH, DASH?

C'MON, YOU TWO. I FOUND US A WAY INSIDE.

Stage Door

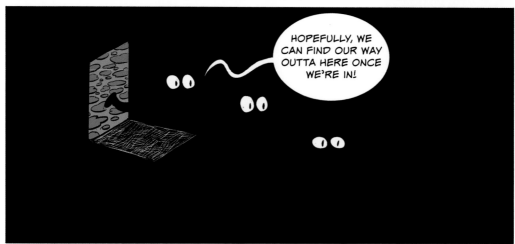

HOPEFULLY, WE CAN FIND OUR WAY OUTTA HERE ONCE WE'RE IN!

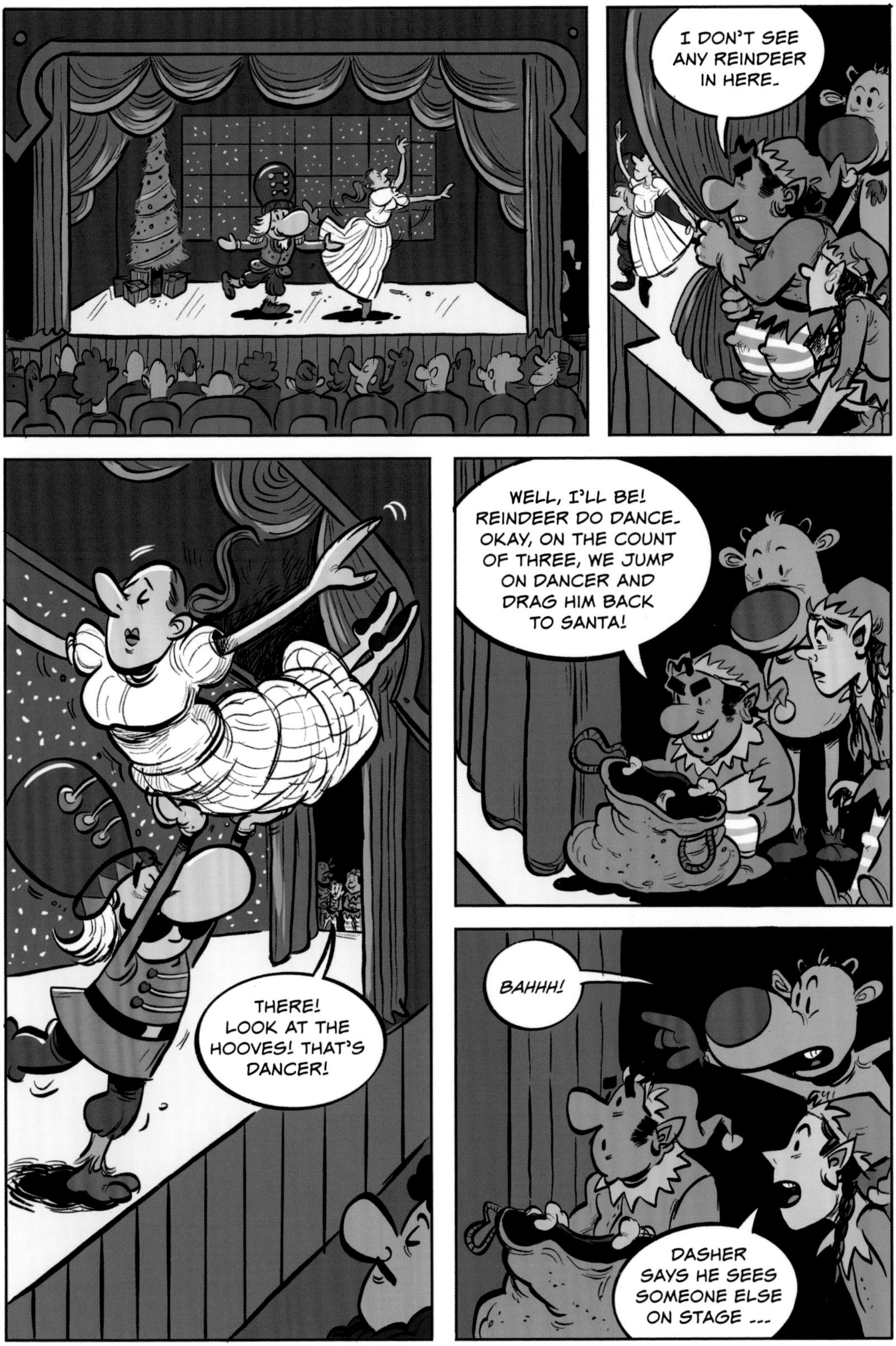
I DON'T SEE ANY REINDEER IN HERE.
WELL, I'LL BE! REINDEER DO DANCE. OKAY, ON THE COUNT OF THREE, WE JUMP ON DANCER AND DRAG HIM BACK TO SANTA!
THERE! LOOK AT THE HOOVES! THAT'S DANCER!
BAHHH!
DASHER SAYS HE SEES SOMEONE ELSE ON STAGE ...

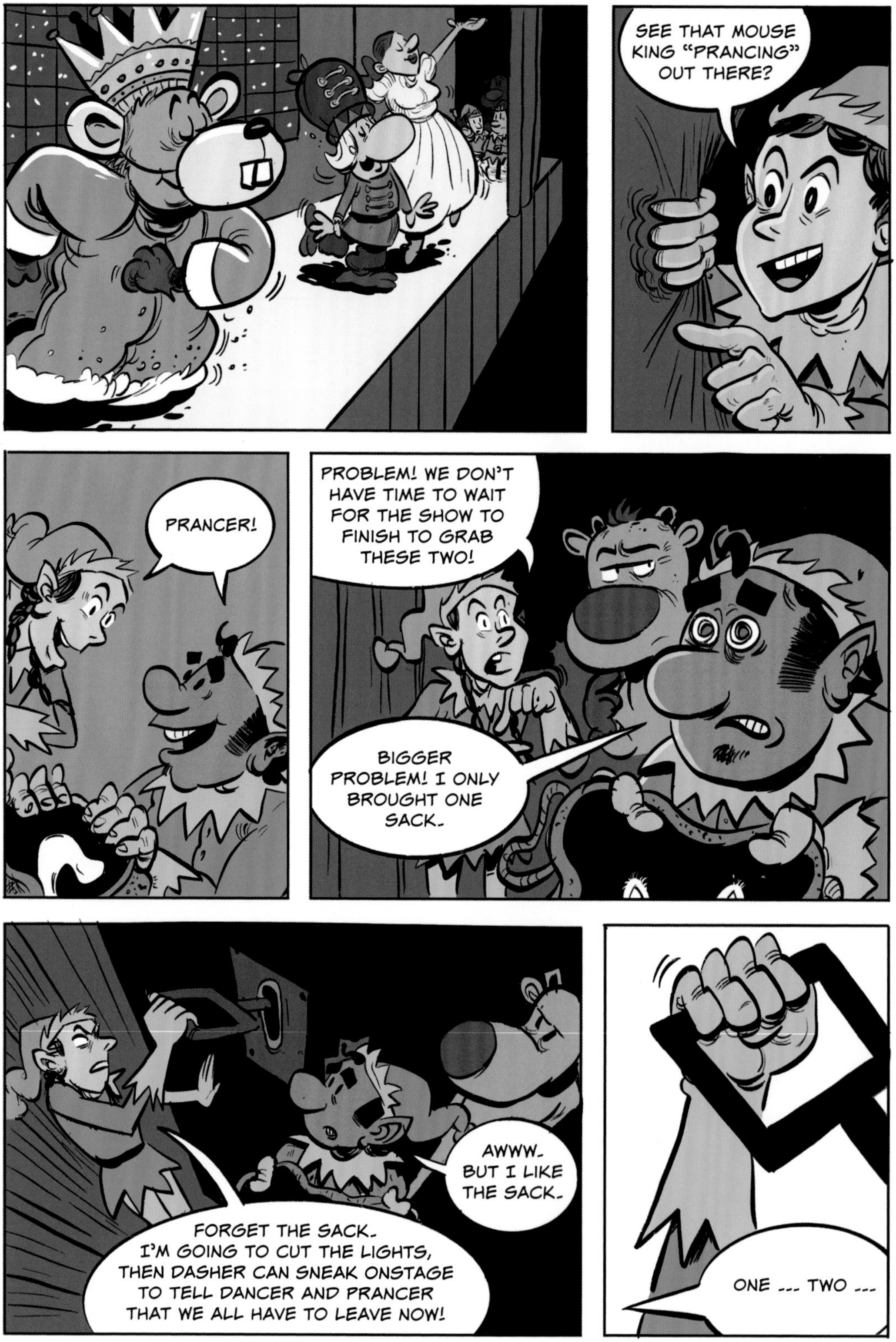
SEE THAT MOUSE KING "PRANCING" OUT THERE?
PRANCER!
PROBLEM! WE DON'T HAVE TIME TO WAIT FOR THE SHOW TO FINISH TO GRAB THESE TWO!
BIGGER PROBLEM! I ONLY BROUGHT ONE SACK.
AWWW. BUT I LIKE THE SACK.
FORGET THE SACK. I'M GOING TO CUT THE LIGHTS, THEN DASHER CAN SNEAK ONSTAGE TO TELL DANCER AND PRANCER THAT WE ALL HAVE TO LEAVE NOW!
ONE ... TWO ...

THREE!
THE POWER WENT OUT!
IT'S PITCH BLACK IN HERE!
I CAN'T SEE ANYTHING!
I SUDDENLY HAVE A BAD FEELING ABOUT THIS.
YOU'RE ONLY GETTING A BAD FEELING NOW? I'VE HAD BAD FEELINGS ABOUT EVERYTHING SINCE THE BEGINNING OF DECEMBER!
I'M AFRAID OF THE DARK!
GET ME OUT OF HERE!
HEAD FOR THE STAGE DOOR!
NOT ANOTHER STAMPEDE! HOW MUCH MORE CAN TWO ELVES TAKE?!
RUNNN!!!!!

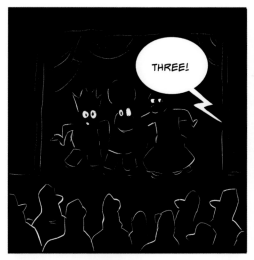

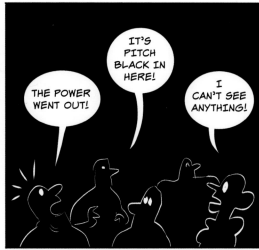

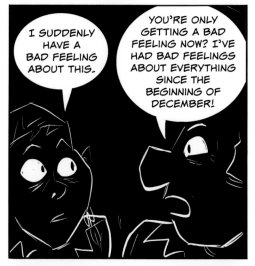

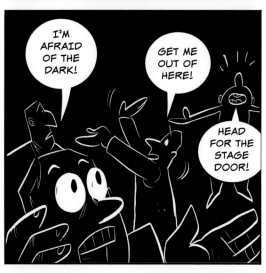

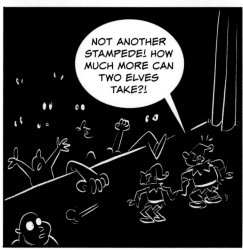

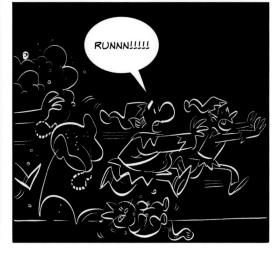

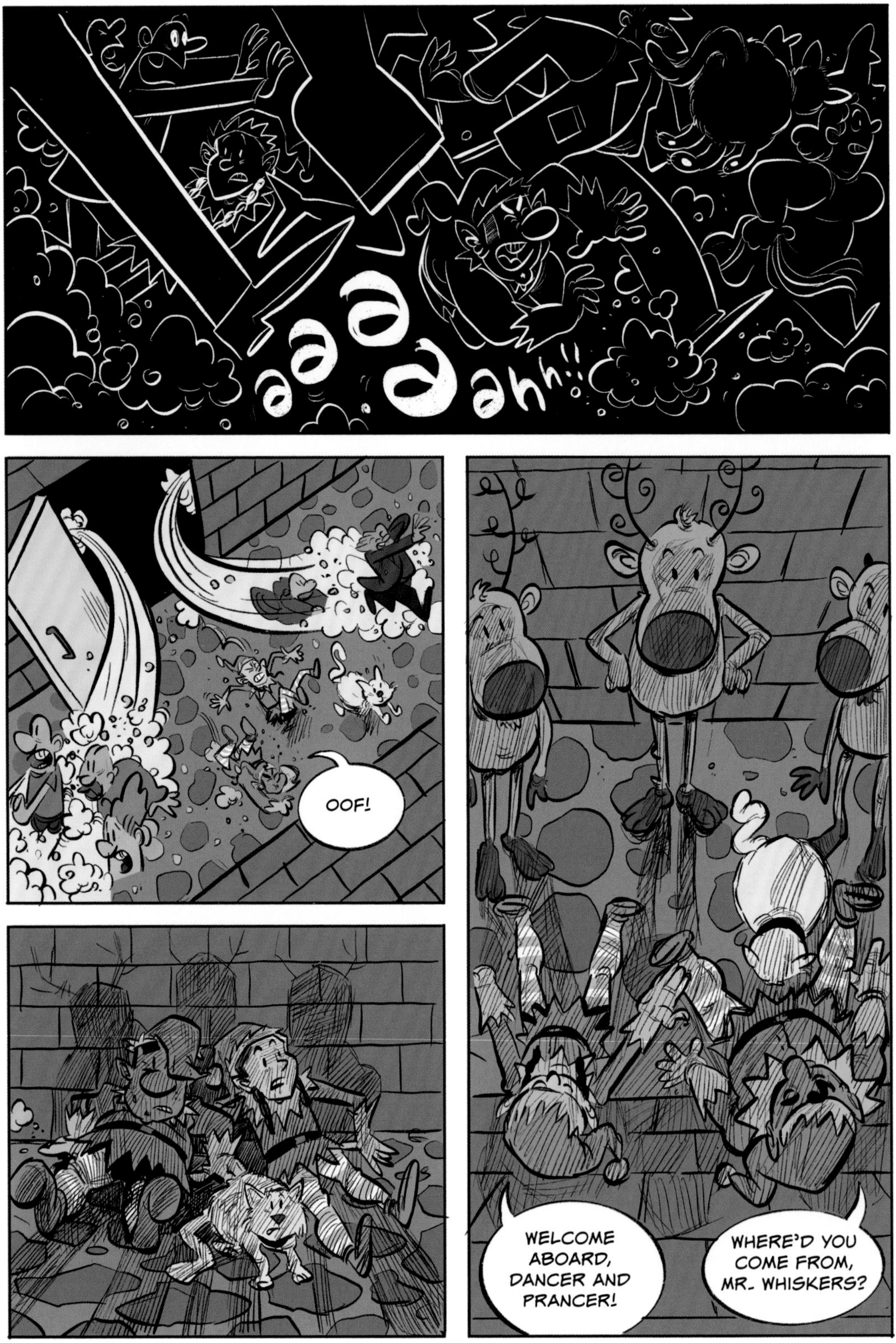
aaaaahh!!
OOF!
WELCOME ABOARD, DANCER AND PRANCER!
WHERE'D YOU COME FROM, MR. WHISKERS?

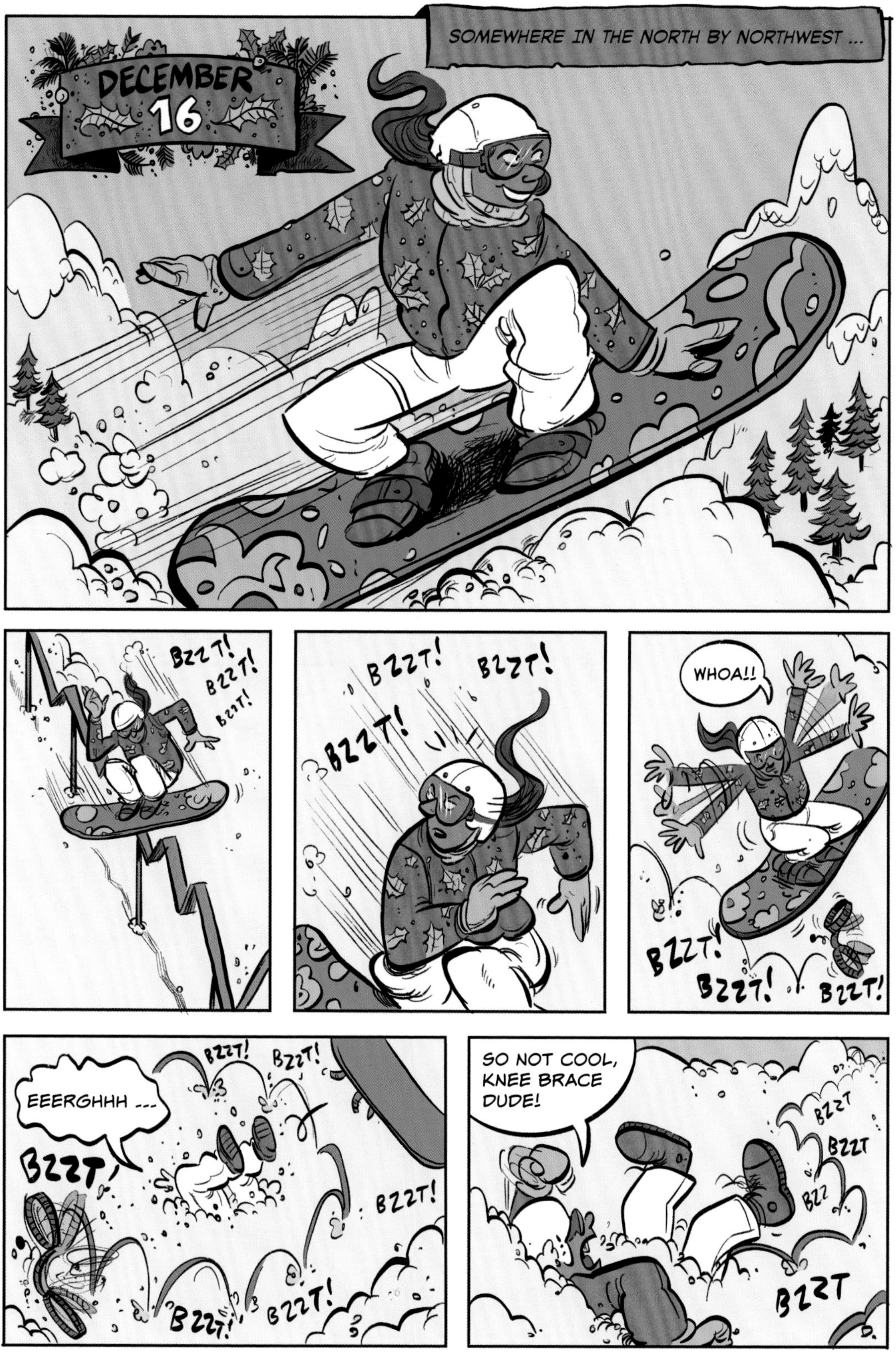
DECEMBER 16
SOMEWHERE IN THE NORTH BY NORTHWEST ...
BZZT! BZZT! BZZT!
BZZT! BZZT! BZZT!
WHOA!!
BZZT! BZZT! BZZT!
EEERGHHH ...
BZZT! BZZT! BZZT! BZZT! BZZT! BZZT!
SO NOT COOL, KNEE BRACE DUDE!
BZZT BZZT BZZ BZZT

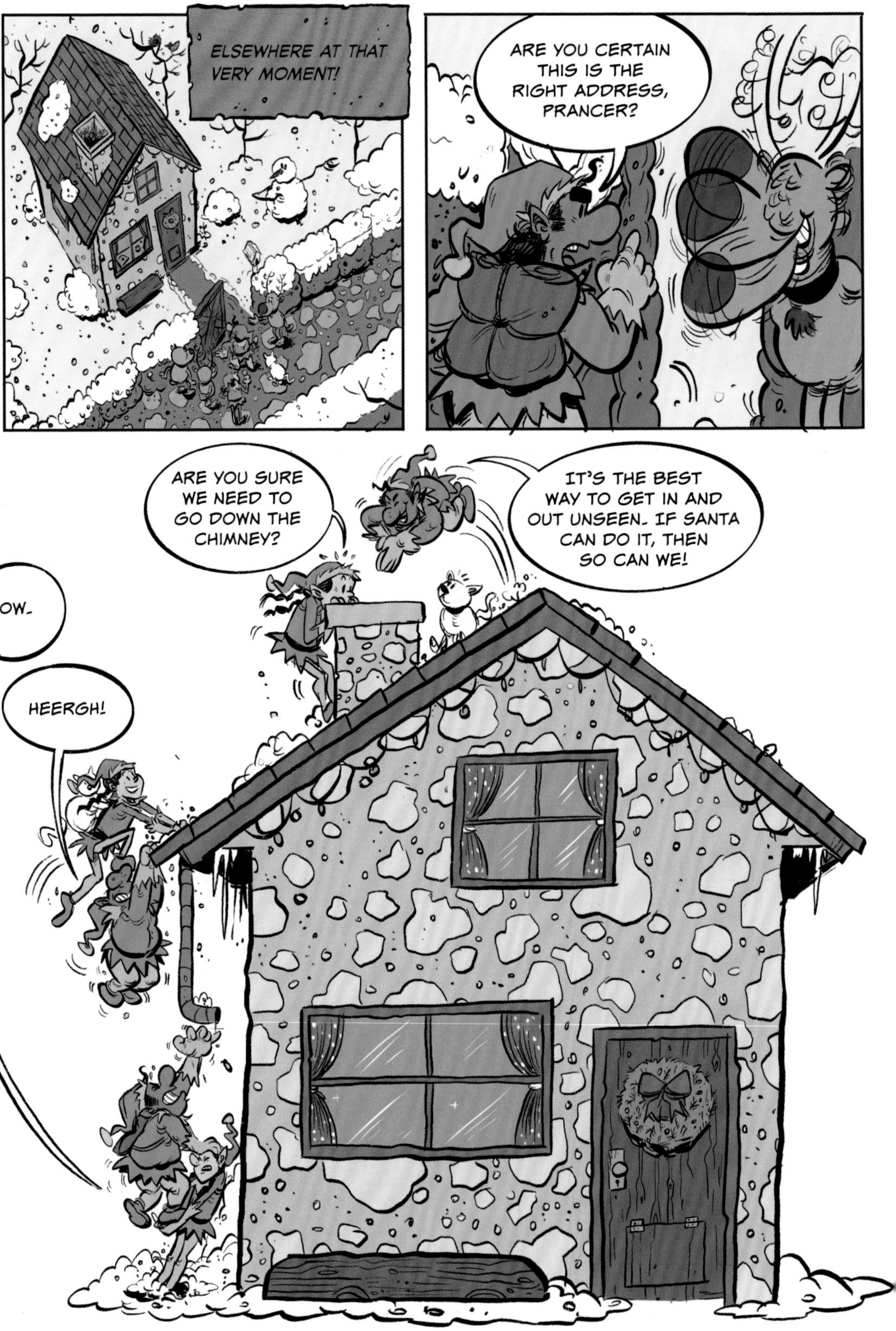
ELSEWHERE AT THAT VERY MOMENT!
ARE YOU CERTAIN THIS IS THE RIGHT ADDRESS, PRANCER?
ARE YOU SURE WE NEED TO GO DOWN THE CHIMNEY?
IT'S THE BEST WAY TO GET IN AND OUT UNSEEN. IF SANTA CAN DO IT, THEN SO CAN WE!
OW.
HEERGH!

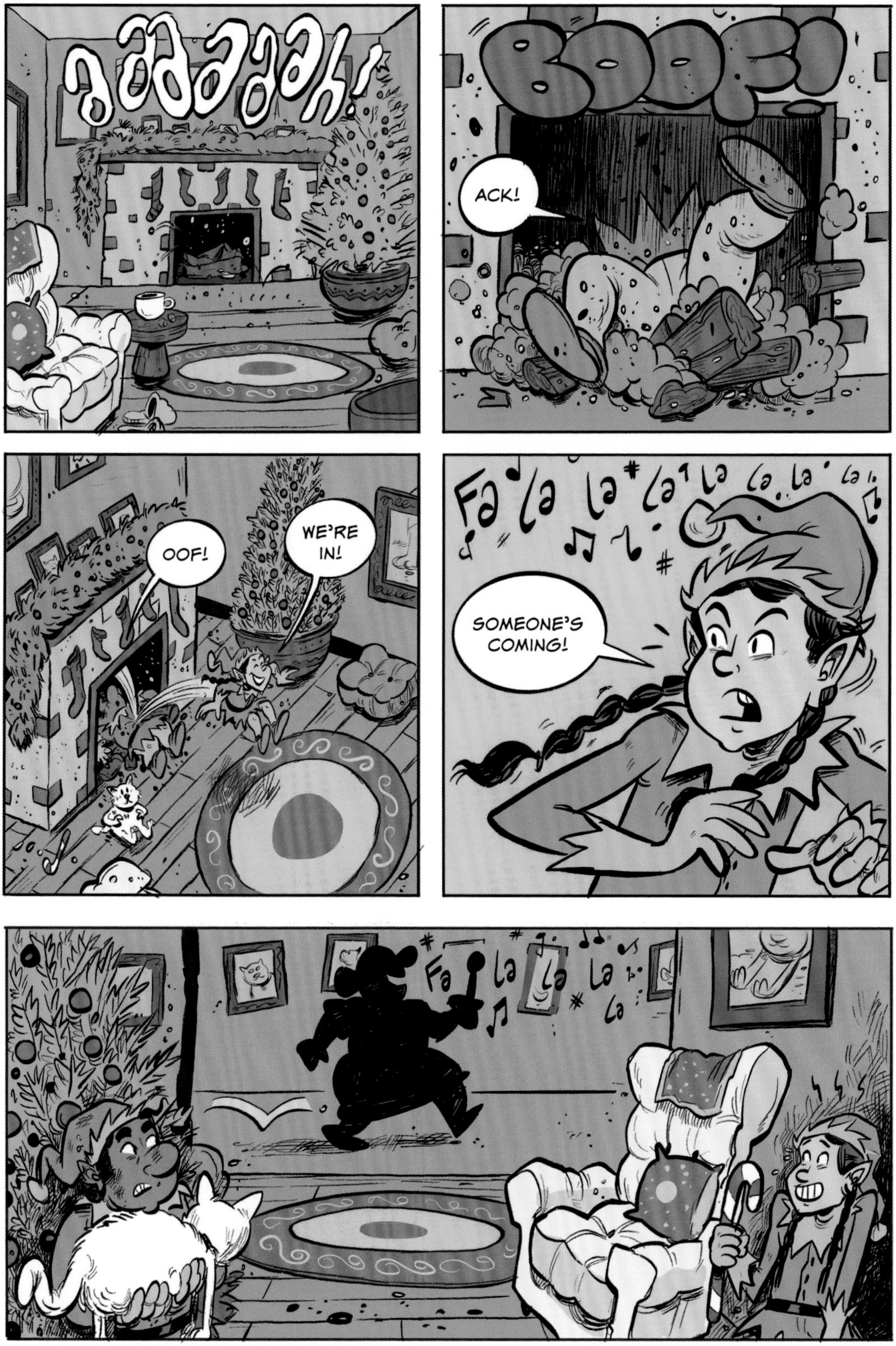
aaaaaah!
BOOF!
ACK!
OOF!
WE'RE IN!
Fa la la la la la la la la
SOMEONE'S COMING!
Fa la la la la la

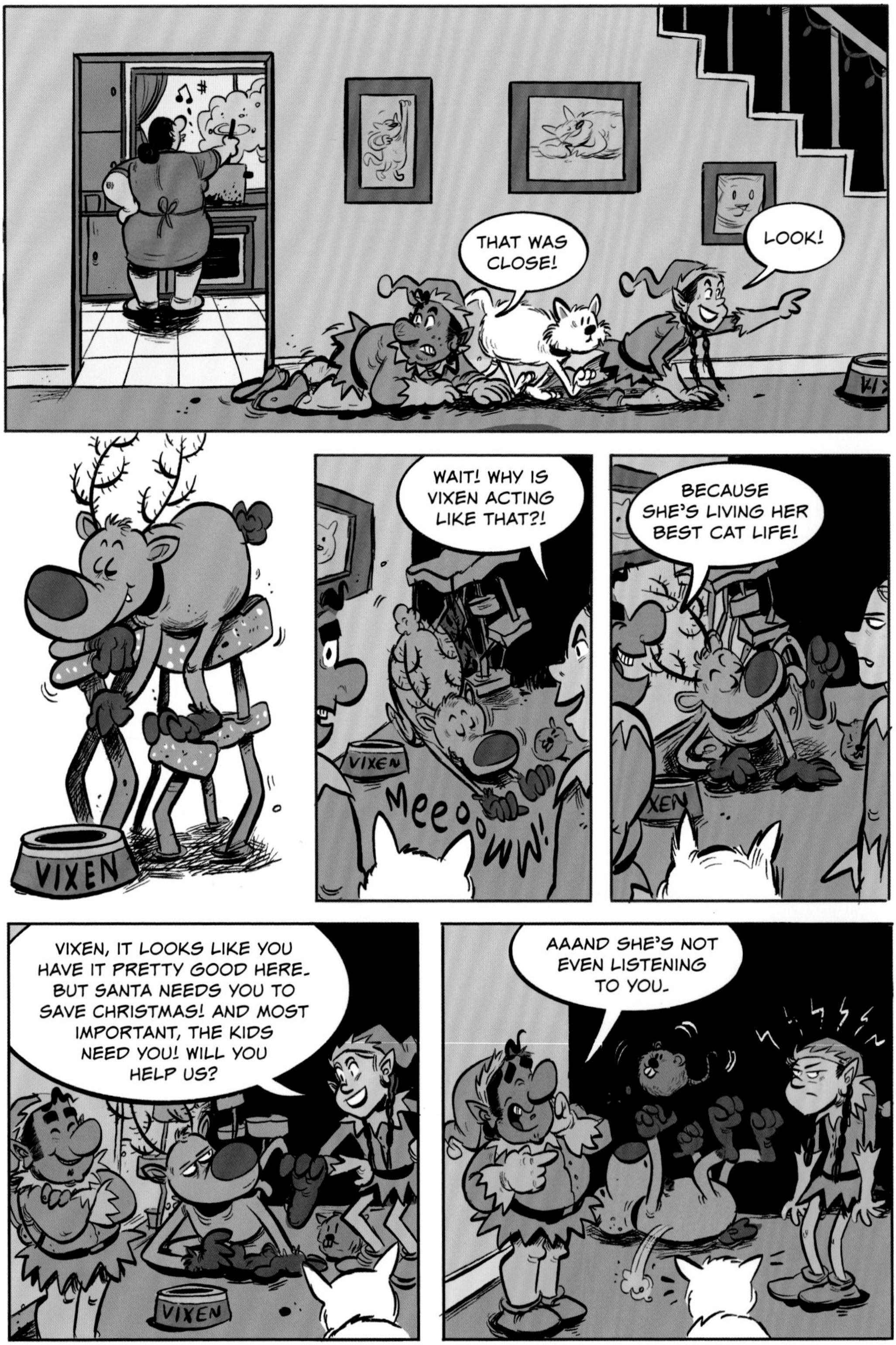
THAT WAS CLOSE!
LOOK!
WAIT! WHY IS VIXEN ACTING LIKE THAT?!
MEEOOWW!
BECAUSE SHE'S LIVING HER BEST CAT LIFE!
VIXEN, IT LOOKS LIKE YOU HAVE IT PRETTY GOOD HERE. BUT SANTA NEEDS YOU TO SAVE CHRISTMAS! AND MOST IMPORTANT, THE KIDS NEED YOU! WILL YOU HELP US?
AAAND SHE'S NOT EVEN LISTENING TO YOU.

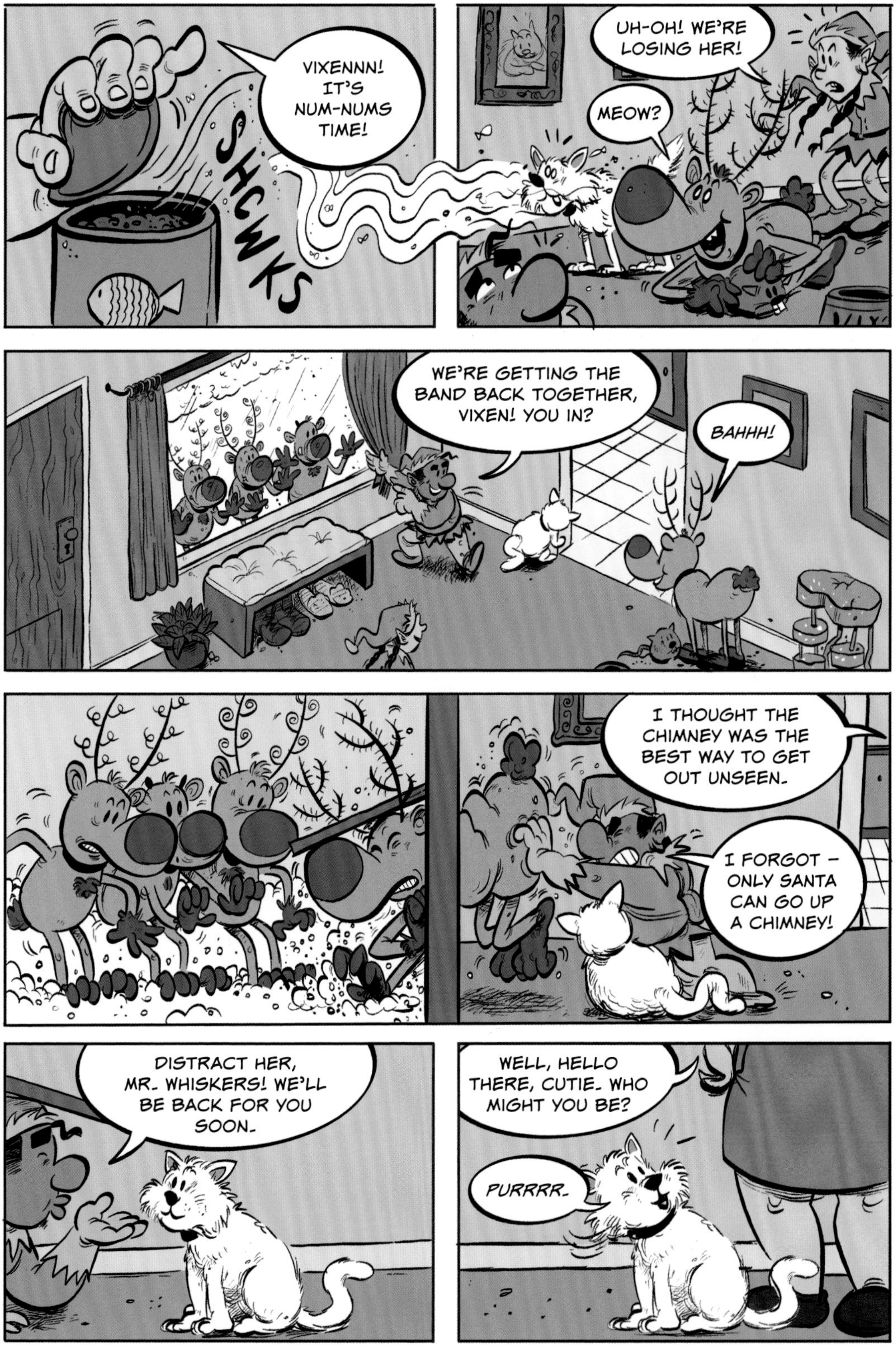
VIXENNN! IT'S NUM-NUMS TIME!
SHCWKS
UH-OH! WE'RE LOSING HER!
MEOW?
WE'RE GETTING THE BAND BACK TOGETHER, VIXEN! YOU IN?
BAHHH!
I THOUGHT THE CHIMNEY WAS THE BEST WAY TO GET OUT UNSEEN.
I FORGOT – ONLY SANTA CAN GO UP A CHIMNEY!
DISTRACT HER, MR. WHISKERS! WE'LL BE BACK FOR YOU SOON.
WELL, HELLO THERE, CUTIE. WHO MIGHT YOU BE?
PURRRR.

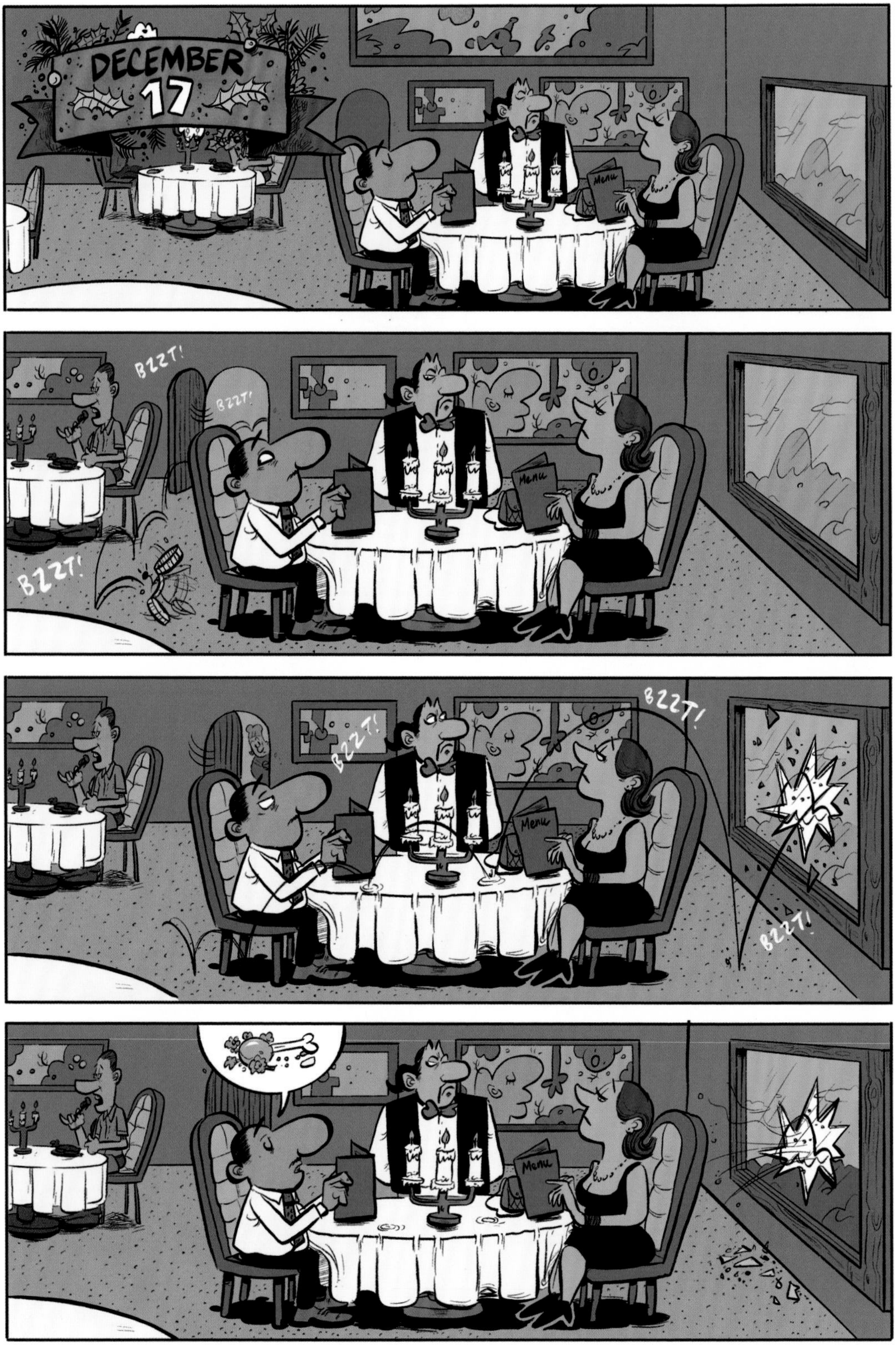
DECEMBER 17
BZZT!
BZZT!
BZZT!
BZZT!
BZZT!
BZZT!
Menu

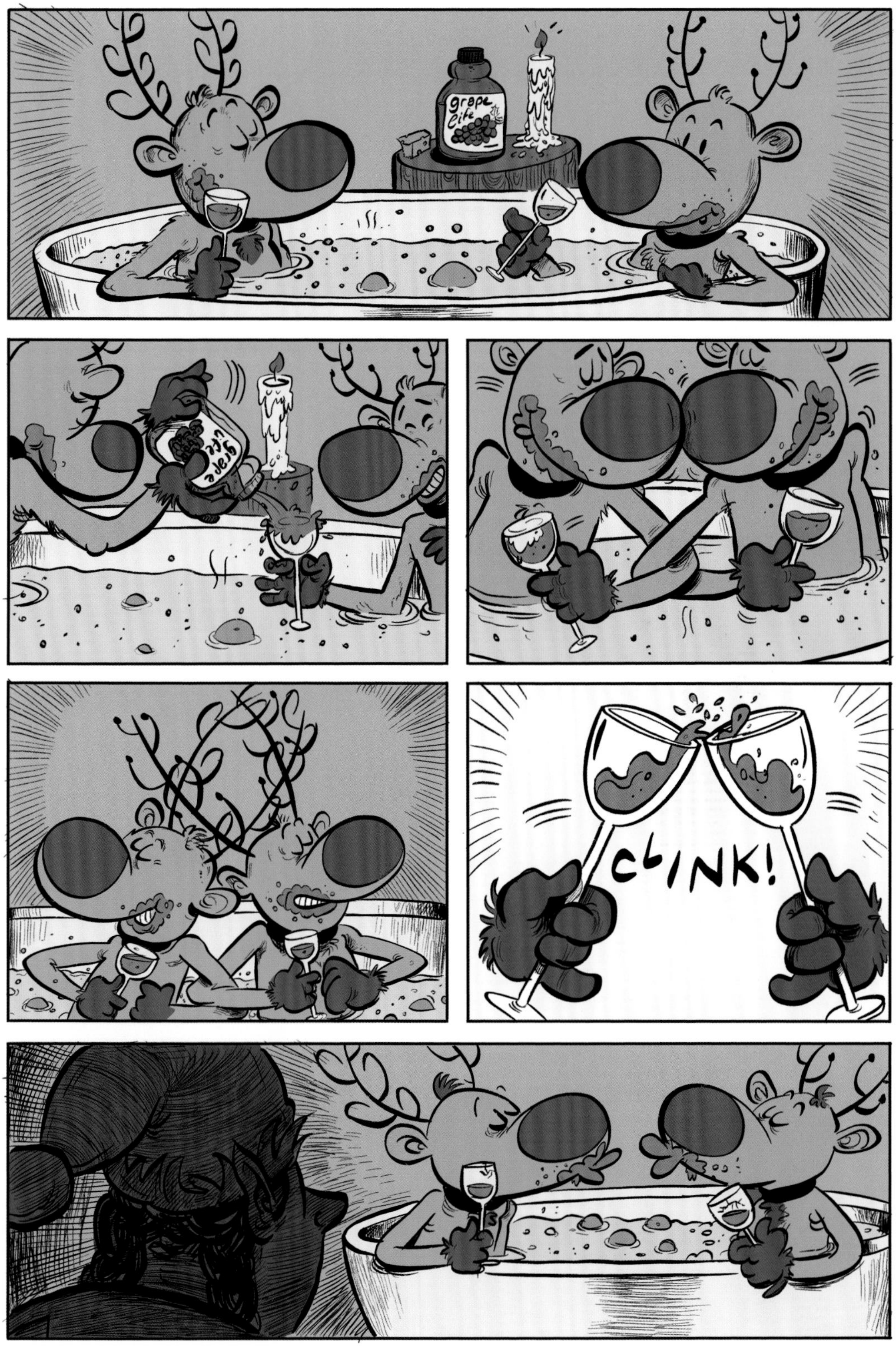
grape Life
CLINK!

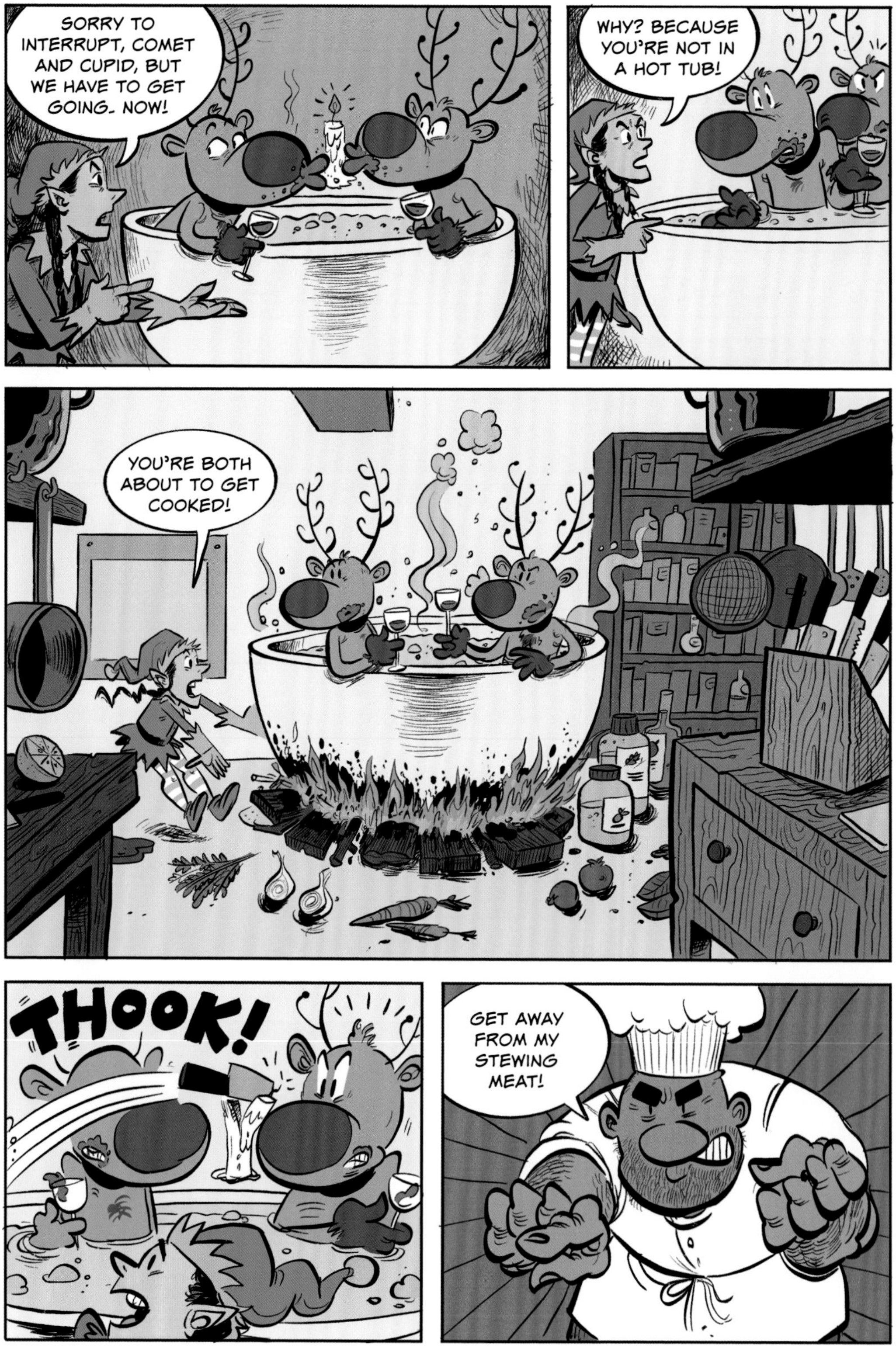
SORRY TO INTERRUPT, COMET AND CUPID, BUT WE HAVE TO GET GOING. NOW!
WHY? BECAUSE YOU'RE NOT IN A HOT TUB!
YOU'RE BOTH ABOUT TO GET COOKED!
THOOK!
GET AWAY FROM MY STEWING MEAT!

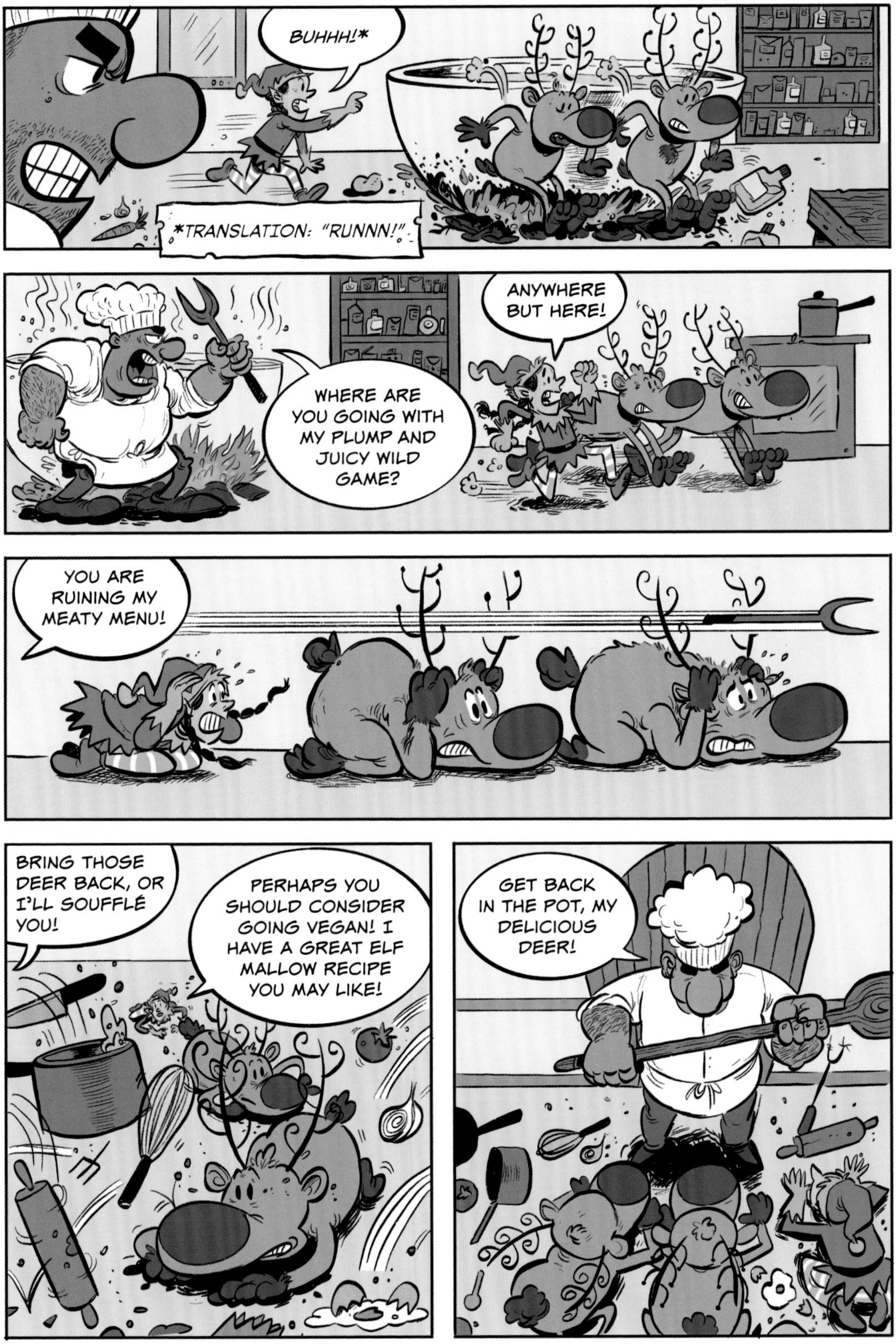
BUHHH!*
*TRANSLATION: "RUNNN!"
WHERE ARE YOU GOING WITH MY PLUMP AND JUICY WILD GAME?
ANYWHERE BUT HERE!
YOU ARE RUINING MY MEATY MENU!
BRING THOSE DEER BACK, OR I'LL SOUFFLÉ YOU!
PERHAPS YOU SHOULD CONSIDER GOING VEGAN! I HAVE A GREAT ELF MALLOW RECIPE YOU MAY LIKE!
GET BACK IN THE POT, MY DELICIOUS DEER!

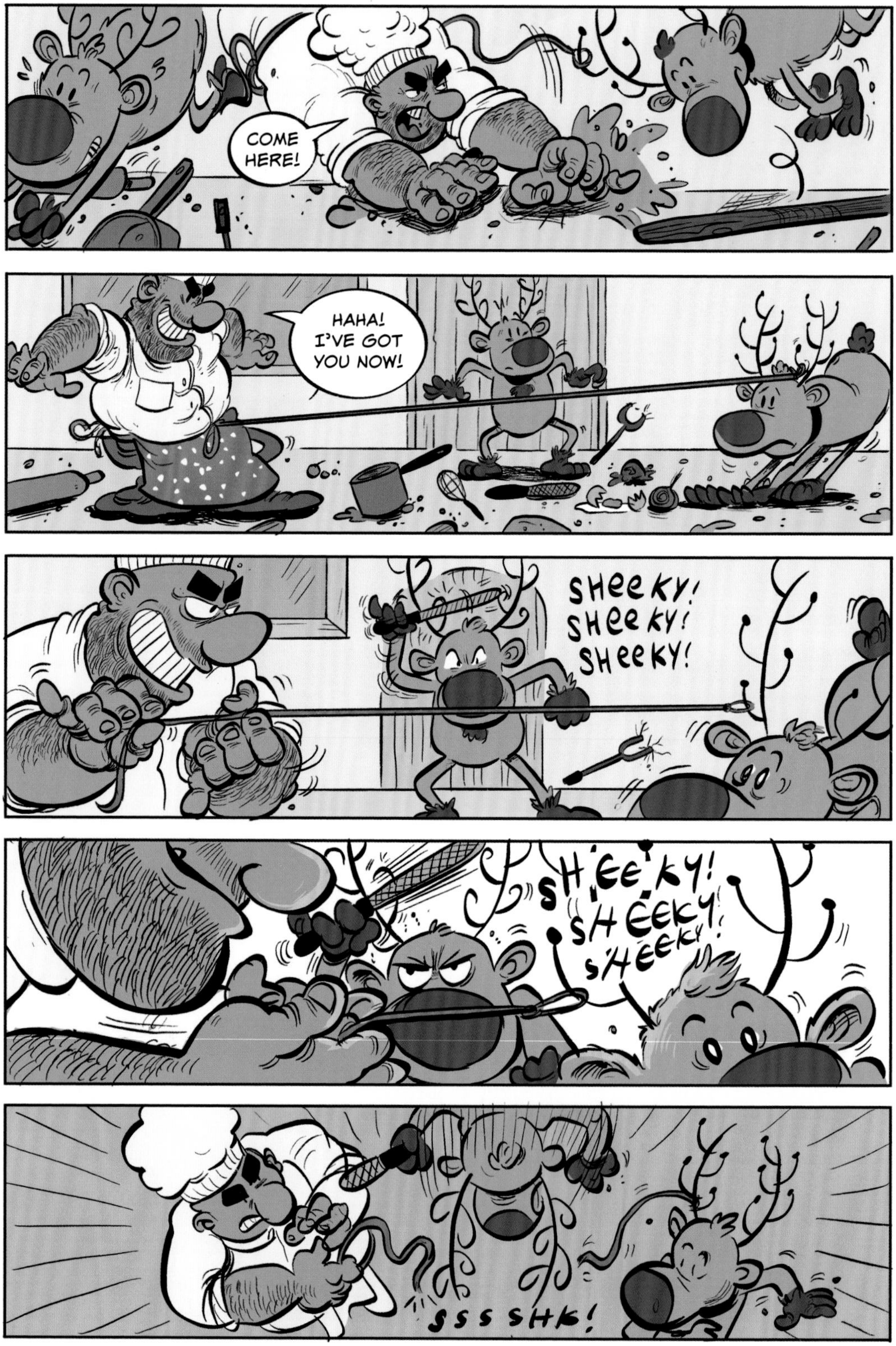
COME HERE!
HAHA! I'VE GOT YOU NOW!
SHEEKY! SHEEKY! SHEEKY!
SHEEKY! SHEEKY! SHEEKY!
SSSSHK!

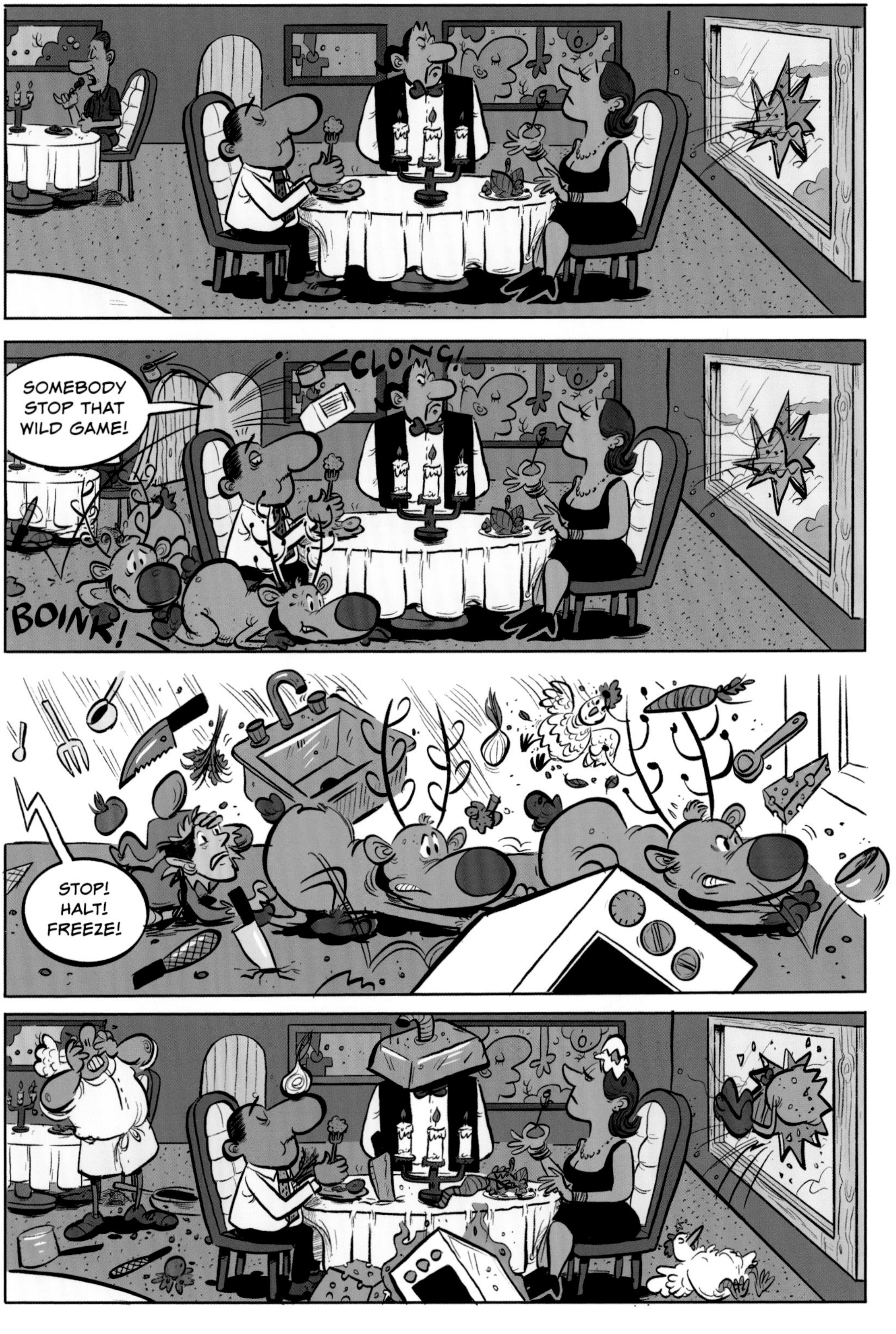
CLONG!
SOMEBODY STOP THAT WILD GAME!
BOINK!
STOP! HALT! FREEZE!

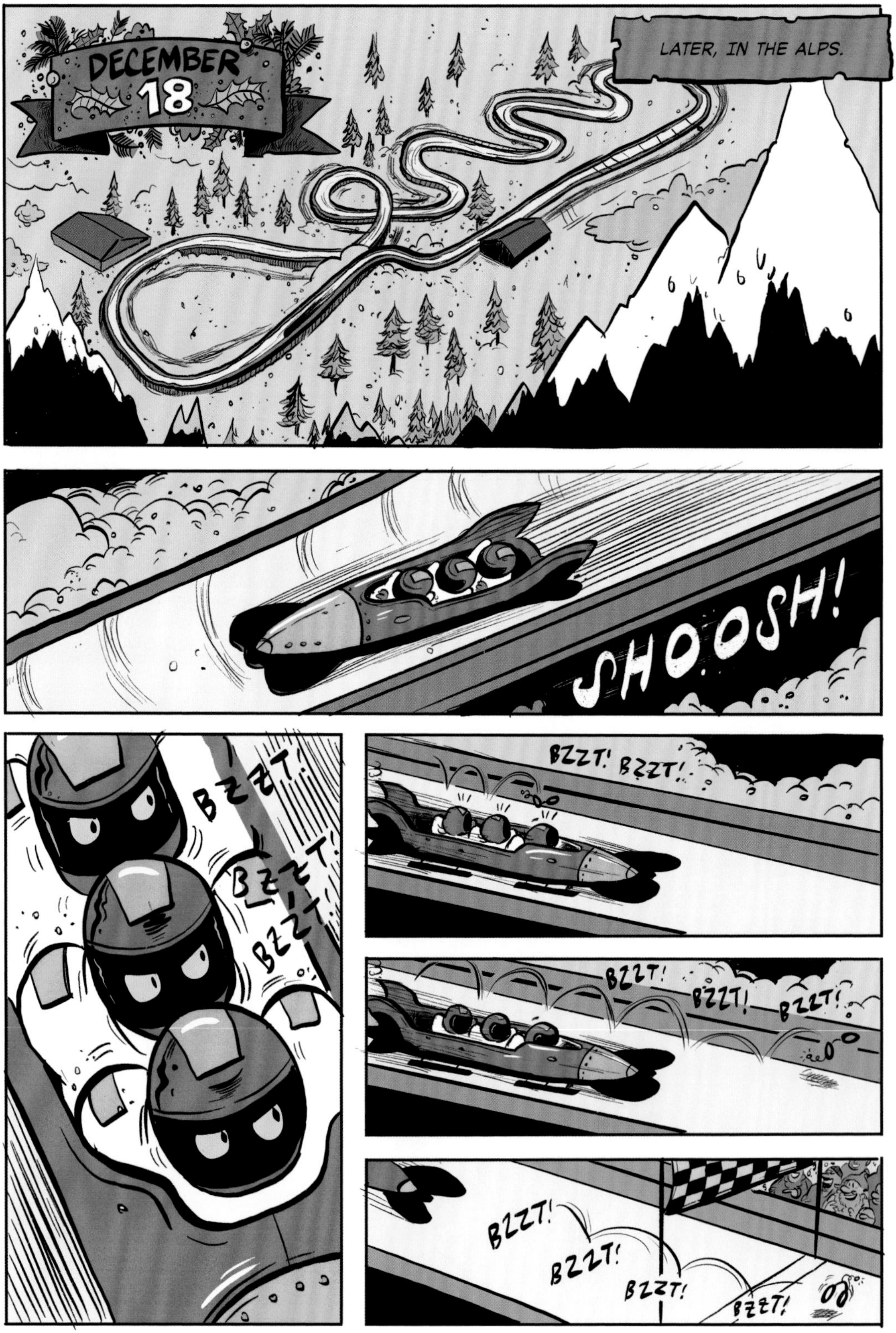
DECEMBER 18
LATER, IN THE ALPS.
SHOOSH!
BZZT!
BZZT!
BZZT!
BZZT! BZZT!
BZZT!
BZZT!
BZZT!
BZZT!
BZZT!
BZZT!
BZZT!

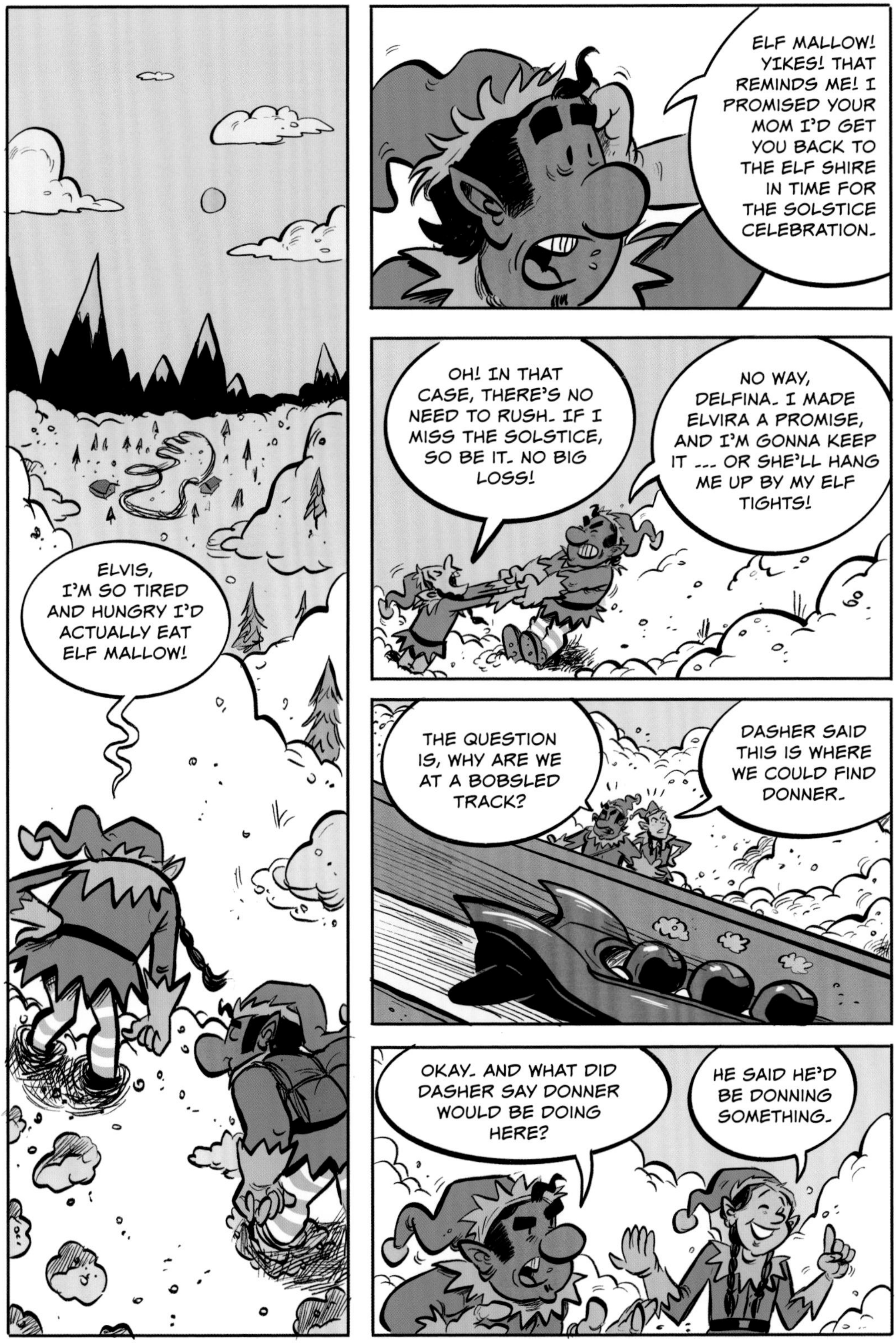
ELVIS, I'M SO TIRED AND HUNGRY I'D ACTUALLY EAT ELF MALLOW!
ELF MALLOW! YIKES! THAT REMINDS ME! I PROMISED YOUR MOM I'D GET YOU BACK TO THE ELF SHIRE IN TIME FOR THE SOLSTICE CELEBRATION.
OH! IN THAT CASE, THERE'S NO NEED TO RUSH. IF I MISS THE SOLSTICE, SO BE IT. NO BIG LOSS!
NO WAY, DELFINA. I MADE ELVIRA A PROMISE, AND I'M GONNA KEEP IT ... OR SHE'LL HANG ME UP BY MY ELF TIGHTS!
THE QUESTION IS, WHY ARE WE AT A BOBSLED TRACK?
DASHER SAID THIS IS WHERE WE COULD FIND DONNER.
OKAY. AND WHAT DID DASHER SAY DONNER WOULD BE DOING HERE?
HE SAID HE'D BE DONNING SOMETHING.

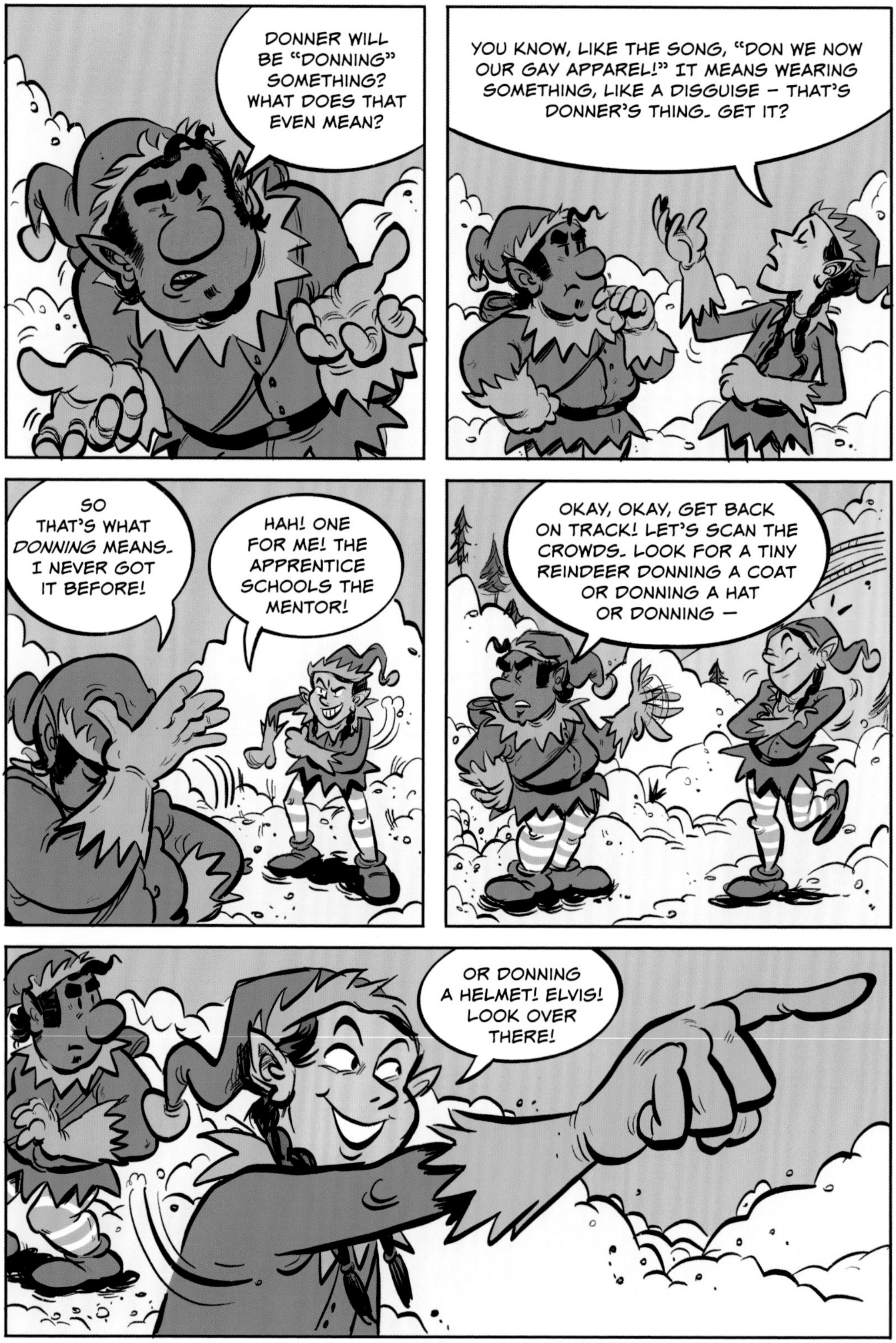
DONNER WILL BE "DONNING" SOMETHING? WHAT DOES THAT EVEN MEAN?
YOU KNOW, LIKE THE SONG, "DON WE NOW OUR GAY APPAREL!" IT MEANS WEARING SOMETHING, LIKE A DISGUISE – THAT'S DONNER'S THING. GET IT?
SO THAT'S WHAT *DONNING* MEANS. I NEVER GOT IT BEFORE!
HAH! ONE FOR ME! THE APPRENTICE SCHOOLS THE MENTOR!
OKAY, OKAY, GET BACK ON TRACK! LET'S SCAN THE CROWDS. LOOK FOR A TINY REINDEER DONNING A COAT OR DONNING A HAT OR DONNING –
OR DONNING A HELMET! ELVIS! LOOK OVER THERE!

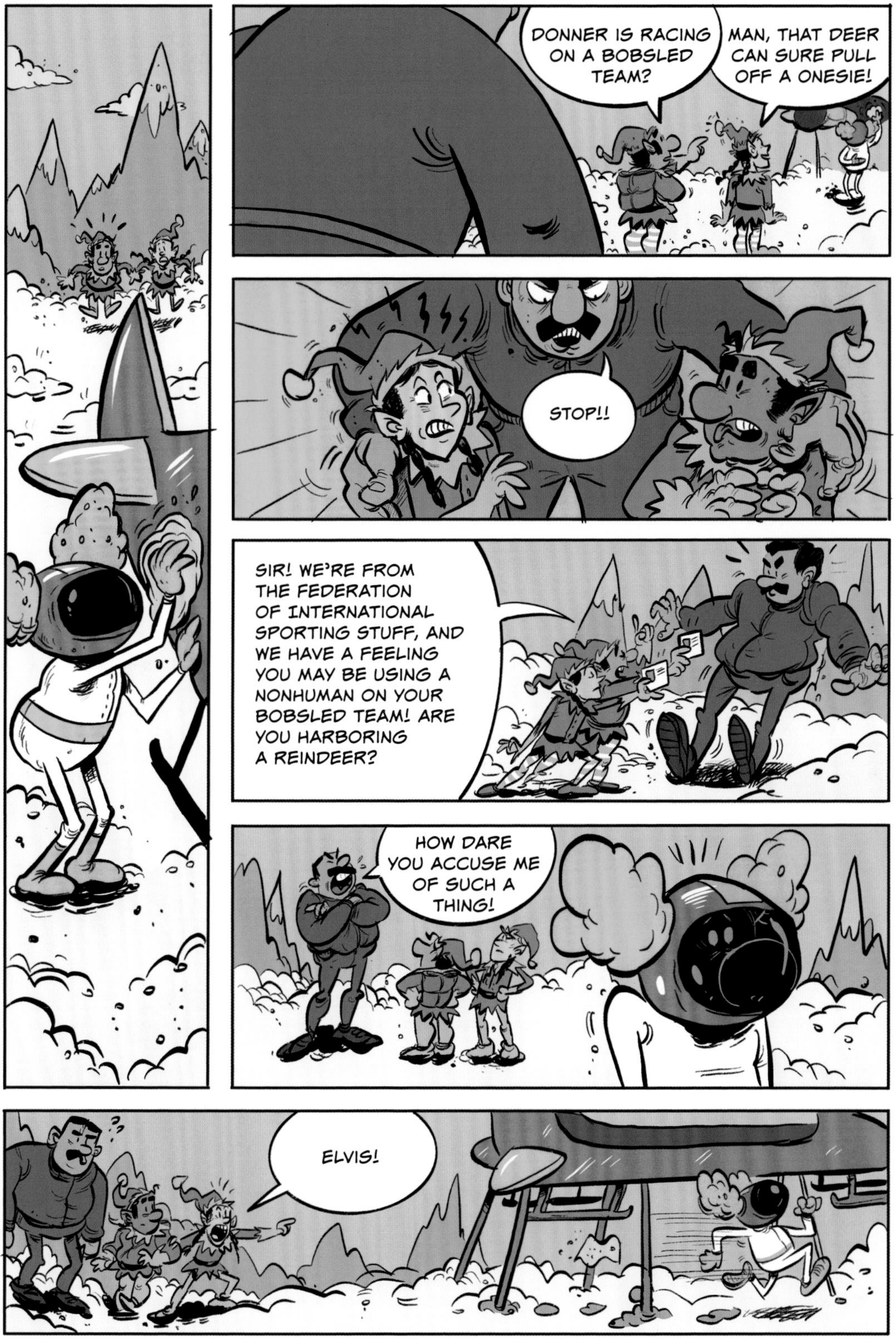

DONNER IS RACING ON A BOBSLED TEAM?
MAN, THAT DEER CAN SURE PULL OFF A ONESIE!
STOP!!
SIR! WE'RE FROM THE FEDERATION OF INTERNATIONAL SPORTING STUFF, AND WE HAVE A FEELING YOU MAY BE USING A NONHUMAN ON YOUR BOBSLED TEAM! ARE YOU HARBORING A REINDEER?
HOW DARE YOU ACCUSE ME OF SUCH A THING!
ELVIS!

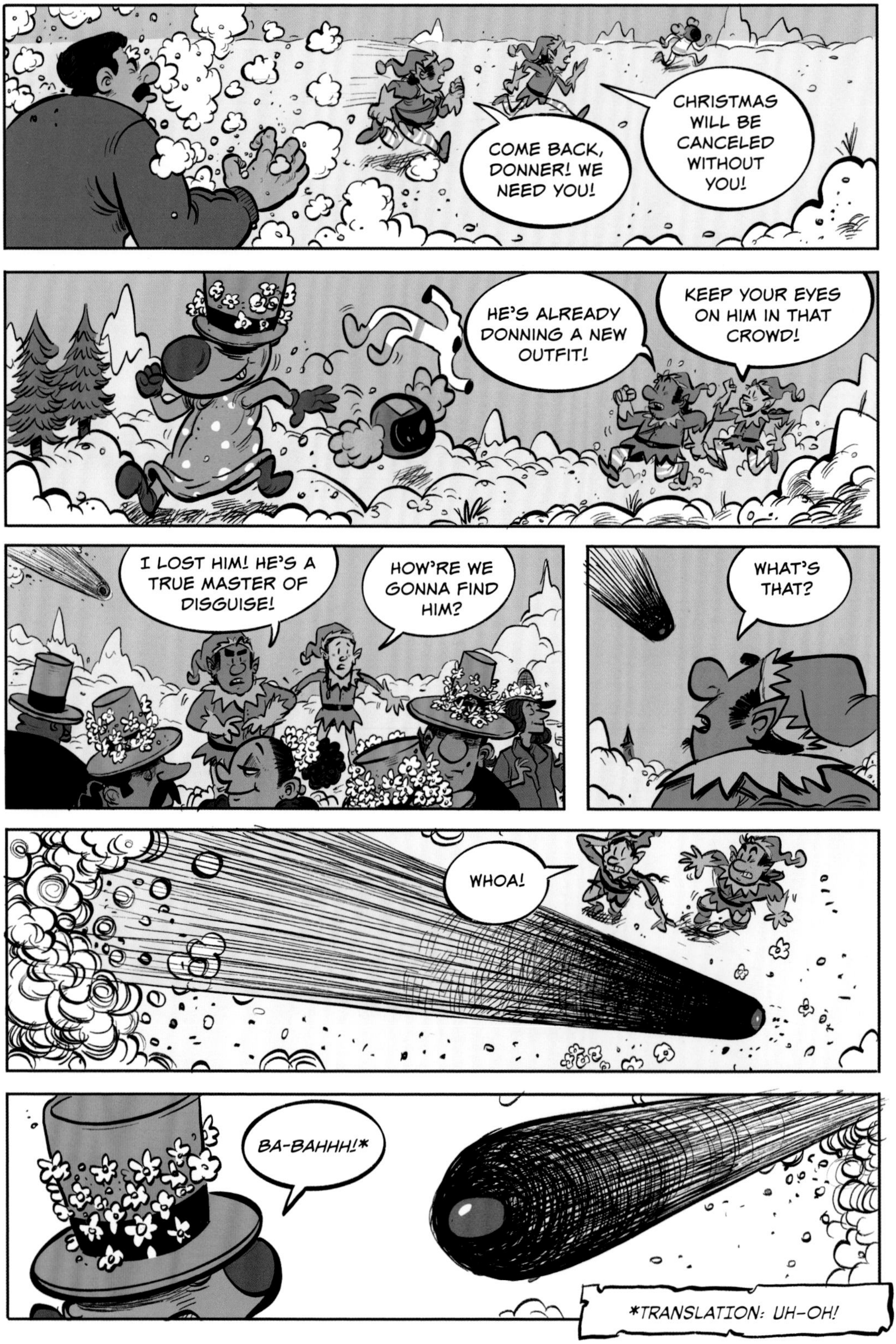
COME BACK, DONNER! WE NEED YOU!
CHRISTMAS WILL BE CANCELED WITHOUT YOU!
HE'S ALREADY DONNING A NEW OUTFIT!
KEEP YOUR EYES ON HIM IN THAT CROWD!
I LOST HIM! HE'S A TRUE MASTER OF DISGUISE!
HOW'RE WE GONNA FIND HIM?
WHAT'S THAT?
WHOA!
BA-BAHHH!*
*TRANSLATION: UH-OH!

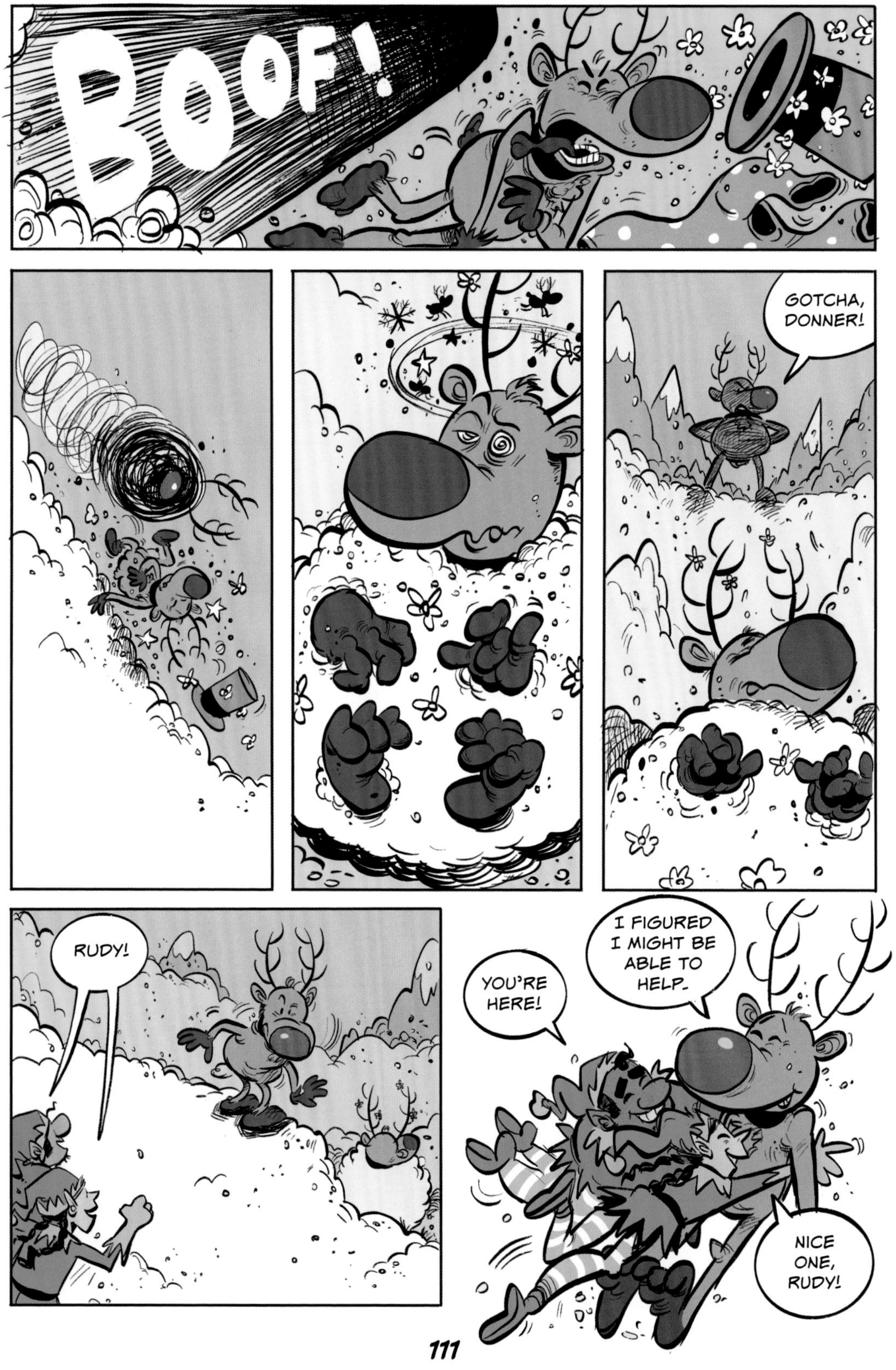
BOOF!
GOTCHA, DONNER!
RUDY!
YOU'RE HERE!
I FIGURED I MIGHT BE ABLE TO HELP.
NICE ONE, RUDY!

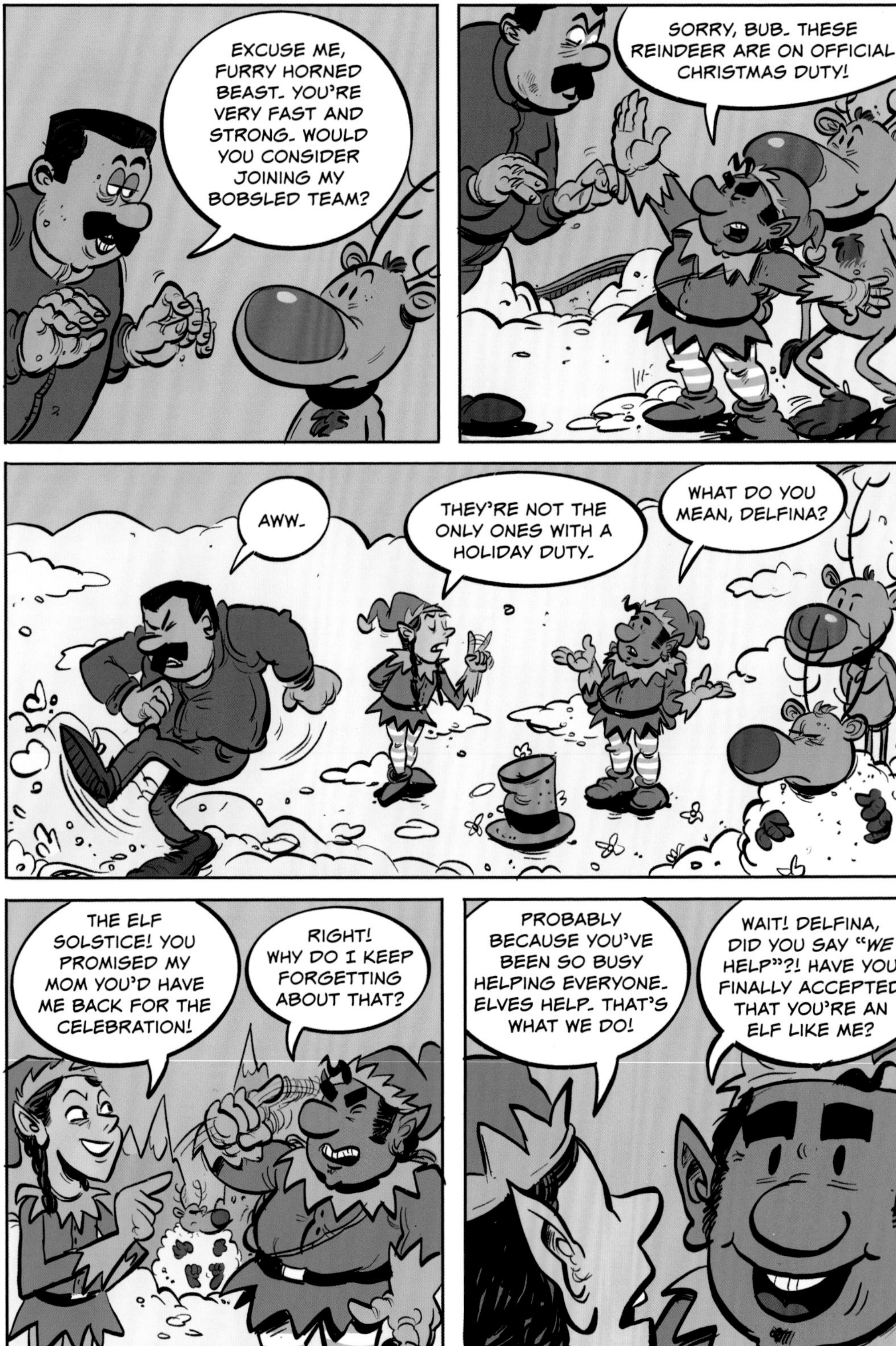
EXCUSE ME, FURRY HORNED BEAST. YOU'RE VERY FAST AND STRONG. WOULD YOU CONSIDER JOINING MY BOBSLED TEAM?
SORRY, BUB. THESE REINDEER ARE ON OFFICIAL CHRISTMAS DUTY!
AWW.
THEY'RE NOT THE ONLY ONES WITH A HOLIDAY DUTY.
WHAT DO YOU MEAN, DELFINA?
THE ELF SOLSTICE! YOU PROMISED MY MOM YOU'D HAVE ME BACK FOR THE CELEBRATION!
RIGHT! WHY DO I KEEP FORGETTING ABOUT THAT?
PROBABLY BECAUSE YOU'VE BEEN SO BUSY HELPING EVERYONE. ELVES HELP. THAT'S WHAT WE DO!
WAIT! DELFINA, DID YOU SAY "WE HELP"?! HAVE YOU FINALLY ACCEPTED THAT YOU'RE AN ELF LIKE ME?

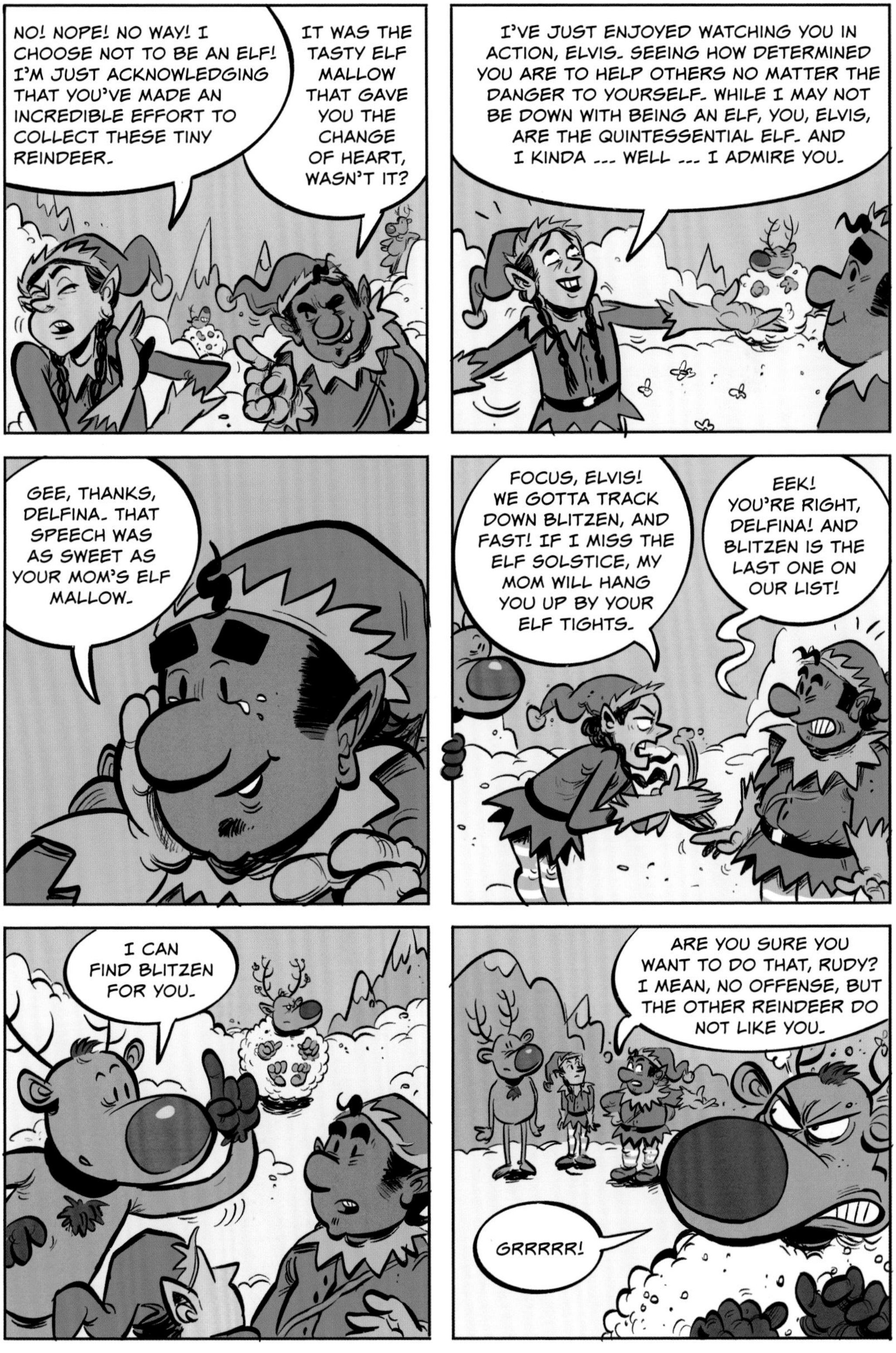
NO! NOPE! NO WAY! I CHOOSE NOT TO BE AN ELF! I'M JUST ACKNOWLEDGING THAT YOU'VE MADE AN INCREDIBLE EFFORT TO COLLECT THESE TINY REINDEER.
IT WAS THE TASTY ELF MALLOW THAT GAVE YOU THE CHANGE OF HEART, WASN'T IT?
I'VE JUST ENJOYED WATCHING YOU IN ACTION, ELVIS. SEEING HOW DETERMINED YOU ARE TO HELP OTHERS NO MATTER THE DANGER TO YOURSELF. WHILE I MAY NOT BE DOWN WITH BEING AN ELF, YOU, ELVIS, ARE THE QUINTESSENTIAL ELF. AND I KINDA ... WELL ... I ADMIRE YOU.
GEE, THANKS, DELFINA. THAT SPEECH WAS AS SWEET AS YOUR MOM'S ELF MALLOW.
FOCUS, ELVIS! WE GOTTA TRACK DOWN BLITZEN, AND FAST! IF I MISS THE ELF SOLSTICE, MY MOM WILL HANG YOU UP BY YOUR ELF TIGHTS.
EEK! YOU'RE RIGHT, DELFINA! AND BLITZEN IS THE LAST ONE ON OUR LIST!
I CAN FIND BLITZEN FOR YOU.
ARE YOU SURE YOU WANT TO DO THAT, RUDY? I MEAN, NO OFFENSE, BUT THE OTHER REINDEER DO NOT LIKE YOU.
GRRRRR!

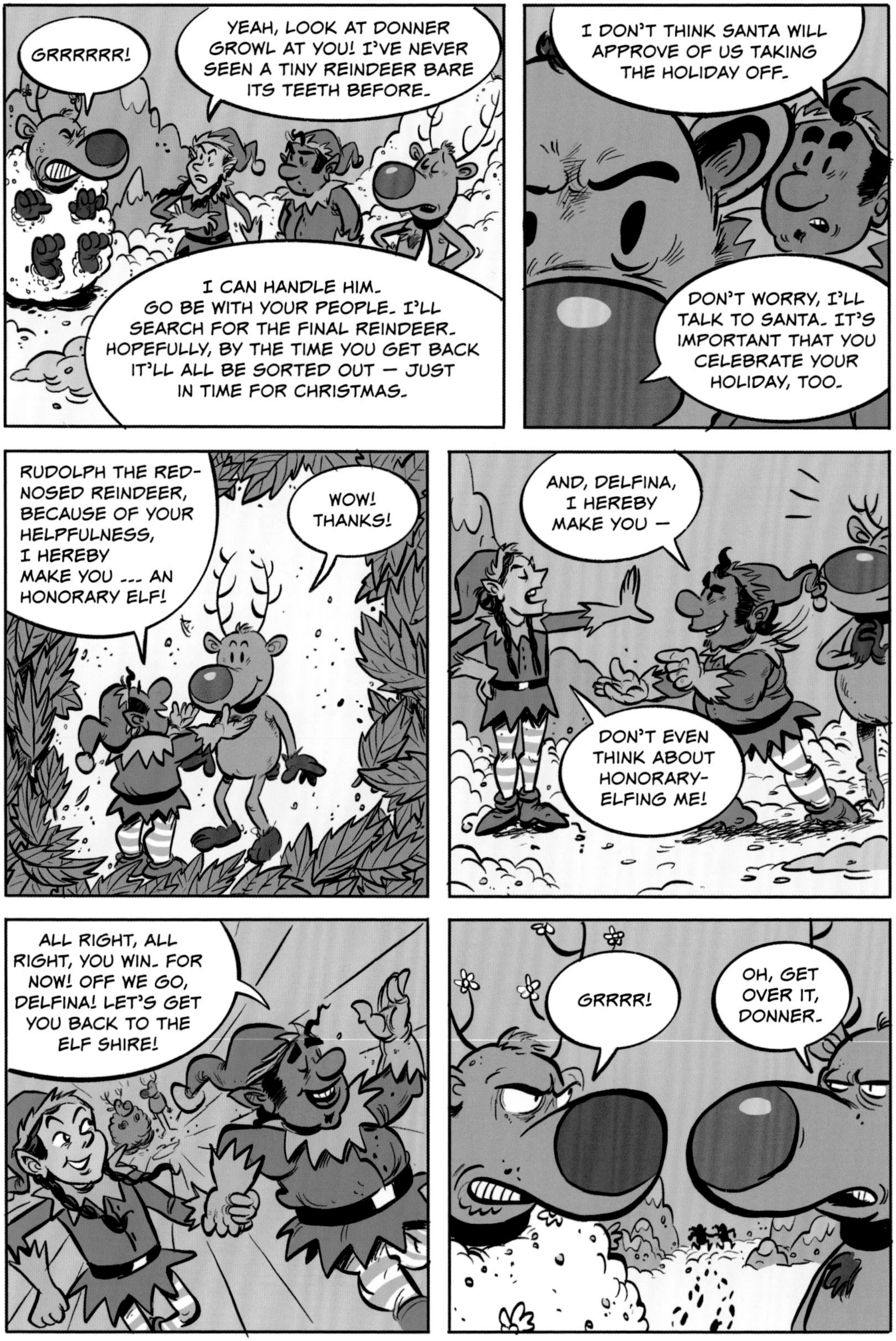
GRRRRRR!
YEAH, LOOK AT DONNER GROWL AT YOU! I'VE NEVER SEEN A TINY REINDEER BARE ITS TEETH BEFORE.
I CAN HANDLE HIM. GO BE WITH YOUR PEOPLE. I'LL SEARCH FOR THE FINAL REINDEER. HOPEFULLY, BY THE TIME YOU GET BACK IT'LL ALL BE SORTED OUT — JUST IN TIME FOR CHRISTMAS.
I DON'T THINK SANTA WILL APPROVE OF US TAKING THE HOLIDAY OFF.
DON'T WORRY, I'LL TALK TO SANTA. IT'S IMPORTANT THAT YOU CELEBRATE YOUR HOLIDAY, TOO.
RUDOLPH THE RED-NOSED REINDEER, BECAUSE OF YOUR HELPFULNESS, I HEREBY MAKE YOU ... AN HONORARY ELF!
WOW! THANKS!
AND, DELFINA, I HEREBY MAKE YOU —
DON'T EVEN THINK ABOUT HONORARY-ELFING ME!
ALL RIGHT, ALL RIGHT, YOU WIN. FOR NOW! OFF WE GO, DELFINA! LET'S GET YOU BACK TO THE ELF SHIRE!
GRRRR!
OH, GET OVER IT, DONNER.

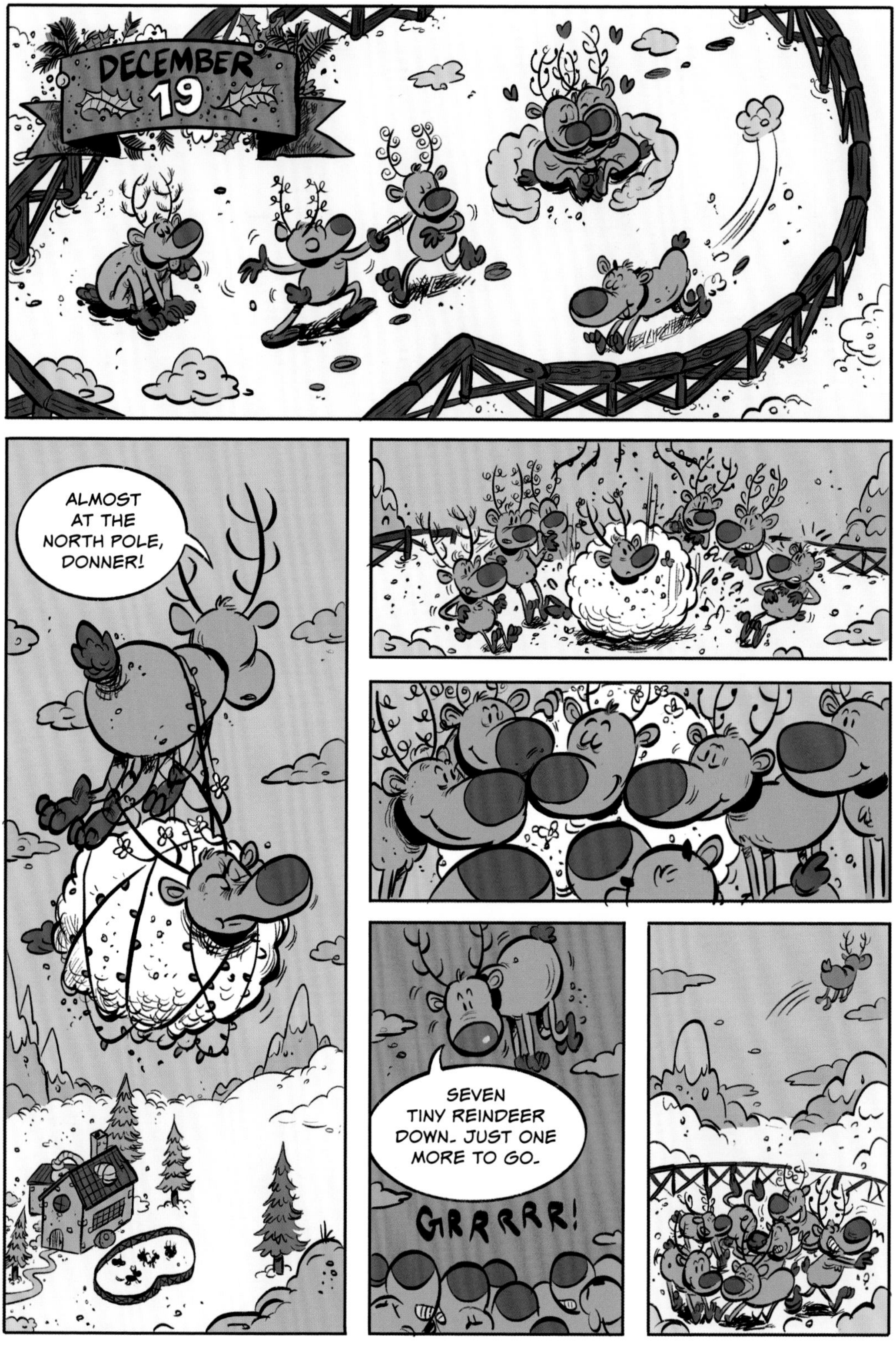
DECEMBER 19
ALMOST AT THE NORTH POLE, DONNER!
SEVEN TINY REINDEER DOWN. JUST ONE MORE TO GO.
GRRRRR!

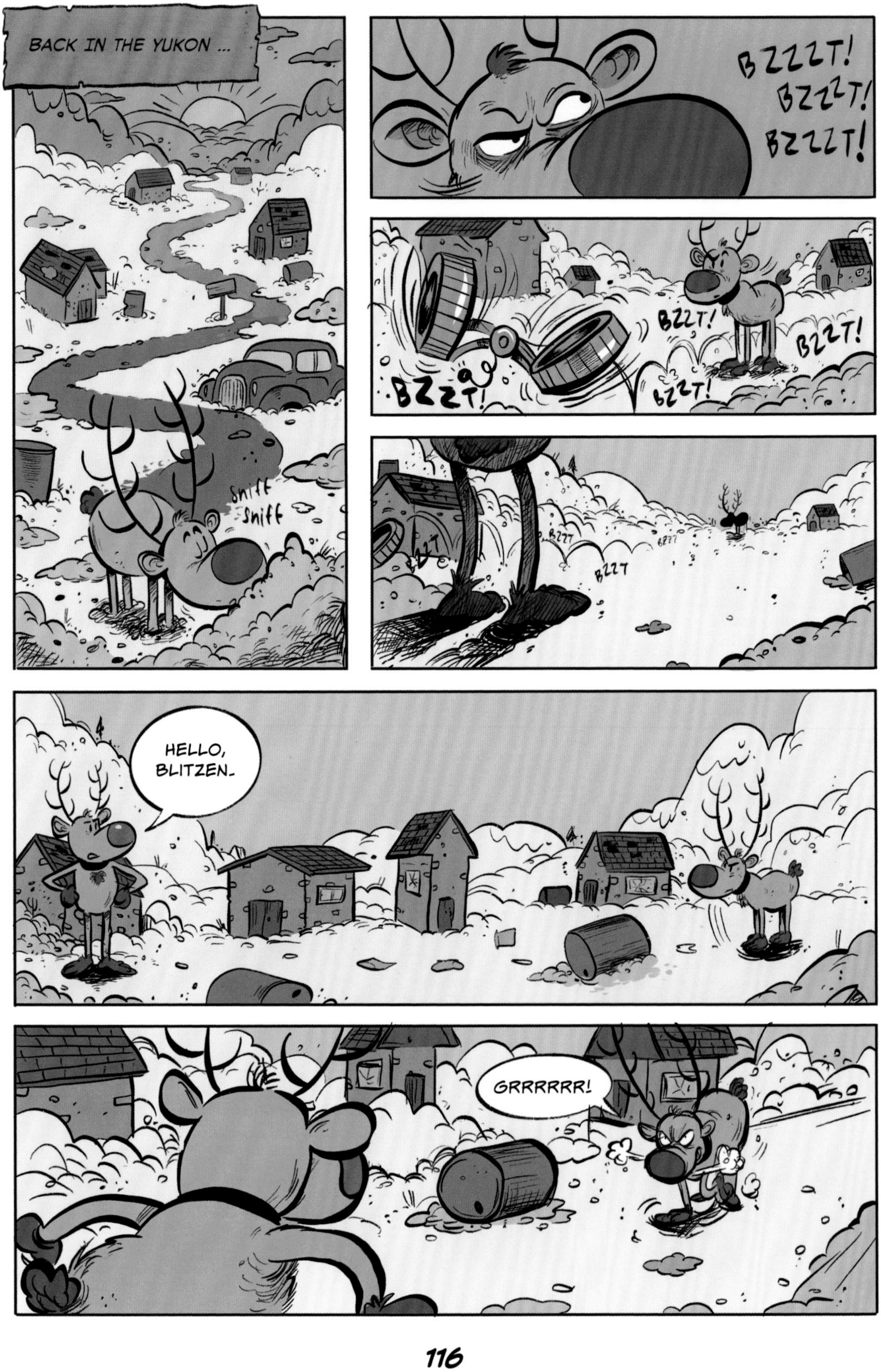
BACK IN THE YUKON ...
SNIFF
SNIFF
BZZZT!
BZZZT!
BZZZT!
BZZT!
BZZT!
BZZT!
BZZT!
BZZT
BZZT
BZZT
BZZT
HELLO, BLITZEN.
GRRRRRR!

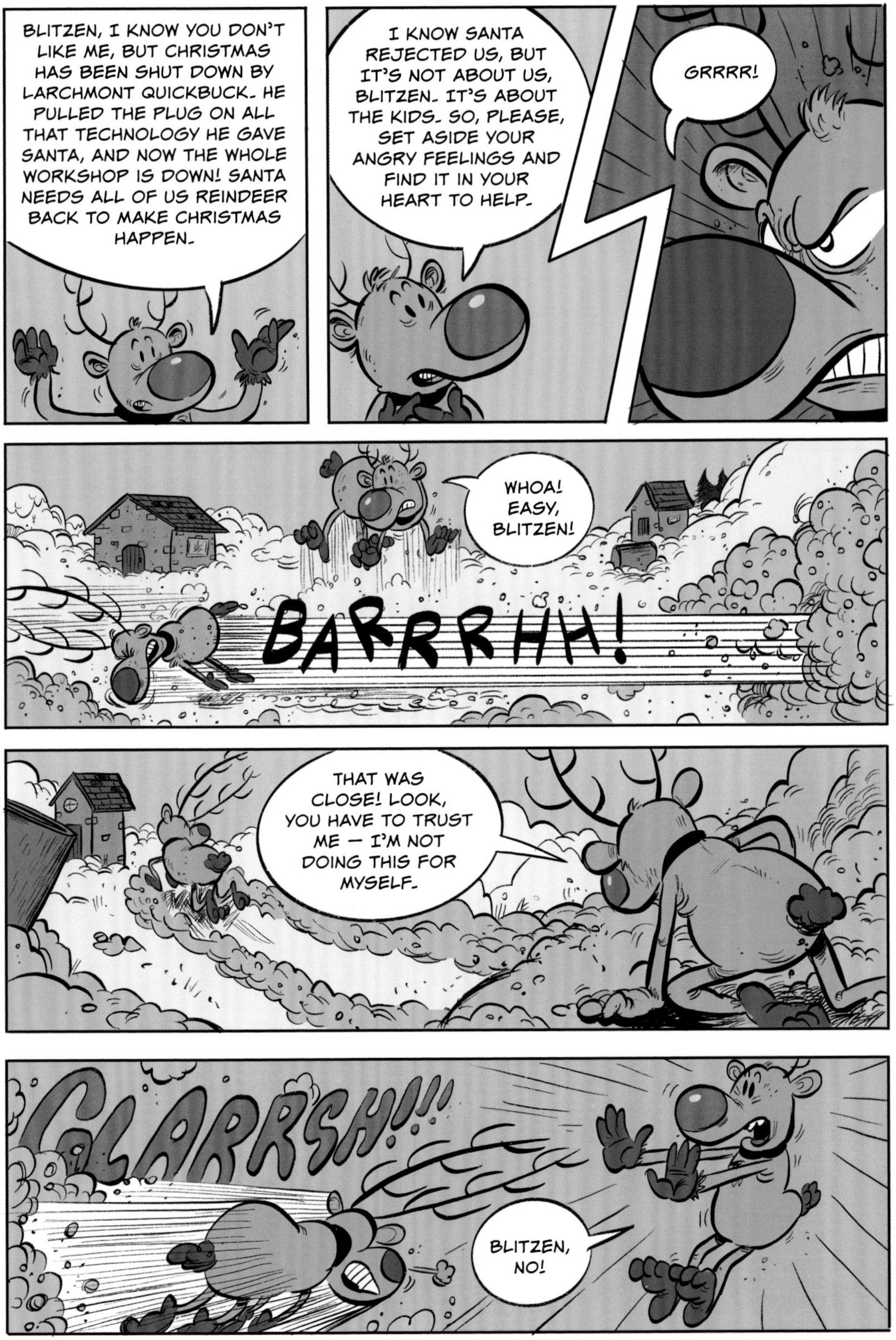
BLITZEN, I KNOW YOU DON'T LIKE ME, BUT CHRISTMAS HAS BEEN SHUT DOWN BY LARCHMONT QUICKBUCK. HE PULLED THE PLUG ON ALL THAT TECHNOLOGY HE GAVE SANTA, AND NOW THE WHOLE WORKSHOP IS DOWN! SANTA NEEDS ALL OF US REINDEER BACK TO MAKE CHRISTMAS HAPPEN.
I KNOW SANTA REJECTED US, BUT IT'S NOT ABOUT US, BLITZEN. IT'S ABOUT THE KIDS. SO, PLEASE, SET ASIDE YOUR ANGRY FEELINGS AND FIND IT IN YOUR HEART TO HELP.
GRRRR!
WHOA! EASY, BLITZEN!
BARRRHH!
THAT WAS CLOSE! LOOK, YOU HAVE TO TRUST ME — I'M NOT DOING THIS FOR MYSELF.
GLARRSH!!!
BLITZEN, NO!

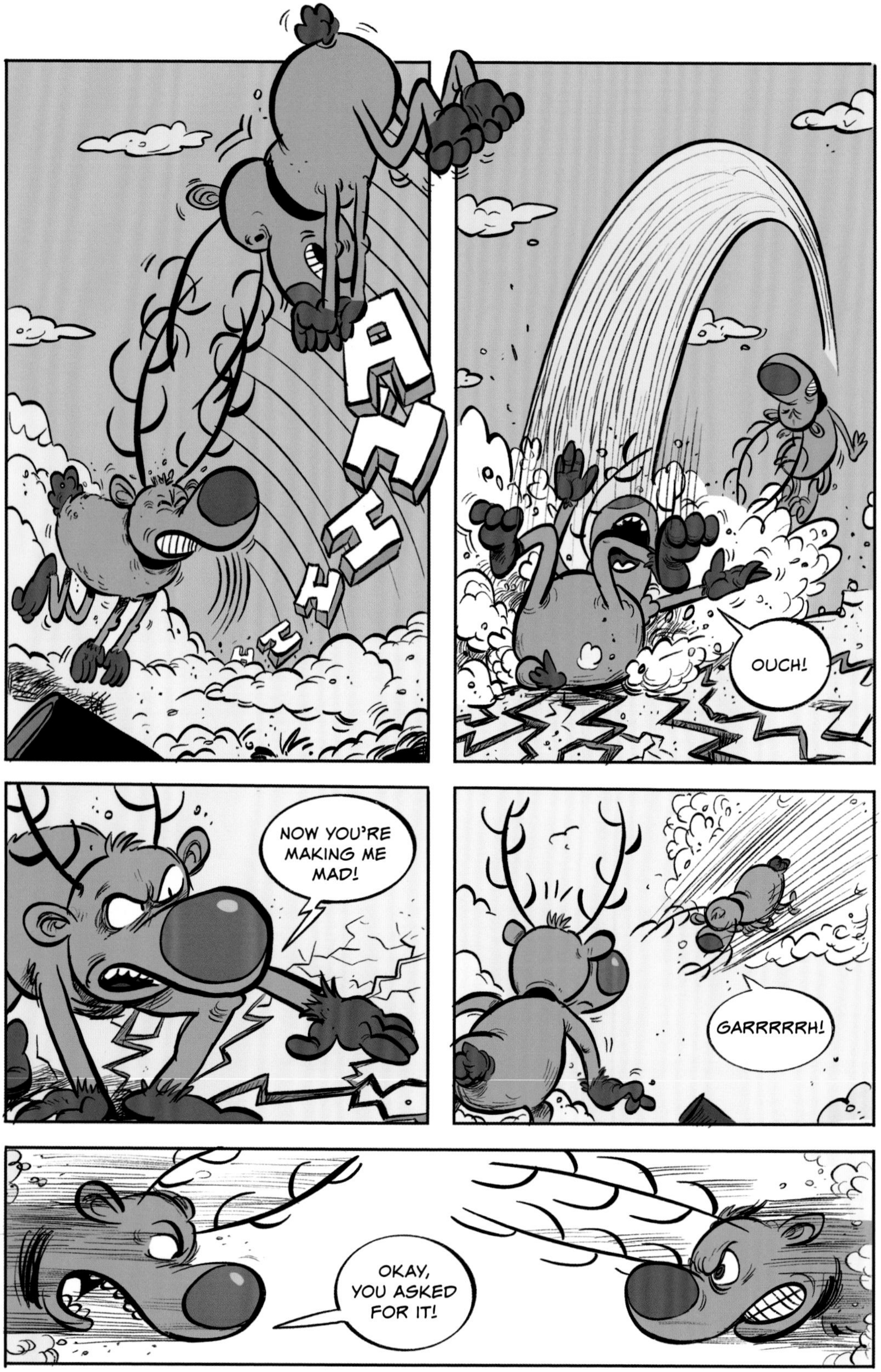
OUCH!
NOW YOU'RE MAKING ME MAD!
GARRRRRH!
OKAY, YOU ASKED FOR IT!

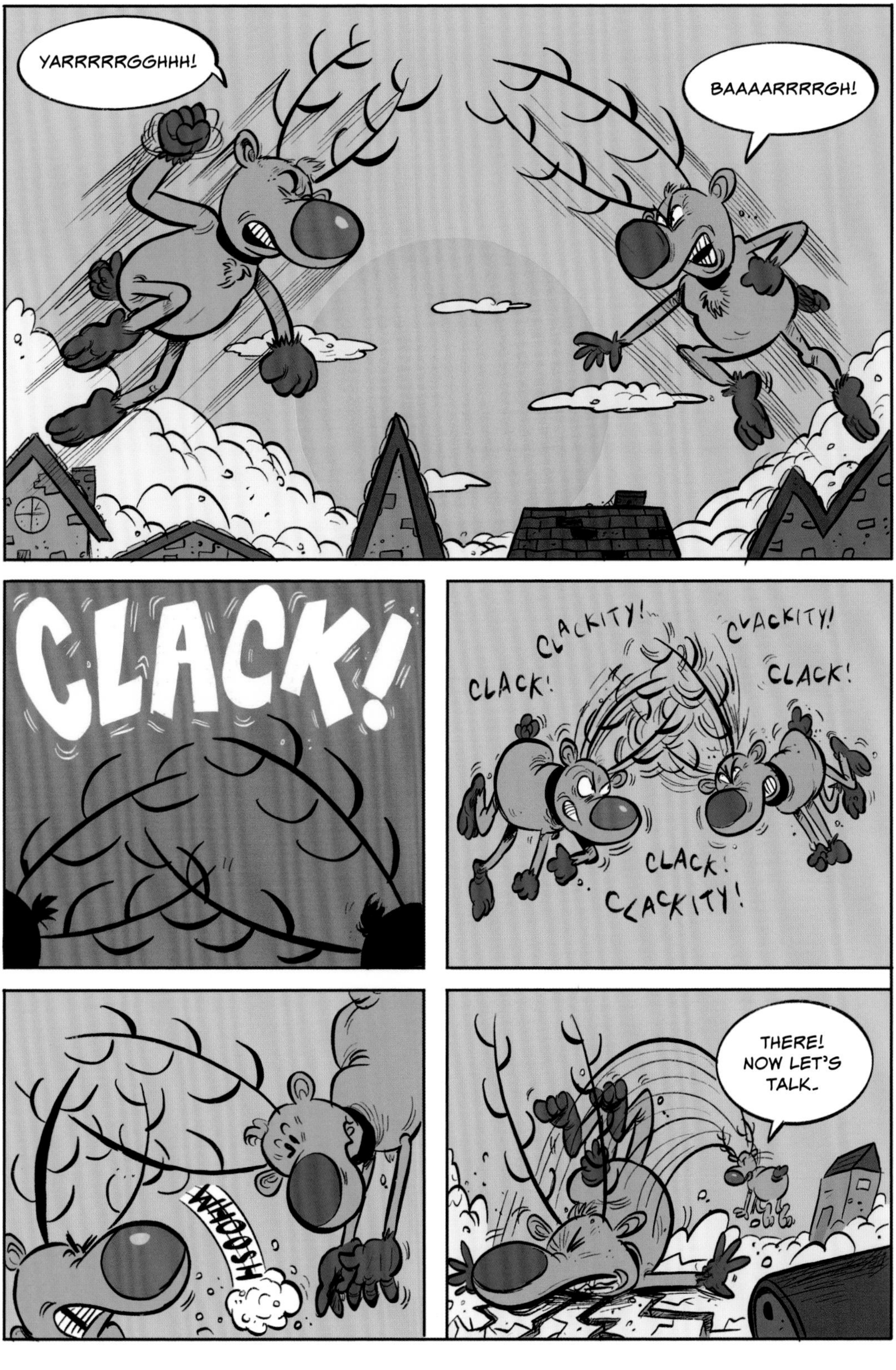
YARRRRRGGHHH!
BAAAARRRRGH!
CLACK!
CLACKITY!
CLACKITY!
CLACK!
CLACK!
CLACK!
CLACKITY!
WHOOSH
THERE! NOW LET'S TALK.

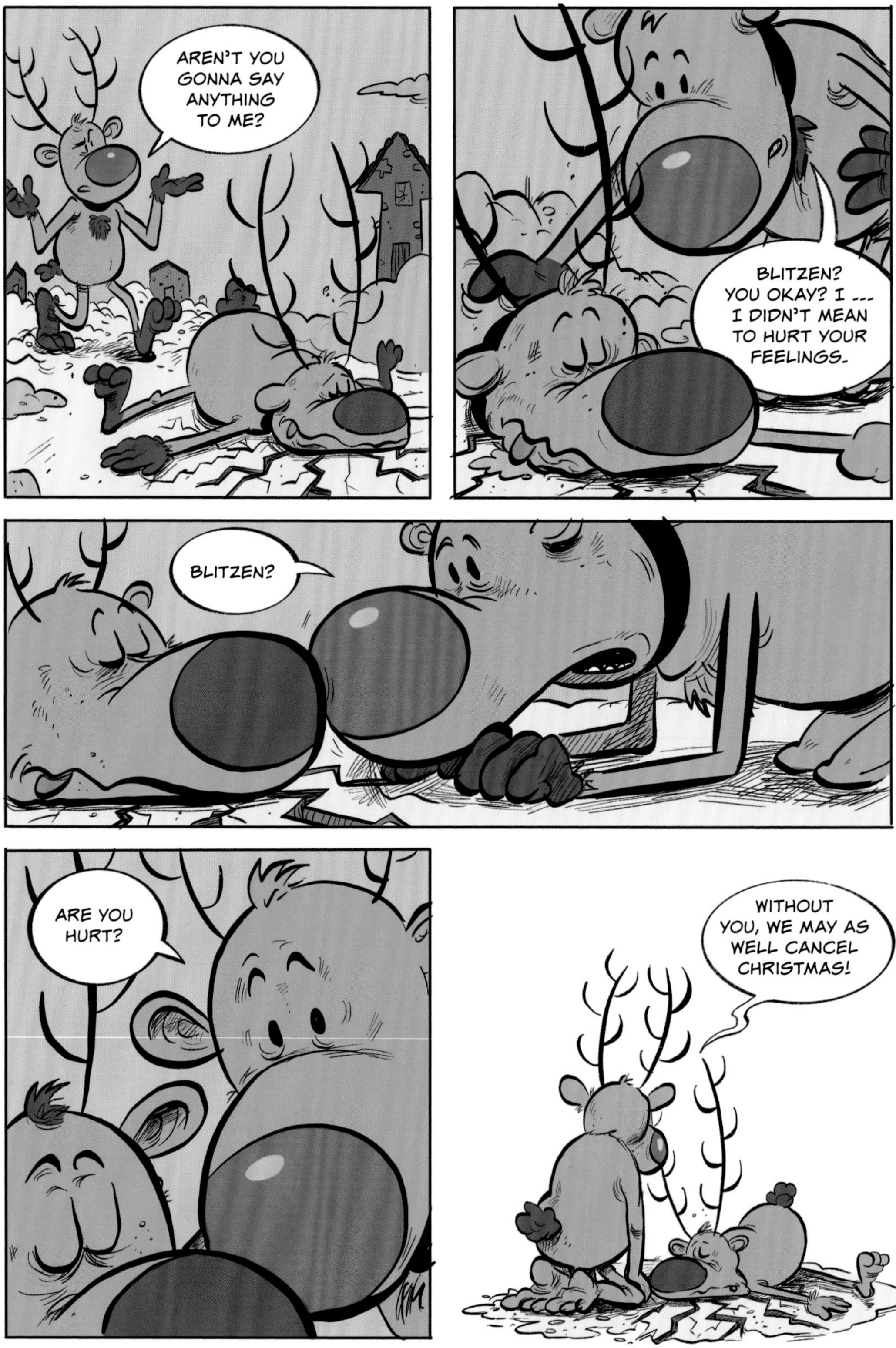
AREN'T YOU GONNA SAY ANYTHING TO ME?
BLITZEN? YOU OKAY? I --- I DIDN'T MEAN TO HURT YOUR FEELINGS.
BLITZEN?
ARE YOU HURT?
WITHOUT YOU, WE MAY AS WELL CANCEL CHRISTMAS!

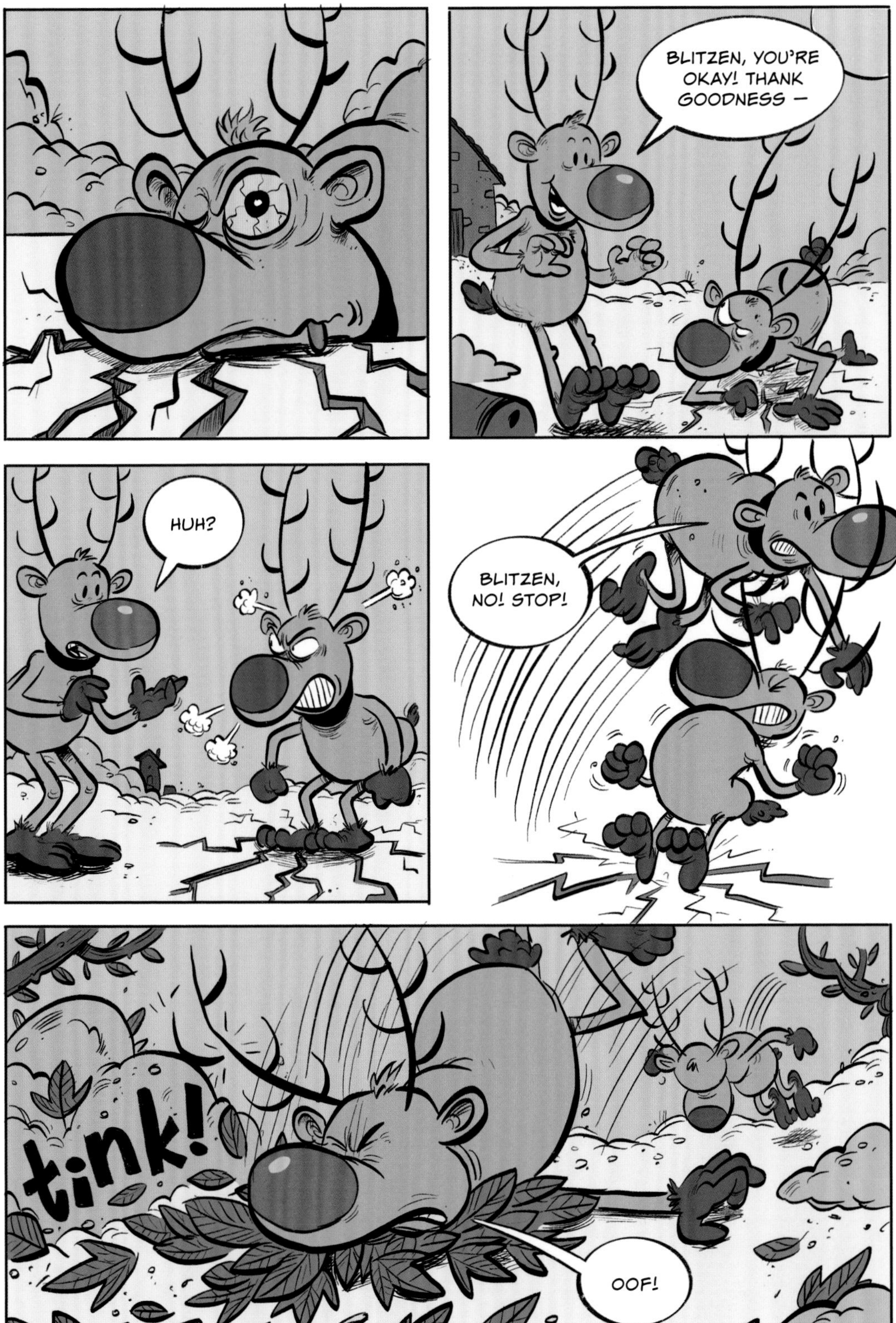
BLITZEN, YOU'RE OKAY! THANK GOODNESS —
HUH?
BLITZEN, NO! STOP!
tink!
OOF!

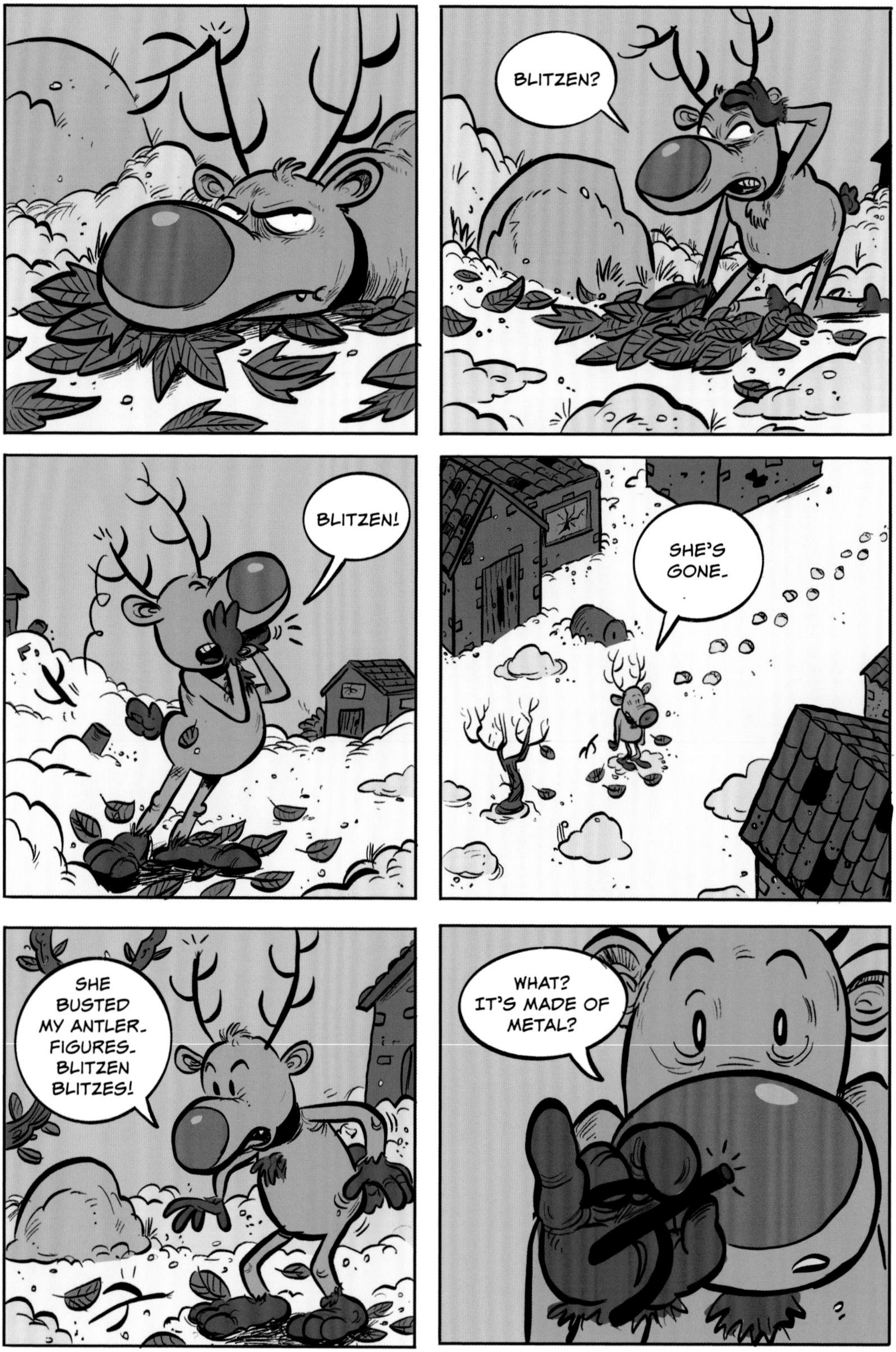
BLITZEN?
BLITZEN!
SHE'S GONE.
SHE BUSTED MY ANTLER. FIGURES. BLITZEN BLITZES!
WHAT? IT'S MADE OF METAL?

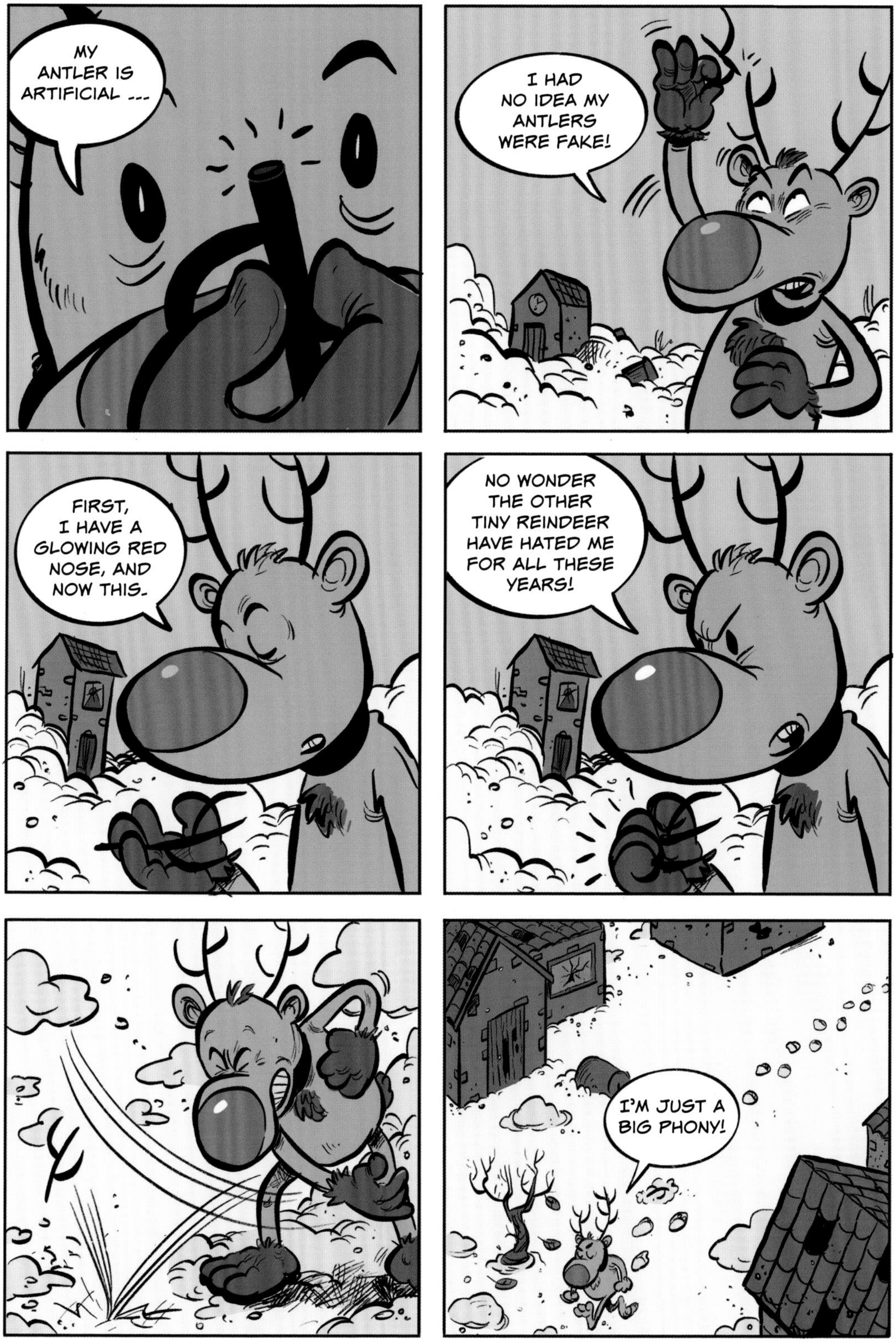
MY ANTLER IS ARTIFICIAL ...
I HAD NO IDEA MY ANTLERS WERE FAKE!
FIRST, I HAVE A GLOWING RED NOSE, AND NOW THIS.
NO WONDER THE OTHER TINY REINDEER HAVE HATED ME FOR ALL THESE YEARS!
I'M JUST A BIG PHONY!

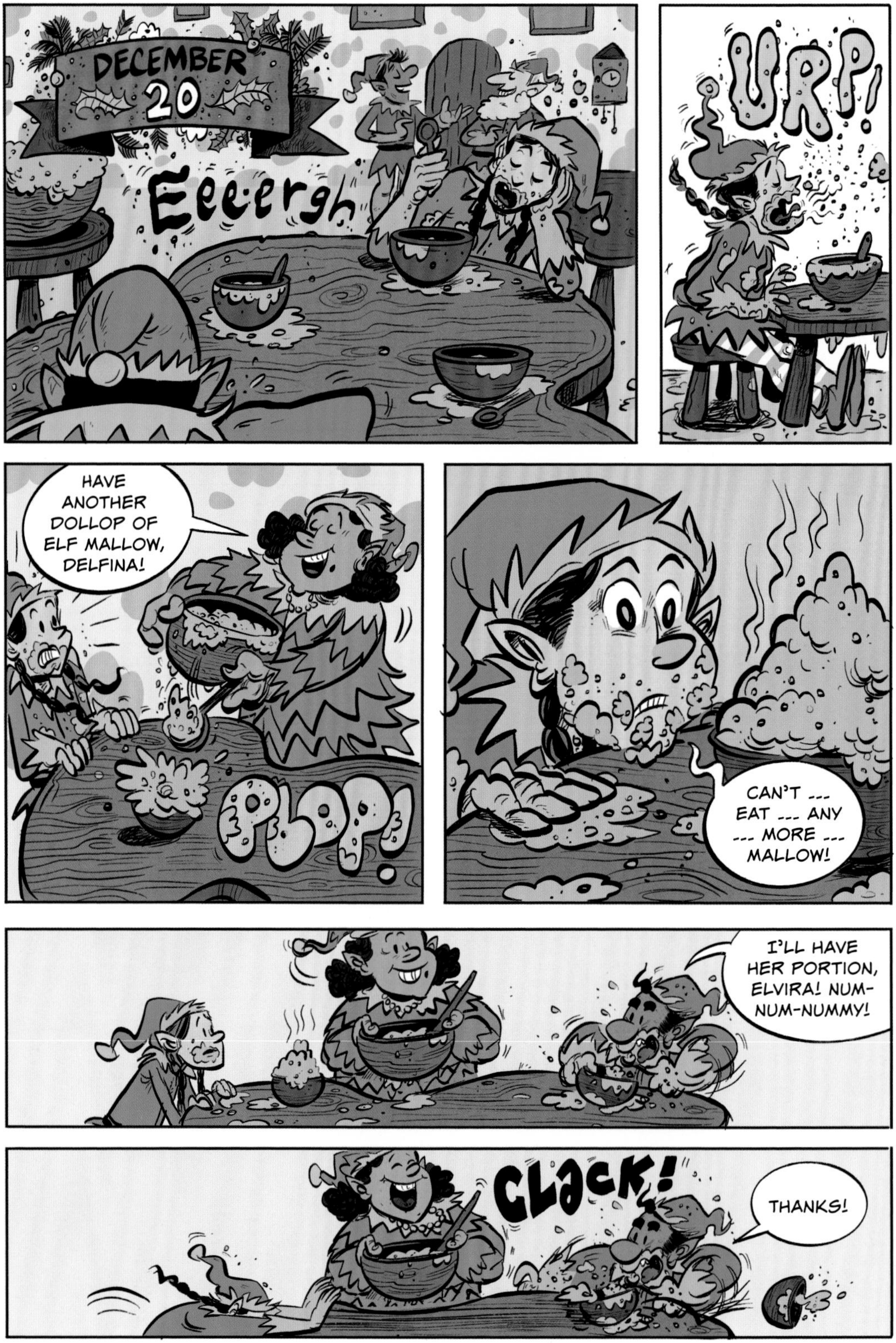
DECEMBER 20
Eeeergh
URP!
HAVE ANOTHER DOLLOP OF ELF MALLOW, DELFINA!
PLOP!
CAN'T --- EAT --- ANY --- MORE --- MALLOW!
I'LL HAVE HER PORTION, ELVIRA! NUM-NUM-NUMMY!
CLACK!
THANKS!

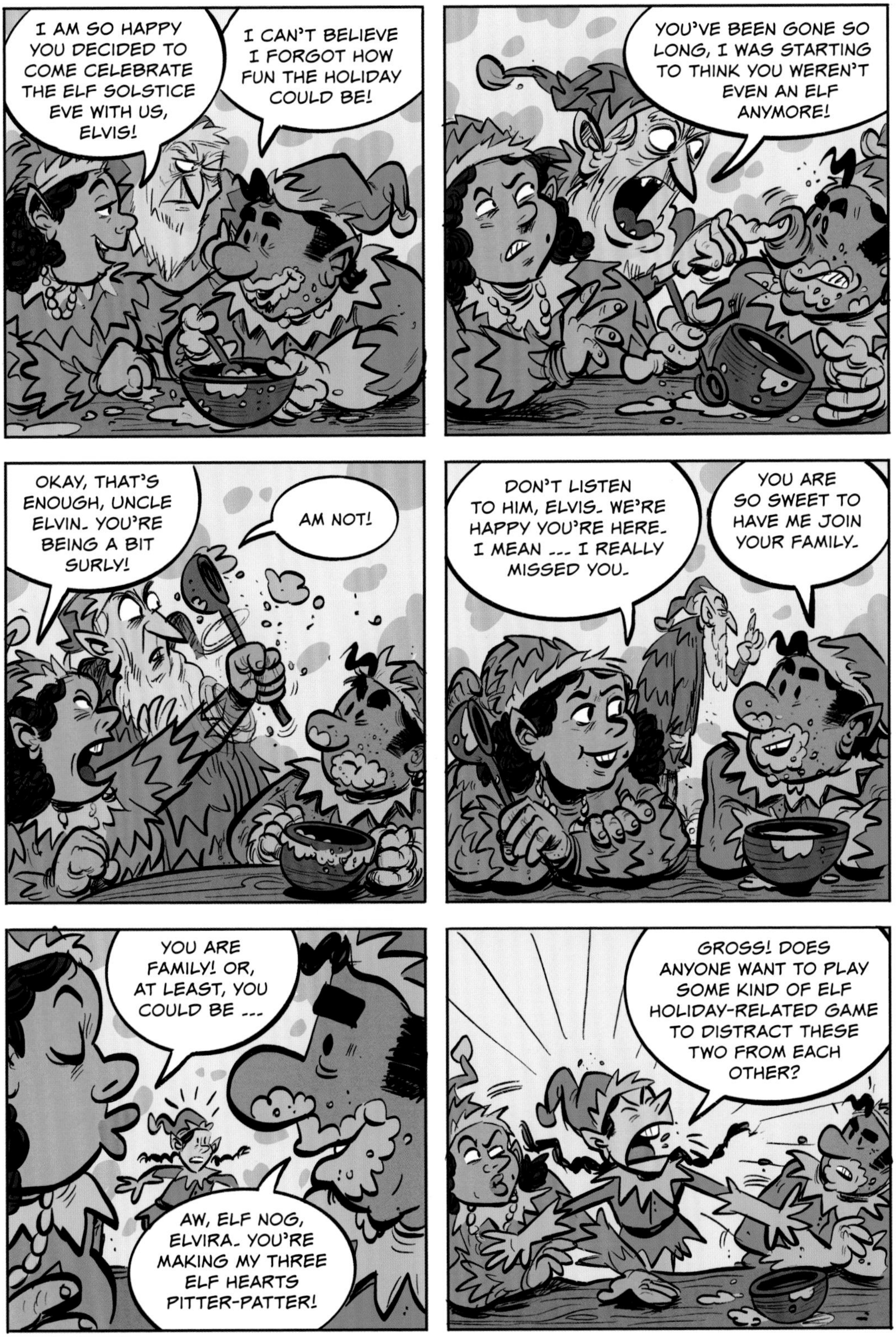
I AM SO HAPPY YOU DECIDED TO COME CELEBRATE THE ELF SOLSTICE EVE WITH US, ELVIS!
I CAN'T BELIEVE I FORGOT HOW FUN THE HOLIDAY COULD BE!
YOU'VE BEEN GONE SO LONG, I WAS STARTING TO THINK YOU WEREN'T EVEN AN ELF ANYMORE!
OKAY, THAT'S ENOUGH, UNCLE ELVIN. YOU'RE BEING A BIT SURLY!
AM NOT!
DON'T LISTEN TO HIM, ELVIS. WE'RE HAPPY YOU'RE HERE. I MEAN ... I REALLY MISSED YOU.
YOU ARE SO SWEET TO HAVE ME JOIN YOUR FAMILY.
YOU ARE FAMILY! OR, AT LEAST, YOU COULD BE ...
AW, ELF NOG, ELVIRA. YOU'RE MAKING MY THREE ELF HEARTS PITTER-PATTER!
GROSS! DOES ANYONE WANT TO PLAY SOME KIND OF ELF HOLIDAY-RELATED GAME TO DISTRACT THESE TWO FROM EACH OTHER?

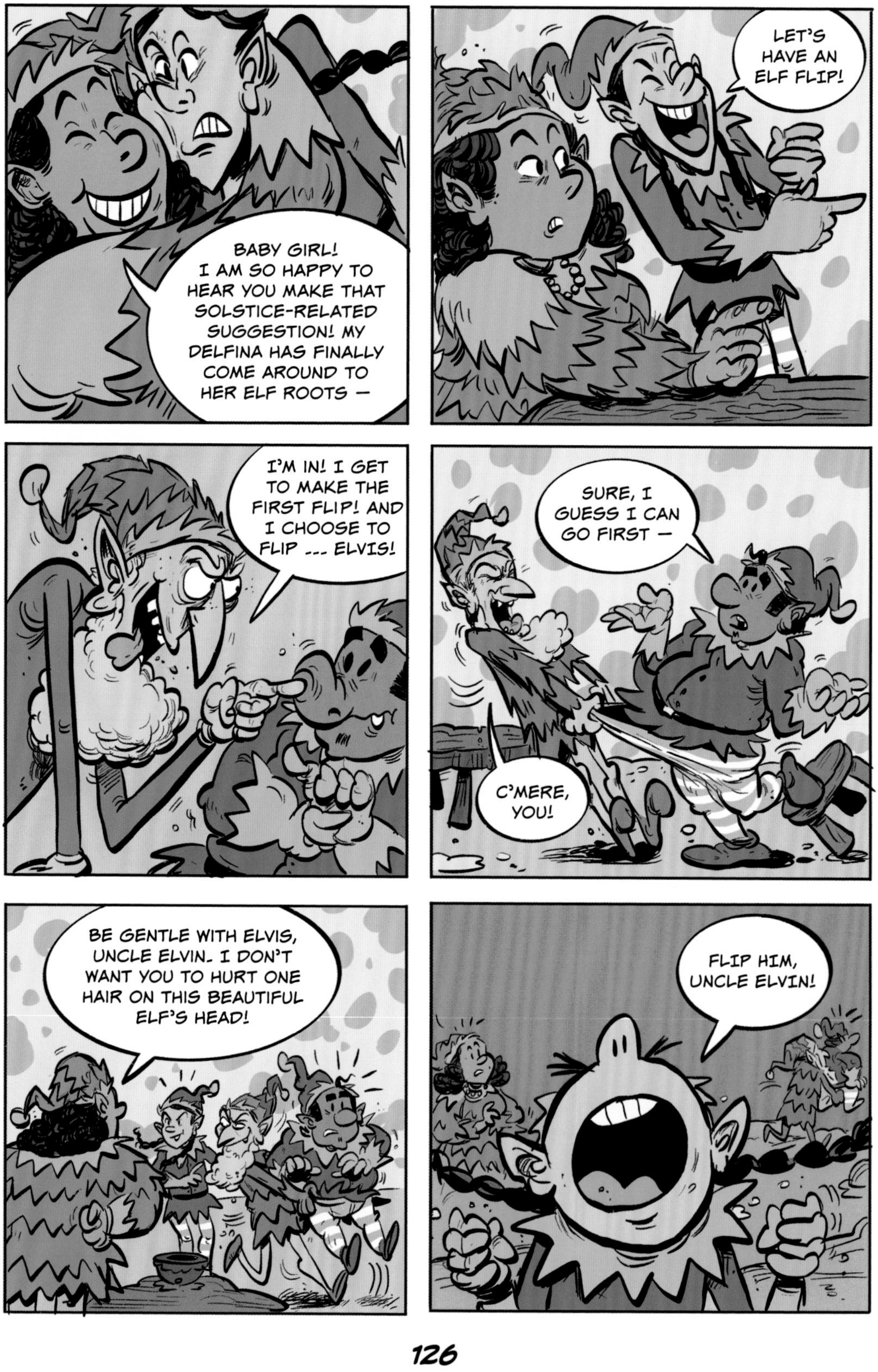
BABY GIRL! I AM SO HAPPY TO HEAR YOU MAKE THAT SOLSTICE-RELATED SUGGESTION! MY DELFINA HAS FINALLY COME AROUND TO HER ELF ROOTS —
LET'S HAVE AN ELF FLIP!
I'M IN! I GET TO MAKE THE FIRST FLIP! AND I CHOOSE TO FLIP ... ELVIS!
SURE, I GUESS I CAN GO FIRST —
C'MERE, YOU!
BE GENTLE WITH ELVIS, UNCLE ELVIN. I DON'T WANT YOU TO HURT ONE HAIR ON THIS BEAUTIFUL ELF'S HEAD!
FLIP HIM, UNCLE ELVIN!

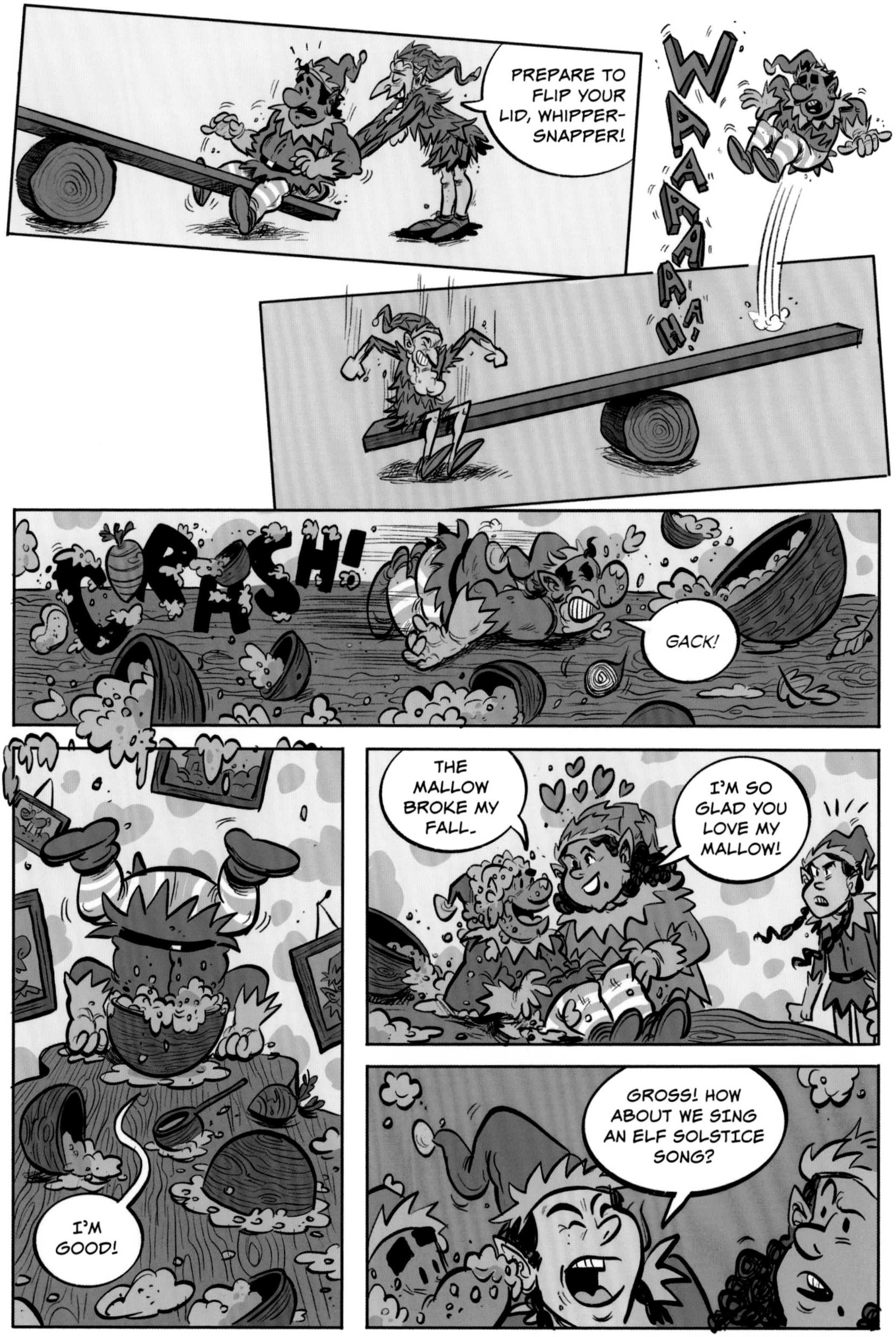
PREPARE TO FLIP YOUR LID, WHIPPER-SNAPPER!
WAAAAAAH!
CRASH!
GACK!
I'M GOOD!
THE MALLOW BROKE MY FALL.
I'M SO GLAD YOU LOVE MY MALLOW!
GROSS! HOW ABOUT WE SING AN ELF SOLSTICE SONG?

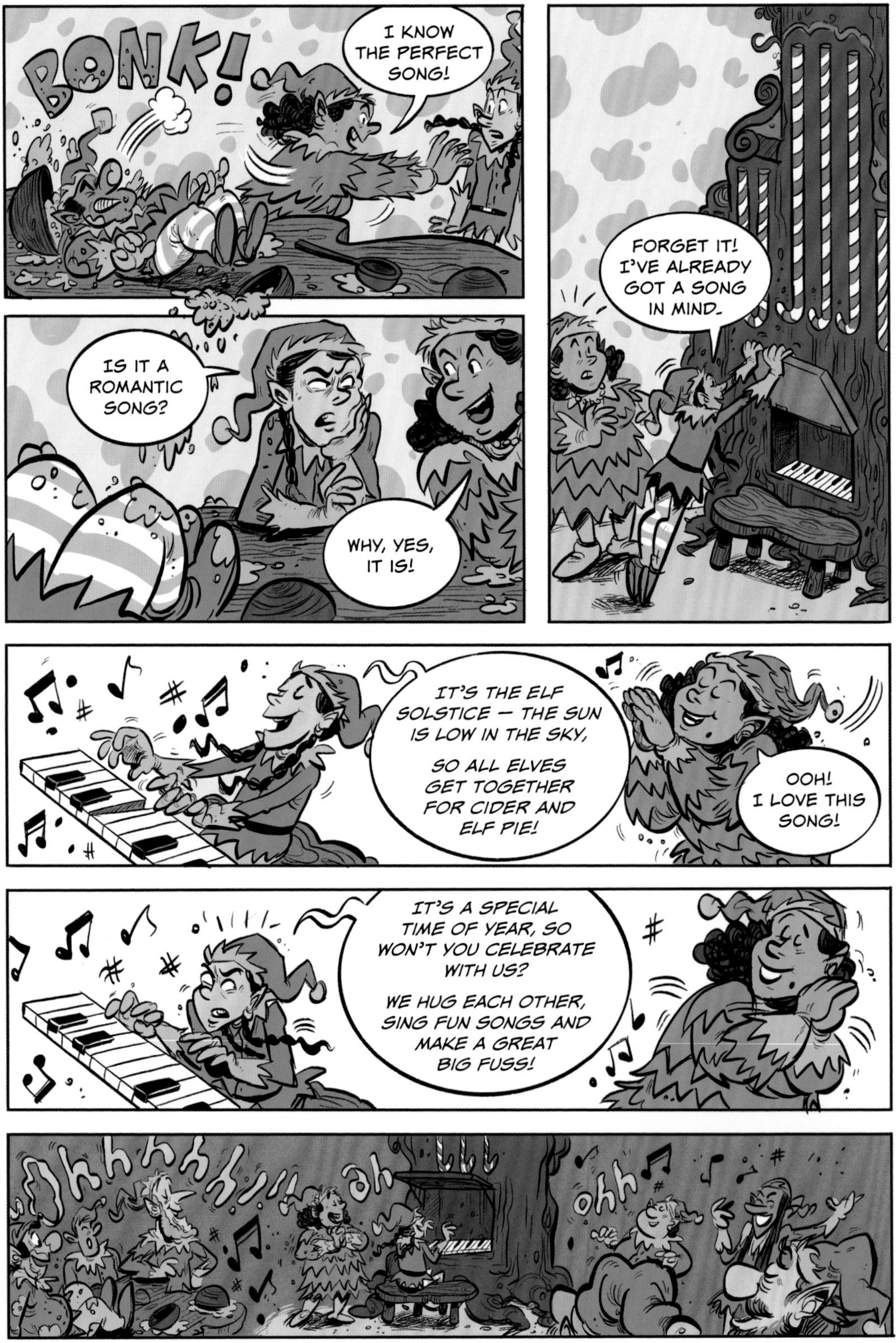
BONK!
I KNOW THE PERFECT SONG!
FORGET IT! I'VE ALREADY GOT A SONG IN MIND.
IS IT A ROMANTIC SONG?
WHY, YES, IT IS!
IT'S THE ELF SOLSTICE — THE SUN IS LOW IN THE SKY,
SO ALL ELVES GET TOGETHER FOR CIDER AND ELF PIE!
OOH! I LOVE THIS SONG!
IT'S A SPECIAL TIME OF YEAR, SO WON'T YOU CELEBRATE WITH US?
WE HUG EACH OTHER, SING FUN SONGS AND MAKE A GREAT BIG FUSS!
Ohhhhhh!!
oh
ohh

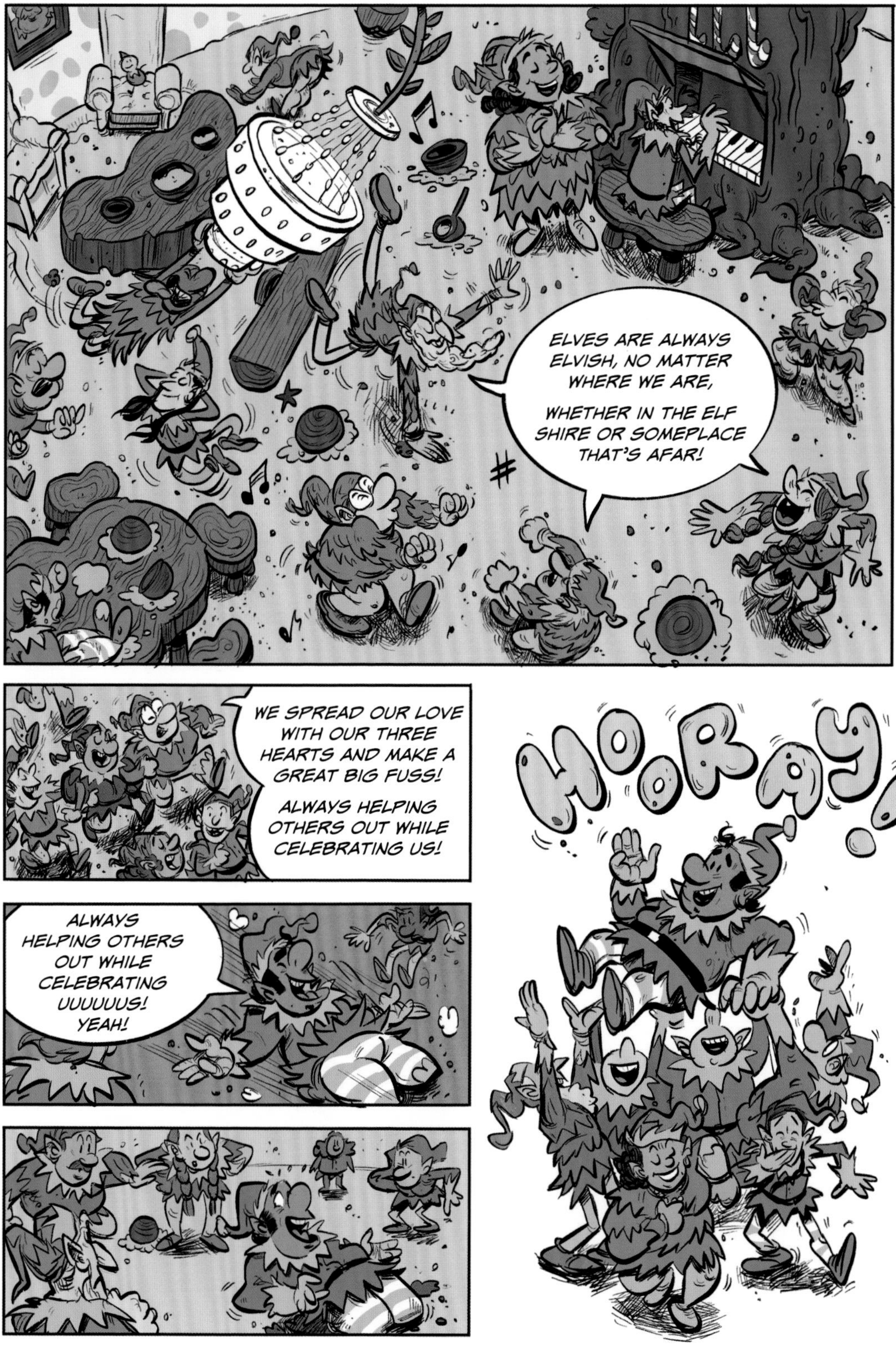
ELVES ARE ALWAYS ELVISH, NO MATTER WHERE WE ARE,
WHETHER IN THE ELF SHIRE OR SOMEPLACE THAT'S AFAR!
WE SPREAD OUR LOVE WITH OUR THREE HEARTS AND MAKE A GREAT BIG FUSS!
ALWAYS HELPING OTHERS OUT WHILE CELEBRATING US!
ALWAYS HELPING OTHERS OUT WHILE CELEBRATING UUUUUUS! YEAH!
HOORAY!

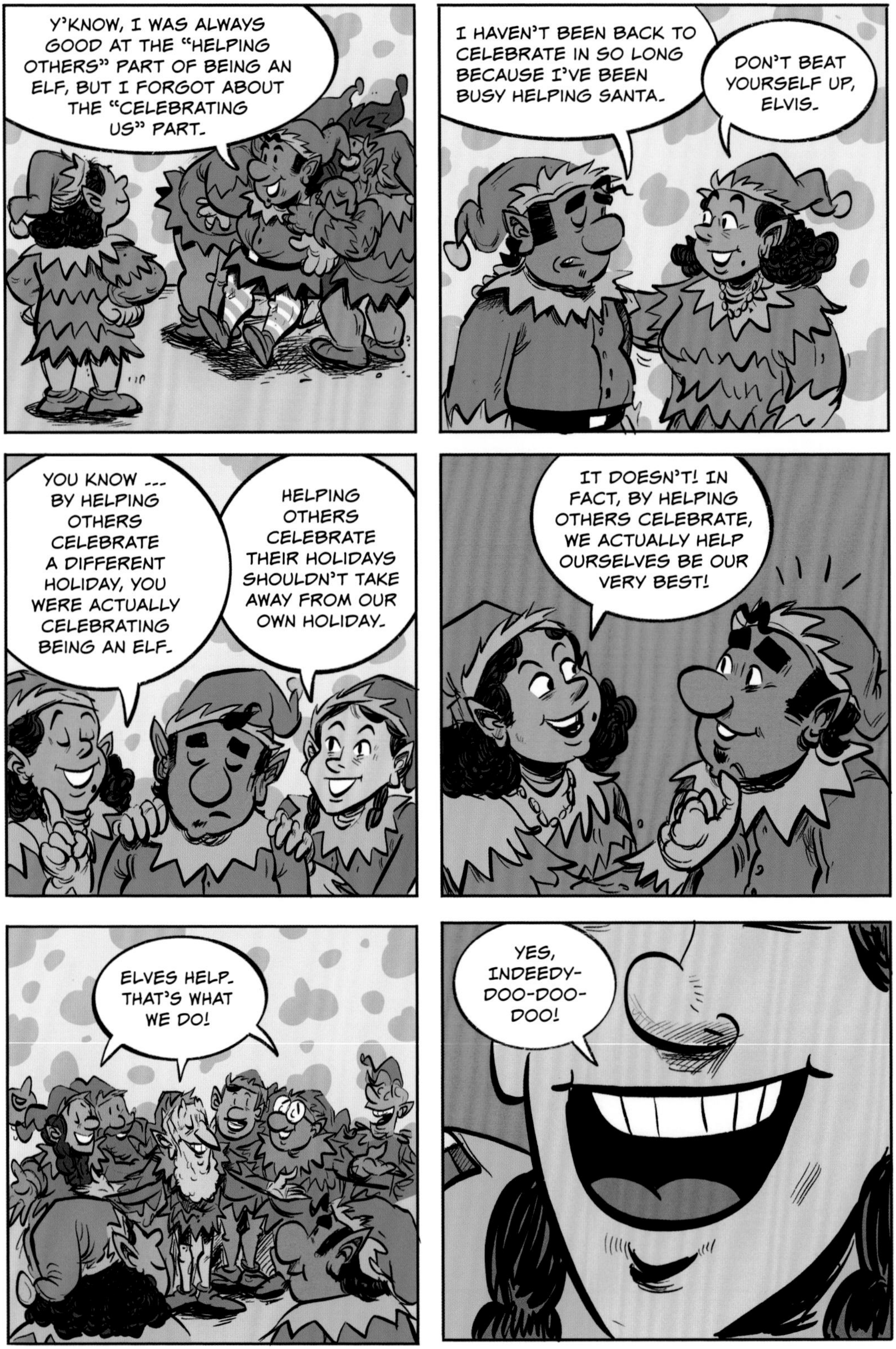
Y'KNOW, I WAS ALWAYS GOOD AT THE "HELPING OTHERS" PART OF BEING AN ELF, BUT I FORGOT ABOUT THE "CELEBRATING US" PART.
I HAVEN'T BEEN BACK TO CELEBRATE IN SO LONG BECAUSE I'VE BEEN BUSY HELPING SANTA.
DON'T BEAT YOURSELF UP, ELVIS.
YOU KNOW --- BY HELPING OTHERS CELEBRATE A DIFFERENT HOLIDAY, YOU WERE ACTUALLY CELEBRATING BEING AN ELF.
HELPING OTHERS CELEBRATE THEIR HOLIDAYS SHOULDN'T TAKE AWAY FROM OUR OWN HOLIDAY.
IT DOESN'T! IN FACT, BY HELPING OTHERS CELEBRATE, WE ACTUALLY HELP OURSELVES BE OUR VERY BEST!
ELVES HELP. THAT'S WHAT WE DO!
YES, INDEEDY-DOO-DOO-DOO!

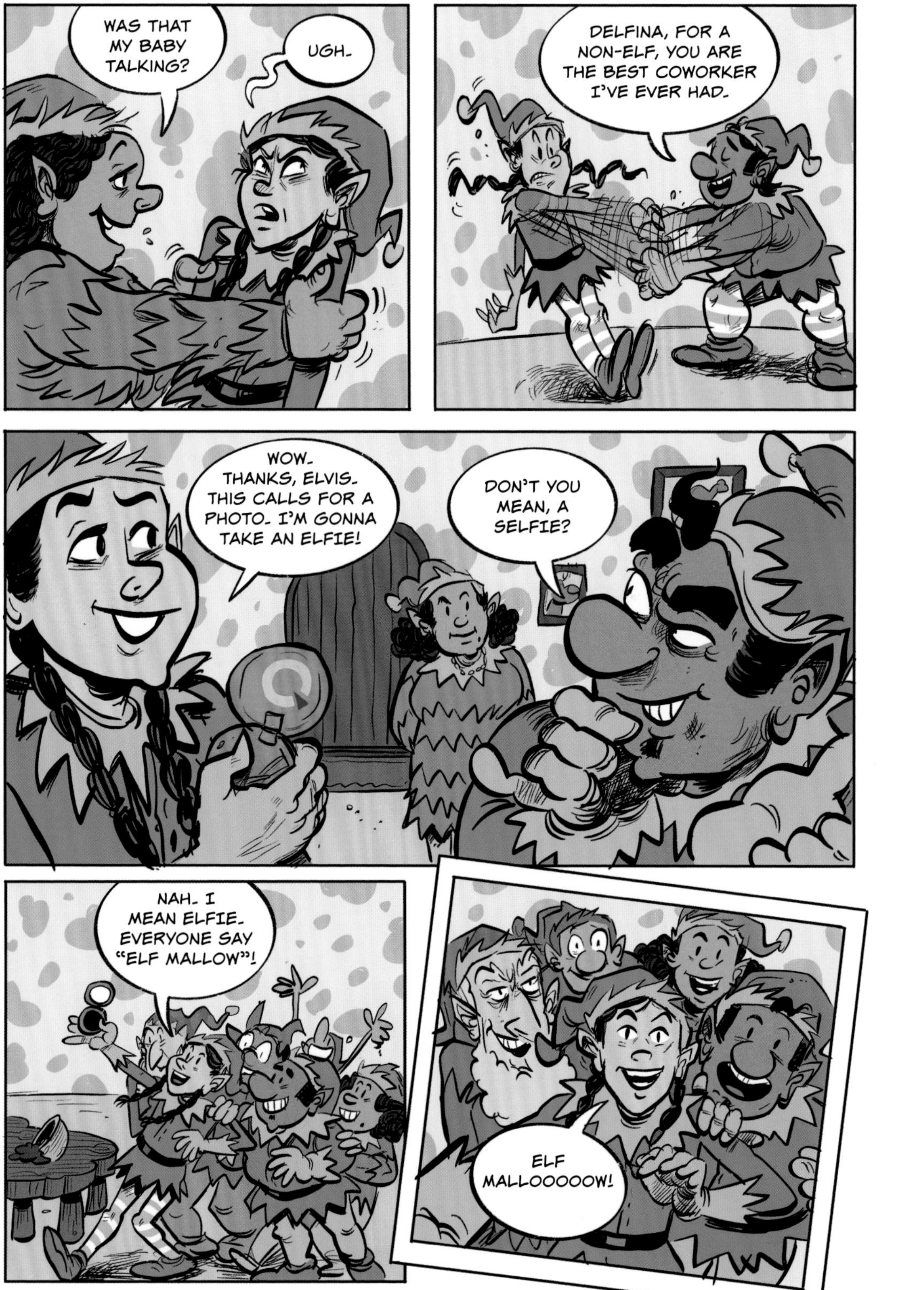
WAS THAT MY BABY TALKING?
UGH.
DELFINA, FOR A NON-ELF, YOU ARE THE BEST COWORKER I'VE EVER HAD.
WOW. THANKS, ELVIS. THIS CALLS FOR A PHOTO. I'M GONNA TAKE AN ELFIE!
DON'T YOU MEAN, A SELFIE?
NAH. I MEAN ELFIE. EVERYONE SAY "ELF MALLOW"!
ELF MALLOOOOOW!

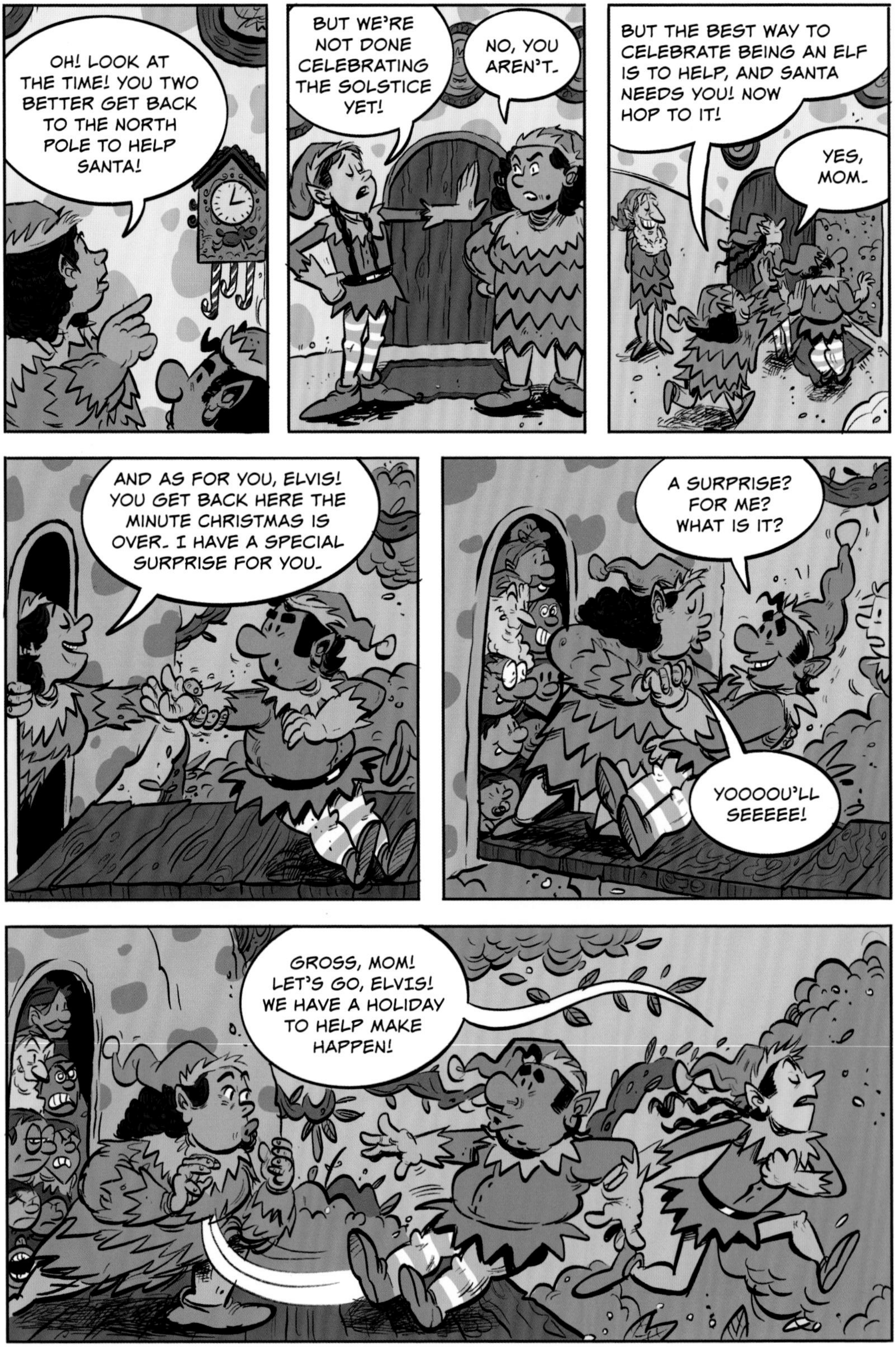
OH! LOOK AT THE TIME! YOU TWO BETTER GET BACK TO THE NORTH POLE TO HELP SANTA!
BUT WE'RE NOT DONE CELEBRATING THE SOLSTICE YET!
NO, YOU AREN'T.
BUT THE BEST WAY TO CELEBRATE BEING AN ELF IS TO HELP, AND SANTA NEEDS YOU! NOW HOP TO IT!
YES, MOM.
AND AS FOR YOU, ELVIS! YOU GET BACK HERE THE MINUTE CHRISTMAS IS OVER. I HAVE A SPECIAL SURPRISE FOR YOU.
A SURPRISE? FOR ME? WHAT IS IT?
YOOOOU'LL SEEEEE!
GROSS, MOM! LET'S GO, ELVIS! WE HAVE A HOLIDAY TO HELP MAKE HAPPEN!

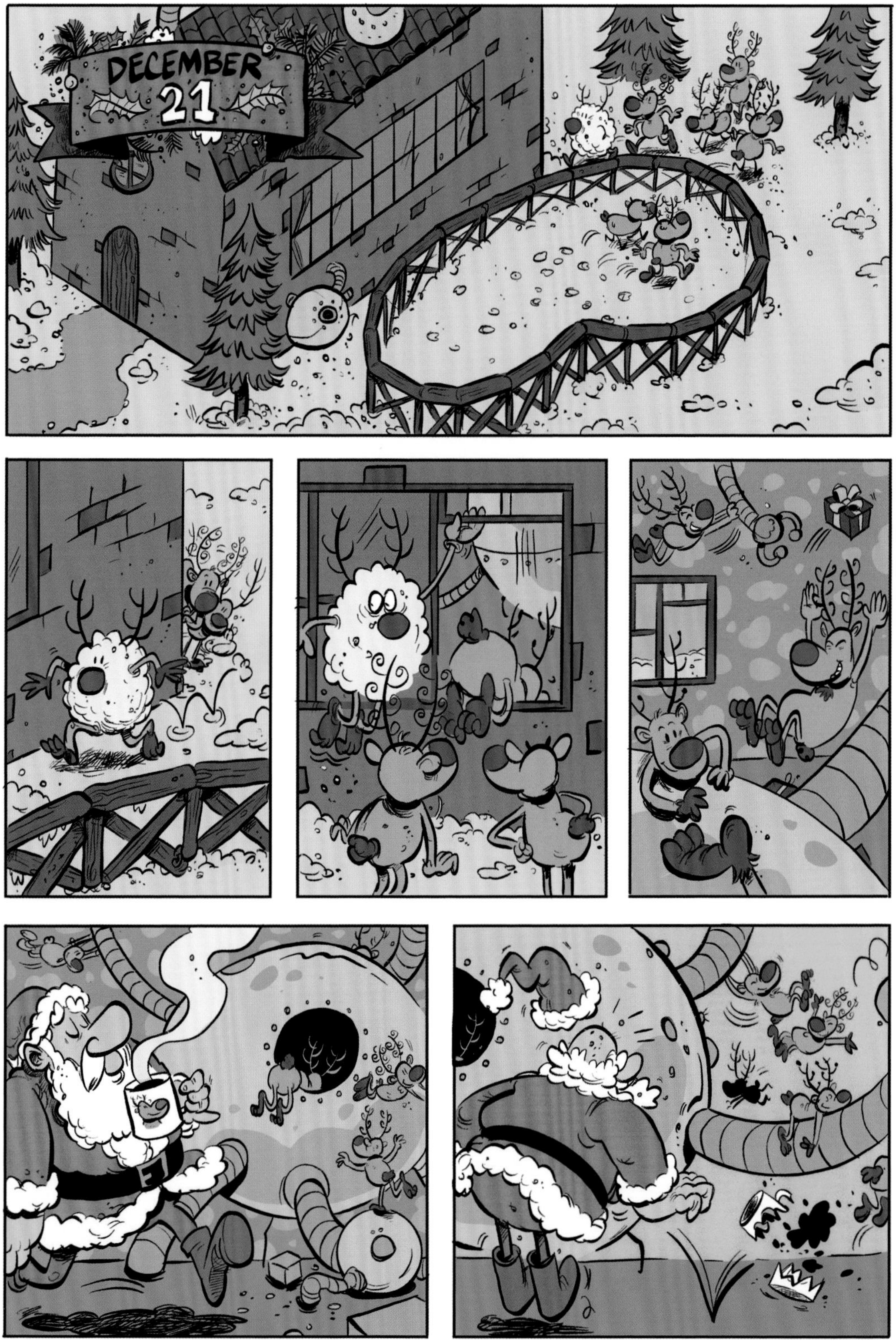
DECEMBER
21

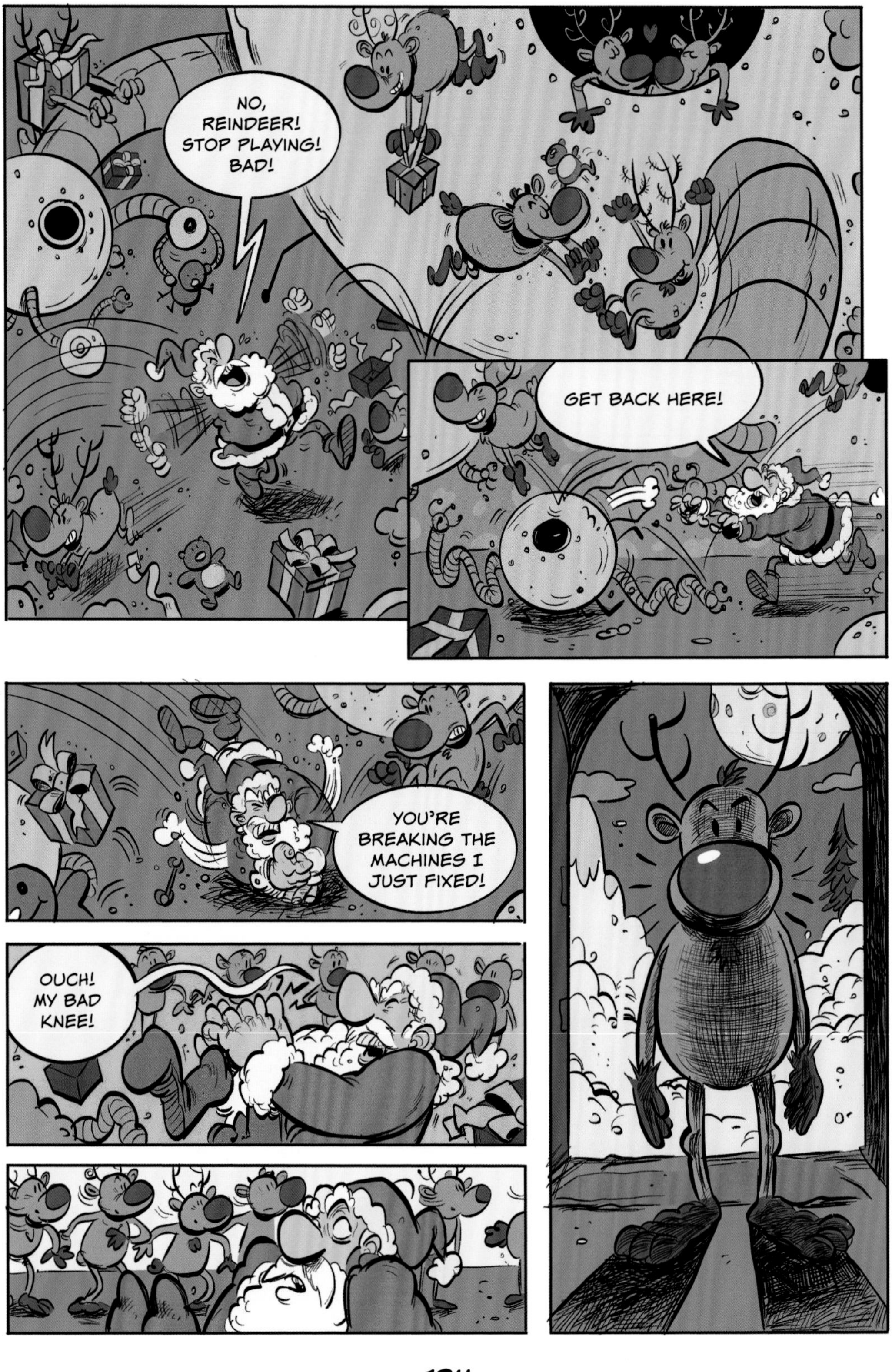
NO, REINDEER! STOP PLAYING! BAD!
GET BACK HERE!
YOU'RE BREAKING THE MACHINES I JUST FIXED!
OUCH! MY BAD KNEE!

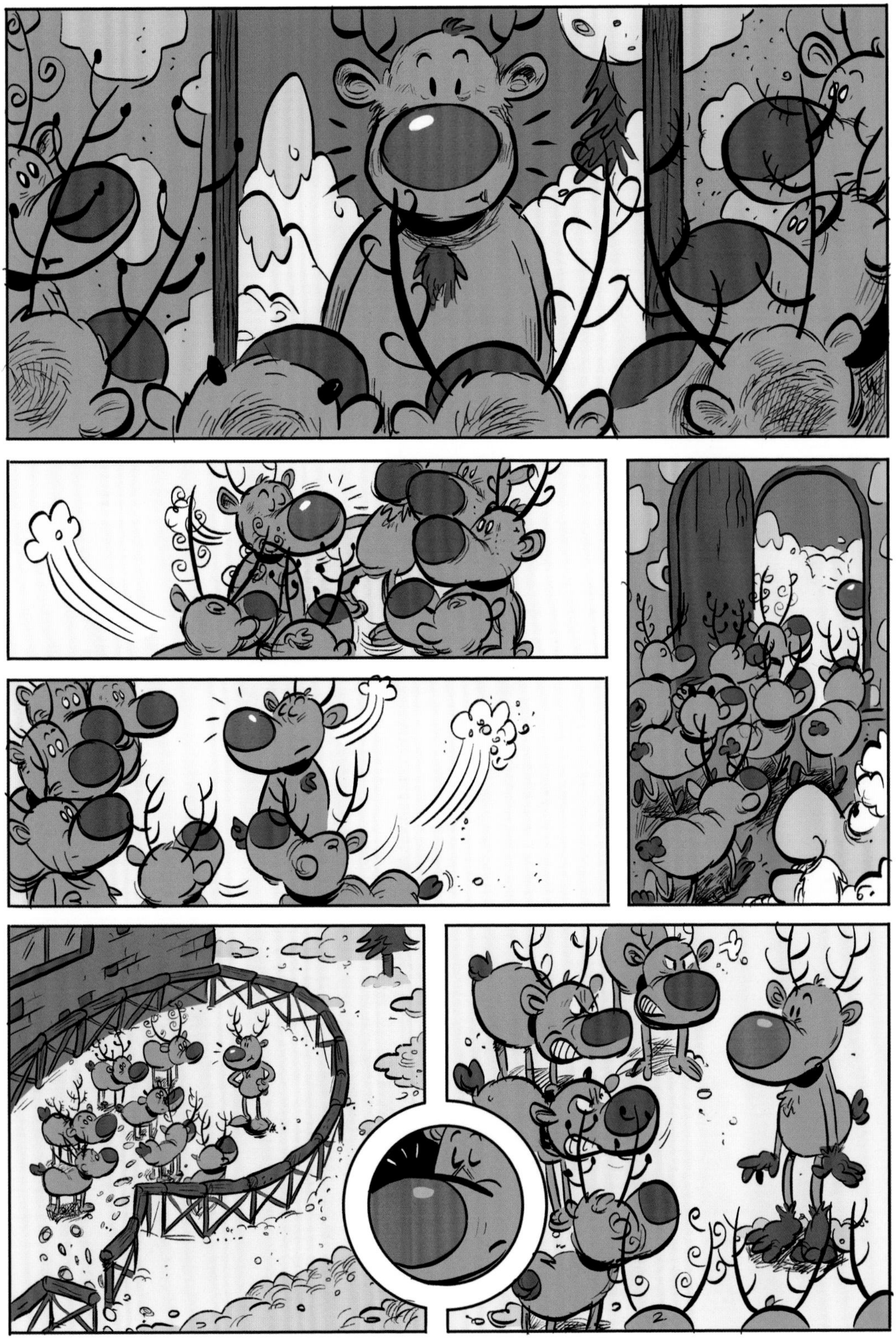

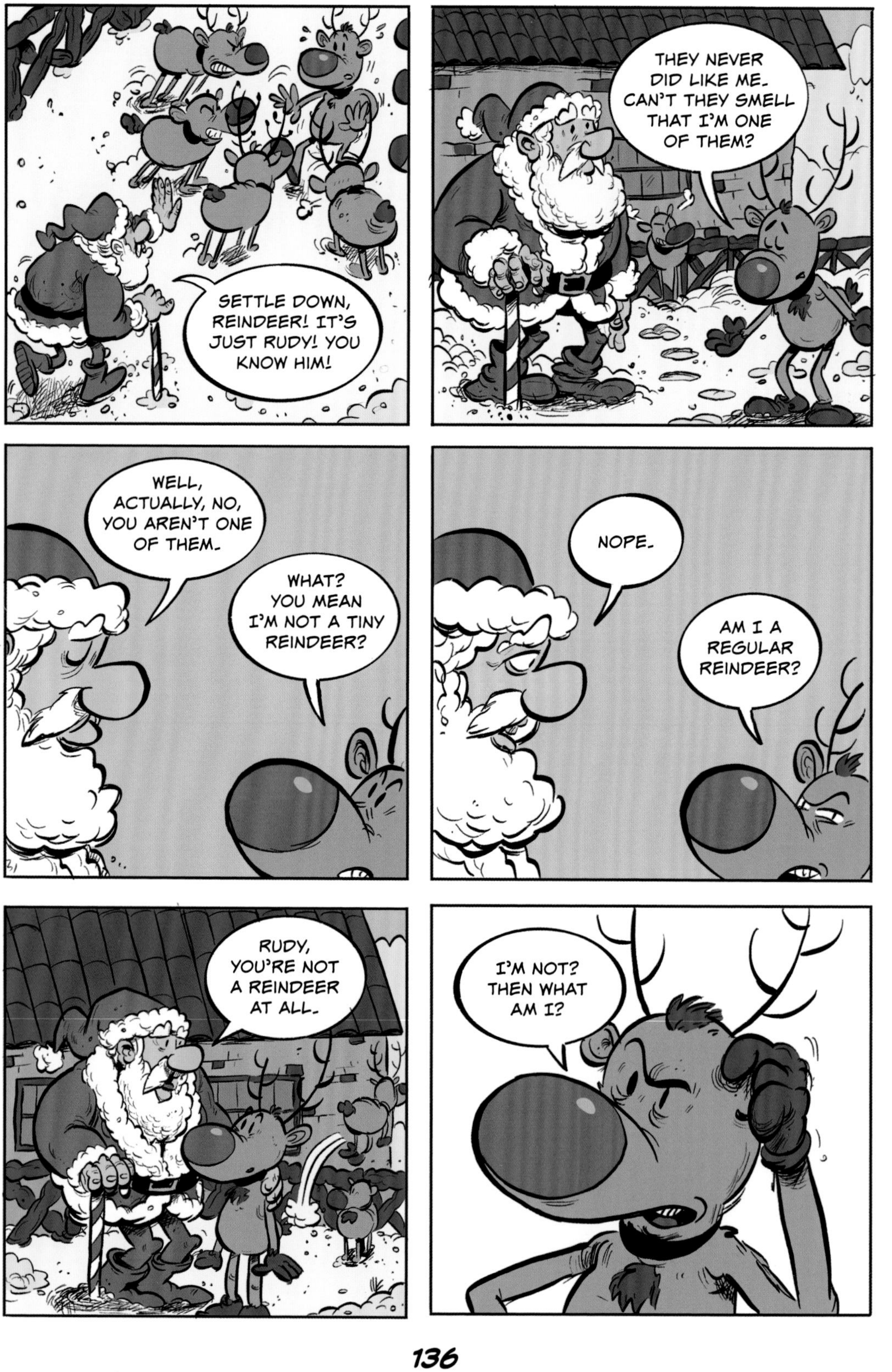
SETTLE DOWN, REINDEER! IT'S JUST RUDY! YOU KNOW HIM!
THEY NEVER DID LIKE ME. CAN'T THEY SMELL THAT I'M ONE OF THEM?
WELL, ACTUALLY, NO, YOU AREN'T ONE OF THEM.
WHAT? YOU MEAN I'M NOT A TINY REINDEER?
NOPE.
AM I A REGULAR REINDEER?
RUDY, YOU'RE NOT A REINDEER AT ALL.
I'M NOT? THEN WHAT AM I?

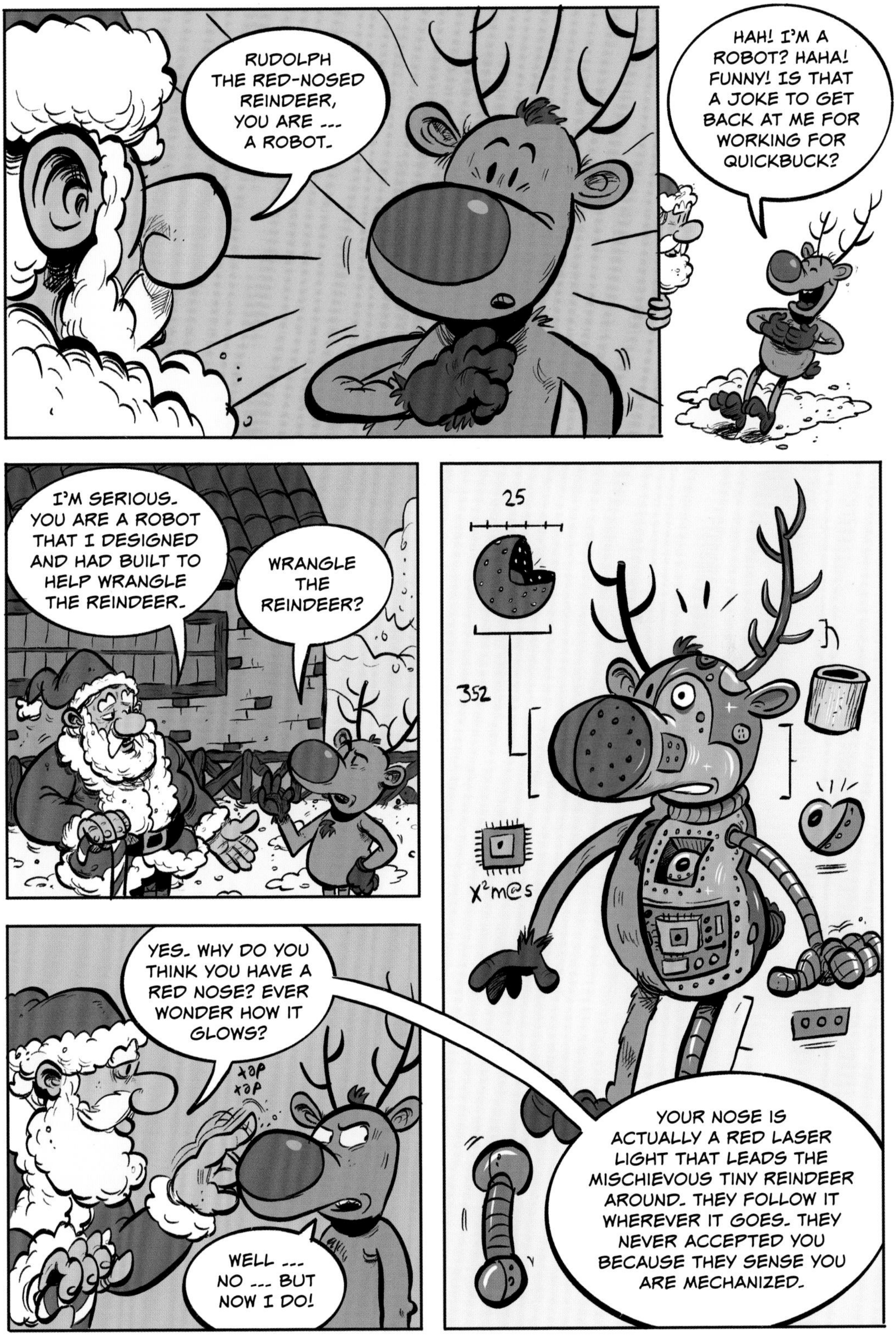
RUDOLPH THE RED-NOSED REINDEER, YOU ARE --- A ROBOT.
HAH! I'M A ROBOT? HAHA! FUNNY! IS THAT A JOKE TO GET BACK AT ME FOR WORKING FOR QUICKBUCK?
I'M SERIOUS. YOU ARE A ROBOT THAT I DESIGNED AND HAD BUILT TO HELP WRANGLE THE REINDEER.
WRANGLE THE REINDEER?
25
352
X²m@s
YES. WHY DO YOU THINK YOU HAVE A RED NOSE? EVER WONDER HOW IT GLOWS?
WELL --- NO --- BUT NOW I DO!
YOUR NOSE IS ACTUALLY A RED LASER LIGHT THAT LEADS THE MISCHIEVOUS TINY REINDEER AROUND. THEY FOLLOW IT WHEREVER IT GOES. THEY NEVER ACCEPTED YOU BECAUSE THEY SENSE YOU ARE MECHANIZED.

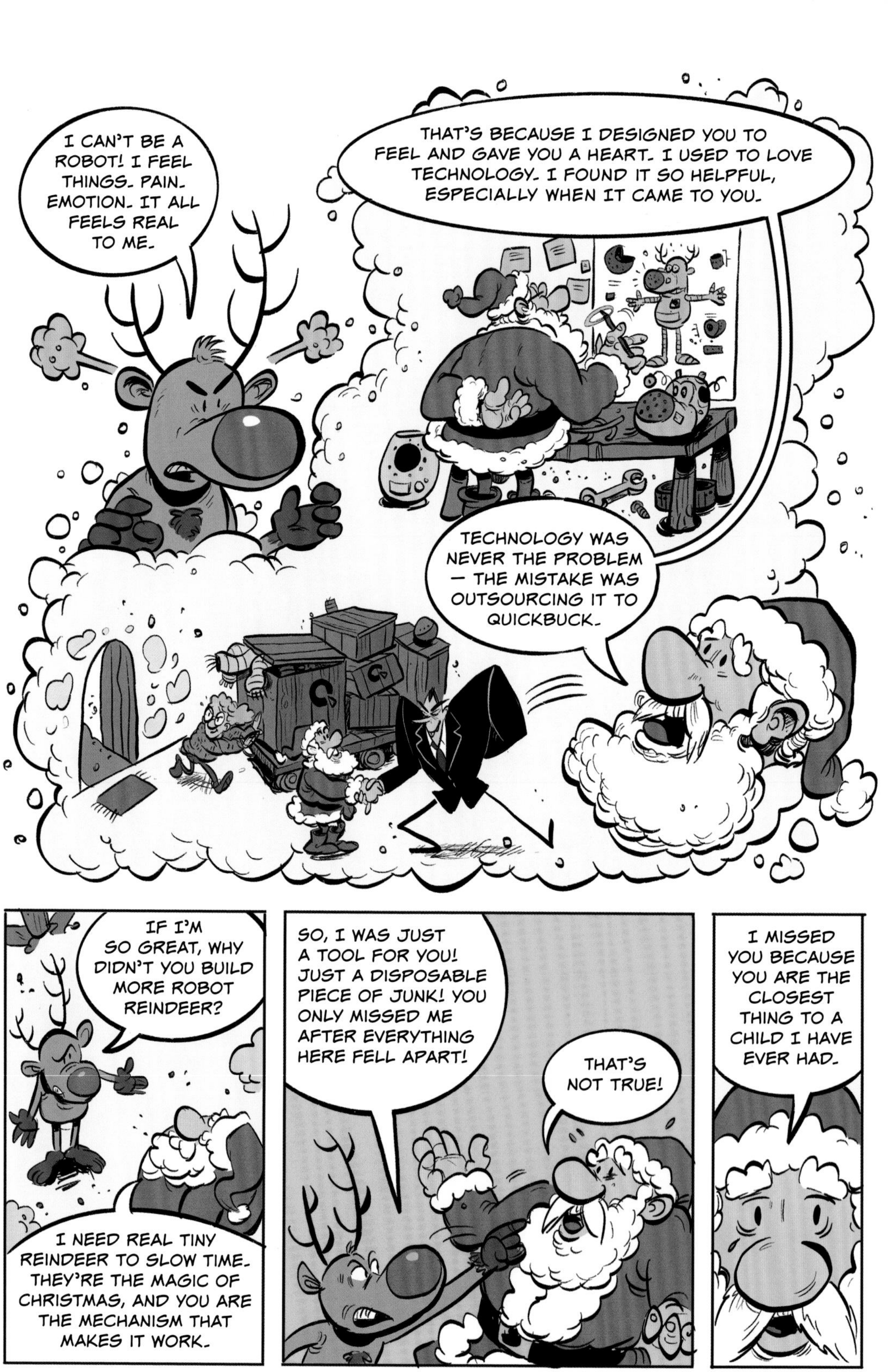
I CAN'T BE A ROBOT! I FEEL THINGS. PAIN. EMOTION. IT ALL FEELS REAL TO ME.
THAT'S BECAUSE I DESIGNED YOU TO FEEL AND GAVE YOU A HEART. I USED TO LOVE TECHNOLOGY. I FOUND IT SO HELPFUL, ESPECIALLY WHEN IT CAME TO YOU.
TECHNOLOGY WAS NEVER THE PROBLEM — THE MISTAKE WAS OUTSOURCING IT TO QUICKBUCK.
IF I'M SO GREAT, WHY DIDN'T YOU BUILD MORE ROBOT REINDEER?
I NEED REAL TINY REINDEER TO SLOW TIME. THEY'RE THE MAGIC OF CHRISTMAS, AND YOU ARE THE MECHANISM THAT MAKES IT WORK.
SO, I WAS JUST A TOOL FOR YOU! JUST A DISPOSABLE PIECE OF JUNK! YOU ONLY MISSED ME AFTER EVERYTHING HERE FELL APART!
THAT'S NOT TRUE!
I MISSED YOU BECAUSE YOU ARE THE CLOSEST THING TO A CHILD I HAVE EVER HAD.

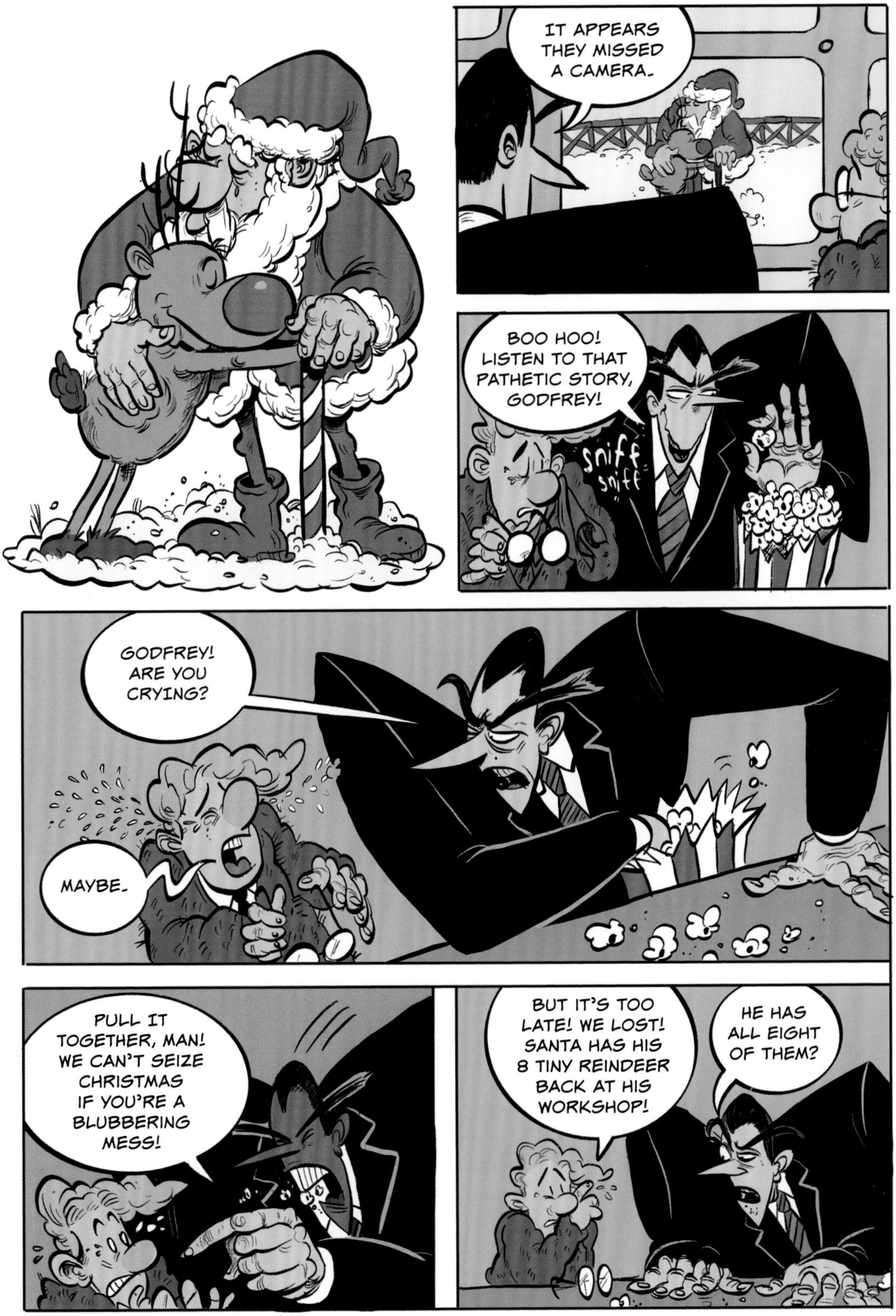
IT APPEARS THEY MISSED A CAMERA.
BOO HOO! LISTEN TO THAT PATHETIC STORY, GODFREY!
sniff sniff
GODFREY! ARE YOU CRYING?
MAYBE.
PULL IT TOGETHER, MAN! WE CAN'T SEIZE CHRISTMAS IF YOU'RE A BLUBBERING MESS!
BUT IT'S TOO LATE! WE LOST! SANTA HAS HIS 8 TINY REINDEER BACK AT HIS WORKSHOP!
HE HAS ALL EIGHT OF THEM?

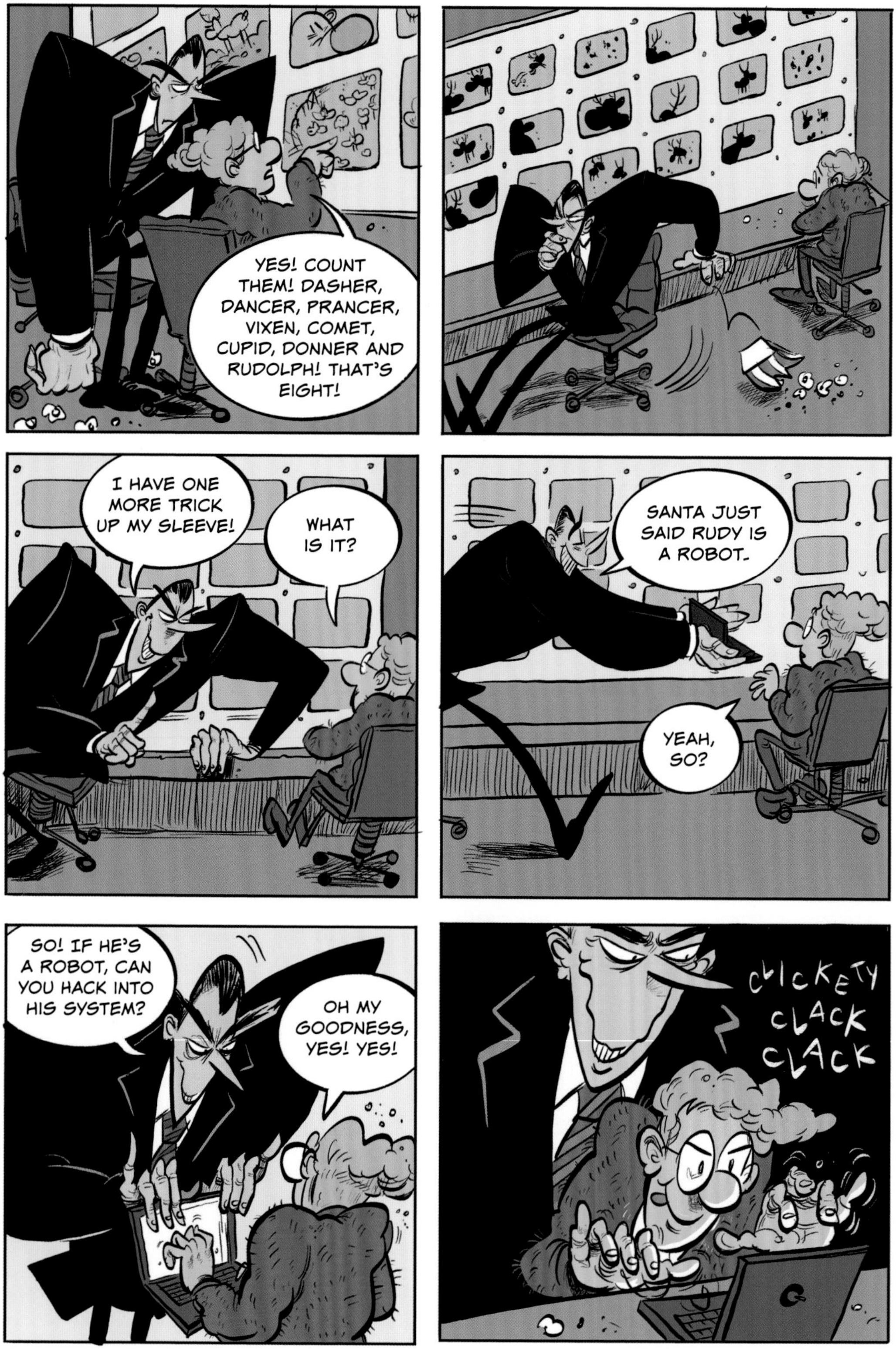
YES! COUNT THEM! DASHER, DANCER, PRANCER, VIXEN, COMET, CUPID, DONNER AND RUDOLPH! THAT'S EIGHT!
I HAVE ONE MORE TRICK UP MY SLEEVE!
WHAT IS IT?
SANTA JUST SAID RUDY IS A ROBOT.
YEAH, SO?
SO! IF HE'S A ROBOT, CAN YOU HACK INTO HIS SYSTEM?
OH MY GOODNESS, YES! YES!
CLICKETY CLACK CLACK

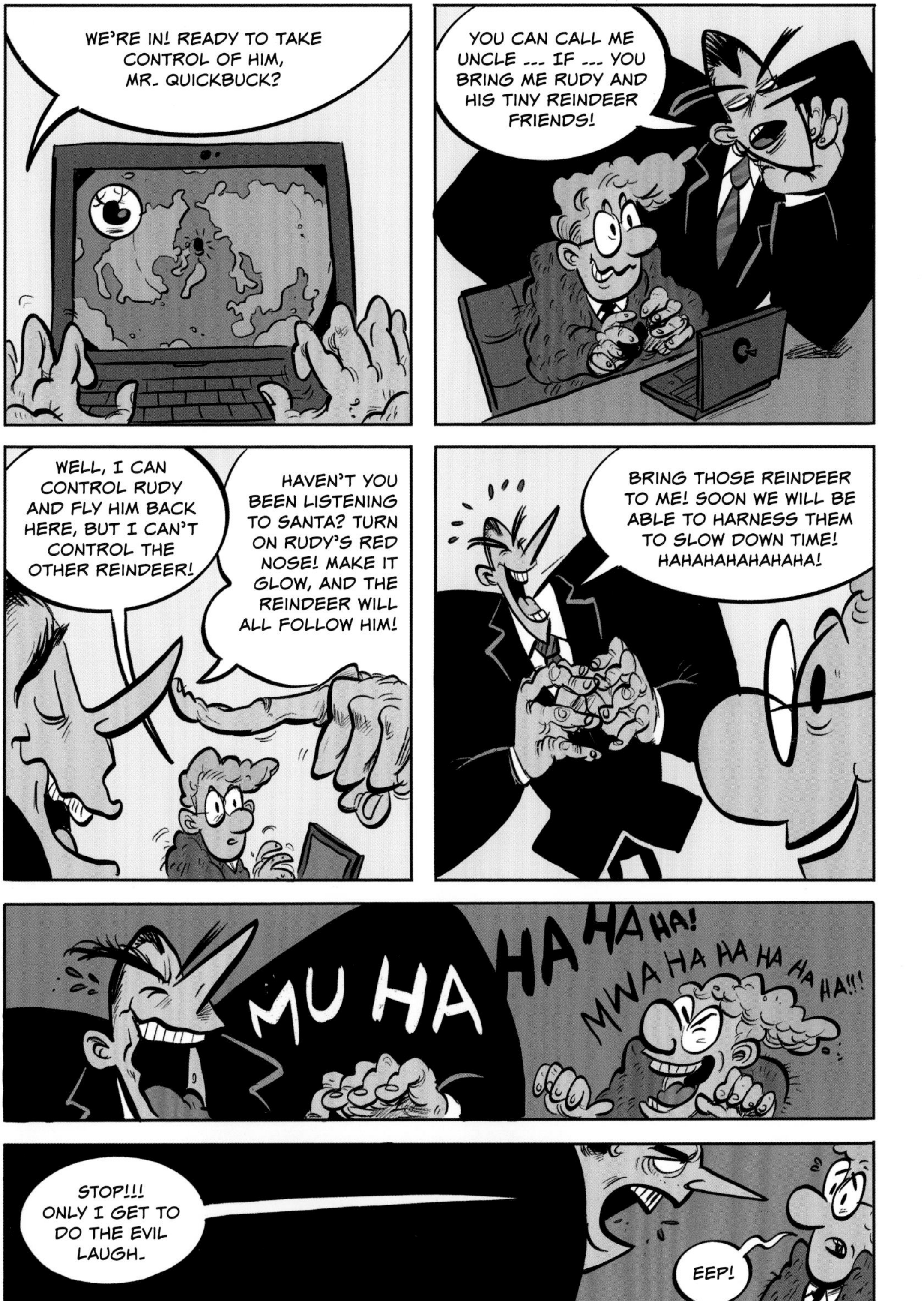
WE'RE IN! READY TO TAKE CONTROL OF HIM, MR. QUICKBUCK?
YOU CAN CALL ME UNCLE ... IF ... YOU BRING ME RUDY AND HIS TINY REINDEER FRIENDS!
WELL, I CAN CONTROL RUDY AND FLY HIM BACK HERE, BUT I CAN'T CONTROL THE OTHER REINDEER!
HAVEN'T YOU BEEN LISTENING TO SANTA? TURN ON RUDY'S RED NOSE! MAKE IT GLOW, AND THE REINDEER WILL ALL FOLLOW HIM!
BRING THOSE REINDEER TO ME! SOON WE WILL BE ABLE TO HARNESS THEM TO SLOW DOWN TIME! HAHAHAHAHAHAHA!
MU HA HA HA HA!
MWA HA HA HA HA HA HA!!!
STOP!!! ONLY I GET TO DO THE EVIL LAUGH.
EEP!

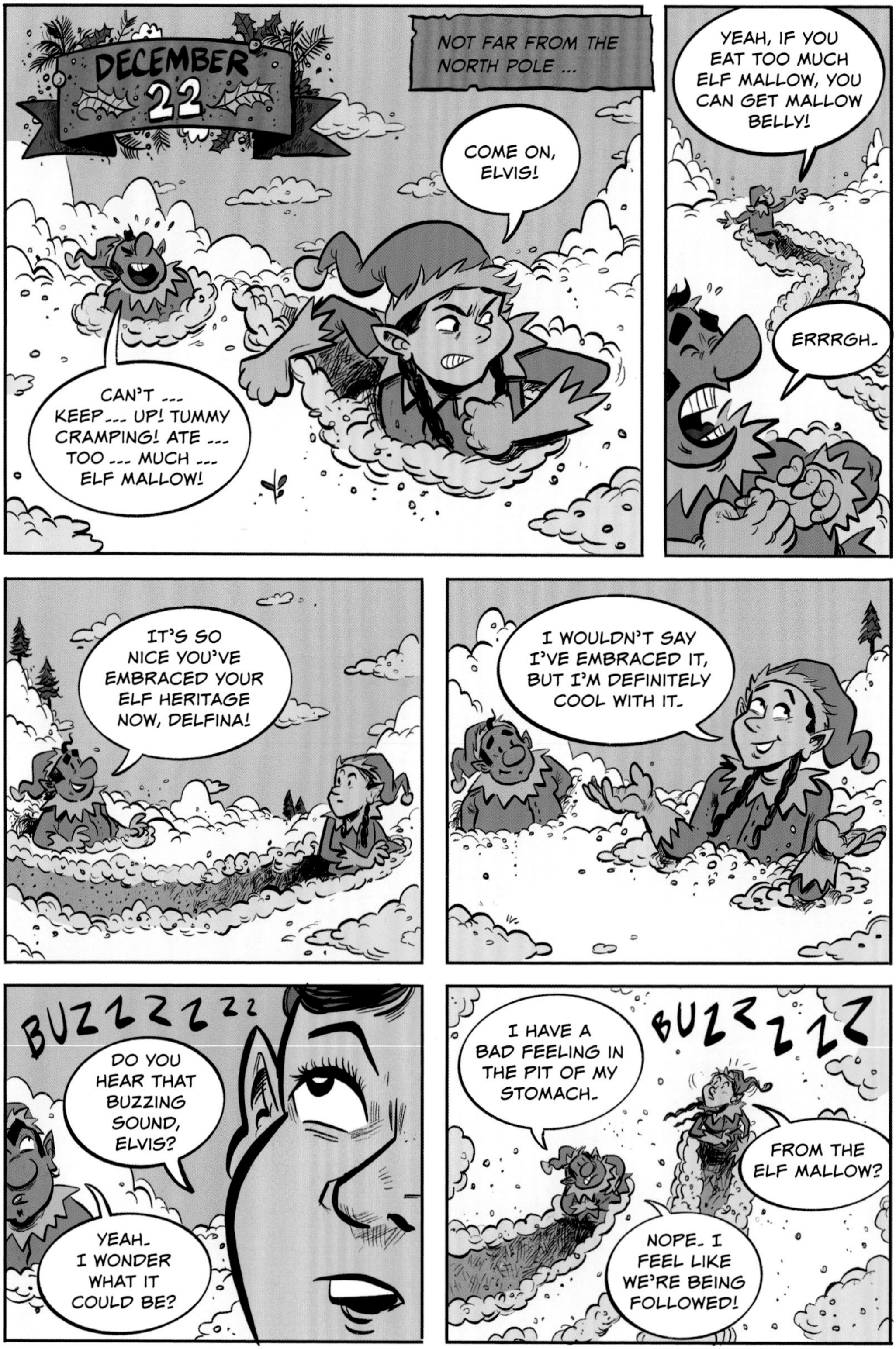
DECEMBER 22
NOT FAR FROM THE NORTH POLE ...
COME ON, ELVIS!
CAN'T ... KEEP... UP! TUMMY CRAMPING! ATE ... TOO ... MUCH ... ELF MALLOW!
YEAH, IF YOU EAT TOO MUCH ELF MALLOW, YOU CAN GET MALLOW BELLY!
ERRRGH.
IT'S SO NICE YOU'VE EMBRACED YOUR ELF HERITAGE NOW, DELFINA!
I WOULDN'T SAY I'VE EMBRACED IT, BUT I'M DEFINITELY COOL WITH IT.
BUZZZZZZZ
DO YOU HEAR THAT BUZZING SOUND, ELVIS?
YEAH. I WONDER WHAT IT COULD BE?
I HAVE A BAD FEELING IN THE PIT OF MY STOMACH.
BUZZZZZ
FROM THE ELF MALLOW?
NOPE. I FEEL LIKE WE'RE BEING FOLLOWED!

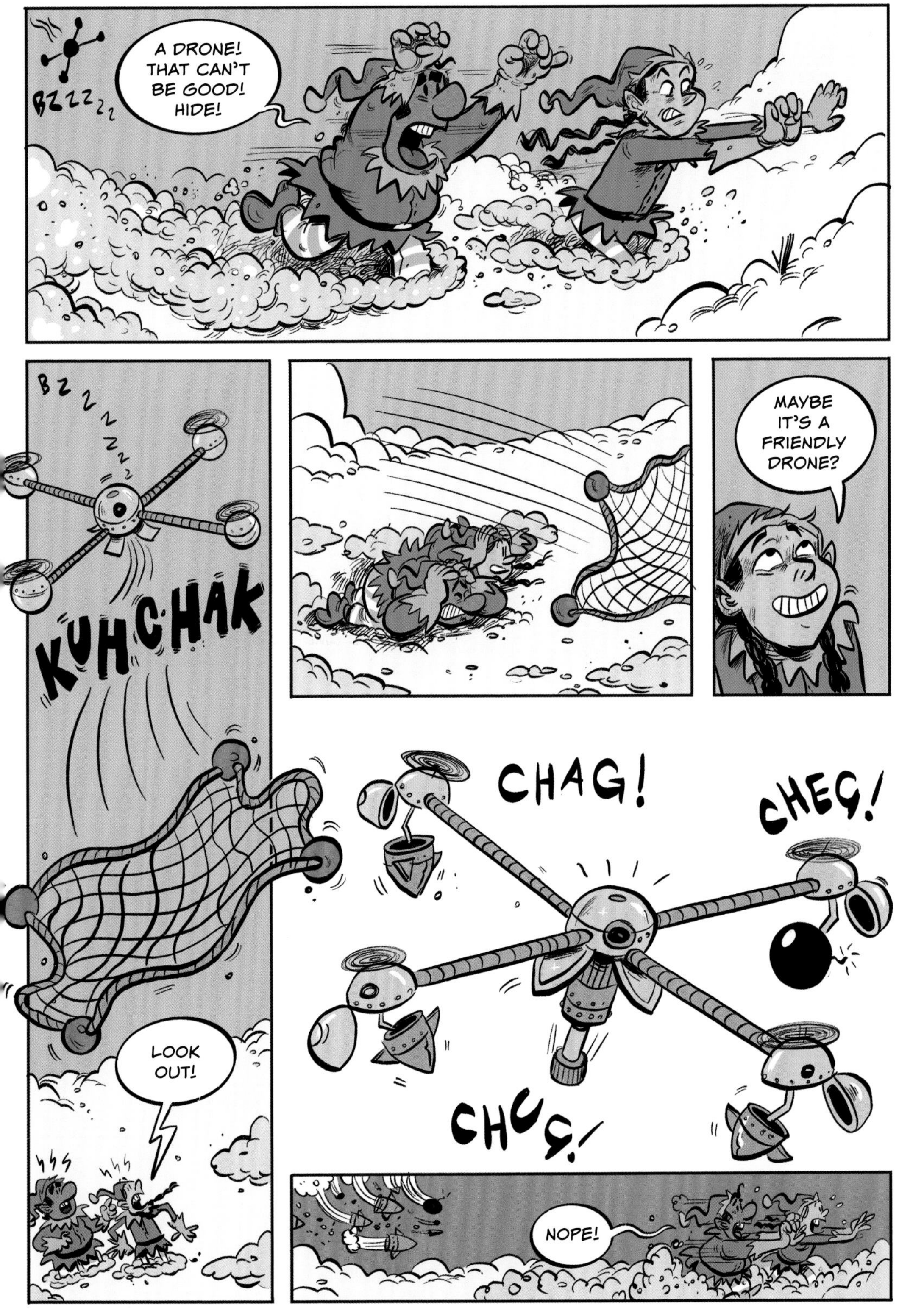
BZZZZZ
A DRONE! THAT CAN'T BE GOOD! HIDE!
MAYBE IT'S A FRIENDLY DRONE?
BZZZZZ
KUHCHAK
LOOK OUT!
CHAG!
CHEG!
CHUG!
NOPE!

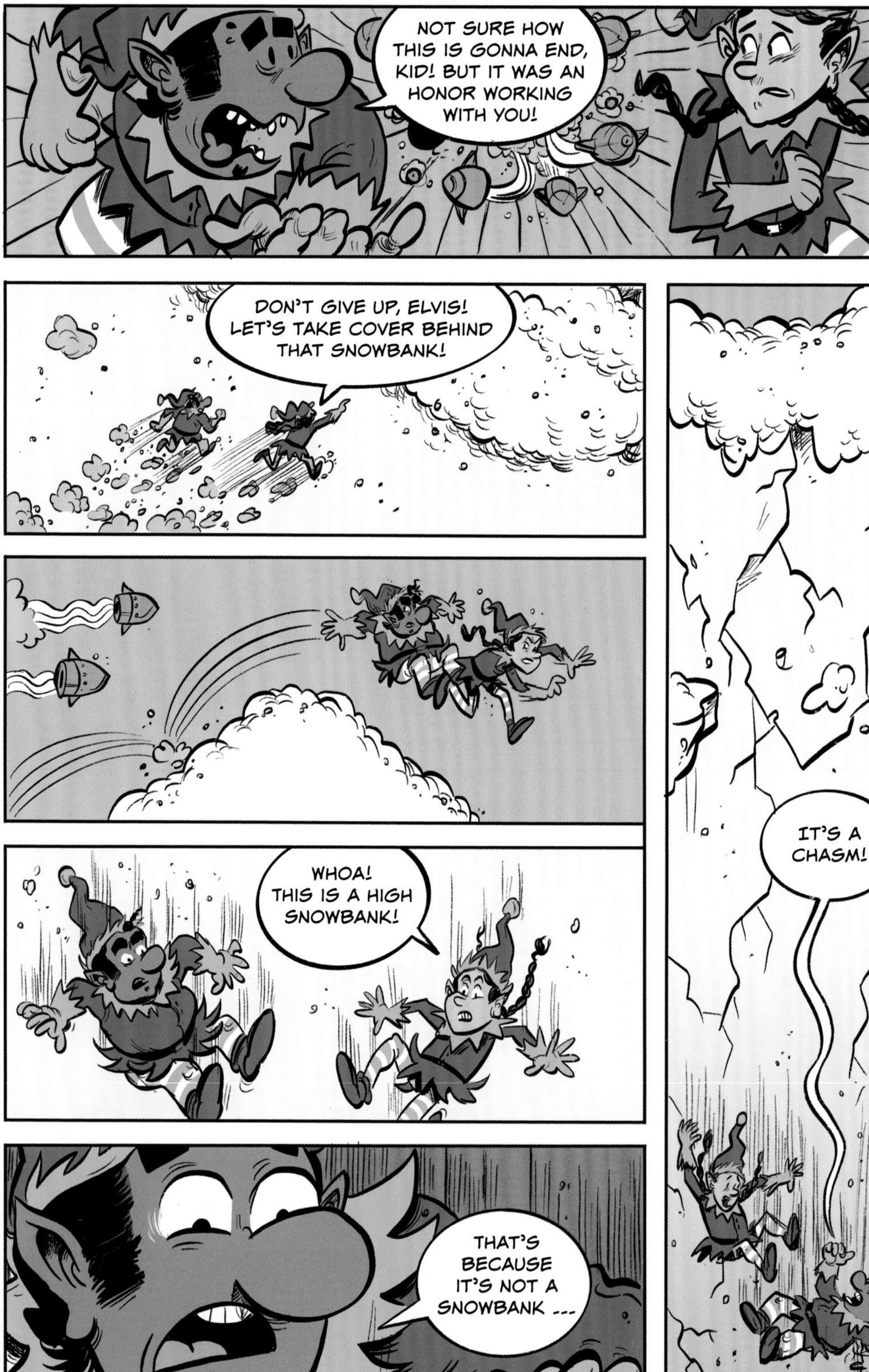
NOT SURE HOW THIS IS GONNA END, KID! BUT IT WAS AN HONOR WORKING WITH YOU!
DON'T GIVE UP, ELVIS! LET'S TAKE COVER BEHIND THAT SNOWBANK!
WHOA! THIS IS A HIGH SNOWBANK!
THAT'S BECAUSE IT'S NOT A SNOWBANK ...
IT'S A CHASM!

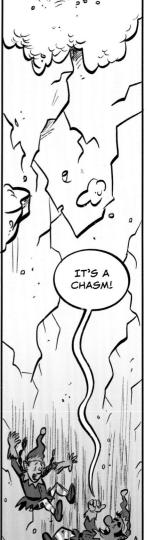

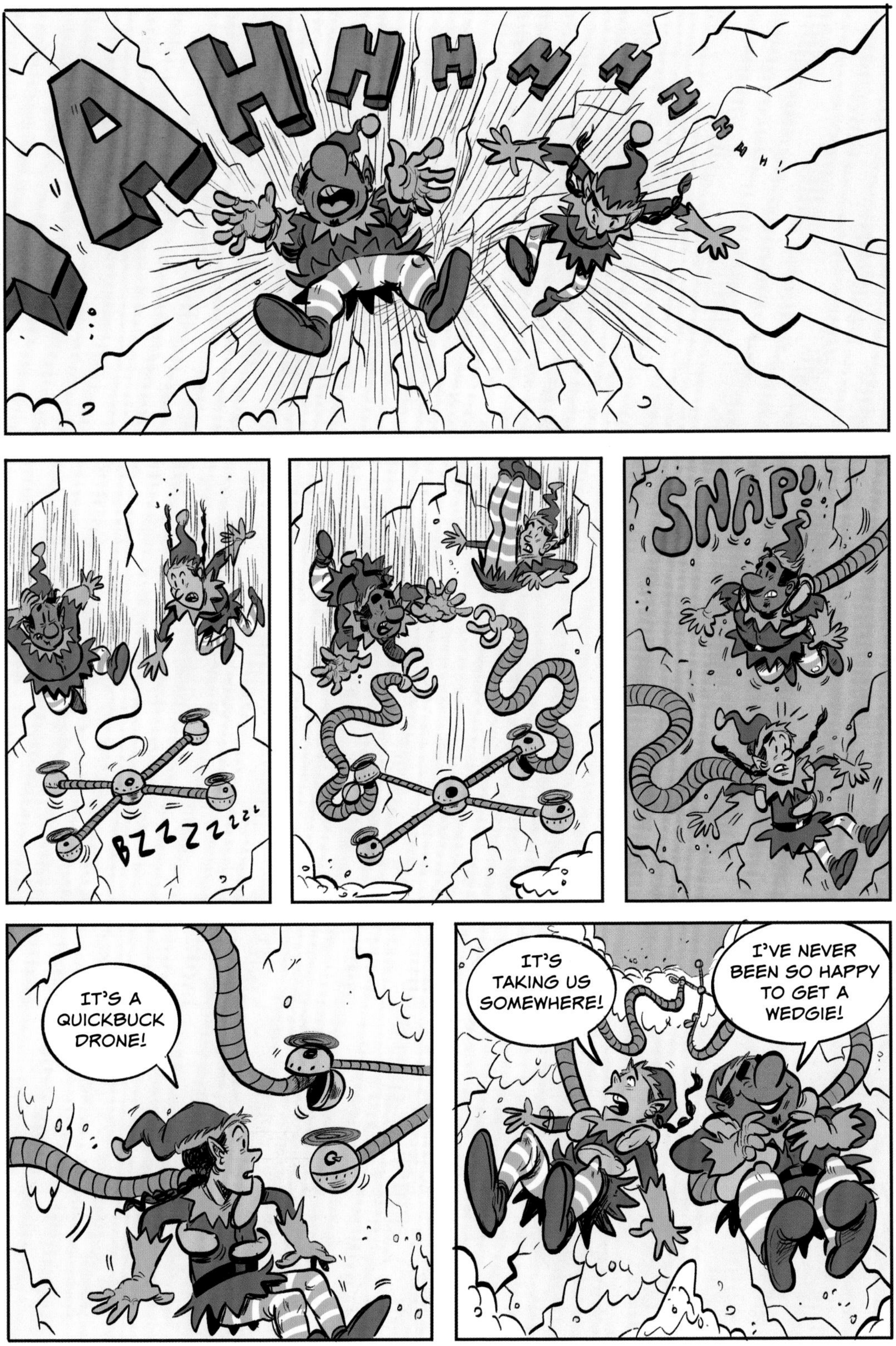
AHHHHHHHHH!
SNAP!
BZZZZZzzz
IT'S A QUICKBUCK DRONE!
IT'S TAKING US SOMEWHERE!
I'VE NEVER BEEN SO HAPPY TO GET A WEDGIE!

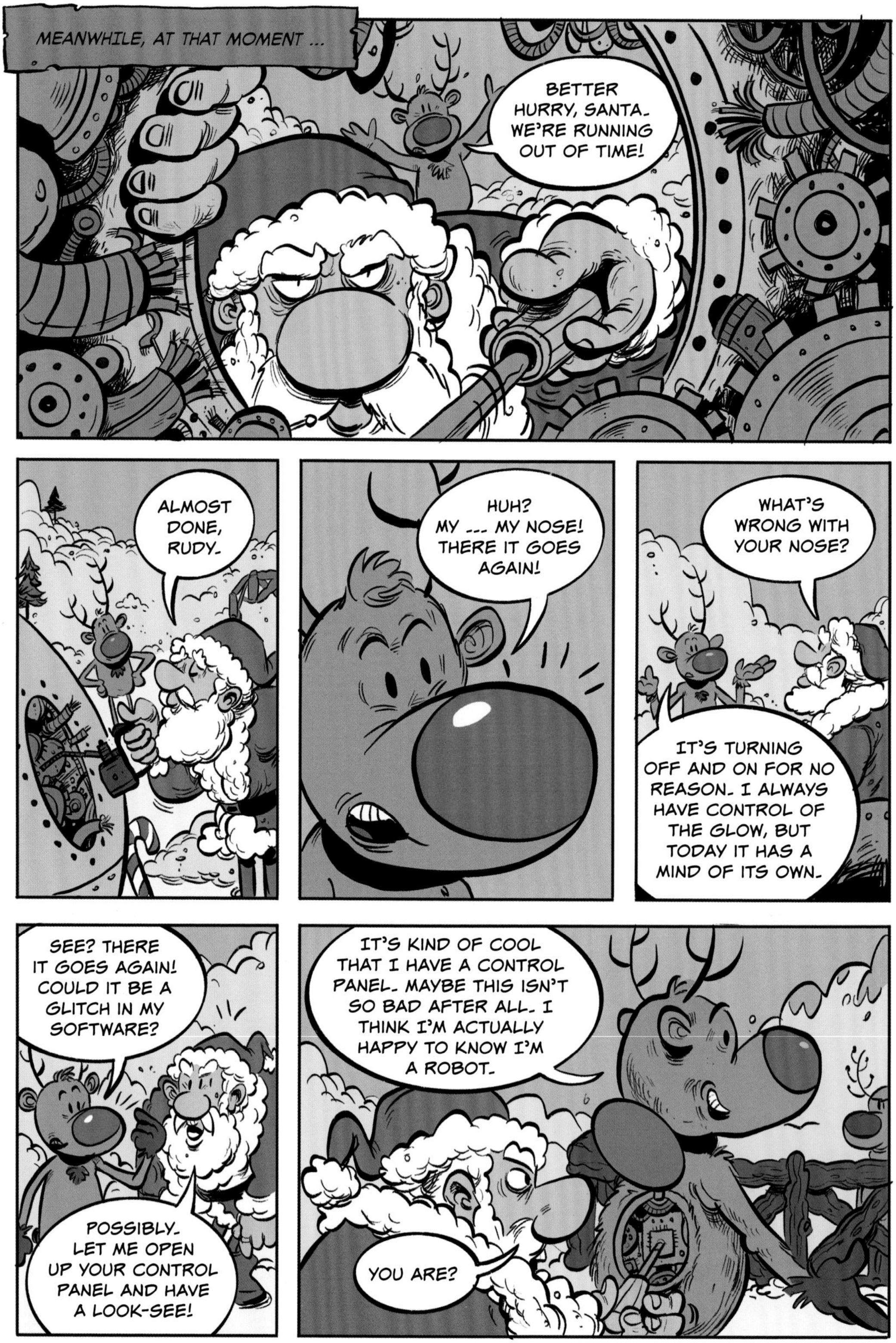
MEANWHILE, AT THAT MOMENT ...
BETTER HURRY, SANTA. WE'RE RUNNING OUT OF TIME!
ALMOST DONE, RUDY.
HUH? MY ... MY NOSE! THERE IT GOES AGAIN!
WHAT'S WRONG WITH YOUR NOSE?
IT'S TURNING OFF AND ON FOR NO REASON. I ALWAYS HAVE CONTROL OF THE GLOW, BUT TODAY IT HAS A MIND OF ITS OWN.
SEE? THERE IT GOES AGAIN! COULD IT BE A GLITCH IN MY SOFTWARE?
POSSIBLY. LET ME OPEN UP YOUR CONTROL PANEL AND HAVE A LOOK-SEE!
IT'S KIND OF COOL THAT I HAVE A CONTROL PANEL. MAYBE THIS ISN'T SO BAD AFTER ALL. I THINK I'M ACTUALLY HAPPY TO KNOW I'M A ROBOT.
YOU ARE?

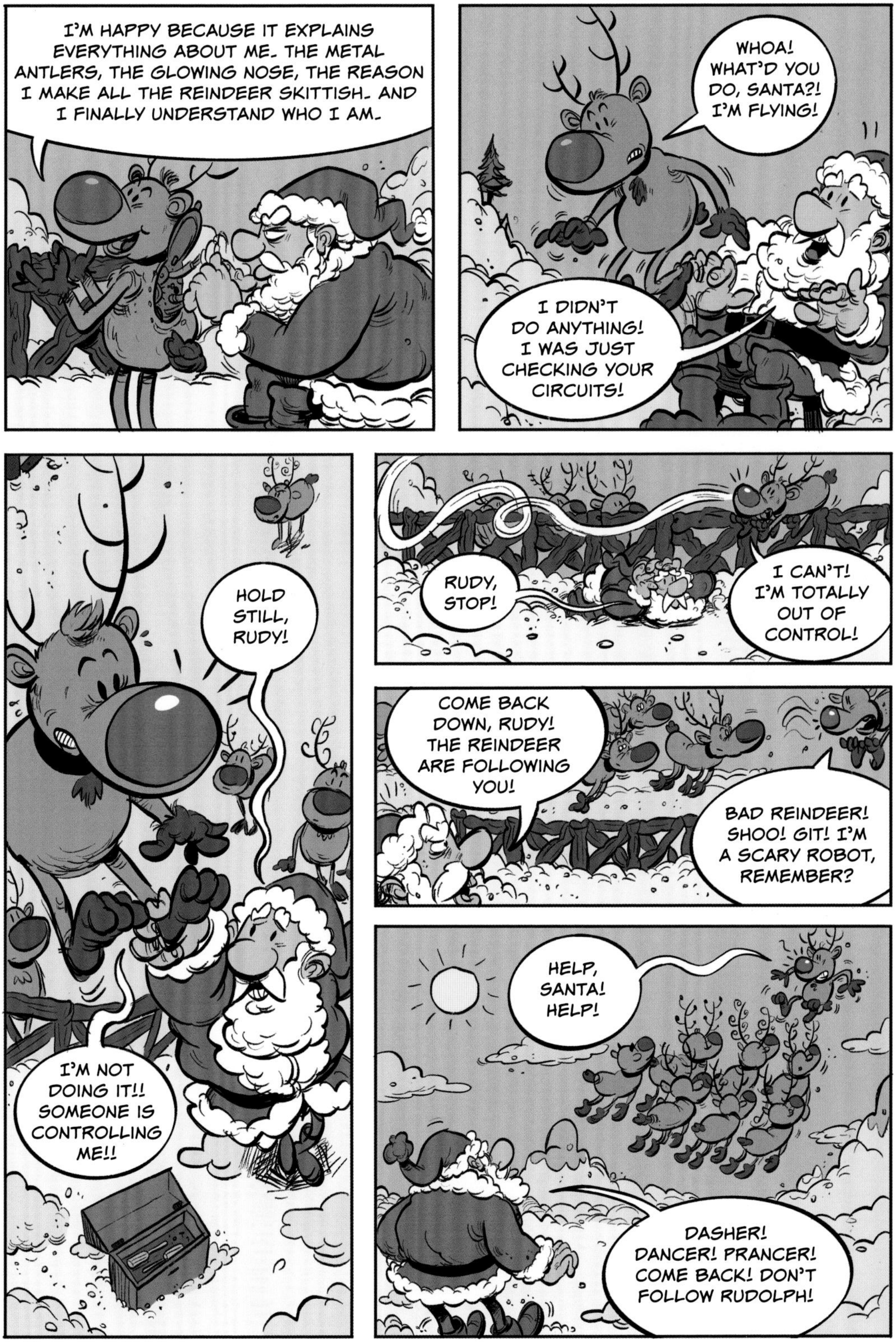
I'M HAPPY BECAUSE IT EXPLAINS EVERYTHING ABOUT ME. THE METAL ANTLERS, THE GLOWING NOSE, THE REASON I MAKE ALL THE REINDEER SKITTISH. AND I FINALLY UNDERSTAND WHO I AM.
WHOA! WHAT'D YOU DO, SANTA?! I'M FLYING!
I DIDN'T DO ANYTHING! I WAS JUST CHECKING YOUR CIRCUITS!
HOLD STILL, RUDY!
I'M NOT DOING IT!! SOMEONE IS CONTROLLING ME!!
RUDY, STOP!
I CAN'T! I'M TOTALLY OUT OF CONTROL!
COME BACK DOWN, RUDY! THE REINDEER ARE FOLLOWING YOU!
BAD REINDEER! SHOO! GIT! I'M A SCARY ROBOT, REMEMBER?
HELP, SANTA! HELP!
DASHER! DANCER! PRANCER! COME BACK! DON'T FOLLOW RUDOLPH!

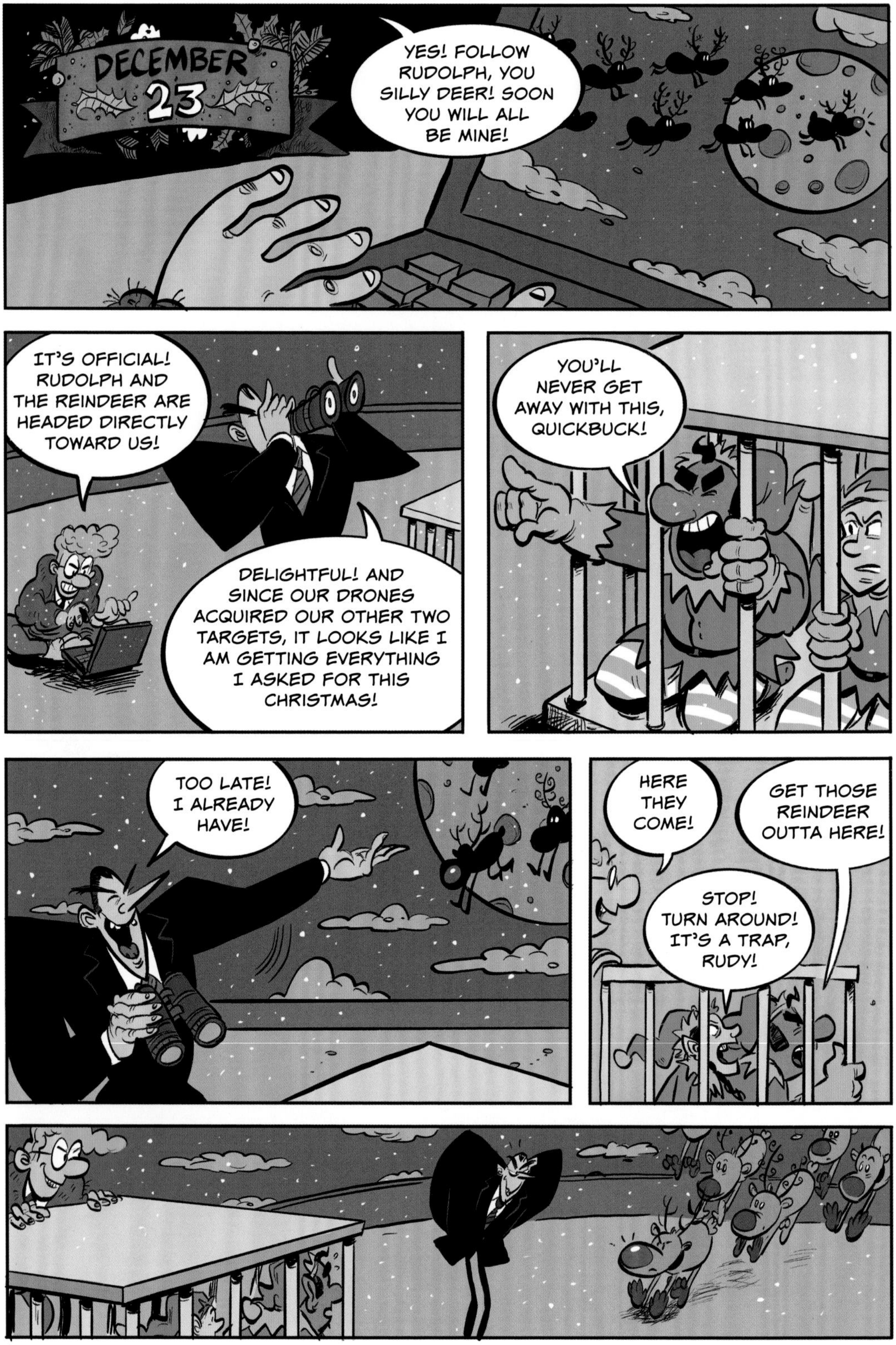
DECEMBER 23
YES! FOLLOW RUDOLPH, YOU SILLY DEER! SOON YOU WILL ALL BE MINE!
IT'S OFFICIAL! RUDOLPH AND THE REINDEER ARE HEADED DIRECTLY TOWARD US!
DELIGHTFUL! AND SINCE OUR DRONES ACQUIRED OUR OTHER TWO TARGETS, IT LOOKS LIKE I AM GETTING EVERYTHING I ASKED FOR THIS CHRISTMAS!
YOU'LL NEVER GET AWAY WITH THIS, QUICKBUCK!
TOO LATE! I ALREADY HAVE!
HERE THEY COME!
GET THOSE REINDEER OUTTA HERE!
STOP! TURN AROUND! IT'S A TRAP, RUDY!

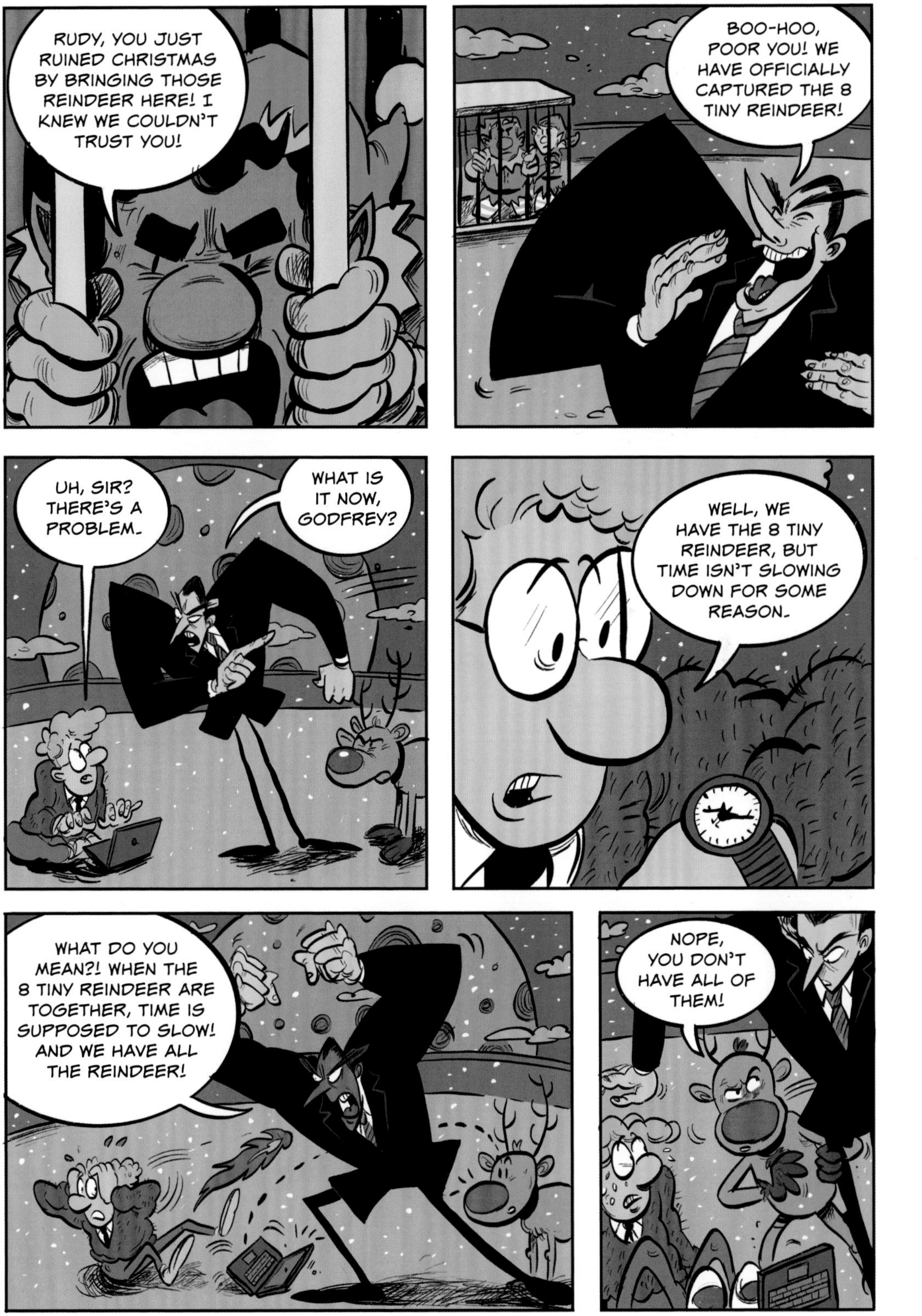
RUDY, YOU JUST RUINED CHRISTMAS BY BRINGING THOSE REINDEER HERE! I KNEW WE COULDN'T TRUST YOU!
BOO-HOO, POOR YOU! WE HAVE OFFICIALLY CAPTURED THE 8 TINY REINDEER!
UH, SIR? THERE'S A PROBLEM.
WHAT IS IT NOW, GODFREY?
WELL, WE HAVE THE 8 TINY REINDEER, BUT TIME ISN'T SLOWING DOWN FOR SOME REASON.
WHAT DO YOU MEAN?! WHEN THE 8 TINY REINDEER ARE TOGETHER, TIME IS SUPPOSED TO SLOW! AND WE HAVE ALL THE REINDEER!
NOPE, YOU DON'T HAVE ALL OF THEM!

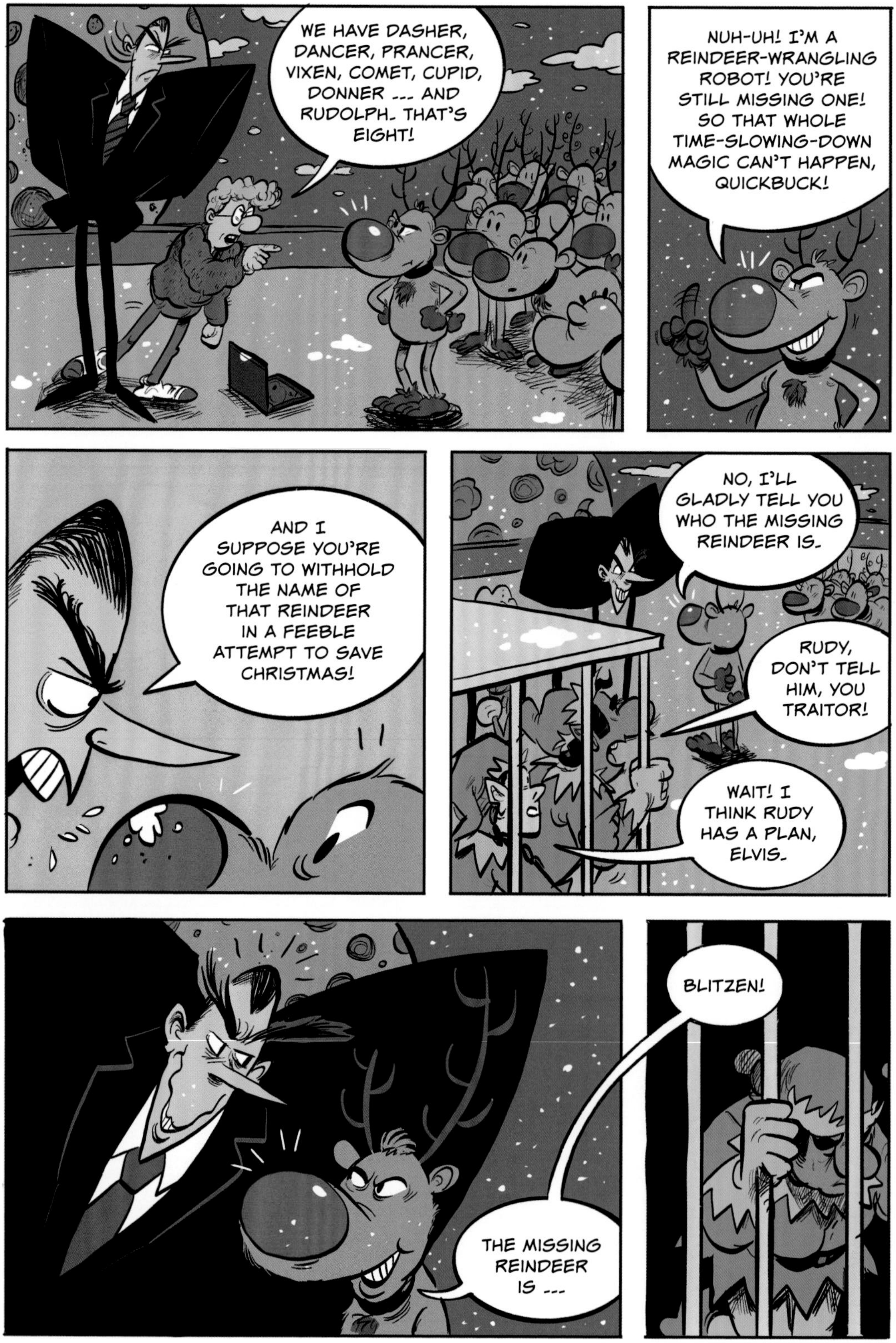
WE HAVE DASHER, DANCER, PRANCER, VIXEN, COMET, CUPID, DONNER --- AND RUDOLPH. THAT'S EIGHT!
NUH-UH! I'M A REINDEER-WRANGLING ROBOT! YOU'RE STILL MISSING ONE! SO THAT WHOLE TIME-SLOWING-DOWN MAGIC CAN'T HAPPEN, QUICKBUCK!
AND I SUPPOSE YOU'RE GOING TO WITHHOLD THE NAME OF THAT REINDEER IN A FEEBLE ATTEMPT TO SAVE CHRISTMAS!
NO, I'LL GLADLY TELL YOU WHO THE MISSING REINDEER IS.
RUDY, DON'T TELL HIM, YOU TRAITOR!
WAIT! I THINK RUDY HAS A PLAN, ELVIS.
THE MISSING REINDEER IS ---
BLITZEN!

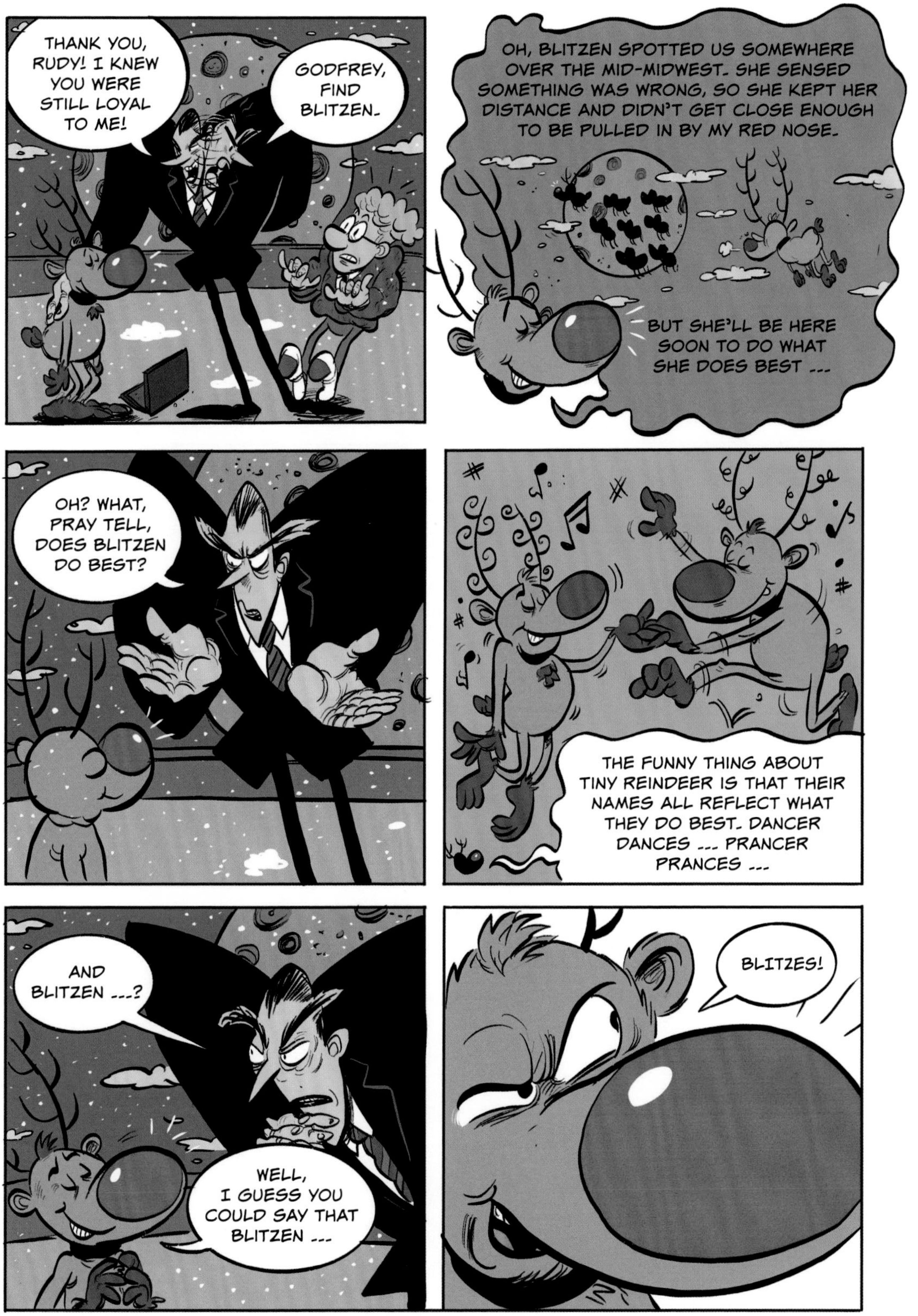
THANK YOU, RUDY! I KNEW YOU WERE STILL LOYAL TO ME!
GODFREY, FIND BLITZEN.
OH, BLITZEN SPOTTED US SOMEWHERE OVER THE MID-MIDWEST. SHE SENSED SOMETHING WAS WRONG, SO SHE KEPT HER DISTANCE AND DIDN'T GET CLOSE ENOUGH TO BE PULLED IN BY MY RED NOSE.
BUT SHE'LL BE HERE SOON TO DO WHAT SHE DOES BEST ...
OH? WHAT, PRAY TELL, DOES BLITZEN DO BEST?
THE FUNNY THING ABOUT TINY REINDEER IS THAT THEIR NAMES ALL REFLECT WHAT THEY DO BEST. DANCER DANCES ... PRANCER PRANCES ...
AND BLITZEN ...?
WELL, I GUESS YOU COULD SAY THAT BLITZEN ...
BLITZES!

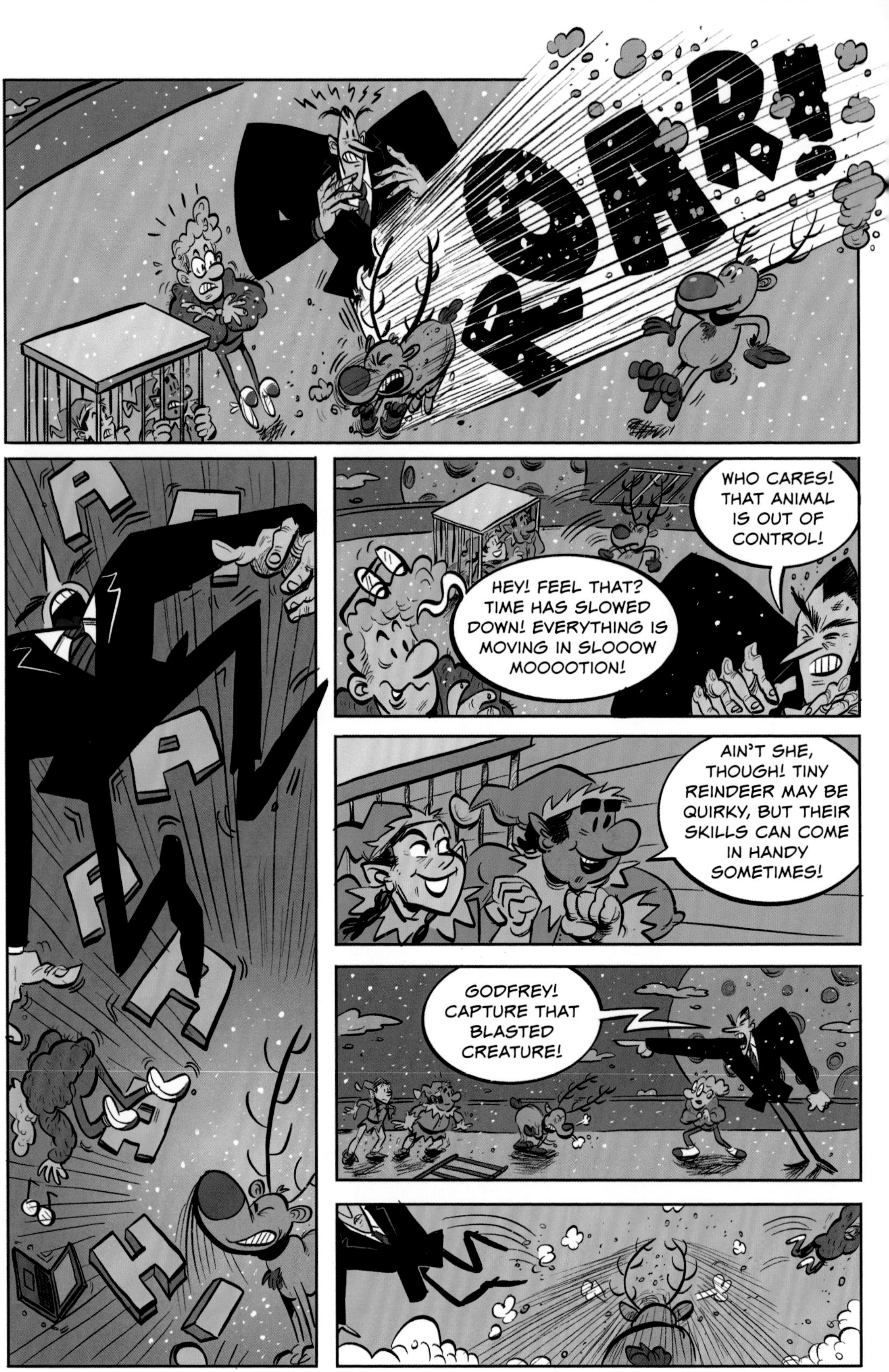
ROAR!
WHO CARES! THAT ANIMAL IS OUT OF CONTROL!
HEY! FEEL THAT? TIME HAS SLOWED DOWN! EVERYTHING IS MOVING IN SLOOOW MOOOOTION!
AIN'T SHE, THOUGH! TINY REINDEER MAY BE QUIRKY, BUT THEIR SKILLS CAN COME IN HANDY SOMETIMES!
GODFREY! CAPTURE THAT BLASTED CREATURE!

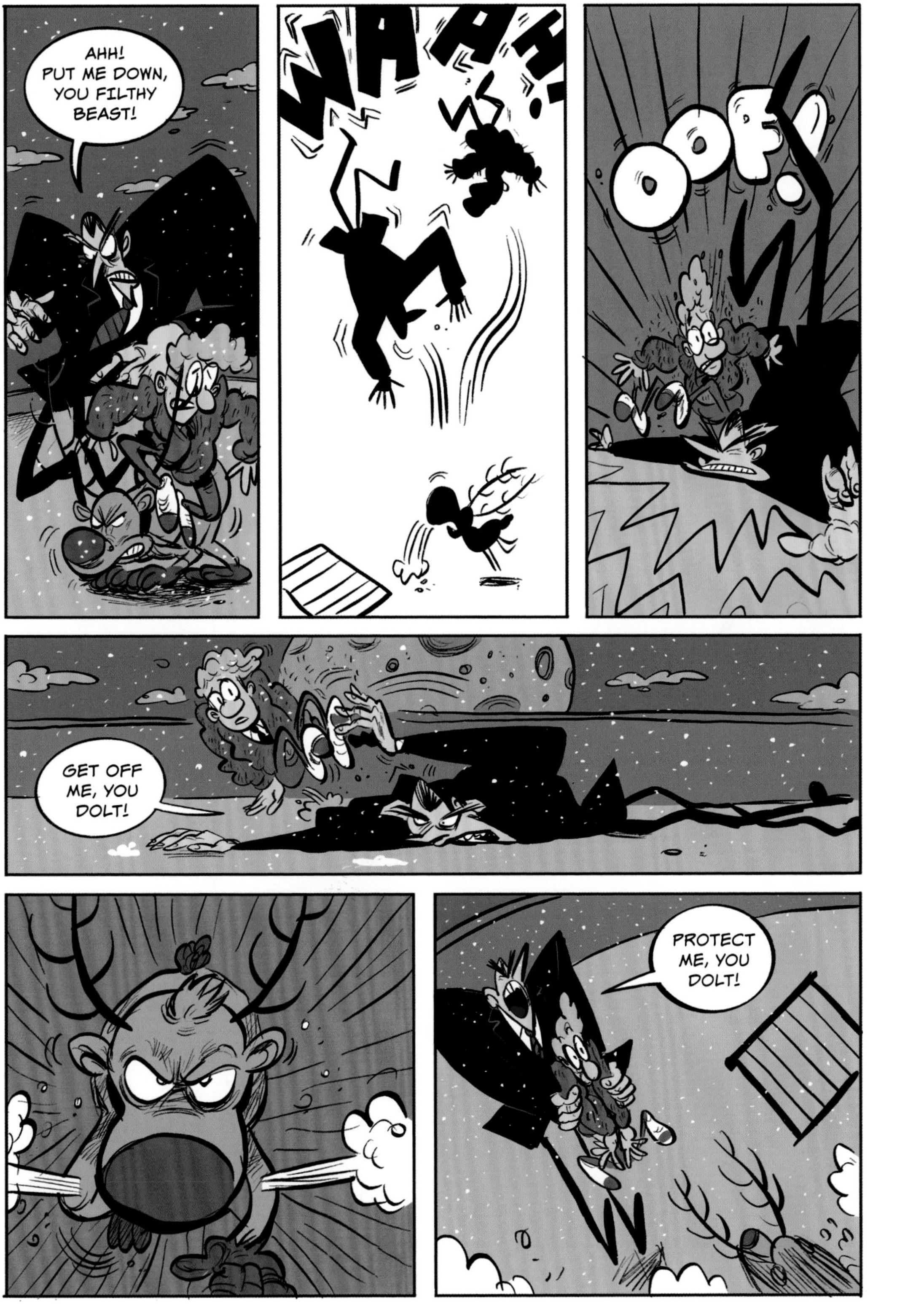
AHH! PUT ME DOWN, YOU FILTHY BEAST!
WAAH!
OOF!
GET OFF ME, YOU DOLT!
PROTECT ME, YOU DOLT!

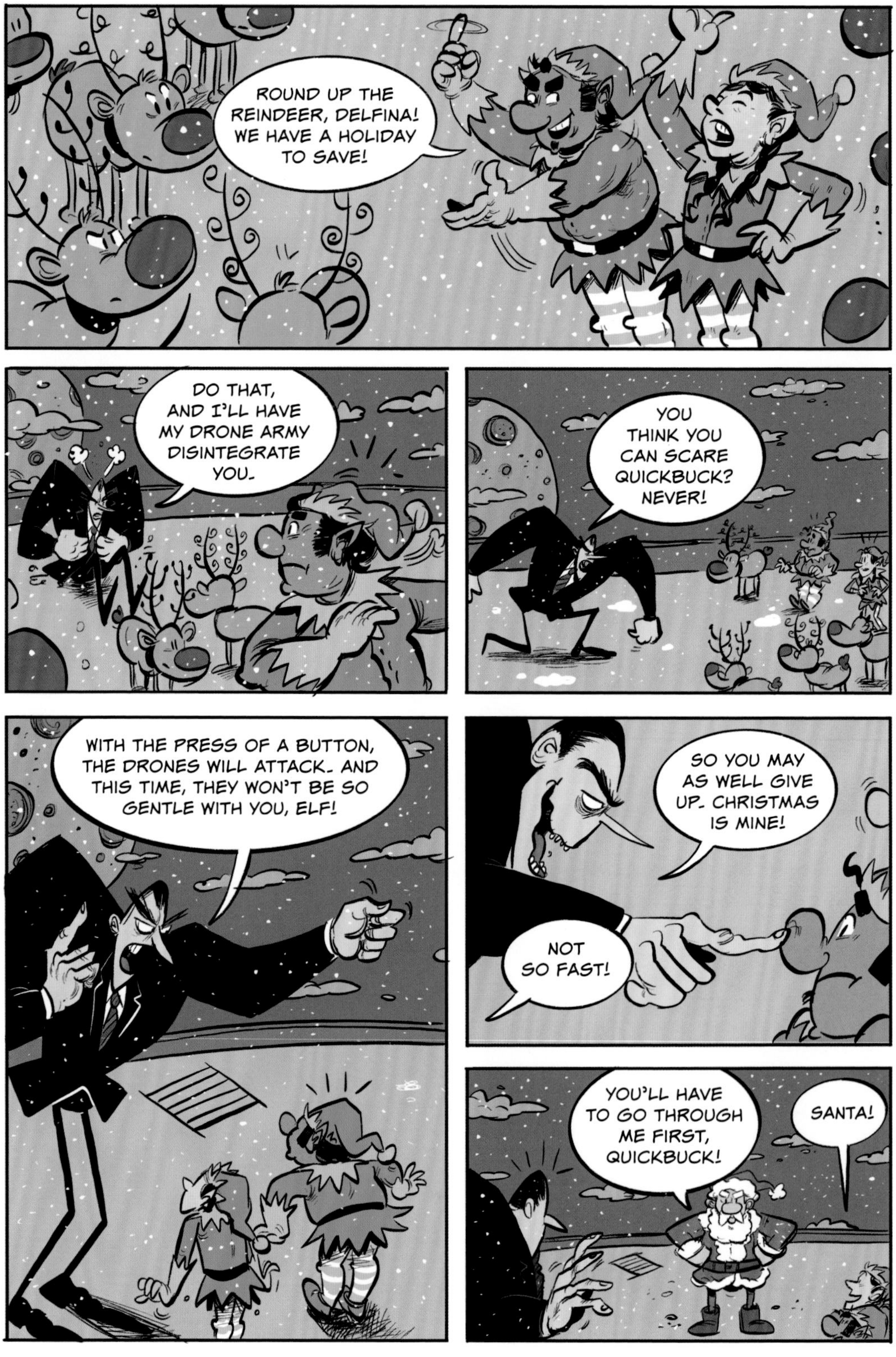
ROUND UP THE REINDEER, DELFINA! WE HAVE A HOLIDAY TO SAVE!
DO THAT, AND I'LL HAVE MY DRONE ARMY DISINTEGRATE YOU.
YOU THINK YOU CAN SCARE QUICKBUCK? NEVER!
WITH THE PRESS OF A BUTTON, THE DRONES WILL ATTACK. AND THIS TIME, THEY WON'T BE SO GENTLE WITH YOU, ELF!
SO YOU MAY AS WELL GIVE UP. CHRISTMAS IS MINE!
NOT SO FAST!
YOU'LL HAVE TO GO THROUGH ME FIRST, QUICKBUCK!
SANTA!

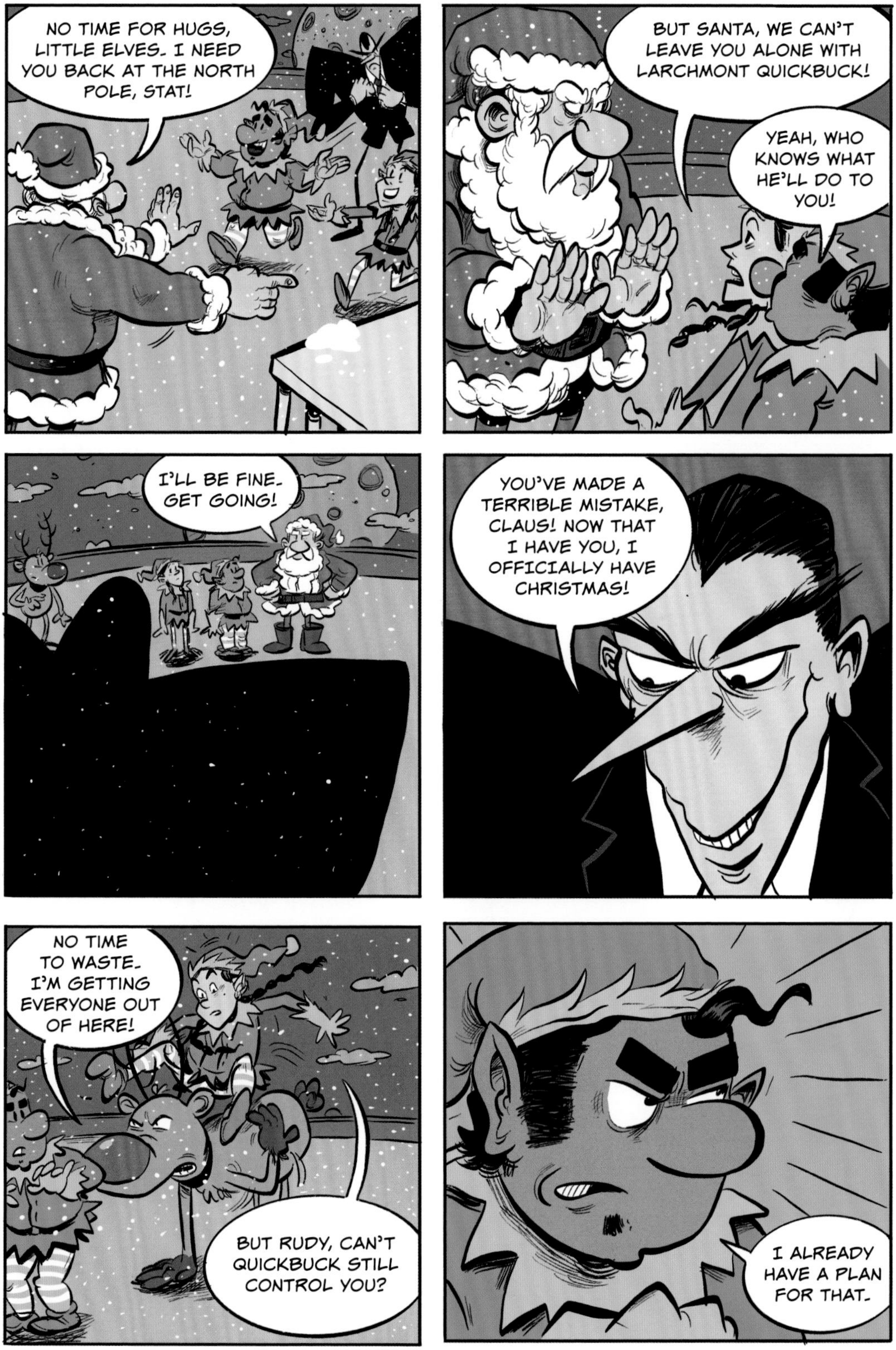
NO TIME FOR HUGS, LITTLE ELVES. I NEED YOU BACK AT THE NORTH POLE, STAT!
BUT SANTA, WE CAN'T LEAVE YOU ALONE WITH LARCHMONT QUICKBUCK!
YEAH, WHO KNOWS WHAT HE'LL DO TO YOU!
I'LL BE FINE. GET GOING!
YOU'VE MADE A TERRIBLE MISTAKE, CLAUS! NOW THAT I HAVE YOU, I OFFICIALLY HAVE CHRISTMAS!
NO TIME TO WASTE. I'M GETTING EVERYONE OUT OF HERE!
BUT RUDY, CAN'T QUICKBUCK STILL CONTROL YOU?
I ALREADY HAVE A PLAN FOR THAT.

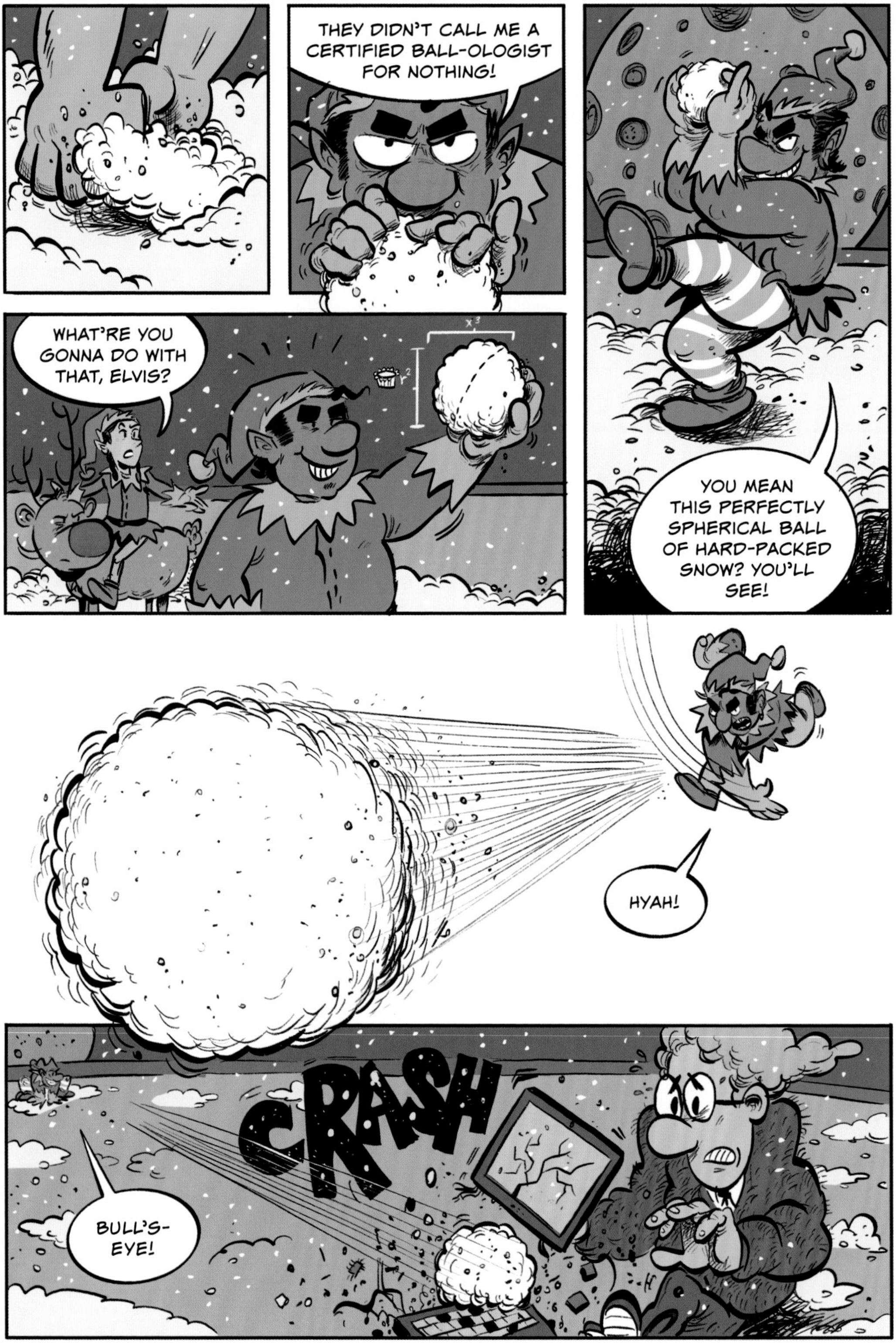
THEY DIDN'T CALL ME A CERTIFIED BALL-OLOGIST FOR NOTHING!
WHAT'RE YOU GONNA DO WITH THAT, ELVIS?
YOU MEAN THIS PERFECTLY SPHERICAL BALL OF HARD-PACKED SNOW? YOU'LL SEE!
HYAH!
CRASH
BULL'S-EYE!

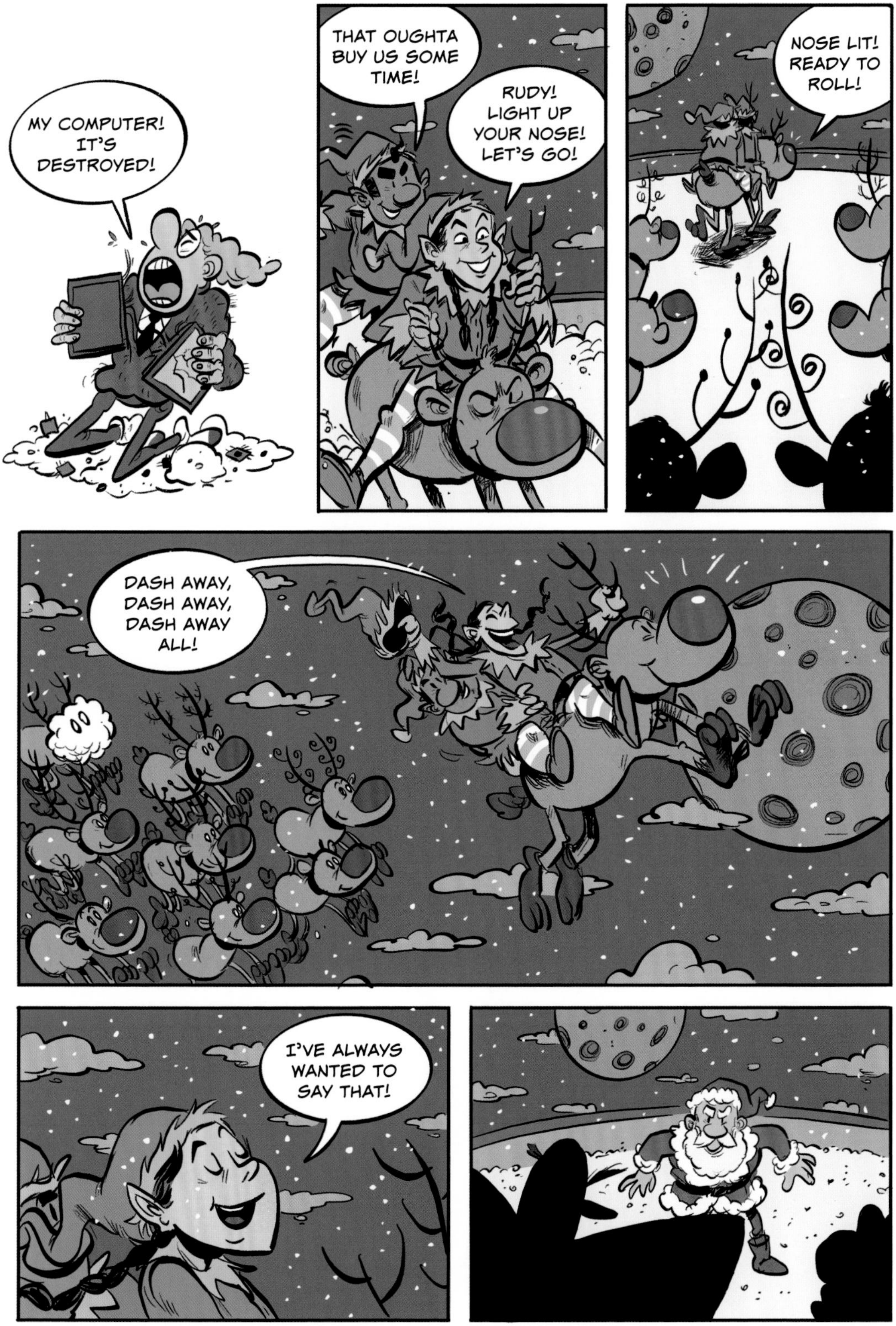
MY COMPUTER! IT'S DESTROYED!
THAT OUGHTA BUY US SOME TIME!
RUDY! LIGHT UP YOUR NOSE! LET'S GO!
NOSE LIT! READY TO ROLL!
DASH AWAY, DASH AWAY, DASH AWAY ALL!
I'VE ALWAYS WANTED TO SAY THAT!

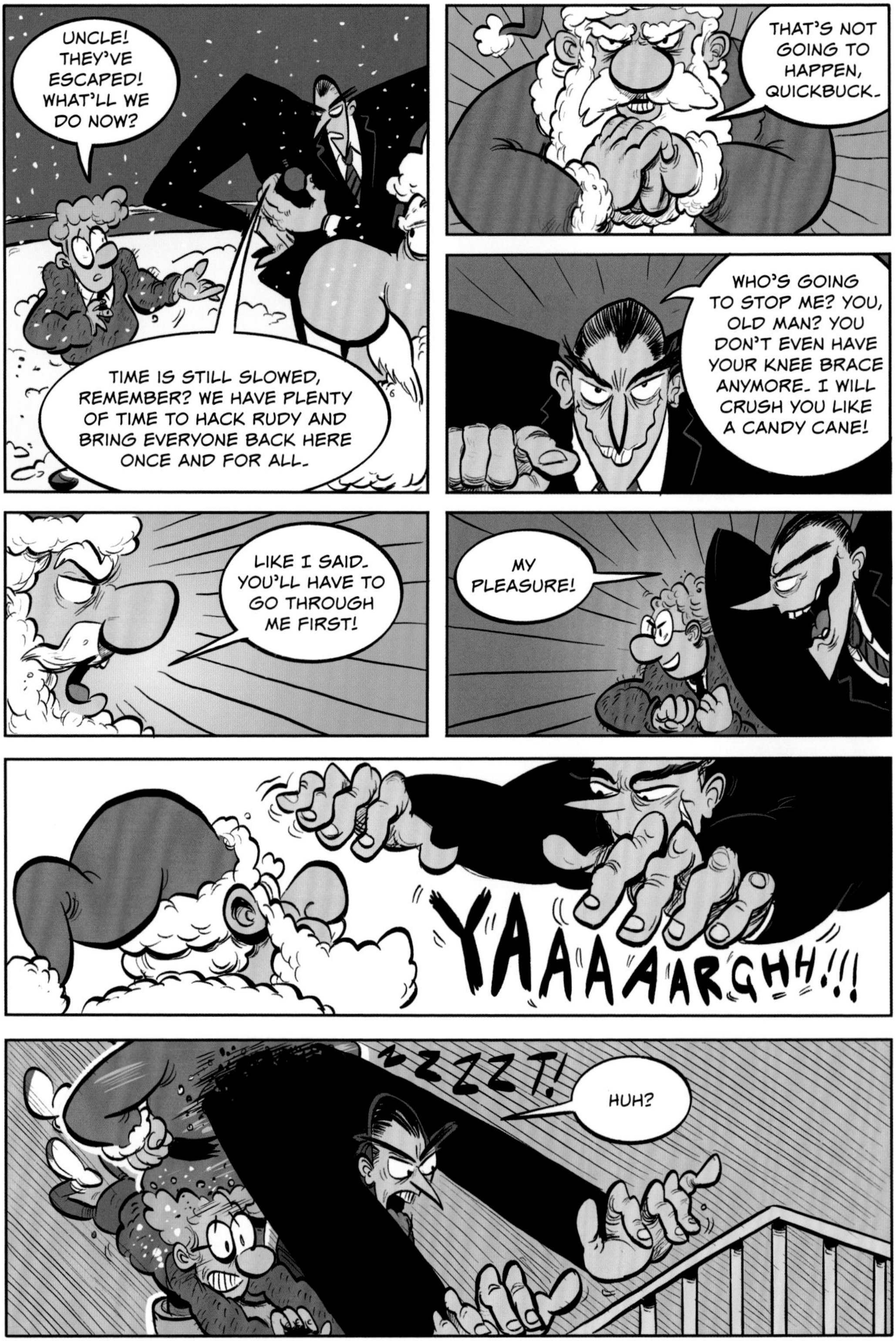

UNCLE! THEY'VE ESCAPED! WHAT'LL WE DO NOW?
TIME IS STILL SLOWED, REMEMBER? WE HAVE PLENTY OF TIME TO HACK RUDY AND BRING EVERYONE BACK HERE ONCE AND FOR ALL.
THAT'S NOT GOING TO HAPPEN, QUICKBUCK.
WHO'S GOING TO STOP ME? YOU, OLD MAN? YOU DON'T EVEN HAVE YOUR KNEE BRACE ANYMORE. I WILL CRUSH YOU LIKE A CANDY CANE!
LIKE I SAID. YOU'LL HAVE TO GO THROUGH ME FIRST!
MY PLEASURE!
YAAAAARGHH!!!
ZZZZT!
HUH?

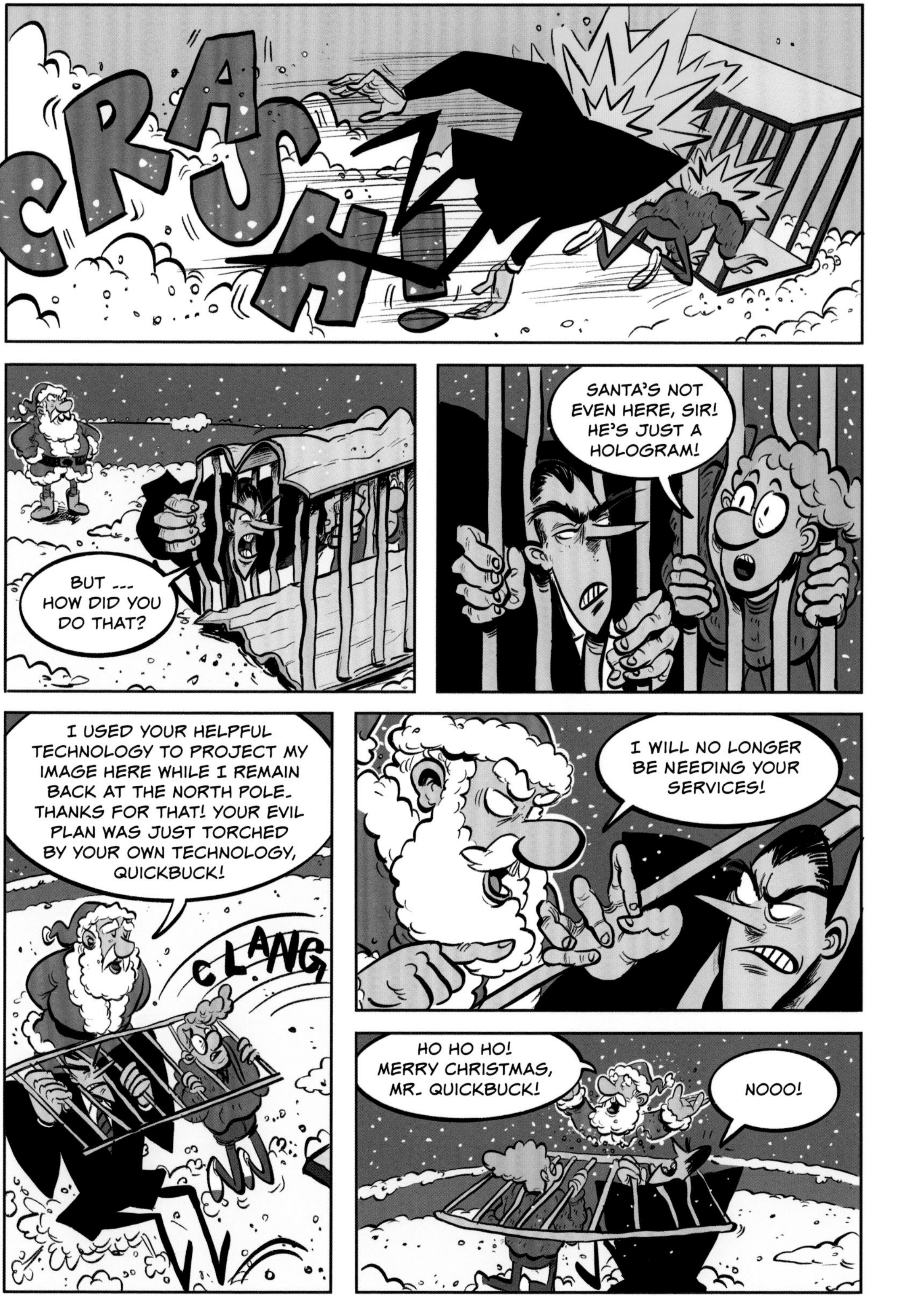
CRASH!
BUT ... HOW DID YOU DO THAT?
SANTA'S NOT EVEN HERE, SIR! HE'S JUST A HOLOGRAM!
I USED YOUR HELPFUL TECHNOLOGY TO PROJECT MY IMAGE HERE WHILE I REMAIN BACK AT THE NORTH POLE. THANKS FOR THAT! YOUR EVIL PLAN WAS JUST TORCHED BY YOUR OWN TECHNOLOGY, QUICKBUCK!
CLANG
I WILL NO LONGER BE NEEDING YOUR SERVICES!
HO HO HO! MERRY CHRISTMAS, MR. QUICKBUCK!
NOOO!

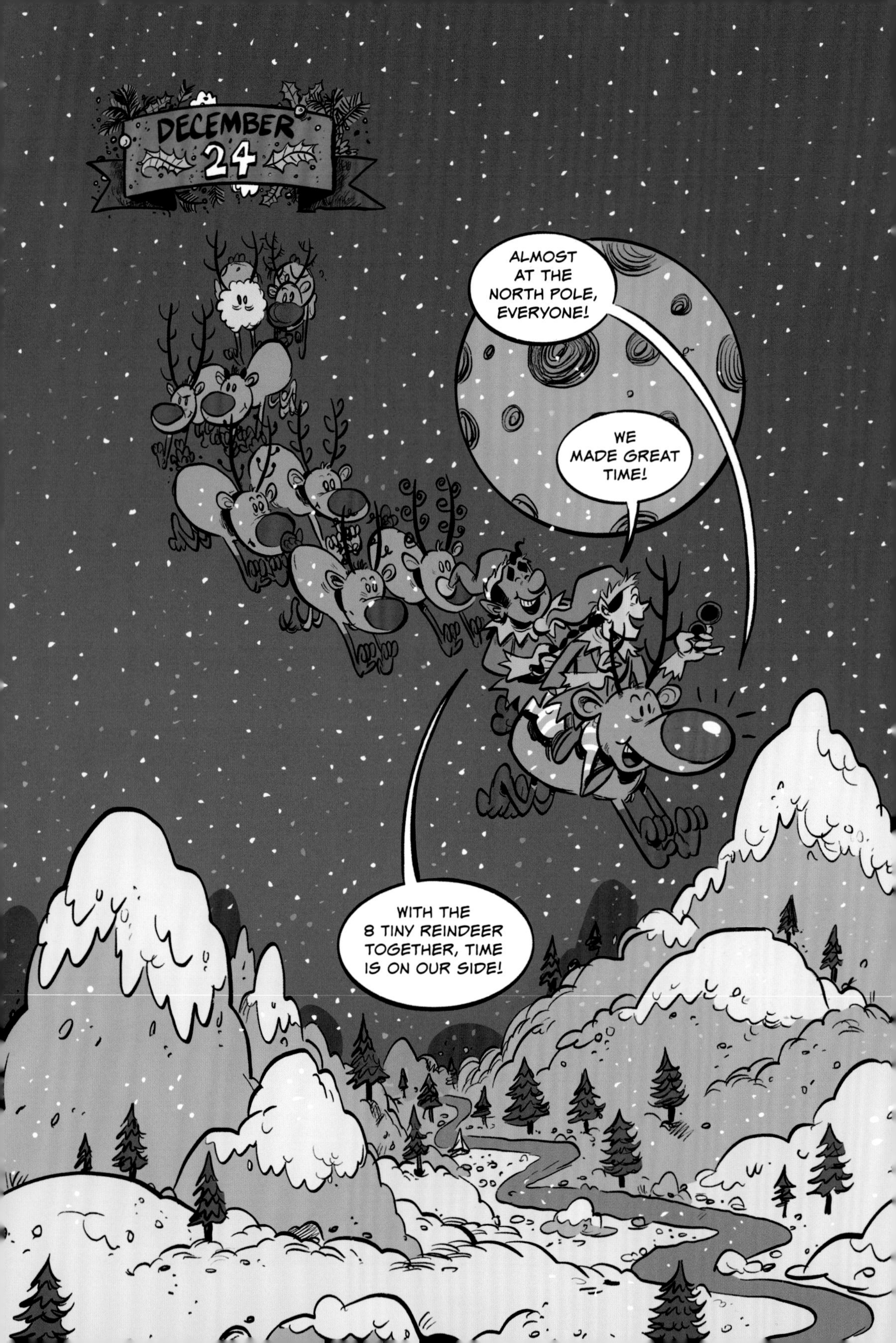
DECEMBER 24
ALMOST AT THE NORTH POLE, EVERYONE!
WE MADE GREAT TIME!
WITH THE 8 TINY REINDEER TOGETHER, TIME IS ON OUR SIDE!

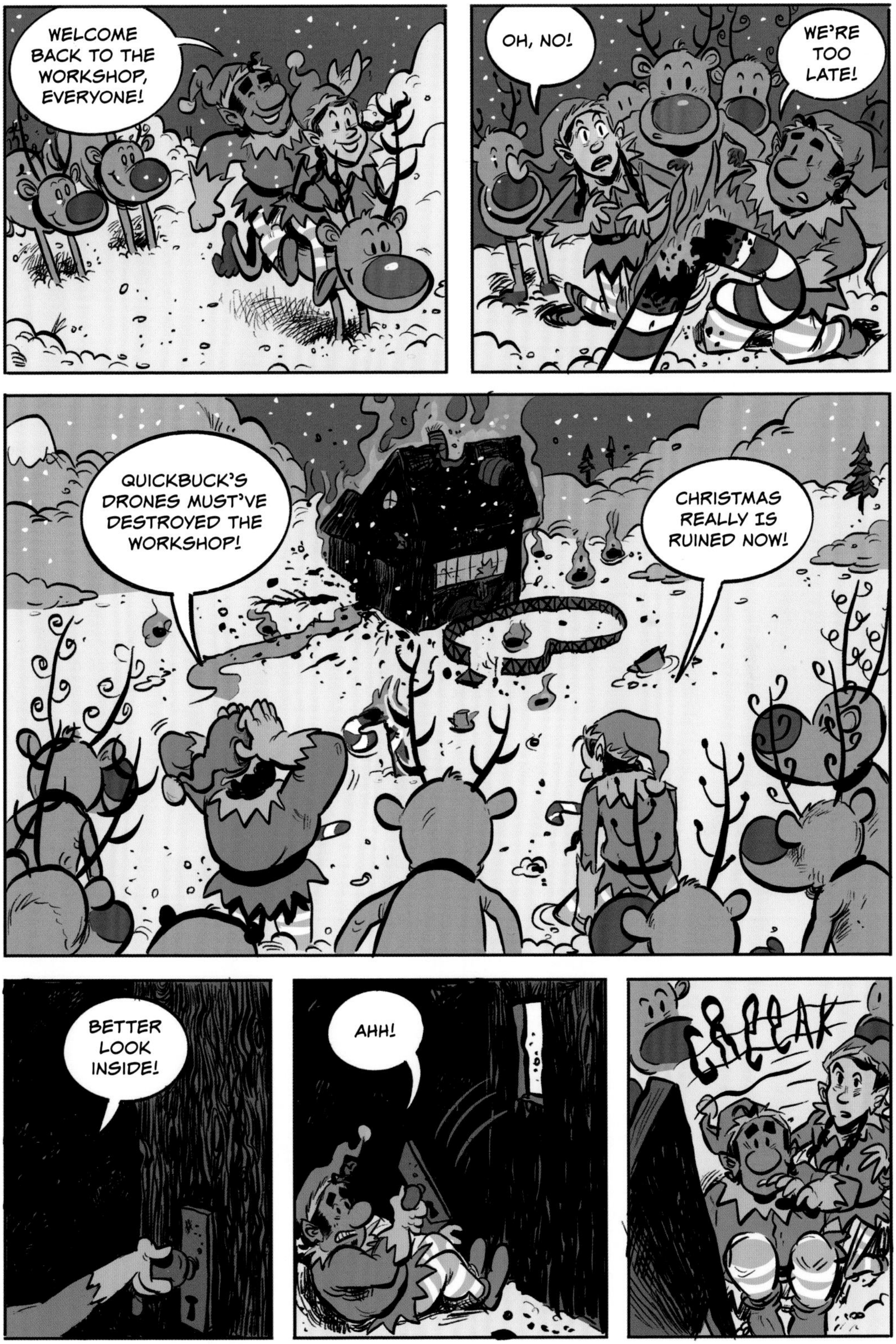
WELCOME BACK TO THE WORKSHOP, EVERYONE!
OH, NO!
WE'RE TOO LATE!
QUICKBUCK'S DRONES MUST'VE DESTROYED THE WORKSHOP!
CHRISTMAS REALLY IS RUINED NOW!
BETTER LOOK INSIDE!
AHH!
CREEAK

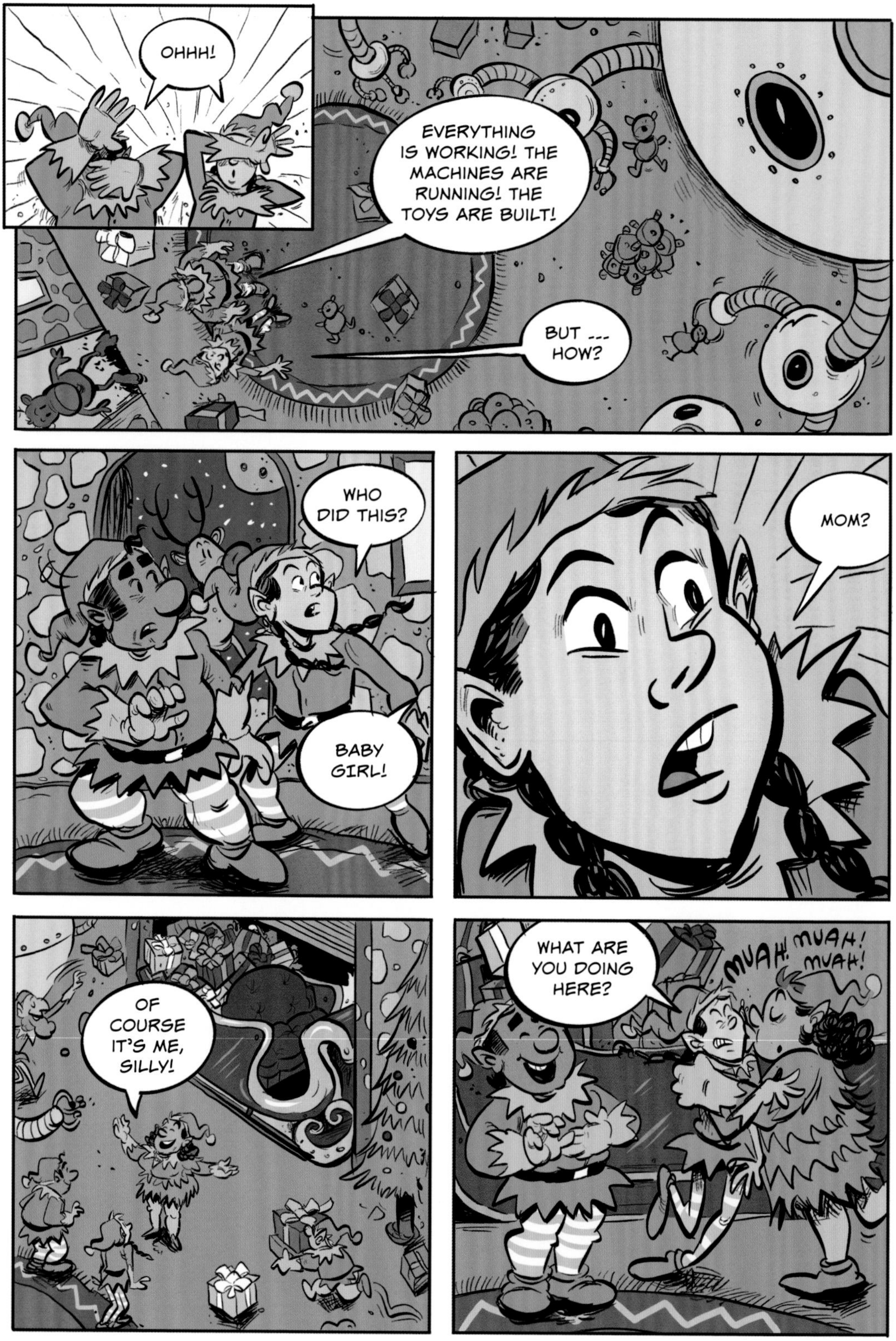
OHHH!
EVERYTHING IS WORKING! THE MACHINES ARE RUNNING! THE TOYS ARE BUILT!
BUT --- HOW?
WHO DID THIS?
BABY GIRL!
MOM?
OF COURSE IT'S ME, SILLY!
WHAT ARE YOU DOING HERE?
MUAH! MUAH! MUAH!

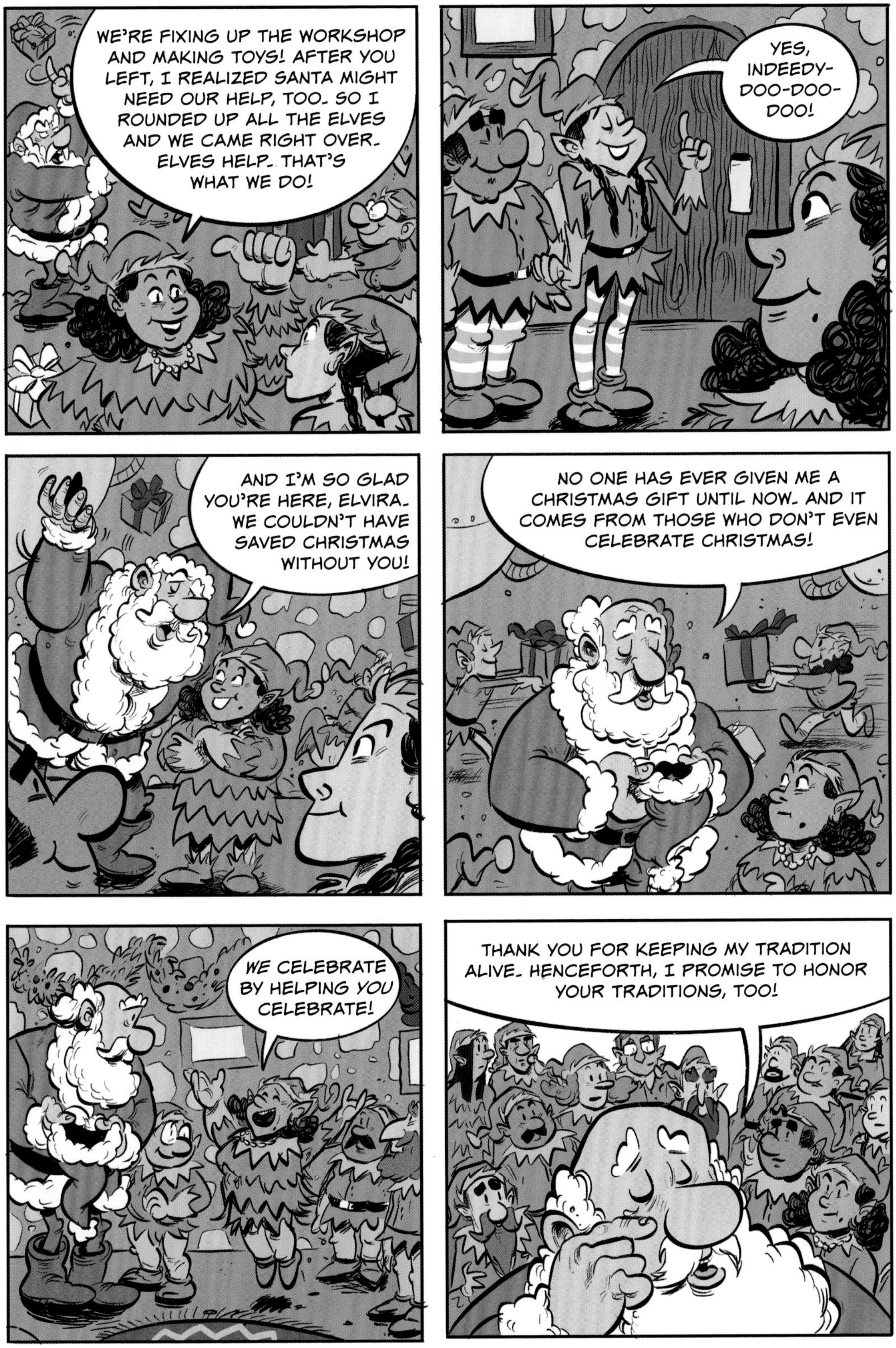
WE'RE FIXING UP THE WORKSHOP AND MAKING TOYS! AFTER YOU LEFT, I REALIZED SANTA MIGHT NEED OUR HELP, TOO. SO I ROUNDED UP ALL THE ELVES AND WE CAME RIGHT OVER. ELVES HELP. THAT'S WHAT WE DO!
YES, INDEEDY-DOO-DOO-DOO!
AND I'M SO GLAD YOU'RE HERE, ELVIRA. WE COULDN'T HAVE SAVED CHRISTMAS WITHOUT YOU!
NO ONE HAS EVER GIVEN ME A CHRISTMAS GIFT UNTIL NOW. AND IT COMES FROM THOSE WHO DON'T EVEN CELEBRATE CHRISTMAS!
WE CELEBRATE BY HELPING *YOU* CELEBRATE!
THANK YOU FOR KEEPING MY TRADITION ALIVE. HENCEFORTH, I PROMISE TO HONOR YOUR TRADITIONS, TOO!

I FORGOT THAT CHRISTMAS RUNS ON HEART! BY SHARING YOUR GENEROUS HEARTS WITH ME, YOU HELPED ME FIND MY HEART AGAIN. THANK YOU, ELVES!

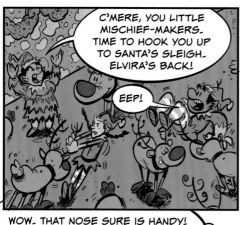

MOM! ELVIS! SO GROSS!

ALL RIGHT, TEAM, WE HAVE CHRISTMAS TO DELIVER BEFORE SUNUP.

C'MERE, YOU LITTLE MISCHIEF-MAKERS. TIME TO HOOK YOU UP TO SANTA'S SLEIGH. ELVIRA'S BACK!

EEP!

MOM, RUDOLPH THE RED-NOSED ROBOT WILL TAKE IT FROM HERE.

C'MON, REINDEER. FOLLOW ME.

OF COURSE HE WILL! THANKS, RUDY!

WOW. THAT NOSE SURE IS HANDY! I GUESS NOT ALL TECHNOLOGY IS BAD, IF IT'S USED IN THE RIGHT WAY.

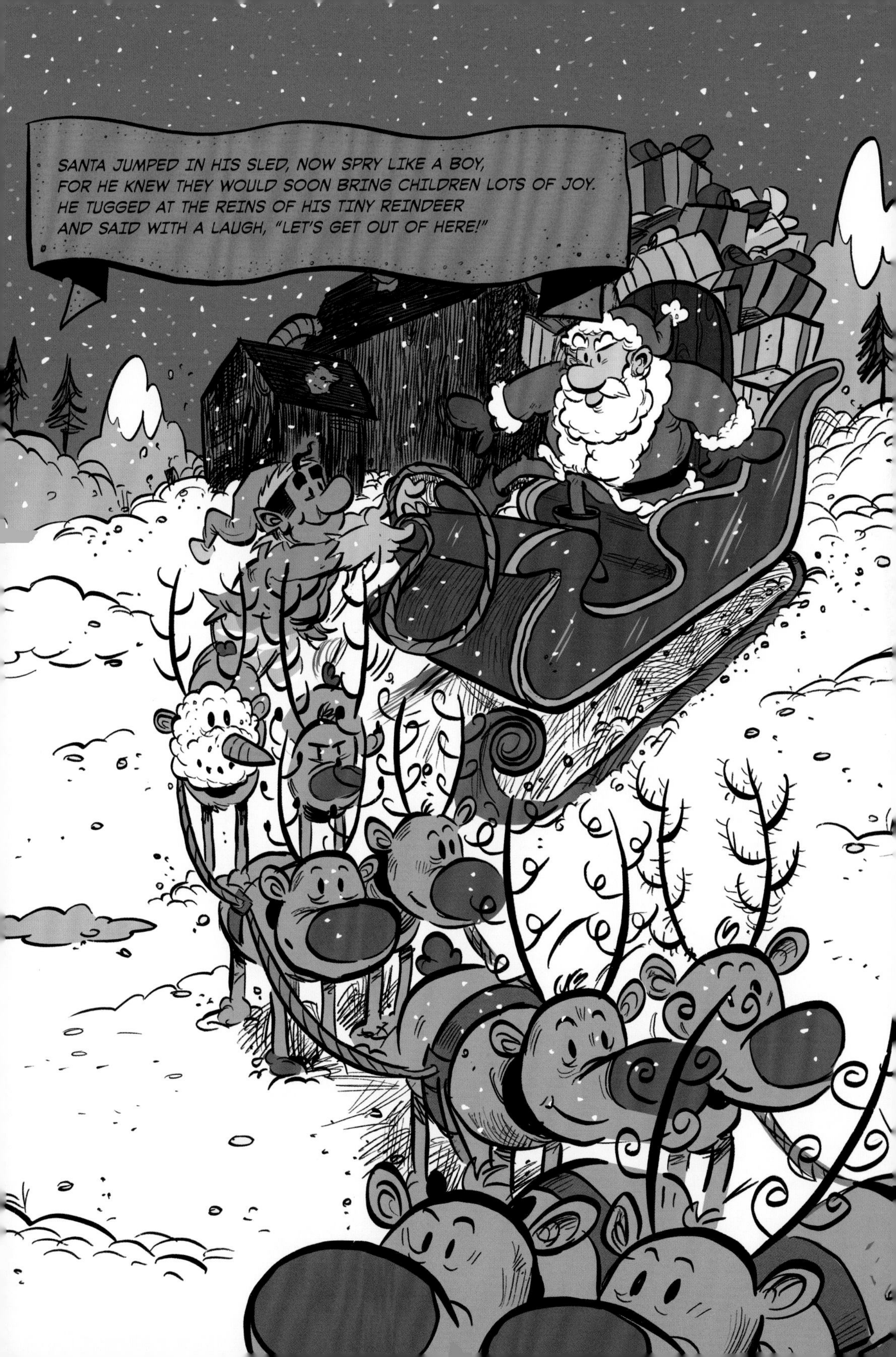
SANTA JUMPED IN HIS SLED, NOW SPRY LIKE A BOY,
FOR HE KNEW THEY WOULD SOON BRING CHILDREN LOTS OF JOY.
HE TUGGED AT THE REINS OF HIS TINY REINDEER
AND SAID WITH A LAUGH, "LET'S GET OUT OF HERE!"

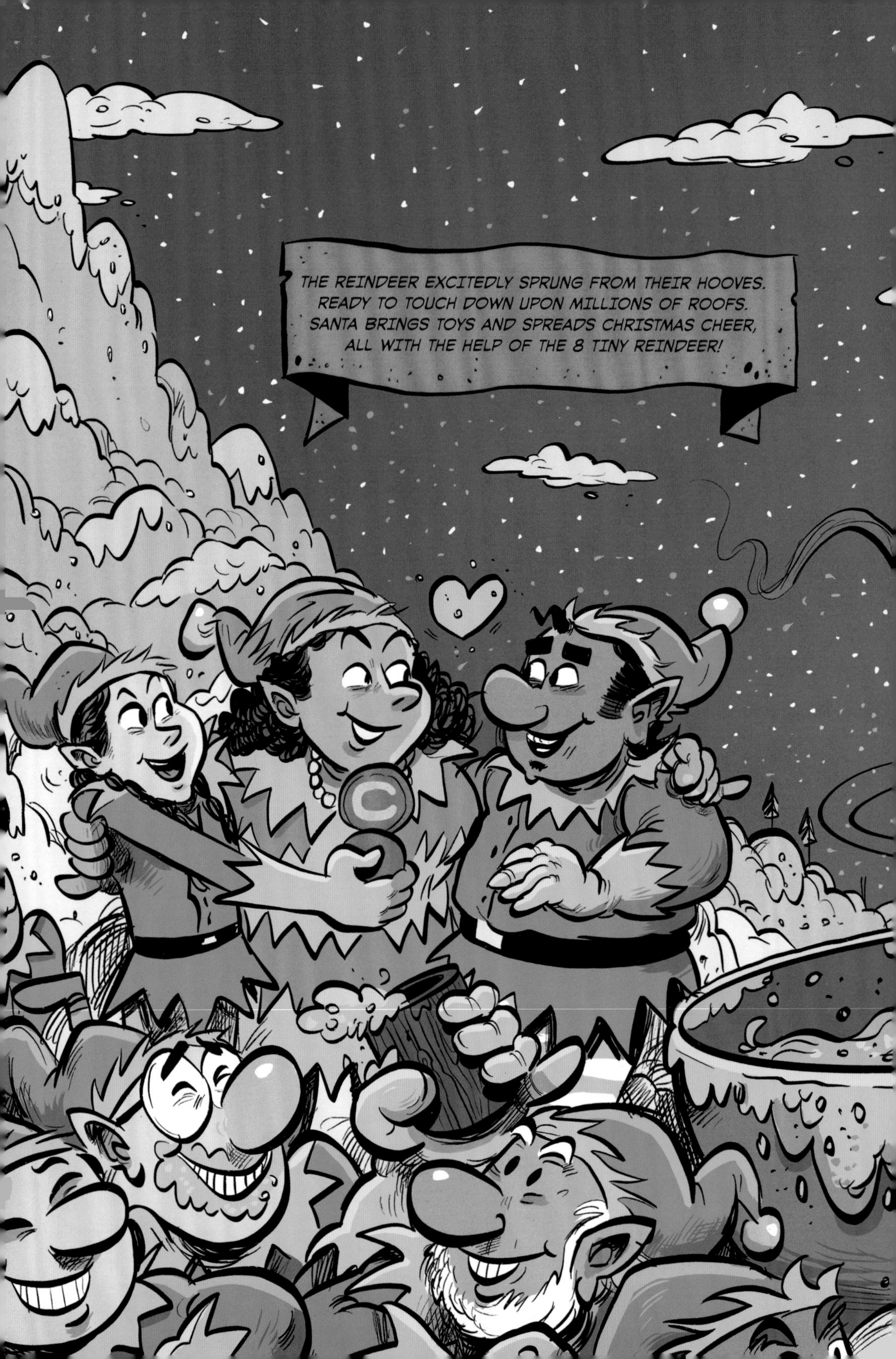
THE REINDEER EXCITEDLY SPRUNG FROM THEIR HOOVES.
READY TO TOUCH DOWN UPON MILLIONS OF ROOFS.
SANTA BRINGS TOYS AND SPREADS CHRISTMAS CHEER,
ALL WITH THE HELP OF THE 8 TINY REINDEER!

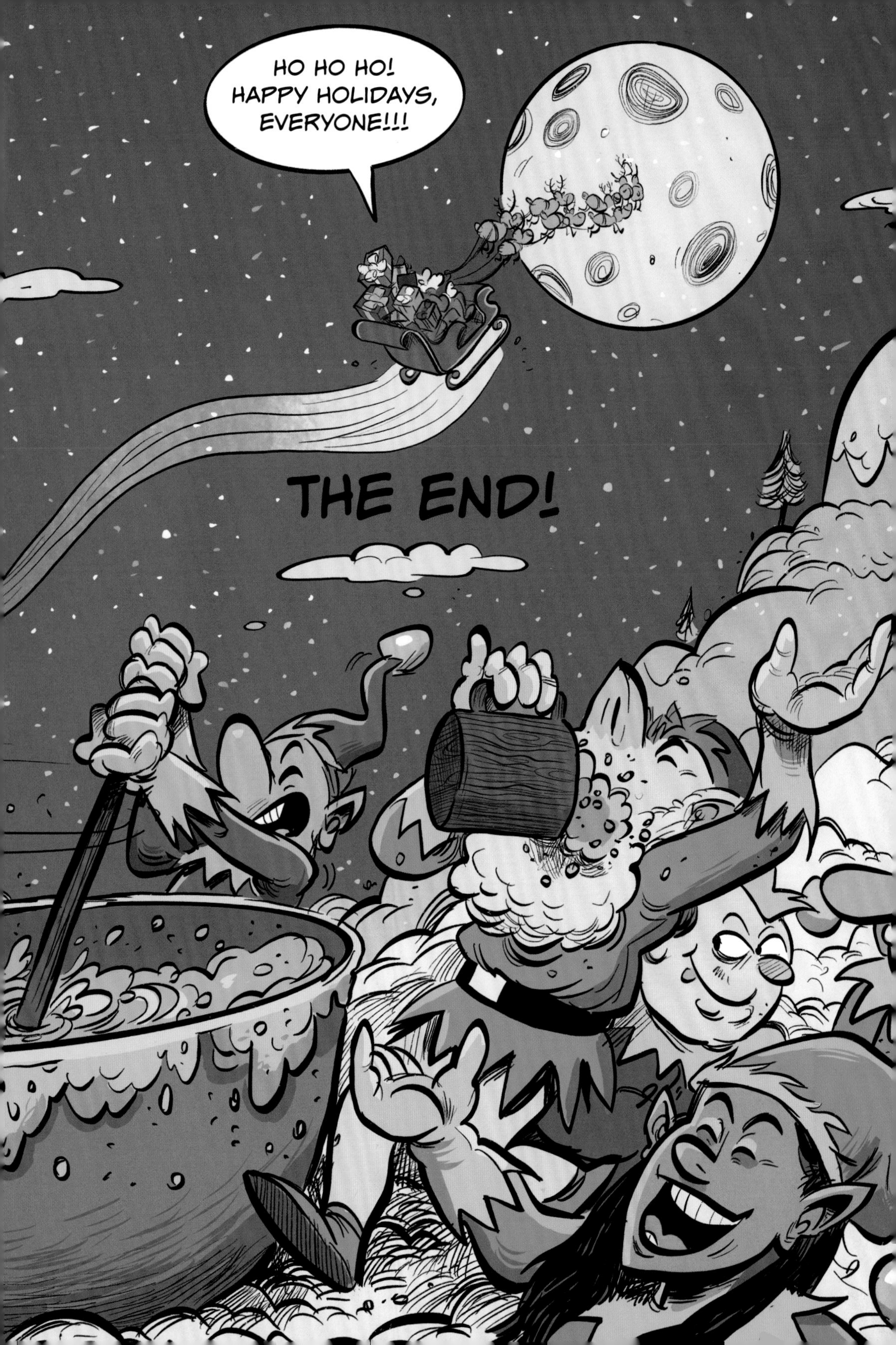
HO HO HO! HAPPY HOLIDAYS, EVERYONE!!!
THE END!

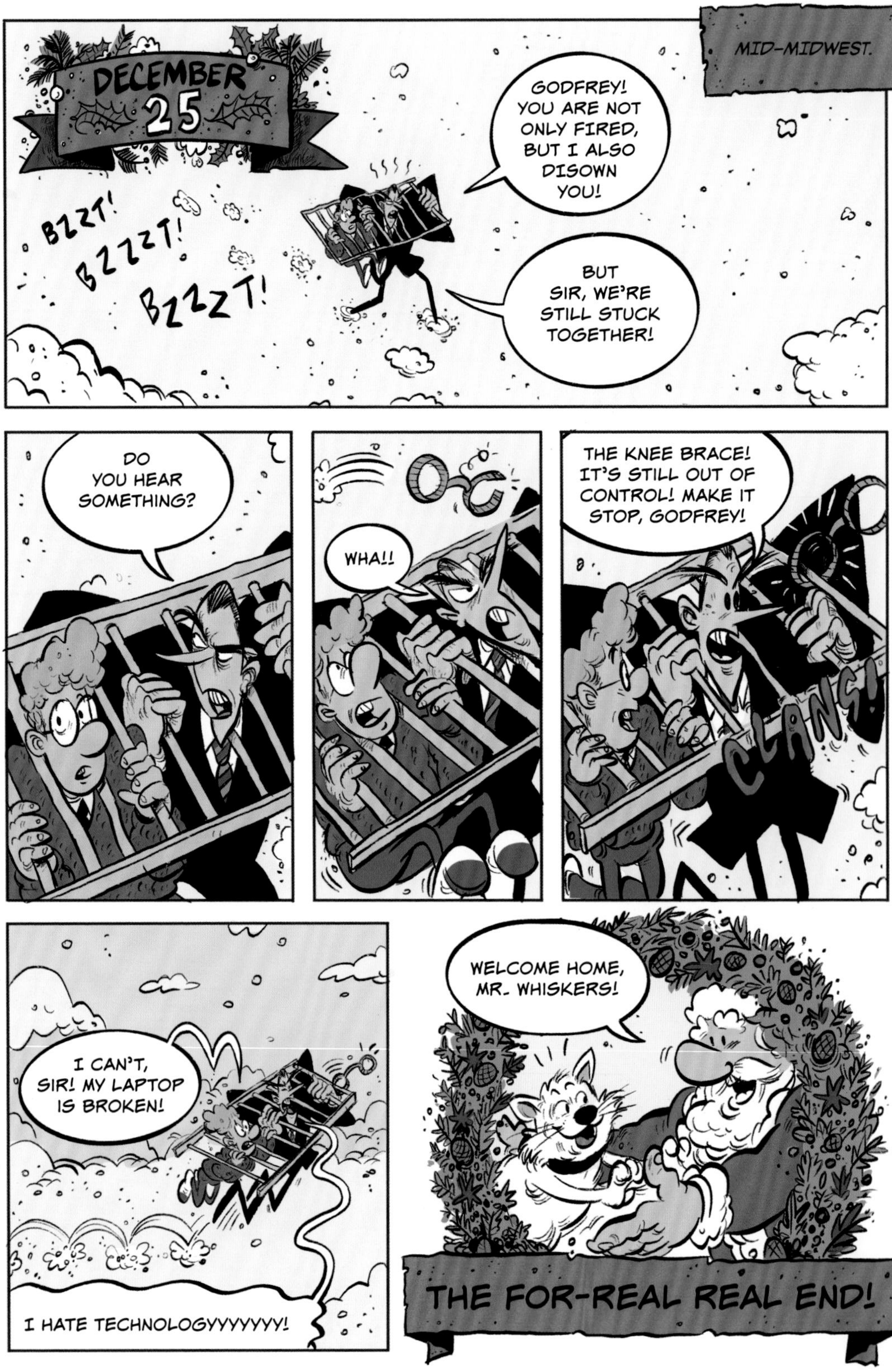
DECEMBER 25
MID-MIDWEST.
GODFREY! YOU ARE NOT ONLY FIRED, BUT I ALSO DISOWN YOU!
BZZT! BZZZT! BZZZT!
BUT SIR, WE'RE STILL STUCK TOGETHER!
DO YOU HEAR SOMETHING?
WHA!!
THE KNEE BRACE! IT'S STILL OUT OF CONTROL! MAKE IT STOP, GODFREY!
CLANG!
I CAN'T, SIR! MY LAPTOP IS BROKEN!
I HATE TECHNOLOGYYYYYYY!
WELCOME HOME, MR. WHISKERS!
THE FOR-REAL REAL END!